When the

Cat's Away

Gilbert Morris

HARVEST HOUSE PUBLISHERS

EUGENE, OREGON

All Scripture quotations are taken from the King James Version of the Bible.

Cover by Abris, Veneta, Oregon

Cover illustrations © Simon Spoon / iStockphoto; Daniel Defabio / iStockphoto

Gilbert Morris is published in association with the literary agency of WordServe Literary Group, Ltd., 10152 S. Knoll Circle, Highlands Ranch, CO 80130.

This is a work of fiction. Names, characters, places, and incidents are products of the author's imagination or are used fictitiously. Any resemblance to actual persons, living or dead, or to events or locales, is entirely coincidental.

WHEN THE CAT'S AWAY
Book 3 of the series Jacques & Cleo, Cat Detectives
Copyright © 2007 by Gilbert Morris
Published by Harvest House Publishers
Eugene, Oregon 97402

Library of Congress Cataloging-in-Publication Data
Morris, Gilbert.
    When the cat's away / Gilbert Morris.
        p. cm.—(Jacques & Cleo, cat detectives ; bk. 3)
    ISBN-13: 978-0-7369-1967-8 (pbk.)
    ISBN-10: 0-7369-1967-8
    1. Cats—Fiction. 2. Cat owners—Fiction. 3. Murder—Investigation—Fiction. 4. Cat shows—Fiction. 5. Alabama—Fiction. I. Title.
    PS3563.O8742W435 2007
    813'.54—dc22

                                                                              2007009154

Printed in the United States of America

    07 08 09 10 11 12 13 14 15 / LB-SK / 11 10 9 8 7 6 5 4 3 2 1

To Johnnie

Thanks for fifty-seven wonderful years—
I couldn't have made it without you!

One

Enola Stern swerved the Hummer violently across the highway to avoid hitting a hammerheaded yellow cat that was meandering across the beach road. "Dumb cat," she muttered. "You're going to wind up flat as a Frisbee!"

Glancing toward the white sands of the beach, Enola took pleasure in the sight, as she always did. She had endured five freezing winters in Fargo, North Dakota, before fleeing to the white sands of the Alabama Gulf Shore. Now she soaked up the vision of the sugar sands, the sparkling aqua-green waters of the Gulf, and the blue sky arching overhead dotted with puffy white clouds—a perfect June day.

A frown touched Enola's face as she saw the construction cranes in the distance. They meant new condos were going up, and like many who had come to the world of white sand beaches, she hated the so-called "progress" brought on by the influx of visitors. She suddenly wished she had lived along the beach when there were only a couple hundred people and a few houses in the town of White Sands, but that day was gone forever. Now progress and ugliness were fast overtaking the Alabama Gulf Coast, once the best-kept secret in America. It was now called the Redneck Riviera. All summer the young kids—loud, crude, and mostly drunk—flowed into the beach. In the winters the snowbirds rushed down from Michigan and other northern states. They were all older people who made life hard for the natives. Groups of them would circle their baskets in the middle of the aisle at Wal-Mart and hold meetings, making it impossible for the natives to get through. Enola suspected that when the snowbirds bought a new car they put the turn signal on and left it on until they traded it in on the next model.

Putting the snowbirds and the loud, vulgar kids out of her mind, Enola pulled up in front of a house set well back from the beach. She smiled as she remembered Zophia Krizova, the previous owner of the lovely home. Enola had met Zophia when she first started her veterinary practice, and the old woman with all her pets had been a gold mine for a newcomer opening up a practice in a strange town. Zophia had loved animals more than anyone Enola had ever seen, and that love had brought the two women close. She thought suddenly of how sad it had made her when the old woman had started going downhill, and she remembered that her greatest fear had not been of death but of what would happen to her many pets when she died. It had been Enola who had suggested that she have it written into her will that the heirs of her estate would be required to take care of the pets royally or lose their inheritance.

By the time Zophia had died, the iron-clad will had been drawn up, witnessed, and signed. In order to inherit the estate the heirs would have to do two things: live in the house and take care of the animals. If they refused either of these, the estate would go to the Society for the Prevention of Cruelty to Animals.

Enola got out of the car, smiling broadly as she thought of the two heirs of Zophia's that had been located. It amused her to think that the animals inside the house were far better adjusted than their new caretakers: Mary Katherine Forrest and Jacob Novak. By now, Enola had come to think of them as simply the Odd Couple. It would have been hard to find two people more mismatched than these two, who were forced by the terms of the will to share the house in order to keep the estate. Mary Katherine Forrest, known to her friends as Kate, was an attractive twenty-nine-year-old widow raising a twelve-year-old son, Jeremy. Kate was a dedicated Christian who doted on animals but was probably the worst housekeeper Enola had ever seen.

Jake Novak was the other heir. He was twenty-nine, the same age as Kate, but their age was the only thing the two had in common. Jake was a former Delta Force soldier and later a homicide detective in Chicago. He was also a wannabe novelist, a wonderful cook, and a meticulous housekeeper—and could not stand animals.

Enola knocked on the door, and as she waited she recalled how Jake and Kate had made a separate peace—Jake living in the upstairs apartment, Kate and Jeremy on the ground floor. The inhabitants of White Sands, of course, were adept at gossip and were convinced Jake and Kate were "a couple" in every sense of the word. In truth, the two heirs got along like cats and dogs.

The door swung open, and Kate smiled, saying, "Come in, Enola. I've been waiting for you." Kate's long auburn hair was tied back in a ponytail. She had a widow's peak, deep-set gray-green eyes set in an oval face, and lips that were wide and very full. She was full-figured with long legs and a rather tiny waist.

Enola stepped inside and said, "Is this a bad time to do the inspection?" Once a month Enola was charged by the will with checking on the health of all the animals. During the time that Kate and Jake had lived in the house, the vet had become good friends with both of them.

"It's a bit hectic, Enola. Did you know that *American Morning*'s sending a crew here to interview Ocie?"

Ocie—Oceola Plank—was an eighty-five-year-old alcoholic Jake had saved from jail by taking him into the house. Jake had seen a tattoo on Ocie that identified him as a member of the Army Rangers, and Jake had then discovered that the old man had been a friend of his own father, who had landed at Normandy. The two had been part of the team that had scaled a cliff under fire. He had also found out that the old man had won the Medal of Honor.

"No. All I heard is the good news—that he won millions of dollars in the lottery."

"He did. I still can't believe it. I'm a little worried, though. Ocie's not here, and the television people are coming soon."

"Where do you think he is?" Enola asked as the two walked into the spacious living area.

"I'm sure he's out getting drunk again, but I don't know what I'll do if those TV people come and he's not here."

"Well, he'll probably show up, or you might have to go get him out of the drunk tank. Kate, let's start with the cats, shall we?"

"Sure." Kate glanced over to the sofa and called, "Come here, Cleo."

A beautiful long-haired Ragdoll feline came at once to Kate's call. She looked up at Kate and her questioning meow sounded like "Wow!" and the look on her face almost certainly seemed like a grin.

Enola, as always, was amused. "I never saw a cat that could grin. She's happy." She reached down and picked up the Ragdoll, who immediately relaxed. Enola put the cat over her shoulder and said, "Ragdolls are the sweetest cats in the world. All they want is lots of loving."

"She's a sweetheart all right," Kate agreed.

Enola checked her and announced, "Well, she's in fine shape. I wish all my patients were as healthy as you, Cleo." She put Cleopatra down and then turned to face the other feline, who was backed up against the wall. "And now for you, Jacques." Reaching into her bag, she pulled out a pair of heavy gloves. They were thick canvas with long gauntlets that went clear up to her elbows. "Jacques, don't you give me any trouble, you hear me?"

The enormous black cat facing her didn't have a white hair on his body. He weighed close to twenty-five pounds, and he hissed at Enola, his body language saying as plainly as if he could speak, *Come on, Doc, you just lay your hand on me. I'll lay you open to the bone!*

"Now Jacques, you stop that," Kate said. She went over at once and put her hand on Jacques' head. "Be a sweet baby now."

Sweet baby? I'm a Savannah! Savannahs aren't sweet babies. Don't you understand I'm half wildcat?

Indeed, Savannahs are half wildcats. They're bred by crossing an African serval, an actual wildcat, with an American domestic. The result is a huge cat...declared illegal in some places.

"No wonder Jake calls him Jacques the Ripper," Enola said as she approached the cat, holding her hands out widely. "Come here, and don't you claw me either."

You come here, baby. I'll show you what it's like to get opened up!

Kate reached out and held Jacques' back while Enola looked him over quickly.

"He's disgustingly healthy," she said, "and as mean and hateful as ever."

Jacques spat at her and made a pass in a motion quicker than light. His claws caught in her glove, and Enola jerked it loose. "No wonder Jake can't stand you." She looked over at Cleo, who was waiting to be petted, and leaned down and stroked her smooth fur. "Kate, have you thought of entering Cleo in that cat show coming to White Sands?"

"What cat show?"

"Why, the International Cat Show's going to be held here this summer. Didn't you know? I think it's in a week or two. It's been in all the papers."

"No, I didn't read about it, but I don't think I'd want to do a thing like that."

"Cleo's registered. You've got the papers, so she'd be eligible."

Suddenly Kate laughed. "I think I'll enter Jacques. That ought to be interesting watching a judge try to go over him."

"No, Jacques doesn't have a chance. I doubt if there's even a category for Savannahs, but Cleo would probably win in her category."

Jacques suddenly made a pass at Enola's legs, but Kate reached down and pulled him back. *You don't see any medals on her, do you?* Jacques hissed. *I'm the one with the medal.*

Indeed, around Jacques' neck was a thin silver chain with a small medal that said *World's Greatest Cat Detective.* Jacques the Ripper had been instrumental in solving at least two murders that had taken place in White Sands, and the newspapers had made much of it.

The cats' examinations finished, Kate walked over to the window and looked out. "I sure wish Ocie would come back. I don't have any way to call those TV people and tell them he's not here."

"Well, I guess the money's changed Ocie a lot," Enola said. She walked over and picked up the resident ferret. "Hello, Abigail. How are you?"

Like all ferrets, Abigail was lean and flexible. She loved to be held, and she cuddled herself up against Enola's neck while the vet examined her.

"I'm just sure Ocie's gone off to get drunk as he always does," Kate said again.

"Well, most winners go a little nuts," Enola said. "Buy a fleet of sports cars and a mansion in Spain...things like that. Ocie ought to be happy with all that money."

"Well, he's not. He's still drinking just as much as ever."

"What's he doing with his money?"

"Well, he's having a house built for the Brices. He's willing to do that, but he says he won't spend any money on himself."

Enola finished a quick inspection of Abigail and said, "She's fine. So what in the world is he going to spend that money on?"

Kate shook her head. "He says God's going to save him some day, and then he'll use the money in whatever way God tells him to." She bit her lip and said, "He makes me furious, Enola, with his hyper-Calvinist nonsense."

"What's 'hyper-Calvinist'?" Enola was half Jewish and half Sioux Indian, a strange mixture, but one that had produced a beautiful woman. She had jet-black hair, an olive complexion, and alluring blue-green eyes almost the same color as the Gulf. She had a sensational figure, and men followed her around like lovesick puppies. Several men in White Sands had bought pets simply for an excuse to come to her office.

"Hyper-Calvinists believe in an extreme form of the doctrine of John Calvin. They believe that all things happen according to a plan, and there's nothing much we can do about it."

"That doesn't make any sense," Enola said. "We've got choices."

"Well, the hyper-Calvinists twist Calvin's words around, and Ocie believes all that stuff. He could have been saved years ago, but he says God's got a plan for certain people to get saved, and it's not his time yet. He's just set in his ways. He makes me so mad, Enola. He won't listen to me."

Just then, the two women heard the sound of a man singing, and Enola said, "It sounds like Jake's happy this morning."

"He is," Kate said. "He fixed us the best breakfast I ever had. I wish I were as good a cook as he is. I can't seem to boil water without burning it."

The door opened that led down from the upstairs apartment, and Jake Novak came in. He was a big man, six-two and weighing close to two hundred pounds. He had coarse black hair, heavy black brows, and deep-set hazel eyes. His mouth was set in a wedge-shaped face, and he had high cheek-bones and a broken nose. His eyes fell on Enola and he went over to her, at once dodging Jacques, who slashed at his leg and missed. Jake put his arm around Enola, squeezed her, and gave her a big kiss on the cheek.

"Hey, stop pawing me!" she said, but not too forcefully.

"You're my favorite veterinarian," Jake grinned. His eyes were usually so sleepy and half-closed that he reminded people of a young Robert Mitchum, the movie star with the sleepy eyes.

Enola pushed him away and said, "Keep your hands to yourself, Jake Novak."

Jake suddenly winked at Kate saying, "Enola and I have this thing, Mary Katherine. She's all over me when we're alone. I have to fight for my honor all the time on our dates, but in public she pretends she doesn't like me much."

Enola snorted and said, "I'm going to check the rest of the animals."

Kate said, "Jake, we've got to find Ocie. That crew from *American Morning*'s coming, and he's gone."

"Well, if we can't find Ocie," Jake grinned, "they can interview me." He whipped out an envelope from his back pocket and took out a slip of paper, which he waved proudly in front of Kate. "It's time to celebrate. I got my advance on the novel. Look at it, and you'll turn green with envy."

Kate took the slip of paper, and her eyes opened wide. "Twenty-five thousand dollars! They're giving you that much money...for your...your scribbling?"

Enola came over and looked at the check. She smiled and winked at Jake. "You know, Jake, for some reason I find you far more attractive than I did five minutes ago."

Jake winked back and then kissed her on the lips.

Kate watched them with displeasure. "Please keep your disgusting flirting out of my sight."

"She's jealous, Enola," Jake laughed. He released Enola, put the check on the table, and went over to embrace Kate, saying, "You want equal time?" But Kate put up her hand. "Keep your grubby mitts off me!"

Jake laughed. Neither Kate nor Enola had ever seen him so happy. He had been working on his novel for a long time, and had grown so despondent of being unable to sell it he had almost taken to drink. Now he was almost bouncing off the walls with joy. "I'll tell you what I'm going to do with part of this money, Enola. I'm going to hire a disaster team to clean up after Mary Katherine." He winked at her broadly. "I figure it'll take about six hardworking maids to clean up the mess she makes."

Kate hated it when Jake made fun of her sloppy housekeeping, but he was right. To change the subject she said, "Enola, come on outside and look at Bandit. Never mind Mr. Rich Man here."

The two women moved toward the door, and Jake followed them.

"Gee, I can't decide whether to buy a Cadillac or a Rolls Royce," he groaned. "I think I'll get a bigger Rolls than that limey who keeps hanging around you, Mary Katherine."

"Never mind about Beverly. He's a far better man than you are."

"You just like him because he's got a hyphen."

The two were speaking of Beverly Devon-Hunt, a thirty-five-year-old lawyer—actually the Earl of Devon when he was at home in England. Bev had dated Kate several times, and Jake didn't care much for that. As they passed through the door, suddenly a parrot came sweeping through the air and landed on Kate's shoulder. He pronounced a vile word very clearly, but Kate grabbed him and said, "Say a good word, Bad Louie. A *good* word."

The parrot squawked, "Hallelujah," and both Enola and Jake laughed. Enola gave him a glance and said, "I pronounce him well except for his vile language."

They stepped outside, and at once Kate said, "Bandit, you stop that!"

Bandit was a full-grown coon looking much like a bandit with his black mask. He had climbed the pole where the birdseed was kept for the visiting birds and was cramming his mouth full of sunflower seeds.

Enola laughed. She went over and began poking at him. "You're feeding him too much, Kate."

"He eats everything!" Kate exclaimed. "He eats the cat food, the dog food, and the bird food. I'm going to have to put a muzzle on him."

Enola laughed. "But he's all right." She heard a bark and turned to see a huge pit bull coming toward her. He was white with soulful eyes, and turned around and sat down on Enola's feet. "I never saw a dog who liked to sit on people's feet," Enola said. "Did you teach him that?"

"No, I guess he was born with some kind of a fascination with feet."

"I wonder why he does it?" Enola said, running her hand over the dog's smooth hide and feeling the powerful muscles.

"Who knows why that dog does anything!" Kate said. "He drags all kinds of junk to the house, he chases cars, and if any of us gets cross with him, he pouts."

"I don't believe that," Enola said. "No dog can pout."

"You don't think so!" Kate exclaimed. "Just watch." She went over to Trouble, pointed her finger at him, and said fiercely, "Bad dog!" Trouble gave her a mournful look, got up, and walked over to the house. He faced the siding and began to howl and moan in a piteous way.

"You'd think we were pulling his claws out," Kate said in disgust.

Enola laughed. "Well, I'm glad you have *someone* sensitive around here. Jake sure isn't."

"What are you talking about?" Jake said in mock disbelief. "I'm the most sensitive living thing in this house."

"*Sure* you are," Enola said wryly, then turned and said to Kate, "I'll check the little birds and Big Bertha."

Big Bertha was a Burmese python, the one animal in the house that Jake seemed to actually be afraid of. Kate thought that was silly, for she loved the big snake. She threatened to put Bertha in Jake's bed when he was making fun of her, and Jake said he'd kill himself if she did.

As the three went inside, Jake said, "I'm going to the bank with this check. And I'm going to make a big noise about it. I want everybody to know how rich I am." He stopped and looked down at the table. "Hey, where *is* that check?"

"You put it right on the table," Kate said.

"Well, it's not here." Jake suddenly bent down and stared under the table and then crawled around to the couch. "Where is it?"

Enola said, "It's got to be here somewhere."

They searched frantically, and then suddenly Jake looked up and yelled, "That beast has my check!"

Enola and Kate looked up to see Jacques the Ripper perched on top of a tall bookcase. He indeed had a slip of green paper that looked like the check, and he was staring down at them with contempt.

Jake yelled, "Give me back that check, you monster!" He ran at the bookcase, reached up and made a grab, but as good as his reflexes were, they weren't up to those of Jacques the Ripper. The claws came out with a quick sweep, leaving Jake with bloody furrows down his hand. Jake let out a yelp, but made another grab at the check. He snatched it away, or at least part of it, from Jacques, who held firmly onto the other part.

Jake ignored his bleeding hand and said, "He *ate* my check!"

"We've got to get some antiseptic on that scratch," Enola said. "A cat scratch can be dangerous."

But Jake shook her off. "*Look* at it. He tore it, and he's eating the signature part. I'll *kill* him."

As Enola cleaned the wound and put on antiseptic, Kate said, "Jake, you can have the publishers stop payment on the check and issue another one."

Novak stared at her. "And won't that make me look good? 'My cat ate my check. Please, pretty please, write me another one.' They'll think I'm an idiot."

As Enola bandaged Jake's hand, the front door opened and Ocie Plank walked into the room. Though he was eighty-five, Ocie's back was as straight as a ramrod. His years of drinking left him looking emaciated. His grizzled white hair and wrinkled face, pale blue eyes, beak of a nose, and badly fitting false teeth made him look like a cartoon character. His clothes were torn, his ears were red, and he was obviously drunk as a lord. "What's going on?" he demanded in a slur.

"Jacques the Ripper, that stupid cat, ate my check!" Jake bellowed. Ocie stared at him. "I thought I was drunk, but I guess you're the one who's drunk, Novak."

Jake glared at Ocie, then at Jacques. He suddenly whirled and disappeared, slamming the back door with a mighty bang. Jacques was watching all this as he nibbled on the check. Cleo stared at him from below. Jacques looked down to her and said, *You see that, Cleo? The Intruder's got no self-control.* Jacques always called the human beings in the house by titles. Kate was *the Person,* her son Jeremy was *the Boy,* and Jake was *the Intruder.* Jacques had hated Jake from the moment he had stepped into their lives. He spit out a part of the check and said, *I wish he'd go drown himself in the ocean. It would do us all a favor.*

But our Person likes him, Jacques, Cleo answered.

Shows she has bad taste, but females never have any sense about good mates.

Cleo suddenly grinned. *Like the Siamese across the road that likes that big yellow tom more than she likes you?*

Shut up, Cleo! You're a female. You wouldn't understand. He reached out with his claws and shredded the remaining fragment of the check and then jumped down with a typically graceful feline movement.

That sure made him lose his cool, didn't it? I like that! He turned and said, *Come on, Cleo. Let's go to that green house down the road and eat the food they put out for that dumb calico.*

He's getting skinny, Jacques. You eat all the food they put out for him. You should be ashamed.

Jacques' eyes gleamed with pleasure. *He'll have to suck it up, baby. It's a jungle out there—and I'm getting mine!*

Two

Jeremy Forrest watched anxiously as a huge bank of low-hanging clouds rolled in from the west. He knew the hurricane season was still months away, but he had seen the devastation the monstrous storms had wreaked on the coast. A movement caught his eye, and he turned to see Rhiannon Brice coming down the beach.

Trouble, the pit bull, came over and sat down on Jeremy's feet. "Get off, Trouble! I don't know why you like to do that."

Trouble reluctantly obliged, and he moved away, giving Jeremy a wounded look.

"Go on. Get your feelings hurt." Jeremy turned from the dog, and watched as the ten-year-old Rhiannon approached. She had a Mediterranean look about her, but Jeremy's gaze went at once to the boy who was following her. He must have been at least sixteen or seventeen, and as they approached, Jeremy heard him saying, "Come on. Whatcha got in your bag there? Lemme have a look."

"Leave me alone," Rhiannon said, without giving the tall, gangly boy a look.

"You think you're something, don't you?" The boy had sandy hair and was peeling from a bad sunburn. Jeremy guessed he was one of the many rowdy young people who flooded the White Sand beaches this time of year, and Jeremy had learned that he disliked most of them intensely.

"Come on. Lemme see what's in the bag." The tall boy made a grab at the bag, and Jeremy, without thinking, ran straight toward him. "Let her alone!" he yelled. He grabbed the bag, but at the same time the boy hit him a blow across the forehead that knocked Jeremy flat on the sand. He rolled over at once, and suddenly something white whizzed by. Trouble was leaping up, knocking the young man backward, and then crouching over him with teeth bared.

"Hey!" the boy yelled, his eyes wide, "get this thing off of me! Will he bite?"

"He'll rip your face right off of you if I tell him to," Jeremy said. He grabbed Trouble by his collar. "Now, you get out of here before I let him have a bite of your ugly hide."

Scrambling to his feet, the boy ran down the beach, then turned and cursed at them.

Rhiannon clucked her tongue. "His language is rude and vile."

"Yes, it is."

"He's uncouth," Rhiannon said. She looked at Jeremy, her eyes the same blue-green as the Gulf.

"How's your grandfather, Rhiannon?"

"Not very well. If he has another heart attack, it might be fatal."

"Aw, that's not gonna happen."

Rhiannon gave Jeremy a withering look. "It happens all the time. You've got to learn to be realistic, Jeremy. You fantasize too much."

As always, Jeremy was half amused and half angry at Rhiannon's strange manner of speaking. Sometimes she talked like a ten-year-old, but more often like a lawyer in court. Jeremy joined her as she walked along the sand. "How's the house coming along?"

At once Rhiannon straightened up, and her eyes were bright as she said, "It's so cool! It's going to be so nice to have a new house all our own."

"You're lucky that Ocie won that lottery."

"It wasn't luck. There's no such thing as luck. I've told you that before, Jeremy. Don't be obtuse."

"I'll be as obtuse as I want to," Jeremy laughed. "It was lucky. The only lottery ticket he ever bought, and Ocie won—instead of any one of the other fifty thousand people who bought tickets, and then he knew you and your grandpa had to have a new house to live in, so he's using part of the money to build it. Now, if that ain't luck, I don't know what is."

Rhiannon sniffed but didn't answer.

"Boy," Jeremy said, shaking his head, "ten million bucks. I wish I had that much money."

"It wouldn't do you any good," Rhiannon said.

"What are you talking about?"

"'Riches make themselves wings: they fly away as an eagle toward heaven.' That's in the book of Proverbs, the twenty-third chapter, in the fifth verse."

Jeremy groaned. "Why do you have to know so much? It gets on my nerves."

"I don't know why I'm so intelligent," Rhiannon said wistfully. "Sometimes I wish I weren't."

Jeremy was surprised. He looked at her and noticed a sadness in her countenance. "Can't you just dumb up, Rhiannon, or at least pretend to be?"

"No, I have to be what I am," she said. "It would be dishonest to pretend to be something I'm not."

"So, what you got in your bag?"

"It's some red snapper. They're all dressed, and I'm taking them to Ocie."

"Well, he sure likes red snapper, but I don't know if he'll want to eat right away. Did you know that *American Morning*'s coming to interview him?"

"What's that?"

"It's a TV program. This woman interviews different people in the morning. Don't you ever watch TV?"

"No, I don't, except for the science and history channels. The rest of it is boring."

The two approached the house, walked around to the side, and entered the cavernous space where two cars and a Harley motorcycle were parked. Going to the door, Rhiannon knocked on it, and when a voice said, "Come in," she went inside.

Jeremy followed her in, and they found Ocie Plank propped up in his bed. The afternoon light streamed through a window, highlighting the craggy face of the old man. Though the rest of him was well-weathered, his eyes were still a bright blue.

"What you doin' here, girl?" he asked.

"Clyde says he's got to have more money to pay off the workers," Rhiannon said matter-of-factly.

Ocie Plank reached over to a table, grabbed up a checkbook and pen. He scribbled on it and said, "There. Take that back to him."

"You didn't put in the amount. He could put a million dollars in there."

"No, he knows I'll cut his liver out if he does that." He smiled. "You anxious to get in that house, sweetheart?"

"Yes, and I have a very good idea, Ocie. You could come and live with us when the house is finished. You're paying for it. It'll be your house too."

"No, it won't," Ocie said with a grin. "I'm giving it to you and your grandpa. Besides, you don't need no drunk living in your house." He reached over to the table beside his bed, picked up a bottle of vodka, took two swallows, and then let out a breath.

"Well, you could buy a condo then," Jeremy said. "One of those penthouses and have everything you ever wanted."

"No, it ain't my money," Ocie said.

"Of course it's your money," Jeremy said. "You won it fair and square."

"No, boy, it's God's money," the old man said. "You see, it's like this. God's in charge of everything. He made me to win that there lottery, and one of these days He's going to save me, and when He does, I'm going to be needin' that money to do what God wants done."

Rhiannon considered this for a second, then said, "I don't believe that."

"Well, sweetie, sometimes I don't either, but I keep trying. What you got in your poke there?"

"You mean my sack?"

"That's what we used to call a poke back in the Arkansas hills where I growed up."

"I got some fillet of red snapper for you, Ocie."

"That's good, honey. You stay and eat with me."

"Okay," the girl said.

"You never turn down a meal, do you?" Jeremy grinned.

"Nope. And I'll cook the fish myself."

"No, *I'll* do it," Jeremy said. "You can't cook as good as I can."

● ● ●

The white van sped down the beach road, and Leslie Madison, the host of *American Morning*, pulled the visor down and studied her face in the mirror attached to it. It was a face that millions were familiar with, oval with perfectly-shaped lips and deep-set blue eyes overshadowed by impossible lashes. Her hair was honey blonde with not a single strand out of place. She pushed the visor up and glanced back at Kyle Summerton, her producer. He had been complaining about their choice of interview subjects, but then Kyle always had to be complaining about something.

"That must be it right up there, the aqua house set back from the beach all by itself," Leslie said.

Will Daniels, the driver, had skin the color of coffee laced with milk. He had a gentle smile and was the best cameraman, sound man, and director in the business. As he pulled off the beach highway and guided the van over the oyster-shell driveway, he said, "This fellow we're interviewing—I heard he got the Medal of Honor. He went up that cliff at Normandy. You remember?"

"So what?" Kyle Summerton snapped. "Nobody wants to hear about worn-out old soldiers." He glanced up. "Nobody's really interested in people winning the lottery anymore either. He'll probably run through the money in six months. This place must have cost a fortune."

"This place doesn't belong to him," Leslie said. "He's staying here with a couple. And for your information, people *are* interested in soldiers, especially now. This could be a good shoot, Kyle, so behave yourself."

"Well, I vote we go down to Tommy Hart's place instead. Now *there's* a story."

Will Daniels winked at Leslie. "That's the guy trying to take over the playboy industry, isn't it? His name is Hart, so he calls the women he employs there the Sweetharts."

"I'm not interested in anything like that," Leslie said. "We came down here to interview Ocie Plank."

"I'm the producer," Kyle said. "We'll do what I say."

Leslie rolled her eyes. Kyle was fully in character today. It was about all Leslie could take. "Well, just fire me then, Kyle," she said.

Kyle Summerton opened his mouth to take Leslie Madison up on her offer—but he knew that without her *American Morning* would go down in flames. She was the most popular host on television.

Leslie was looking at him with a smile playing around her lips. "Being a bully doesn't work, Kyle, unless your victim is weaker than you are—which I'm not."

Kyle swallowed hard. He knew he couldn't bulldoze Leslie as he did everybody else in his sphere, so he said grumpily, "Let's get this loser of an interview out of the way. *Then* we're going down to Hart's place."

• • •

"Mom, the TV people are here!" Jeremy yelled. He shot over to the front window and stared out.

Kate Forrest had been getting ready for the event. She wasn't going to be in the segment, as far as she knew, but she wanted to look nice. She wore a green dress that matched her gray-green eyes and had put her hair up in a flattering style. Going to the door, she opened it and waited until a woman and two men approached.

"Hello," she said. "I'm Kate Forrest."

"Mrs. Forrest, so good of you to have us. I'm Leslie Madison. This is our producer Kyle Summerton, and this is Will Daniels, our director and man of all parts."

"Won't you all come in." After Kate had ushered them inside, Leslie said, "What a beautiful place you have here."

"Thank you. We like it very much. And I must tell you how much I enjoy your work. You seem like an ordinary person. One I could borrow a cup of sugar from," she said with a smile.

Leslie said, "Thank you. I like to think I'm that kind of person."

Will Daniels had been pacing around the spacious interior, and said, "I think if we can get you and Mr. Plank here, we can get a shot of the Gulf in the background."

At that moment something thumped loudly behind Daniels. He turned toward the table behind him and said, "What's going on back there?"

Kate rushed over. "It's our rabbit, Miss Boo. She's bitten into an electric cord and electrocuted herself again."

"Oh, the poor thing! She's dead?" Leslie said.

Kate didn't answer. She ran quickly through the house to the door that led up from the kitchen and called up the stairs, "Jake, get down here quick!"

Leslie Madison and her crew stood back as Jake came barreling into the room. He was wearing a pair of Levi's and a white knit shirt and looked to Leslie like a professional fighter. With his coarse black hair and deep-set eyes Leslie thought he resembled the old movie star Robert Mitchum.

"It's Miss Boo," Kate said. "She's electrocuted herself again."

"I'm getting sick of bringing that varmint back from the dead," Jake said.

He bent down, reached behind the table, picked up the rabbit, and began squeezing her rhythmically.

"You're doing CPR on a rabbit?" Daniels exclaimed.

"It's sort of a specialty of mine," Jake said dryly.

"Are you a medic, Mr. Forrest?" Kyle asked.

Miss Boo had begun to gasp, and Jake shook her and said, "You look stupid enough with those flop ears—now stop biting electric cords." He put her down and said, "I'm not Mr. Forrest. Kate and I aren't married. We just live together."

Kate made a strangled noise and said loudly, "This is Jake Novak. A common relative of ours left us the house, but we have to live in it in order to inherit it. Jake," she said distinctly, "lives upstairs in his own apartment."

"Pretty convenient, isn't it?" Kyle laughed and smirked as he looked at the two.

"You'll have to forgive Kyle," Leslie said. "He sometimes forgets his manners."

Rhiannon, who had been standing beside Jeremy, had said nothing, but now she piped up and said, "He's uncouth, that's his problem."

Kyle Summerton frowned, staring at the black-haired girl. "This your kid, Kate?"

"She's a neighbor," Kate said. "Her name is Rhiannon."

Kyle suddenly grinned. "You're a nice-looking kid. Be nice to me, and I'll put you in the movies."

"I don't want anything to do with you," Rhiannon said flatly. "You're incogitant."

Kyle reddened, and everyone knew he had no idea what the word meant. Jake said, "Incogitant means 'thoughtless or inconsiderate.' You'll have to forgive Rhiannon. She has a bad habit of speaking exactly what she thinks."

Kyle tried to think of a comeback that would put the girl in her place, but suddenly an enormous black cat thumped down from a tall bookcase. Kyle whirled, and as the cat approached him, he said, "Well, there's a good-looking animal." He leaned over, reaching out his hand, but Kate cried out, "Don't—!"

"Too late!" Jake yelled, grinning. Jacques the Ripper slashed the back of Summerton's hand, leaving four bloody furrows. The man reeled backward and bellowed, "What do you mean leaving an animal like that loose? It's dangerous."

"You shouldn't have been trying to pet him, Kyle," Leslie said. "But I do think your hand needs to be treated."

"Oh, I'll do that," Kate said quickly. "We keep the first-aid kit handy." She moved to a table, pulled a first-aid kit out of a drawer, and walked over to the producer. "Here, Mr. Summerton, let me take care of it."

Summerton kept his eye on Jacques and said, "What kind of a cat is that anyhow? It looks like a black panther."

"He's a Savannah," Kate said.

"He's half wildcat," Rhiannon said, her big eyes fixed on Summerton. "That's why he clawed you. He doesn't like to be petted."

Leslie was amused at Rhiannon. "Do you like TV, Rhiannon?"

"No," she sniffed. "I think it's meretricious."

Leslie laughed ruefully. "Is this girl a midget? I don't know what that word means."

Rhiannon said, "It means 'gaudily and deceitfully ornamental.' That's what TV is."

Jake laughed. "You won't win any points against Rhiannon, Miss Madison. She's been reading through the *Encyclopedia Britannica,* and she's got a memory you wouldn't believe. On any subject that's spelled between A and J, she's going to know all about it."

Kyle complained as Kate dressed his wound, and finally he jerked his hand back saying, "Let's get this over with. We've got more important things to do."

"I'm all set," Daniels said.

"Is Mr. Plank here?" Madison asked.

"He's in his room," Jake said. "I'll get him." He turned and left the room, and as soon as he was gone, Leslie asked, "How does it happen that Mr. Plank's living with you?"

Kate hesitated. "Ocie's an alcoholic. You'll find that out soon enough, I guess. He crashed into our car and hurt himself, so to keep him from being taken to the jail, Jake fixed him up a room. He's been with us ever since."

"Well, isn't that noble of you," Kyle said sarcastically. "You starting a branch office of AA?"

"Be quiet, Kyle," Leslie said. She smiled warmly and said, "I think it's wonderful that you would do a thing like that. You didn't know him at all?"

"No, but Jake noticed a tattoo on his shoulder," Kate said. "It told him Ocie was in the Army Rangers who were part of the Normandy invasion."

"I remember seeing that on TV," Daniels said. "That took some nerve."

"Ocie pulled five men out under direct fire and was awarded the Medal of Honor. He never mentions it, though. He won't talk about it."

Leslie Madison managed to get a few more salient facts about Ocie Plank. Then the door opened, and the man himself came in, followed by Jake, who was grinning broadly.

Kate said quickly, "Ocie, this is Miss Leslie Madison. She's the TV host who'll be interviewing you. And this is the producer Mr. Summerton, and this is Mr. Daniels who will be doing the camera work."

"Howdy," Ocie said giving a wave of his hand. "How are y'all?"

He had a half-empty bottle in his left hand, and he obviously had been imbibing of it.

"I think you'd better get the bottle out of his hand," Summerton said to Kate. "Wouldn't make a good impression."

Ocie stared at him, turned the bottle up, drank the remainder and then handed the empty to Kate. "There, Miss Kate, you take care of that business for me."

Kyle was surveying Ocie who was wearing a soiled T-shirt with the arms cut out and a pair of marine fatigue pants. He was barefooted and his hair uncombed. "You can't go on live TV dressed like that."

"Fine with me," Ocie grinned. He turned and started to leave, but Leslie ran forward at once. "Oh, no, don't leave, Mr. Plank. Your clothes are just right. Would you sit on the couch here, and I'll sit on the chair right opposite you, and we'll have a talk."

"You sure do smell good, honey," Ocie said. He turned to Jake and said, "Have you ever noticed how women smell better than men?"

"I've noticed," Jake said. "But when I have my Brut shaving lotion on, I smell better than any woman."

Leslie laughed aloud and said, "I'd like to get a whiff of that, Mr. Novak."

Just then Daniels moved in to put his subjects into the proper lighting and point them in the right direction. Jacques was watching critically. He turned to Cleo and said, *I don't like that sucker.*

You shouldn't have scratched that fellow, Jacques.

I don't like him.

You don't like anybody except our Person.

I'll get him again. You see if I don't. Jacques turned his golden eyes toward Leslie Madison and said, *The woman's not bad. I may let her pick me up and pet me some.*

You don't like to be petted, Jacques.

While the feline conversation was going on, Daniels had satisfied himself. "We're ready when you are, Leslie. The show is about to begin."

"You know what?" the woman said. "I'm going to try something a little different this time."

"I don't like *different*," Summerton growled.

"Be quiet, Kyle," Leslie chided. "Usually we try to give our subjects a list of things to talk about, but I think you and I could just talk like we were off the record, to keep it more natural. Would that be all right with you, Mr. Plank?"

"Call me Ocie."

"Is that your real name, Ocie?"

"No, it's Oceola Cunningham Plank. I didn't like all that, so I made people call me O. C., and it wound up being 'Ocie.'"

"That's fine, Ocie." Leslie turned and said, "I'm ready, Will."

Will counted from five down to one and then pointed a forefinger, and his lips formed the word *Go.*

In a relaxed tone Leslie Madison gave the lead-in. "Welcome to *American Morning*. We're here on the Gulf Coast—specifically, the sunny white shores of White Sands, Alabama. Our guest this morning is Mr. Ocie Plank. How are you this morning, Ocie?"

"Well, I've been drinking," the old man said with a grin. "Did you notice that?"

Jake snorted, then tried to cover up his laugh, but Leslie only smiled. "Yes. That's all right, though."

"No," Ocie said rubbing his cheeks with his fingers, "it ain't right. Gettin' drunk is a sin. Didn't you know that, honey? It says so in the Bible."

"Does it?" Leslie said, already surprised by the turn of the conversation.

"Sure it does. It says the drunkard and the glutton shall come to poverty. That's in Proverbs 23:21, don't you see."

"Well, you certainly haven't come to poverty," Leslie countered gently. "You've come to riches. You've won the lottery and ten million dollars."

"I'm still a drunk, though," Ocie maintained. "A common drunk with ten million dollars is no better off than a drunk with ten dollars."

"Well, if drinking is wrong, in your opinion, why do you do it, Mr. Plank?" Leslie asked.

"I drink because I'm a fool. Why do you drink, sweetheart?"

Leslie's eyes flew open, and for a moment she was speechless. She finally laughed and said, "Well, I guess I'm a fool, too." Then she regained her professional tone and asked, "Have you ever tried to quit drinking, Ocie?"

"No, I ain't never tried to quit."

"Why not?"

"When it's time for me to quit, God will make me quit. That's the way God works."

"I don't understand you," Leslie asked. "You mean you don't have anything to do with your own destiny?"

"I mean we all do what God has us doing."

"Well, He had you win ten million dollars. How are you going to spend the money?"

"That's up to God, honey."

"What does that mean, Ocie? I don't understand you."

Leslie was suddenly cut off when a gaudily colored parrot landed on Kyle's shoulders—and called him a vile name.

"Bad Louie, you hush!" Kate said, her face turning red. "I'm so sorry. He formerly belonged to some construction workers, and they taught him some bad words."

"But Kate's teaching him good words," Ocie said. "Make him say something good, Kate."

"Say a good word, Bad Louie," Kate said, "and I'll give you a peanut."

"Hallelujah! Praise the Lord!" Louie croaked hoarsely and took the peanut that Kate offered.

"You want me to cut that out of the interview?" Daniels grinned.

"No, leave it in," Leslie said. "You always want spontaneity, Kyle. Well, there's some spontaneity for you." She turned back to Ocie and said, "What did you mean when you said that God will have to spend your ten million dollars?"

Ocie scratched his head, then said, "Well, there was a fellow called Calvin, and he taught that we didn't have much say about what we do. If somebody falls down, it's because God meant them to fall down. If somebody wins a million dollars, that was just in the script. You know about scripts, honey. Well, the script's all written, and I ain't got nothing to do with it. I just have to do what God's already got planned."

"Are you a Christian man?" Leslie asked.

"No, I ain't a Christian. I wouldn't be drunk if I was, but some day I'm going to get saved, when it's God's timing. Until then I'm just a drunk. A drunk with ten million dollars."

Leslie stared at him for a moment. Then she turned to Kate and said, "Mrs. Forrest, do you believe this...well, theology Ocie's talking about?"

"No, I certainly don't," Kate burst out. "It's nonsense."

"No, it ain't!" Ocie said.

"Yes, it is," Kate moved forward, forgetting they were on television, and stood in front of Ocie. "You hide behind that warped excuse so you can keep on being a drunk."

"I don't neither," Ocie protested. "I can't help what I do. We do what God makes us do. I'll be saved when God saves me."

"Ocie, the Bible says, 'Today is the day of salvation,' as you well know."

"God chooses people. He ain't chose me yet."

"Of course God chooses people. He chose David to be King of the Jews. He chose Saul to be the apostle to the Gentiles." Kate had completely forgotten that this interview was going out to hundreds of thousands of homes. Daniels made a sign and mouthed, *Do we cut this off?*

Leslie Madison shook her head. *No. Keep on rolling, Daniels.*

"You know very well Jesus said plainly, 'Come unto me all ye that labor and are heavy laden, and I will give you rest.'"

"Well, I ain't sure exactly what that means."

"It means *exactly* what it says! You can come to Jesus right now if you want to. You're denying the power of the blood of Jesus, Ocie. Don't you remember that verse that says, 'Behold, if any man hear my voice, and open the door, I will come in to him, and will sup with him, and he with me.'"

Jake was watching Ocie's face and was surprised to see his ruddy countenance go as pale as a sheet. He also saw that Ocie's hands were beginning to tremble, and he passed them over his face in a strange gesture.

Ocie suddenly stood up, and Jake said, "What's the matter, Ocie?"

Ocie was staring at Kate, and he whispered, "I...I feel awful—"

"You *should* feel awful," Kate continued. "Jesus has been knocking on your door for *years,* and you've been hiding in a bottle of vodka, spouting nonsense about God. You can get saved any time you want to. All you have to do is repent and call on the name of Jesus."

The room grew deathly silent, and suddenly Ocie fell to his knees and began to cry. "Pray for me, Kate. I want to stop running from God."

Will Daniels was confused. He saw that both Kyle and Leslie were frozen by the scene, but he kept the cameras running. *You want me to stop?* He lipped to Leslie.

Not on your life! This is the real thing!

The entire crew watched as Kate went over and knelt down beside Ocie. She put her hands on his shoulders and prayed, and Ocie began to weep great sobbing tears. Then he called on God in a loud voice filled with fear.

Jake was as shocked as anyone else in the room. He could do nothing but stand there and watch. Finally he saw that Ocie's shoulders were no longer shaking, and then he saw the old man look up with a light in his eyes Jake had never seen before. Ocie got to his feet and reached over and grabbed Kate's hand. "I'm saved, Katie! I'm truly saved from sin and from hell! It's finally happened!" Kate, who was weeping, hugged him.

And then Ocie turned and looked right into the camera and said loudly, "All right, you sinners out there, listen to me. I've just been washed in the blood of the Lamb! I'm vowing here and now to never take another drink as long as I live. I'll shout praises to Jesus here for the few years I got left, then I'll transfer to heaven and get me a new body, and I'll really praise God then."

Suddenly he turned and looked right at Leslie Madison. He took two steps toward her and said, "Are you washed in the blood of the Lamb, TV Lady?"

Leslie couldn't speak a word for a moment, and then she quickly turned to the camera and said in a voice not quite steady, "Well, friends of *American Morning*, I hope you enjoyed meeting Ocie Plank. He didn't speak of it, but he's a Medal of Honor winner, and from what I can understand about what's happened right now, he's God's soldier from here on out."

"Cut," Kyle said. He looked confused, but whispered, "Good grief! What are people going to think?"

"They're going to think they just saw a sinner get saved," Ocie said. "Now, what about you, brother? Have you been born again?"

The TV people had left, and the household was having coffee around the table. Jake had said very little, but he was now regarding Ocie steadily. "Did you mean what you said about the money, Ocie?"

"Why certainly I meant it, and I meant the rest of what I said, too."

Ocie put his cup of coffee down and turned and faced Jake. "Jake, you need to get born again."

"Oh, Ocie I'm too far gone. Don't you worry about me."

"Don't make light of it," Ocie warned. "I mean business. I was hiding from God in a bottle, Jake. What are you hiding in?"

"None of your business!" Jake suddenly rose and walked out of the room. He slammed the door to his apartment forcefully.

"I think he's mad at you, Ocie," Jeremy said.

"No, he ain't, son," Ocie said. "He's mad at the truth. We're all going to pray for that big fella. He's tough, but he ain't as tough as God."

Rhiannon said, "We got to pray that God gives Mr. Jake dysphoria."

"What in the world is that?" Jeremy asked.

"You can look it up." Rhiannon grinned at him.

Three

Kate opened a drawer and pulled out her black swimsuit. Quickly slipping into it, she stuffed her beach bag with sunscreen, Jan Karon's latest Mitford novel, and a beach towel. She left the house, making her way down through the white sand where it met the blue-green waters of the Gulf. Spreading the towel on the sand, she applied some sunscreen and slipped on her sunglasses.

For the next half hour she read and let the warmth of the sun soak into her. She grew sleepy finally, and when problems tried to edge into her mind, she firmly slammed the door on them, concentrating by an act of will on her surroundings—the rhythmic crashing of the surf a few feet away, the harsh voices of the seagulls, the sand beneath her, firm but yielding where she shoved her hips and shoulders into it.

Finally she dropped off into a restful sleep. She awoke with a start an hour later. Opening her eyes and sitting up, she looked out over the Gulf, noting that the sun was lower and the air was somewhat cooler.

Kate took off her glasses and ran toward the surf, hitting it at full speed. The white, frothing waves grabbed at her ankles, and then she stepped into a trench cut by the water and dove forward. As she ducked under, the waves rolled over her. She was shaken by the cool water, and she came up shaking her head and snorting. Rising, she waded out into deeper water until finally she reached the point where the waves came in so strongly they rolled her off her feet and flung her back toward the shore. Then with a fell grip, the undertow put cold green arms around her, drawing her out into the depths. She fought against it, coming to the surface and swimming hard to catch the next wave.

After half an hour of hard swimming Kate came wading in to shore exhausted. She wrapped the beach towel around her shoulders and sat down to watch the water. A shiver ran over her in the summer heat, and she drew the red-and-green towel closer, staring hard at the line where sea and sky met, and concentrated on putting grim thoughts out of her head. *We live— but the earth is always pulling at us. We try to put it out of our minds, but we are appointed to die, and none of us knows the day or the hour.*

Suddenly she noticed something breaking the smooth surface of the water out beyond the waves. *Dolphins! Bottle-nosed dolphins!*

Six of them surfaced, but too far away to tell too much about their sizes. Father and mother with young? Perhaps. Perhaps a group of youthful males out for their first adventure away from their folks—or a troop of adolescents trying out their flippers.

Kate watched with delight as the blunt noses broke the water, each followed by a swelling head, and then the curving bodies rose in an arc so beautiful it brought a tightness to her throat.

Finally with a sigh she rose, gathered her towel and her bag, and made her way back to the deck. She paused abruptly—for Jake was sitting in one of the deck chairs staring out moodily at the Gulf. She studied his face and thought, *He's not handsome—not Hollywood pretty anyway.* Then the thought came to her mind, *He looks thoroughly masculine…like a young Burt Lancaster or Clark Gable.* And she studied, for that brief moment, the deep-set eyes, the coarse black hair, and heavy black brows. His eyes were startling, a hazel color that he kept hooded except in moments of intense surprise or pleasure. The wide mouth, the wedge-shaped face, the high cheekbones, and the broken nose all came together in her mind as she thought, *He doesn't know how attractive he is to women—and that's a good thing.*

"You ought to take a swim, Jake," she said, breaking the silence. "The water's fine."

"It's just the same as it was yesterday and the day before," he answered flatly.

"Don't be so peevish." Kate turned and saw Jacques, Cleo, and Trouble all watching her. She sat down in the chair next to Jake, and Trouble came over and tried to crawl up in her lap.

"You're too big, Trouble," she said, shoving him away and watching as he went off and threw himself down facing away from her. The picture of a pouting pit bull if she had ever seen one. Cleo, like all Ragdolls, loved to be held and she leaped up with marvelous grace into Kate's lap. Kate put her over her shoulder and began stroking her. Cleo began purring like a small steam engine.

Jacques watched all this with a critical eye and made a move toward Jake, who said, "Get away from me or I'm going to have you put to sleep."

"Don't be mean, Jake," Kate said.

And then in that instant Jacques the Ripper made one of his famous lightning moves. Jake was wearing a pair of worn blue jeans, which the big cat's claws caught readily, and there was a distinct ripping sound.

"Get away from me before I turn you into hamburger!" Jake yelled with a swipe at the cat.

"Don't fuss at him, Jake," Kate said. "He didn't mean anything bad."

"Oh yes, he did! He did it because he hates me."

Jacques sat down and licked one paw as if he were totally innocent. *Cleo, he's the one that needs to be put to sleep. I'd like to feed the Intruder to the sharks.*

Cleo stopped purring long enough to turn her big eyes on Jacques. *You're just as mean as he is, Jacques. As a matter of fact, you two are a lot alike.*

Alike! What are you talking about? I'm twice as intelligent as he is and five times better-looking. You ever see him try to climb a tree? It's pitiful!

Persons don't climb trees like cats.

They certainly don't. They can't do anything as well as we can.

This, of course, was all in the silent eloquence of cat language, expressed by peculiar looks in the eyes and body language.

"I've got something I want to read to you, Jake," Kate said. "I think it might be good for you." She picked up her beach bag and fished out part of a newspaper. She rustled as she turned the pages and then said, "Here it is. It says, 'In the home of Mary Beth and Ian Samways, cats rule and people serve. Emelie, the eight-year-old Maine coon, just won second place in *Cat Fancy* magazine in the Year's Most Spoiled Cat Contest.'"

Jake stared at her. "There's no such thing as a spoiled cat contest. You're making that up."

"I am not. Listen to this. 'Her favorite ritual is a delightful afternoon catnip tea with warm apricot–sour cream scones and some freshly whipped cream. She takes her high tea accompanied by a rendition of Bach's "Goldberg Variations" on the piano, after which she requires her owner's warm lap for her beauty rest.'"

"That's the craziest thing I ever heard of," Jake said.

"It goes on to say a lot more. For example, 'Several times a week Emelie is hand-fed thinly sliced wild salmon and other select fish. The baking mix for the apricot scones is mail-ordered from Vermont. She sleeps in the baskets of fresh-out-of-the-dryer laundry, and she has premium indoor bird-watching accommodations: floor pillows and a view of four outdoor bird feeders.'"

A look of disgust crossed Jake's rugged features. "They ought to put that woman in the nuthouse! Anybody would have to be crazy to treat a cat like that."

Jacques had been listening intently to Kate as she read about the spoiled cat. *Now that's what I'm talking about, Cleo! That's what I deserve around here. Furthermore, I'm going to demand my rights.*

You can't do that. You're treated better than ninety-nine percent of the cats in the world anyway, Jacques. Why don't you just enjoy it?

Nothing doing. I'm going to demand a lot better care than I've been getting around here.

Jacques' thoughts were interrupted as Jake suddenly pulled off a flip-flop and heaved it at Jacques. It hit the big cat right in the chest, and with a wild, outlandish growl deep in his throat, he leaped at Jake and slashed at one of his pant legs. Jake pushed him away with the other foot.

Jacques stared at the fuming Jake. *Look at him, Cleo. He's just eaten up with envy because he's not as good-looking and smart as I am. Come on, let's go catch a cardinal and eat it...*

● ● ●

Rhiannon placed three of her Scrabble pieces down on the board and counted up. "There, I have a three-way win. That's two hundred-and-sixty points for me."

Jeremy was staring down at the board. They had been playing Scrabble for an hour, and he had been totally humiliated. He was well aware that it was dangerous to play Scrabble with any human being who liked to read the dictionary as if it were an interesting novel. Now with disgust he glared at Rhiannon and snapped, " 'Sanguineous?' You made that up just to make it fit in there. There ain't no such word as 'sanguineous.' "

Rhiannon gave Jeremy a superior look mixed with pity for what she felt was his apparent lack of education. " 'Sanguineous' *is* a word."

"What does it mean?"

"It means something involving bloodshed—like, for instance, if someone said, 'This is a sanguineous novel.' It would mean there'd be lots of people blown up and shot or stabbed."

"Wait a minute. I'm going to look that up." He began thumbing through the dictionary as Kate entered, having changed out of her swimming clothes into a pair of white shorts and a lime-green top. "How are you kids doing?"

"Jeremy's mad at me," Rhiannon said.

"Why are you mad at her, Jeremy?"

"He's mad at me because I'm smarter than he is."

Kate laughed and gave Rhiannon a warm hug. She had grown to love the ten-year-old, and she had reaped infinite amusement from the girl's intelligence and ability to speak about the most arcane subjects. "You never ought to tell a man that you're smarter than he is, Rhiannon."

"He's not a man," Rhiannon corrected, "but why not?"

"Because men don't like to hear that. They like to think they're smarter than us females."

"They can't help it if they're not."

"Some men are smarter than some women—just like some women are smarter than some men," Kate said. Then, changing the subject as she noticed the flush on Jeremy's face, she asked, "How's your house coming along?"

"Oh, it's fine." Rhiannon brightened up, and her green eyes seemed to glow. "Ocie is paying for all of it. Now he's a real Christian."

"He sure is, Mom," Jeremy said, "but did you know he's getting into trouble with his witnessing?"

"What do you mean, Jeremy?" Kate asked.

"Well, he's going into all the bars and passing out tracts. He's already been thrown out of three or four of them."

"Who's been thrown out?" Jake suddenly appeared, having exchanged his slashed blue jeans for a fresh pair looking just as disreputable.

"Ocie. He's going into the bars and telling people about Jesus and handing out tracts."

"Well, I expect that's what the early disciples did in the book of Acts," Kate said.

"But, Mom, he's making a public nuisance out of himself!" Jeremy said.

"That's what they said about Socrates," Rhiannon said.

"How do you know?" Jake shot back. "You're only up to the J volume of the encyclopedia."

"Granddad told me. He said that when people have the truth and try to get others to believe it, they get in trouble like Socrates and Jesus."

"Well, he's getting in trouble all right," Jeremy said. "He asks everybody he meets if they're saved. That's not right, is it, Jake?"

Jake shot a quick look at Kate. He had no religion himself, but he had come to respect the real thing, which he saw in Kate. "There are worse things than that, Slick."

"There certainly are," Kate nodded. "By the way, Jake, I've asked Ocie, Enola, and Beverly to have supper with us tonight. And *I'm* going to cook it."

Jake made a face. "I suppose you've been down at the Winn-Dixie and bought some frozen dinners."

Kate flushed and started to speak, but Jake cut her off. "No, *I'll* do the cooking." He got up and left the porch. Rhiannon called out, "I think it's noble of you to do the cooking, Jake."

Jake turned and winked at her. "I do it in self-defense, sweetheart."

● ● ●

Rhiannon was interested in everything. She had pulled a chair up and was standing on it, watching Jake as he was preparing the supper. "What are you cooking, Jake?"

"We're going to have Lobster Newburg. You'll love it."

Rhiannon watched as Jake melted butter in a skillet, blended in flour, and added cream. Then he stirred until the sauce thickened and bubbled.

"It's a lot of trouble, isn't it, Mr. Jake?" Rhiannon said.

"Anything good is worth trouble." Jake stirred small amounts of the hot mixture into egg yolks and finally added the lobster. He then added wine, lemon juice, and salt, and sprinkled it with paprika.

Rhiannon watched carefully as he poured the mixture into small pastries. "Did you buy those little pie crusts at the store?"

"Certainly not! I made them myself. Nothing you get at the store ready-cooked is any good. Remember that, Rhiannon."

"All right, I will."

Jake finished filling the pastries and placed them in the oven. He looked up at Kate, who had been setting the table. "They better get here quick. This cooks in ten to twelve minutes, and it won't stay hot long when it's out of the oven."

He had no sooner spoken than the phone rang. Kate picked it up and said, "Hello," and then listened for a moment. She turned and said, "It's for you, Jake."

"Put it on the speakerphone. I'm cooking."

Kate did so, and Jake said, "Hello, this is Jake."

The voice on the other end said, "Mr. Novak, this is James Aldridge from Enterprise Publications. I understand that you wish a new check issued."

"That's right, Mr. Aldridge."

"Surely I got it wrong. My report said that your cat ate it."

Jake was embarrassed, and he said loudly, "The mentally defective cat that ate it is *not* my cat. He eats everything. He ate my only lavender thong. Would you believe it?"

Mr. Aldridge was silent and then said stuffily, "Perhaps I'd better have this sent electronically to your bank so that your cat won't get at it."

"You can send it by Pony Express—"

Kate suddenly interrupted him, saying, "Be quiet, Jake. You cook, and I'll take care of Mr. Aldridge." She turned to the speaker and said, "It's true, Mr. Aldridge. The cat did get to it. I'm awfully sorry that it's made trouble for you."

Mr. Aldridge was somewhat mollified. "Very well. I'll see that a new check gets cut and issued. It will be in the mail tomorrow."

"Thank you so much, Mr. Aldridge." Kate punched the button to disconnect.

"What kind of an idiot is that guy? He can't understand a cat eating a check?" Jake looked over to Jacques the Ripper, who had taken all this in from his position on top of the refrigerator. He looked pleased and said to Cleo, *There, that showed him a thing or two, didn't it? I'll eat the next one, too! You see if I don't.*

The doorbell rang, and Jacques came down smoothly and accompanied Kate as she went to the front door. *This might be a chance,* he said, *to whack somebody.*

Kate opened the door and was pleased to see all three of her guests— Ocie, Beverly, and Enola.

"Come on in. Jake's cooking dinner."

As the three went inside, they all greeted Rhiannon and Jeremy and Jake. Enola was wearing a David Meister graphic dress. The scarlet and white colors formed an intricate pattern; it was self-belted with a square neckline, and for all its simplicity it practically shouted, *This is an expensive dress.* Enola went over to Jake and smiled at him. "I think it's wonderful that you're so certain of your masculinity that you don't mind doing woman's work."

Jake grinned crookedly at her. "Thanks. You look beautiful, Enola. If you drop dead, we won't have to do anything to you."

Rhiannon piped up. "That's a sanguineous remark, Mr. Jake."

"Rhiannon's just showing off," Jeremy said, glaring at the girl. "She memorizes a new word just so people will think she's smart."

"She *is* smart," Enola said. She went over to give the girl a kiss on the cheek. "You're the most beautiful young woman I've ever seen."

"Really?" Rhiannon said, amazed.

"Really. If you're this pretty at ten, think what you'll look like by the time you're eighteen. Why, the streets will be filled with the bodies of men shooting themselves because you refuse them."

Rhiannon seldom laughed aloud, but she found this amusing. "I'd like that a lot," she said, her bright green eyes sparkling.

"So would I," Enola said. "So, Jake, what are you cooking?"

"Lobster Newburg."

"My word! That's pretty ambitious, isn't it?" Beverly was wearing a pair of patterned wool trousers, a light brown cashmere turtleneck, and a bone windowpane sports coat.

"You look like an ad for *GQ*," Kate smiled.

"*Gentleman's Quarterly?* I wouldn't wear their ratty-looking clothing to the funeral of my worst enemy!"

Ocie laughed and said, "You limeys sure like to dress up. You look good, though. I'll have to admit that."

Jake stood with a platter in his hands. "So, how does it feel to be rich, Ocie?"

"I ain't rich, I keep sayin'."

"Sure you are," Jeremy said. "You got millions of dollars out of that lottery."

"Ain't my money, son. It all belongs to God. He's the one who's rich."

"I like that," Kate said. "The only man I've heard of who gave away everything he had was a missionary named C.T. Studd."

"Why, I know about him. He was English," Beverly said.

"Yes," Kate said. "He was a cricket star. A national idol. He inherited a large fortune, and he gave it away. Every dime."

"You mean every shilling." Bev smiled.

"Whatever. Anyway, he went on the mission field to China, India, and Africa."

"He gave it all away?" Jake said, a disbelieving look on his face. "I never heard of a man doing that."

"Jesus did," Ocie said. "He made the world, and it was all His. He came down to this earth and didn't even have a house to live in."

Jake said, "Let's get this food on the table before it gets cold."

They moved over to the dining table, and Enola helped with the drinks. When they all sat down, Kate reached her hand out and said, "Let's have the blessing."

Jake gave her the same rolling-eyes look he always did when Kate wanted to say grace, but he reached out and held Enola's hand with his left and Jeremy's with his right. They all bowed their heads, and Kate said, "Ocie, you ask the blessing."

"Be right proud to," he grinned. "Lord, we thank you for this food, for every bite of it. We thank you for everybody here at this table. God, I pray that you just give us all something hard to do and then give us the grace to do it. In the name of Jesus. Amen."

Kate served the lobster, and Jeremy said, "I don't like lobster. They look like big bugs."

"Good, I'll eat yours then." Jake grinned.

"Wait a minute!" Jeremy said. "Maybe I'll try it."

"You'd better," Beverly said. He had tasted his Lobster Newburg and said, "This is tastier than anything I've had in the fanciest restaurants in England, Jake. My compliments to the chef."

The others all tasted the lobster and agreed that Jake had outdone himself. Then to change the subject, his eyes glinting with humor, Jake said, "I was talking to Police Chief O'Dell, Ocie. He says some folks want him to lock you up. They say you're a public nuisance."

"That's nonsense," Kate piped up.

"I'm just telling the truth as I see it," Ocie said.

"You believe people always ought to tell the truth, Kate?" Jake asked.

"Why, of course I do," Kate said.

"Just say what's on your mind...all the time?" Jake pressed.

"Certainly."

Jake turned to Enola and gave her a wink. "Enola, I crave your body."

Enola laughed, knowing Jake's sense of humor.

Kate sputtered, "Jake—you can't—you can't say things like that!"

"I thought you admired men who told the truth," he said.

Bev was amused. "Telling the truth can get a man into trouble, Jake. Thomas More, for instance. Henry the Eighth cut his head off for telling the truth."

"I admire that man though I don't know nothin' about it," Ocie said.

As the meal continued, Jake's eyes fell on Rhiannon. She was eating like a machine. "Don't you ever get a meal at home, Rhiannon? You eat like a starved wolf every time you come here."

"At home I eat only what I can make."

Enola gave Rhiannon a careful look. "What about your grandfather? How is he?"

Rhiannon didn't answer. She just shook her head, but her eyes were troubled.

Quickly Enola changed the subject. "Have you all been reading about the upcoming cat show? You know, I've been hired to be the resident vet."

Jake groaned. "A cat show is like getting a bunch of rocks off the ground and having a judge. You can't get rocks to perform, and cats won't do anything you want them to either."

Jacques had come in to watch the proceedings, hoping he could catch someone off guard and snatch whatever it was they were eating. He looked at Cleo and then toward Jake. *That's what you think, Intruder! Cats are a lot more talented than humans!*

Enola said, "Kate, you ought to enter Cleo in the show. She's a beauty."

Jacques glared at Enola. *What do you mean, 'Cleo'? What about me?*

Enola went on to say, "I doubt if there's a category for Savannahs like Jacques. Not enough of them."

I could be my own category, babe, Jacques said. He glared at Cleo, who was licking herself as if in readiness to receive a trophy.

Kate said thoughtfully, "I've never even seen a cat show."

"Well, the cats aren't the most interesting part," Enola said. "It's the owners who put on the show."

"What are you talking about, Enola?" Bev said. "You mean the owners are more interesting than the cats?"

"They certainly are. They'll kill to win. They're just like the owners of racehorses, except somehow they're more—" she glanced over at Rhiannon and said, "more *sanguineous* than racehorse owners."

Jacques suddenly leaped up on the table and grabbed a piece of lobster, and when Kate shooed him, he ignored her. Jake said, "You want me to cut him down to size, Kate?"

"No, he just felt lonesome." Kate got up, picked up Jacques and set him on the floor. Then she picked up Cleo and stared into her lovely eyes. "Do you really think Cleo would have a chance?"

"I'm sure she would," Enola said. "She's the most beautiful cat I've ever seen. And I've seen a *lot* of cats."

"All right then, I'll do it," Kate decided. "Then *she'll* get a medal to put around her neck. She and Jacques will both have one."

Jacques glared at them and then turned and walked huffily away. He passed by Abigail, the ferret, who was watching intently. Jacques made a slash at her, but Abigail did a backflip and scurried away. *Get out of my way, you overgrown rat, or I'll eat you for supper! A medal for you, Cleo? That'll be the day—when a female is as important as a gorgeous male like me!*

Four

Rhiannon opened the oven door, took out the pan inside, and then turned and moved to the table. She set the pan down on hot pads and looked at it with satisfaction. She was wearing a faded T-shirt with a picture of John Wayne on the front. The shirt was far too big for her, so large in fact that she could almost have turned around in it. Her shorts were too big also, and she kept them up with a leather belt that had belonged to her grandfather. She'd had to poke holes in it with an ice pick so she could tighten it, and though she looked like a ragamuffin, Rhiannon gave little attention to her personal appearance.

She looked around the new kitchen and felt a glow of satisfaction. "Ocie did a good job," she said aloud. Everything was brand, shiny new, and although the house wasn't completely finished, Rhiannon and her grandfather had moved in at once.

Ocie had insisted on buying all new furniture for the house and, much to her delight, he had taken Rhiannon with him to pick it out.

She especially enjoyed it because Ocie hadn't questioned any of her choices but had simply told the furniture salesman, "We'll take it," every time she picked something out. The dining-room table had cost a lot, and Rhiannon had hesitated. It was made out of some sort of wood from South America. It was two inches thick and had beautiful swirls and patterns in the wood, and the finish made it glow richly.

Going into the living room, Rhiannon found her grandfather sitting in his recliner with his eyes closed. The television was on the Fox Channel, his favorite, and she said, "Granddad, come on. Dinner's ready."

Morgan Brice opened his eyes slowly. He was a tall man with silver hair and a beard cut short. He was tall, gaunt, and handsome, but illness had sapped him. He took pain pills, something he'd tried unsuccessfully to conceal from Rhiannon. Eventually she had assumed the responsibility for his medication and gave him his pills when she felt he needed them.

"I'm not very hungry, honey," he said in a tired voice.

"You've got to eat, Granddad," Rhiannon insisted. "Come on now." Rhiannon pulled at his arm, and Morgan got slowly to his feet. He had the look a very ill person has—which made it impossible for him to hide his sickness from Rhiannon, although he could conceal it from strangers who didn't know him well. The two walked into the kitchen, and she pulled the chair out, and as he sat down, she said, "Look what I've got."

"That looks good. What is it?"

"I got this from the frozen-food department at Winn-Dixie. It's Marie Callender's fettucine with chicken and broccoli. You always like it, Granddad."

"It looks delicious," Morgan said. As a matter of fact, the old man had little appetite, but for Rhiannon's sake he made a show of eating the entire meal.

As usual, Rhiannon ate as if she were being timed. Her table manners were no more attractive or formal than her dress code. She ate noisily and with great gusto. Jeremy had once said, "Gosh, Rhiannon, I'd rather listen to you eat than anybody I know!"

"You don't feel good today, do you, Granddad?" Rhiannon asked during an uncharacteristic pause in her eating.

"Oh, not really bad," he fibbed.

"Yes, it is bad. I can tell."

Morgan smiled. It was so hard to hide anything from this child. She was a constant miracle to him. He had had her IQ tested when she was eight but would never tell her how high it was. He knew that it wasn't good for children to know such things.

"I'm just a little off my feed," he admitted.

Rhiannon leaned forward, the fettucine smearing her lips, and stared at her grandfather so directly that he felt like a bug under a microscope. Then without warning, she asked, "Are you going to die, Granddad?"

The question didn't take Morgan completely off guard. He had raised his granddaughter since her parents had been killed in an automobile accident. She had been only two years old when he had taken over, and most of his friends had told him he couldn't handle it. But she had turned out to be the joy and delight of his life. Carefully he replied, "Why, of course I am. We've all got to do that, sweetheart."

"I know that," Rhiannon said impatiently. "But I mean are you going to die *soon?*"

"Well, the Bible says no man knoweth the day nor the hour of his death. So, it's possible I might outlive you, as young as you are and as old as I am."

"But I'm not sick."

Her logic put Morgan into a dilemma. He had discovered long ago that Rhiannon needed to be told the exact truth. It disturbed her greatly when anybody tried to avoid speaking the truth. "You know, Rhiannon," Morgan said thinking quickly, "I've had such a good life and a long life, too."

"Sixty years," Rhiannon prompted.

"Yes, indeed, and I had a good life with your parents. Your father was a good man, and he married a good woman. And then since you came to live with me, we've had such good times. And, you know, not everybody believes there's a better life after this. The Vikings, for instance, didn't."

Rhiannon shook her head, her curly black hair shaking with emotion. "I haven't gotten to the Vikings yet in the encyclopedia."

"Well, let me tell you what they were like." Morgan stroked his jaw thoughtfully and began to speak. "One of the Viking poets said that life is like a bird coming out of a raging storm all wounded and beat, just about dead. This bird flies into a nice warm building where there's light and heat and peace. He gets his feathers all dry, and he eats until he can't eat anymore, but then, as soon as that's over, he flies out into the storm once more."

"Why didn't he stay inside?"

"The poet didn't say. What he meant was the Vikings thought life was coming out of nothingness into a warm place where there was a little joy and a little fun and a little light and then flying out into the cold."

"I don't like it," Rhiannon said. "It's not good theology."

"It's not good theology, and it's not true. The Bible tells us we're just pilgrims on this earth. Our real home isn't here. You remember when we were reading about Abraham? It said God called him, and he went out not knowing where he went. So it is with us. We're pilgrims, but we have God with us, and He loves us."

Morgan saw that Rhiannon was troubled by the conversation. Suddenly she got up, came over, and sat down on her grandfather's lap, and put her arms around him. He held her tightly. Her voice was muffled as she whispered, "I'm afraid, Granddad."

"No, no, you mustn't be afraid," he said warmly.

"I don't want you to leave me."

"Well then, we'll just have to ask Jesus to let me stay with you for a long time," he said through misting eyes.

"Let's do it now, Granddad."

"All right." Morgan was always impressed at how Rhiannon was willing to pray at the mention of prayer. He held her as Rhiannon began with earnest. "God, let my granddad live a long time. He's a good man, and we need each other. In Jesus' name. Amen." She looked up at him and said, "Now I feel better."

"So do I," Morgan said. "I think maybe I can eat a little more of Mrs. Callender's dinner."

After the meal Rhiannon cleaned up the few dishes then said, "I'm going fishing, Granddad. Maybe I'll catch a red snapper or a speckled trout."

As soon as she left the house, Morgan picked up the phone and dialed a number.

When a voice answered, he asked, "Is that you, Kate?"

"Yes, Morgan. How are you?"

"I need to see you. I've got a little problem. Could you come over and talk with me?"

"I'll be there in five minutes."

Morgan put the phone down and went out on the front porch. Ocie had insisted on building a large deck and buying the very best deck furniture. He sat down in one of the chairs and watched until he saw Kate moving along the beach. She was running with a smooth, easy motion, and when she walked up on the porch, he said, "You didn't have to run, Kate."

"Oh, I like to run on the beach," Kate said, taking a seat beside him. "What can I help you with, Morgan?" she asked. She didn't mention how bad he looked. His face had little color in it, and it bothered her, as she had been noticing him go down steadily.

"Kate, I'm having trouble with the school," Morgan said.

"The school? But school's out."

"I know, but it's the new superintendent. His name is Lowell Jackson. He paid me a visit."

"What did he want?"

"He wants me to enroll Rhiannon in school in September."

"But I thought that was all settled," Kate said. "You went through this once, didn't you?"

"Yes, they tested her, and she knew more than those administering the test," he smiled faintly. "I think the teachers were afraid to have her in their room, she's so smart. But Jackson sees it differently. He's a man who's got a little book. If it's not written in the book, it's not so."

"Well, surely something can be worked out."

"I wish you'd help me with this, Kate," Morgan said. "I can't fight much of a battle, but I know you love Rhiannon, and you can do what has to be done."

"Of course I will," Kate said without hesitation. "Now, I don't want you to worry about this. If there's *anything* you need, just ask."

A gleam came to Morgan's eyes. "Well, there *is* one more thing...would you make us some sassafras tea? Rhiannon bought some roots from a woman selling them on the street. Used to drink that when I was a child."

"I'll do my best," Kate said. "But I'm no expert."

"There's no wrong way to make sassafras tea," Morgan said. He caught at her hand as she passed by, and when she looked down he smiled, and she saw that he was troubled. "Thank you, Kate."

"No charge. Kate Forrest's prompt tea service. We never close."

● ● ●

The sun was setting, but Jake persisted in working on his Harley-Davidson. It wasn't a new machine, and he had replaced practically every part, but he took great pride in it and refused to let a mechanic touch it. He was stripped down to a pair of old shorts liberally decorated with oil and other unidentifiable stains. He turned to pick up a wrench and instead of that touched something warm and furry. He jerked his hand back and let out a yelp, then looked with disgust at the coon that had moved in close to watch him.

"Bandit, you scared me to death. You've got to be more careful how you sneak up on a fella."

Bandit moved closer, his bright eyes glowing. He reared up on his hind legs and extended his front paws, his clever little hands—Jake could never think of them as paws because they were little hands, actually—and uttered a chirping noise.

"Why, you beggar! You're always looking for a handout," Jake said. He reached into his pocket, pulled out three pecans. He cracked one of them, extracted the meat and then extended it to Bandit. He watched, as always delighted by the delicate way the coon would eat. His little hands manipulated the nut, and Jake cracked the other two. Then he reached over and got a bottle of water he had been swigging on. "Here, have some of this." He held the bottle out, and Bandit tilted his head up. He reached up and grabbed the bottle as Jake held it and swigged at it noisily.

"Now, go pester somebody else," Jake ordered.

Jake watched as the coon headed for the shade in the house. Bandit loved his comfort, and his favorite place was in the kitchen. Jake had been forced to put child locks on all the cabinet doors, for Bandit could open a door more adeptly than any child. Jake had found that out when he had come home one day and found every door open, every package of cereal open, and everything that had a top untopped. It had taken him nearly two days to do the cleanup job and replace the ruined groceries.

Jake turned to go back to work on the Harley when he heard footsteps. He looked up and saw Jeremy coming out of the house. "Hey, Slick, give me a hand on this contrary machine," Jake called.

As Jeremy approached, Jake saw that he had a bruise on his right cheek and a cut on his swollen lower lip. "Carburetor's not running right on this machine, but I'll fix it or know the reason why," Jake said.

Jeremy said nothing but sat down on a wooden box. Jake made small talk, more or less to keep a silence from building up. Finally he turned and tried to look surprised. "Hey, Slick, what happened to your face?"

"Nothing."

"Nothing? Looks to me like you ran into a brick wall or something. Lemme see that." He reached out and pulled Jeremy's head around. "Not too bad," he said, "but you gonna tell me what happened?"

Jeremy struggled with himself. He was a wiry boy of twelve, almost skinny, but would clearly be a big man some day. He had auburn hair and blue eyes, and he had grown very fond of Jake, who had spent a great deal of time with him.

"Carl Bailey beat me up."

"He did, huh? Why'd he do that?"

"Because I faked him out in a basketball game and stole the ball from him. He just jumped on me. I didn't have a chance."

"Didn't the coach stop it?"

"He wasn't there. It was just a pickup game with a bunch of us guys."

"He's bigger than you, I take it?"

Jeremy looked up, misery drawing his mouth into a pale line. "He's bigger than anybody in our class."

Jake picked up a rag and wiped the grease off his hands, went over, and sat down in the sand facing Jeremy. He studied the young boy, thought of his own adolescence when he had been beaten up by a bully. It seemed to him that all boys went through that. He said, "When I was in the eighth grade a big kid named Duane Thayler did the same thing to me. I couldn't see out of either eye for a day or two. Sure does discombobulate a fellow to take a beating like that."

"It does what?" Jeremy said. "You sound like Rhiannon, using them big words."

"Oh, it just means it hurts your feelings and you feel rotten."

"Well, that's the way I feel all right," Jeremy conceded. "He'll do it again, too. He's a bully. He beats up on all the guys."

Jake hesitated. He didn't know exactly how to handle the situation. His first impulse was to go find the boy and turn him over his knee and thrash him, but that would just make things worse for Jeremy. He said, "You want some help, Jeremy?"

"You can't help me. He wouldn't pick on me if you were there."

"No, he wouldn't, but maybe I can show you a few things, and you'll be able to handle him next time."

"He's so much bigger than I am, Jake."

"You ever hear of Robert Fitzsimmons?"

"No, who's he?"

"He was a prizefighter back in the early days of the ring. He was only a middleweight. It means he had to weigh no more than a hundred and sixty pounds, but somehow Fitzsimmons always fought bigger guys. He scheduled a fight with the world's heavyweight champion, Jim Jeffries, who was big as a house. When somebody told Fitz about how big Jeffries was, he just grinned and said, 'The bigger they are, the harder they fall.'"

Jeremy grinned, suddenly forgetting his cut lip. "I like that. I bet he won, didn't he?"

"No, he got beat."

"Oh." Jeremy looked disappointed. "I thought you were going to say he won."

"That's only in storybooks. But nobody beat Jeffries when he was in his prime. I don't think Muhammad Ali could have beat him, he was so big and strong. But you know, it's okay to lose."

Jeremy scowled. "Well, I sure know about that."

"It's okay to lose—it's not okay to quit," Jake said.

Jeremy sat there thinking and finally said, "He's going to make life miserable for me as long as I'm in that school."

"I can help you," Jake repeated. "It may take a while, but one of these days, sooner or later, if you let me help you, you'll get the best of him."

Jeremy swallowed hard and finally said, "Okay. I want you to help me, Jake."

"Why, sure I will, Slick. Come on."

"Where we going?"

"We're going down and buy memberships at the Bodenheimer Health Club. Every day we're going down there, me and you."

Jake rose, and Jeremy rose with him, hope in his eyes. "Do you really think so, Jake, that I can do it?"

"Is the Pope Catholic? Come on, let's go."

● ● ●

Jake had dismantled his Glock and was carefully oiling the parts. It was the gun he had carried when he had been a homicide detective, and he kept it in first-class shape. Abigail had climbed up his pants leg, then propped herself up on the table in the acrobatic way ferrets have at times. She sniffed around at the different parts, then hunched herself up on her back high in the air, and jumped up on his shoulder.

"You just can't resist me, can you, girl?" Jake reached up and tickled Abigail's back. He had actually grown rather fond of the little creature. When he had first come to the coast he had thought ferrets were without personality. He had discovered, however, that Abigail, at least, had a scintillating personality. She loved to play games, and nothing was more to her liking than coming up to his bedroom, where he would throw a cover over her and grab her and shake her. She would fight her way out and make a run at him as if she were a full-grown lion, whereupon he would roll her on her back, and she would nip him until she loosed her. She was careful never to hurt him, though, and now he looked at her shiny beady eyes and said, "I'll bet you're a real prize among ferrets. Maybe we ought to get you a boyfriend, and then we could raise little ferrets." Jake suddenly realized how far this was from his usual attitude toward animals. "I'm getting senile," he grumbled. "You're not getting a boyfriend."

A door closed, and he looked up to see Kate come out of her room. He stared at her—she was wearing an outfit he'd never seen before. Kate felt somewhat self-conscious. The outfit was a Shin Choi design. It consisted of an embroidered, gathered full skirt with dark green figures on a sparkling white background, a solid-white tank-top pullover cut lower than her usual, and a cardigan with a button front and deep pockets, jet-black in contrast to the top. She had paid more for it than she was accustomed to paying, but it was the first new outfit she had bought since moving to the coast.

"Well, you're certainly all dressed up. Where are you going?"

Kate gave him a direct look. "I'm going out with Beverly."

"Oh? And why are you wearing such a sexy dress?"

"This is *not* a sexy dress!" Kate protested.

"It is too," Jake said. He proceeded to tell her why, and she interrupted him.

"I don't want to talk about it, Jake."

"Maybe it's not the dress that's sexy. Maybe it's you."

"That's an awful thing to say, and it's not true."

"Well, if you say so—but be sure you explain it carefully to Devon-Hunt. Anybody with a hyphen in his name can't be very bright, so you'll have to explain carefully that the dress isn't sexy and you aren't either."

"I don't want to hear any more about this, Jake."

"Okay. Well then, there's something else I've been meaning to talk to you about, Kate."

"Oh? What?" Kate's voice was suspicious.

"It's about a physical problem."

"I didn't know you had any physical problems. Mental, yes. Physical, no."

"Very funny. Gee, and I was hoping you'd help me out."

Kate relented. "Why, of course I will, but I don't know what I could possibly do. I'm not a nurse."

Jake got up and came close to her. He always made her feel small and fragile when he did this. "It's a dental problem, Kate."

"Well, I can't help you with a dental problem either. I'm not a dentist."

"No," Jake said, "But I've discovered a home-treatment plan, but I need some help to make it work. Will you help me, Mary Katherine?"

"Well...I guess so. If I can."

"Oh, you can. I'm sure of that," Jake said. "It goes like this." He moved forward, reached out, pulled her to him by her shoulders and kissed her firmly on the lips. Kate was taken so completely aback she couldn't move, and then she pushed him in the chest with her fist and cried, "Why, you—you liar!"

"No, I'm not a liar. It's a treatment."

"It is not!"

"Sure it is. Look at this." Jake whirled and moved over to the table where there was a magazine. "It's a health magazine, and look at this on page forty-five."

Kate was furious but looked down and saw a man and a woman kissing. "Read what it says," Jake said.

Kate read the first of the article, which said, "Kissing can help prevent cavities. It stimulates the flow of saliva, which naturally cleans away cavity-causing food particles."

"This is the most arrant nonsense I ever heard!"

"No, we have to think of our dental health, Kate," Jake said, but his eyes were dancing with merriment. "I think three or four treatments a day for a couple of weeks, and I wouldn't have any cavity problems at all." He moved toward her again, and she cried out, "You stay away from me, you beast!" Kate whirled and made for the door, her head held high, and just before she closed it, he called out, "Don't you believe in medical help for the unfortunate?" He at once went to the window and saw that Beverly had driven up in his Rolls. When Kate got in and slammed the door so loudly he could hear it, he laughed and said, "Well, I guess she's not interested in proper dental hygiene."

Jacques and Cleo had been watching the whole thing, and Jacques said, *I like that. That's teaching that woman a thing or two. She needs it. She's all swollen up with pride.*

She is not, Jacques, and it was mean of Jake to play a trick on her like that.

Jacques the Ripper moved in closer and touched noses with Cleo. Their eyes met, and he whispered in cat talk, *All's fair in love and war, baby....*

● ● ●

Bev noticed immediately that something was wrong with Kate. She said very little, and he had to keep the conversation going.

"I've picked out a fine place for us to eat," he said brightly. She looked up to see that he had turned west on Fort Morgan Road. "We're not going to the Fort, are we?"

"Some other time when the sun's shining, and we want to just get out and increase our historical knowledge," he answered. Fort Morgan had been built to protect Mobile Bay during the Civil War. It had failed, of course. Visitors now came to view the remnants fairly often.

"Where are we going?"

"You've heard of the Beach Club, haven't you?"

"No, I haven't," Kate said.

"Well, it's probably the fanciest place to eat on the coast. I always find out the most expensive restaurant to take my dates to. I don't have the manly attractiveness of Jake, so I have to impress young ladies with my money. Pitiful, isn't it?"

"You don't have to do that, Bev," Kate said.

"Well, I did do some scouting around looking at all the restaurants. It came down to a dead heat between the Beach Club and a place called Hooters."

"Hooters! Have you ever eaten there?"

"Oh, yes, I go there quite often. They make wonderful hamburgers."

"It's nothing but a—a peep show. The waitresses there wear—they don't wear enough clothes, or they're too tight or something."

"Oh, I didn't notice that. I was too interested in my hamburger."

"I'll bet," Kate said.

Bev's mild teasing enabled Kate to put Jake's behavior out of her mind. They arrived at the Beach Club which was, indeed, a lovely restaurant facing the Gulf. Kate had lobster, while Beverly had crab cakes and fried shrimp. "This helps build up my cholesterol," Bev said. "My arteries are getting a little bit empty."

"Isn't it amazing that everything that tastes good is bad for you?"

"They're a bunch of moralists, those doctors, that's all they are," Bev said.

Afterward Bev and Kate went to the civic auditorium, where a classical guitarist was performing.

On their way home Kate talked about the guitarist, and when Bev finally stopped the car in front of her house, she said, "Bev, it's been a wonderful evening—"

"Kate, there's something important I want to talk to you about," Bev interrupted.

Kate was well acquainted with what men wanted when they parked in front of a date's house in the wee hours of the morning. "What is it, Bev?" she asked cautiously.

"Something's been on my mind lately. I was watching an old film on the Turner Network. I don't know the name of it. Got in on the middle of it, don't you see? But it had a young man and a young woman. Mickey Rooney, I think it was. I don't know the young woman."

"Could have been Judy Garland."

"Yes, I think it was."

Kate wondered where he was going, and noted he had put his hands on the seat behind her. "What does a Mickey Rooney movie have to do with anything?" she asked.

"Well, I'm not quite certain about some American phrases nor about dating habits in this country. But at one point in the movie Mickey asked his date to do something, and I wasn't sure about it."

"What did he ask her to do?" Kate asked.

"He asked her to go steady with him. I'm not exactly sure what that means," Beverly said, "but I think it means that they make sort of a pact that neither of them will go with anybody else."

Kate smiled. "That's exactly what it means. That expression isn't used much anymore, but it was big when I was in high school."

"Well, what I'm getting at is...will you go steady with me, Kate?"

Kate was surprised—and a little amused.

"I can't imagine why you would ask me that. We've only been dating a short while."

"Well, I'm interested in taking it to the next level, as I believe they say," Beverly said. He moved closer to her, and his hand dropped on her shoulder. "Eventually I want to get married and have a family." He paused, then when she didn't reply, he went on. "I'd like for us to see if an arrangement like going steady would work out for us."

Kate's amusement increased. Bev had cupped his hand on her shoulder and was softly caressing it.

"And if I don't work out as a potential wife, you'll try another woman?"

"Well, I haven't thought that far," Bev admitted.

"Bev, I like you very much, but I can tell you right now it won't work between us."

"Why not?" he asked as he moved another fraction of an inch or so closer to her, and his grip on her tightened. "Do you find me...unsuitable?"

"Of course I don't find you unsuitable. I find you rich, English, a man with a title—and with a hyphen. All the things that are totally alien to me. We might as well be living in different universes."

"Well, if it bothers you, Kate, I could get rid of the hyphen. It doesn't mean anything to me if that's all it is. People in love don't have to be alike in every way. I find you very appealing. As a matter of fact, Kate, I'm quite sure I'm falling in love with you."

The pressure of his hand grew greater, and he pulled her around until she was facing him. Kate had lifted her head, and her two hands came against his chest, but she didn't push him away.

And then he kissed her, heavy and long, and for an instant all the loneliness she had known since her husband had died came rushing back to her. For a moment she was once again a complete woman, with a woman's dreams and desires, and as he held her, she was flooded with old memories. And then as she pulled back, and her breath rushed out, she couldn't speak for a moment. And she realized she liked this man much more than she had thought.

"You're a lovely woman, Mary Katherine Forrest," Bev said quietly. He withdrew his hand and moved slightly away from her, which pleased her. He wasn't a man to pressure a woman—she knew that—and now she said, "You're a real gentleman, Bev. There aren't many left. Almost an endangered species."

"I never want to force myself on a woman. Love is a two-way street."

Kate wanted to break the moment. She knew she wouldn't forget his kiss easily. To change the rhythm of what had happened, she knew she must change the subject, so she said, "I can't answer your question now—about going steady, but I do want to ask you to do something for me."

"Anything."

"Don't agree until you've heard what it is." Then she quickly outlined

Morgan Brice's problem with the superintendent of schools and said, "I've got a plan. Morgan's too sick to do much teaching, but you could tutor Rhiannon in English literature."

"But Kate, I've never taught anybody."

"She's ten years old, Bev."

"Yes, though she's the smartest ten-year-old I've ever seen. But Kate, I'll do it if it means that much to you."

"Thank you, Bev. It does."

He grinned. "How many points do I get?"

Kate laughed, reached out and touched his cheek. "Quite a few. And even more for tonight. I had a lovely time. Good night, Bev."

"Good night, Kate dear. I'll go home and brush up on my Shakespeare. That child probably has all of the plays memorized."

"She probably does," Kate agreed. She gave Bev one small kiss on the cheek and then went in the house. In the kitchen she found Jake at the table writing.

He looked up and said, "It's a little late, Mary Katherine."

Kate smirked. "Jake, you are not my father or my husband."

"No, but if either one of them were here, they'd say it was too late."

"You're impossible," Kate said. She turned to see Trouble who had come to sit down on her feet. "Get off of my feet, Trouble! Why does that dog like to sit on feet? He's a pervert."

I've always said that, Jacques remarked. He had been sitting on the table watching Jake work, and he now licked his front paw and said, *All dogs are perverts.*

"Jake, I need you to do something for me."

"If you'll promise me to get in earlier on your future dates, I will."

"I won't promise you that."

"Well, what is it you want?" Jake conceded, curious about what Kate would ask. "Maybe I'll do it anyway."

She explained the problem Morgan had with the school superintendent, and she said, "I'm going to get enough tutors for Rhiannon to satisfy the superintendent that she's getting a good education."

"I'm a professional thug," Jake said. "What do you want me to teach her—how to use a blackjack?"

"You were a history minor in college. You can tutor her in history. Will you do it?"

"I suppose. But she probably knows everything already—or at least everything beginning with the letter J."

"Thank you, Jake. That's kind of you." She turned and headed for her room.

"Did that sexy dress get the job done?" he called after her.

Kate didn't answer. She shut the door and prepared for bed. When she finally slipped between the covers and turned out the light, she lay there for a while, thinking about Bev's proposal, and she thought, *I wonder what it would be like to be Lady Katherine.* The notion amused her, and as she drifted off to sleep, she dreamt of her evening with the lovely British man with the hyphen in his name.

Five

Kate had spent the morning cleaning house and feeding all the animals. She had just taken a frozen mouse out of the freezer for Big Bertha, the Burmese python, when Jake and Jeremy entered. They had been gone all morning without giving her any hint as to where, and both of them were carrying small canvas bags.

"Well, where have you two been?"

Jake didn't answer for a moment. He was looking at her clothing, which was the rattiest pair of shorts and the most dilapidated shirt she could find. "Nice outfit," he said. "I see you've been shopping at Neiman Marcus again."

"I'm cleaning house. I don't need a dress from Neiman Marcus to clean house."

Jake looked around the room, turning his head to one side. "It looks nice," he said. "Doesn't it, Jeremy?"

"Sure does, Mom," Jeremy said. He added, "You'll be as good a house-keeper as Jake if you keep this up."

"I'm already a good housekeeper," Kate said.

"Oh? Let me just take a look at your room," Jake said with a grin. He turned and headed toward the door that led off of the main area of the house into Kate's room, but she ran and got in front of him. "You stay out of my room!" she said, her face turning red.

"Well, if you need help," Jake said, "I'll go outside and get the rake."

"My room isn't that bad." She started to wave her finger at him and saw she still had the frozen mouse in her hand.

"Is that for supper?" Jake said. "I don't think there'll be enough to go around."

"What I do in my bedroom is my own business. You just take your nose out of it."

For Jake Novak, teasing Mary Katherine Forrest was a major form of entertainment. The two were so different in so many ways that he found no difficulty ribbing her, especially so far as housekeeping and cooking were concerned. She was very defensive about it, and Jake needled her with the words, "You know, *my* mother always made me put on clean underwear."

"Jake Novak, you have the worst habit of saying things that have nothing to do with the conversation."

"It has everything to do with the conversation."

"What does your underwear have to do with keeping a house clean?"

Jake winked at Jeremy broadly and said, "Well, she always made me put on clean underwear because she said I might be in an accident, and they would take me to the hospital, and there the doctor and the nurses would see that I was wearing dirty underwear, which would be a reflection on her as a mother."

Kate stared at him. "What in the world does that have to do with keeping my room clean?"

"Well, just think about this, Mary Katherine. Suppose we had a fire here—not a bad one, just a minor blaze. We'd call the fire department. They'd come rushing in, and one of the first things they'd do would be to open the doors to the bedrooms and see if the blaze had damaged anything there. They'd see the beautiful house—and then they'd open your door and, well, I hate to say it, Mary Katherine, but you know what your room looks like. Like a bomb has gone off in it, and you know how those firemen are. They're the worst gossips in the world."

"Oh, sure."

"No, they really are," Jake insisted. "Of course they get it from their mothers. And just think—it would get out in the newspapers, and on the front page of the *Morning Register* would be the huge headline 'MARY KATHERINE FORREST'S BEDROOM IS THE PITS.' And there would be photos, of course."

"You think you're so smart!"

"Oh, I suppose I'm of average intelligence. You're *sure* you don't want me to clean your room?"

"You just think you're better than I am because you can cook better."

"Certainly."

"But *I'm* cooking supper tonight."

"Aw, Mom, let Jake do it," Jeremy said.

Kate stared at her son. "You never complained about my cooking before we moved here."

"You're a good cook, Mom, but Jake is a real chef."

"All right, then." Kate threw up her hands and noticed the mouse was still in her right one. She stared at it for a moment and then went over to the refrigerator and stuck it back in the freezer section.

"I wish you'd keep those frozen mice out of the refrigerator," Jake said. "I might make a mistake, and we'd have fried mouse for supper."

"Jake, can we have blueberry pancakes and sausage tonight?" Jeremy asked.

"That's not supper. That's breakfast," Kate said.

"A foolish consistency is the hobgoblin of little minds," Jake intoned.

"What does that mean, Jake?" Jeremy asked.

"It means you don't have to do the same thing over and over just because you've always done it that way." He moved over to Kate and put his hands on her shoulders and looked down into her eyes. "Launch out into the unknown, Mary Katherine. Get off the beaten track. Grab your hat and get your coat. Leave your worries on the doorstep. Put your feet on the sunny side of the street."

Mary Katherine slapped his hands away and said huffily, "I'd love to, but instead I'm going to take Cleo to the vet."

"What's wrong with her, Mom?" Jeremy said quickly.

"It's time for her shots, and she needs something for hair balls."

Jake said, "Come on, Slick. Let's go catch a shark."

Mary Katherine started toward her room to change clothes, but she couldn't help but ask, "Why do you want to catch those things? You can't eat them."

"It's a man thing, Mom," Jeremy said. "You wouldn't understand it."

Mary Katherine whirled and glared at Jake, "You taught him to say that, Jake Novak!"

"Didn't either."

"You are so awful! I'd hate to think how terrible you must have been when you were younger."

"When I was younger I was shorter."

"And your behavior was worse."

"No, Mary Katherine. When I was Jeremy's age here," he put his hand on Jeremy's shoulder and looked down at him fondly, "I went to church every Sunday and helped old ladies across the street all the time."

"I'll just bet you did!"

Kate slammed the door, and Jeremy looked up. "Why do you tease Mom like that?"

"It's good for her, Slick. It keeps her juices all swishing around. It makes her prettier, don't you think?"

"If you say so, Jake."

● ● ●

Enola was checking Cleo carefully while the cat simply sat there looking up lovingly at her. Then Cleo suddenly grinned, and as the edges of her mouth turned up, Enola laughed. "This is the only cat I've ever seen who grins—except for the Cheshire cat in *Alice in Wonderland*."

"Is she all right?"

"She's in great shape. She'll do wonderfully in the cat show. I bet there won't be another cat there that will grin at the judge. That'll get her the blue ribbon for sure."

"Well, I hope so," Kate said. "But in the meantime, what am I supposed to do about her hair balls?"

Enola opened the door of a nearby cabinet and took out a small box, opened it, and extracted a tube. "Here, this will fix the hair-ball problem. You might give some to Jacques as well, though he's mean enough that he'll probably pass hair balls without it."

Kate took the green tube and read the word *Laxatone*. "How am I supposed to get *this* down her?"

"You don't have to feed it to her orally. Just put a small amount on her front leg above the claws. She'll lick it off."

"Does it taste bad?"

Enola laughed. "How do I know? I've never tasted it. But you know how cats are. They clean themselves all the time. She'll take care of administering her own medicine. Now, Kate, could you use some coffee?"

"Yes, that would be wonderful."

"Come along. I think I've got a treat for Cleo as well."

The two women moved into a smaller room that had a table with three chairs. On the table, against the wall, was a coffeemaker with a full carafe, and over it hung a stainless-steel cabinet. Enola opened its door, took out two cups, and filled them with coffee. "I like it strong," she warned.

"So do I." The two women sat down at the small table and Kate tasted the coffee. It was hot just like she liked it. "Enola, you should have seen it. Jake had a fit the other day when I was making coffee with Folgers instant. He dumped the whole jar down the garbage disposal. I thought he was going to put me in after it."

Enola laughed, her dark eyes dancing. "Must be interesting to live with Jake Novak."

"I'm not *living with him!*"

"Well, you know what I mean." Enola said, still amused. "Everybody in White Sands thinks you're living with him in every sense of the word—if you know what I mean."

"Do *you* think so?"

"I don't know," Enola said, setting her cup down momentarily. "Are you?"

"No!" Kate protested loudly.

"Why so emphatic, Kate? When you answer a question like that, all you have to do is to say gently, in a most feminine manner, 'Why no, Enola, I'm not sleeping with Jake.' Speak sweetly. Don't shout no. It makes people think you're guilty."

"Well, I'm not. Not of that anyway."

The two women drank their coffee, and Enola asked, "You've been here in White Sands long enough to know if you like it. Do you?"

"Yes, I suppose so. My life is so different, that's for sure. When I lived in Memphis I got up, worked a shift at Wal-Mart and then a shift at McDonald's. I was barely able to stagger home. And I was trying to take care of Jeremy and keep house."

"It sounds pretty bad."

"It *was* bad."

"But you're all right now. You've got that beautiful house and lots of interesting pets, including Mr. Jake Novak. You have cash money coming in every month. You don't have to work, and you've got Lord Beverly Devon-Hunt chasing you with his tongue hanging out."

"Oh, Enola, you exaggerate. He is not chasing me, and his tongue is not hanging out."

"You two are hitting it off pretty heavy. How many times did you go out with him last week?"

"I forget."

"It was three."

"What, are you keeping score?" Kate said with a smile. "You have a private detective following me?"

"Jake tells me these things. You have no secrets in that house. Jake is as gossipy as a woman when he wants to be. But tell me more about Beverly. You want to confess any improper behavior?"

"No, he's not like that. He's a gentleman."

"Yes, he *is* 'like that.' *All* men are 'like that.' He just knows you're a Puritan."

"I am not!"

"Of course you are. I do yard work in less clothing than you have in that swimsuit of yours."

"I can't stand those skimpy bikinis."

"I like them. It gives a girl a sense of freedom."

Kate sipped her coffee, and then she giggled. "You know what he asked me to do?"

Enola leaned forward, her enormous eyes opening wider. "Tell me. This is just like being on *The Young and the Restless*. What did that scamp want you to do?"

"He asked me to go steady."

Enola laughed aloud. "'Go steady'! Why, I haven't heard that phrase used since I was in junior high. Where'd he hear that?"

"Oh, he was watching some movie with Mickey Rooney and Judy Garland. He pretended not to know what going steady meant."

"He must have an eye for you, Kate. You'd be crazy not to grab that guy."

"But I don't love him."

"Love is a many-splendored thing." Enola grinned crookedly. "The best advice I could give you is *learn* to love him."

"How do I do that?"

"You don't have to actually do it. All you have to do is make him *think* you love him."

"I couldn't do that," Kate said, surprised at Enola's frankness.

"Why not?" Enola said. "It's not hard. A woman has a few advantages over a man."

"Like what?"

"Well, we're smarter, for one thing."

Kate laughed. "Jake would hand you your head if you said a thing like that to him. He doesn't think women are very smart at all."

"Ah, and that's where we have the advantage," Enola said. "Men are so dumb that they don't know that we're the smart ones. So, we can do things that catch them off guard. That's what you need to do with Devon-Hunt."

"Things like what?"

"Oh, *lean* on him."

"Lean on him?"

"You know what I mean. Put yourself up against him, and look up at him, and flutter your eyelashes, and act helpless."

Kate laughed. "I can't do that kind of thing and keep a straight face!"

"Well, *I* can," Enola said. "It wouldn't be any harder than working a double shift at Wal-Mart and McDonald's. Here, I've got some great magazines that will give you all kinds of hints."

"I'm not reading those awful things," Kate said.

"Why, they're the Bible of fifty million women, Kate."

"Not the kind of Bible they need," Kate said.

Enola glanced at her watch and said, "Uh-oh! I'm going to be late for my luncheon. Kate, why don't you come with me?"

"Who'll be there?"

"Oh, just a group of cat owners and judges for the cat show. You need to meet some of your competition."

"What will we do with Cleo?"

"We'll leave her here. I've got a room with a color TV and a Simmons mattress and a door that leads to a fenced-in area. She'll be fine. Come on."

"But I'm not dressed for a fancy place."

"Well, we're going to a fancy place all right. We're going to Gauthier's."

"I've never been there. Too expensive."

"We won't be paying for it. Some of the rich owners are footing the bill. Come on. It'll be fun."

● ● ●

Enola pulled her Hummer into the parking lot at Gauthier's. As the two women approached the door, Kate said, "Enola, I'll be out of place here."

"They'll all be snobby, most of them anyway. Just be snotty right back at them."

"It's out of my league."

"You need to learn how to bluff, Kate. These jet-set phonies put on their pants one leg at a time. Spit in their eye before they spit in yours."

As soon as Kate entered the restaurant, she was almost baptized in the luxury of the place. It even smelled like money! What appeared to be a maitre d' approached them—a small man with a wealth of chestnut hair, attractive brown eyes, and a good smile. "May I help you, ladies?" he said.

"We're part of the cat-show luncheon," Enola said.

"Yes, of course. Follw me, ladies. They're in one of our private dining rooms."

The maitre d' led the women into an ornate dining room dominated by a large, oval table. To one side was a longer table where a waiter was fixing drinks. "Here you are, ladies," the maitre d' said. "Enjoy your meal."

"Thank you, we will," Enola said.

Kate was looking over the guests. There were only a few people there, no more than a dozen. They were all talking loudly, but one of them, a small woman with silver hair and a pair of careful brown eyes, left her place by the bar and approached the two women.

"Raina Bettencourt," Enola whispered. "She'll be the final judge, so don't spit in the soup while she's around."

"Good afternoon," the woman said with a wide smile, "I'm Raina Bettencourt."

"Yes, I know." Enola smiled. "I was present when you did the judging in Buffalo two years ago. I thought you made an excellent choice, Mrs. Bettencourt. I'm Dr. Enola Stern. I've been asked to be the resident veterinarian at the show."

"I'm so glad to meet you, Dr. Stern."

"And this is Mary Katherine Forrest. She'll be entering a Ragdoll in the competition."

"I love Ragdolls," Raina said. "Come along. I'll introduce you to some of the other owners."

"I think I've seen her on television," Kate whispered. "Didn't she host that special on the big cats in Africa?"

"Yes, she did. She's very famous. Be careful around her, Kate. She can be mean as a snake when she's riled."

A large man stepped forward and put his hand out. He held onto Mary Katherine's a little longer than was necessary, and then he turned his charm toward Enola.

"Watch out," Raina whispered. "This is Harrison Phelps. You've probably seen him on television."

Enola turned toward the man and smiled cooly as she said, "I understand you're very rich, Mr. Phelps. I need all the rich friends I can get. I'm just a poor vet myself."

Phelps laughed, clearly charmed by Enola's forward approach. "Well, we'll see if we can talk about that, my dear. We'll have plenty of time between showings to get better acquainted. What are you entering in the show?"

"I won't be entering, but my friend, Mary Katherine, has a Ragdoll she'll be showing."

Harrison Phelps grinned and shook his head. "Well, that's bad news, Mary Katherine, or may I call you Kate?"

"Everyone does," Kate said. "Why is it bad news that I'll be entering my Ragdoll?"

"Well, I hate to tell you, but I have the Ragdoll award nailed down myself. Paid three hundred big ones for her. Her name is Princess Grace."

"Money doesn't buy awards," Raina said with a small smile, "although I'm sure you might disagree with that, Harrison."

"Money buys *anything*."

Mary Katherine grinned slyly and said, "You must know the Bible very well, Mr. Phelps."

"The Bible?" the man looked at her quizzically. "I don't know anything about the Bible. Does the Bible say that, that money buys anything?"

"Yes, it does." Everyone turned to look at Kate.

"I've read the Bible quite a bit, but I never read that," Raina said.

"It says in Ecclesiastes 10:19, 'Money answers all things.'"

Harrison Phelps was delighted. "Hey, that's been my philosophy. Money will buy anything, but I sure didn't know the Bible confirmed that. I thought it said everybody had to be a monk or a nun and give all their money away."

"It doesn't say that either, Mr. Phelps," Kate said.

"Dear, just call me Harrison."

"Very well, Harrison," Kate smiled. "It says money answers all *things*. Money will buy any *thing*, but it won't buy something that isn't a *thing*."

"I'd be interested to know what you mean." The speaker was a woman in her sixties. "I'm Hannah Monroe," she said. "I'm not a Bible scholar. As a matter of fact, I haven't read much of it. But what do you mean by saying that some things aren't *things*?"

Kate began, "Well, I mean Mr. Phelps here can probably buy any car he wants because it's a thing. He can buy any house he wants because a house is a thing." She turned then and looked directly at Harrison Phelps. "But you can't buy love because love isn't a thing. You can't buy peace in your heart because that's not a thing. So, you see, money has its limitations."

"You'll never make him believe that." A woman had crossed over to stand next to the two women. "I'm Eileen Saban. I'm Harrison's ex-wife. He thinks money is all there is, so I suggest you watch your wallet. He has no morals whatsoever."

"Eileen, I'd appreciate it if you'd stay out of my business," Harrison said, obviously annoyed. "When we were married you had something to say about my behavior, but not now."

"Well, that's a lie, but you always were a liar. You never took any advice from anyone. Miss Forrest is right. Money won't buy some things, and you're going to find that out. And you're going to find it out in this show, too."

"What do you mean by that?" Phelps snapped.

"Why, I mean Byron Blue Diamond is going to win." She turned and smiled at the two women. "She's a beautiful Russian blue. I got her as part of the settlement when I divorced Harrison."

"You didn't divorce *me*. I divorced *you*, and that crook of a lawyer got the Blue Diamond out of me. You're only here to embarrass me, but you won't do it, because we all know what kind of a woman you are."

"Er, I think perhaps it's time we sat down and ate," Raina Bettencourt said, smiling as if she enjoyed the battle between the two, but also embarrassed by their public squabbling.

Raina seemed to be in charge of the table, for she indicated where she wanted people to sit.

"Why do these people let her boss them around like that, Enola?" Kate whispered.

"Because she's the judge."

"And you two ladies sit here," Raina said, indicating two nearby chairs.

A very striking woman was seated across from Kate. She looked vaguely familiar, so Kate said, "I don't think we've met before, but you seem familiar."

Eileen Saban said, "You've seen her picture in fashion magazines. This is Olga Ivanov. She has a Siamese that has won several shows. Cats are her hobby."

Kate was impressed with the woman. She had a model's body, tall and lean, enormous brown eyes, auburn hair, and a wide mouth. "It must be exciting to be a fashion model, Miss Ivanov," Kate offered.

"Just Olga," the woman replied. "No, it's not particularly exciting. I'm often bored to tears. A waitress at a truck stop has a more exciting life than I do."

Everyone at the table laughed, and Raina said, "Oh, don't believe her! She loves all that attention."

Seated beside Olga was a nice-looking man with coal-black hair. He had gray eyes, and there was something intriguing about him that Kate couldn't quite put her finger on.

"I'm Victor Mandel," he said with a nod.

"I'm glad to know you, Mr. Mandel," Kate replied.

"Just Vic will do. I'm a gangster out of Philadelphia."

A laugh went around the table, and Harrison said, "Well, there's one honest man among us."

"Are you really a gangster?" Enola said.

"Yes, I am."

"How do you stay out of jail?"

"Money answers all things. Isn't that what you said, Kate?"

"Yes, I did."

"Well, money buys judges and politicians. That's how I stay out of jail."

Just then the servers brought in the food. The meal consisted of spicy tomato-basil soup, a small salad of fresh baby greens with cherry tomatoes, cucumbers, mandarin oranges and almond slices bathed in a fresh raspberry vinaigrette dressing, poached salmon, smoked cheese grits, and asparagus.

As she ate, Kate noticed a vivacious young woman with a healthy tan. She introduced herself as Mary Beth Pickens and told Kate, "I feel so out of place here."

"So do I," Kate said. "I'm just a working girl, or I was until a few months ago."

"Did you strike it rich?" Vic Mandel smiled. He was really a rather attractive man, but there was an aura of violence about him. It was nothing obvious, but Kate knew she would hate to cross him, for he would not be a man to forgive easily.

"No, I didn't," Kate said briefly, then turned back to the young woman. "What do you do, Mary Beth?"

"Oh, I ride the barrels. Rodeo, you know."

"That must be exciting," Kate said.

"Oh, I love it. My horse is named Cherry. She's a quarter horse. I'm going to win the nationals this year. You wait and see if I don't."

"And you have a cat entered in the show?"

"Yes, I do. I don't have much money, but an aunt of mine died recently, and she knew I loved cats. So when she died, she left her beautiful Persian to me."

"Well, good luck to you. I hope you win."

"What kind of cat do you have entered, Kate?" Vic Mandel asked.

"A Ragdoll, but I have another cat too. A Savannah."

"Don't believe I know that breed."

"There aren't too many of them. It's illegal to own a Savannah in some places. New York, for example."

"Why illegal? Sounds right up my alley."

"Well, there are laws against keeping wild animals in New York."

"You mean this cat is wild?"

"He's half serval—that's an African wildcat—and half domestic. He's about twice the size of most cats. His name is Jacques." She smiled and said, "You'd like him. We call him Jacques the Ripper. His hobby is ripping people's flesh off the bone."

Vic Mandel laughed. "Yes, that's my kind of cat all right."

"I don't think I'll enter him though," Kate said. "I doubt if it would be legal, would it, Raina?"

"I'm not sure. There aren't many Savannahs around. I can check into it."

"No, he's nothing but a troublemaker," Enola said. "You don't want Jacques the Ripper mixing in with the respectable cats. I love him, but his manners aren't all that good."

● ● ●

The meal had been very elegant, but tasty, and the company had been fascinating. As Kate and Enola drove away, Enola said, "That food was pretty good for an expensive restaurant. Sometimes the more it costs, the less I enjoy it."

"Jake could do it better," Kate said. "I hate to say anything positive about that man. He drives me crazy, but he *is* a great cook."

"What did you think of the cat owners?"

"Well, I like Mary Beth Pickens," Kate said.

"Like her all you please. She'll get trashed," Enola said cynically. "Phelps will win, or maybe Vic Mandel."

"Have you seen the cats, Enola?"

"Don't have to. Those two owners are the carnivores here. Far more dangerous than any of the cats. Both of them will do anything to win. Spend any amount."

"But that's not fair," Kate said.

Enola laughed and cast a glance at Kate. "Life ain't fair, honey. If it were, we'd all be born to rich daddies."

Six

Kate had taken her daily swim, then showered and put on fresh clothing. She exited her bedroom and found Jake cooking. "What are we having for supper?"

"Whatever you want to go buy," he said. "This isn't for us."

"Who's it for? It smells really good."

"It's crawfish etouffée. I can't stand to eat it myself. A friend of mine from Arkansas said they use crawfish for fish bait there. I don't think I want to start eating fish bait at my advanced age."

"What are you going to do with it?"

"I'm taking it to Morgan and Rhiannon. They both love it."

"Can I come along? I need to talk to Morgan."

"Sure. I just made a sour cream–walnut cheesecake."

"Sour cream in a dessert? It sounds awful."

"Well, just for that you don't get any," Jake said. "Come on. You can carry the cake. I'll take the etouffée."

The two left the house and were followed by Cleo and Jacques. They hadn't gone far before Jacques said, *Cleo, look at that dumb dog.*

Cleo looked down the beach to see Trouble trying to haul an enormous piece of driftwood. It was at least eight feet long and waterlogged. Trouble had his big jaws clamped on it, and his feet dug in. He could move it a few feet, and then he'd have to stop and wait until he got his breath.

Look at that dumb dog, Cleo. You won't find cats wasting their energy on something they can't eat.

Don't say bad things about Trouble. He's a nice dog.

He's dumb. You want proof that dogs are dumb and cats are smart? You never see six cats hooked up to a sled, do you? Only a dog's dumb enough for that.

I heard Jake say that they like it.

What does he know? He's only a biped. How would he like to be hooked up with five other bipeds to a sled? See what I mean? But dogs might like it. They're stupid.

Jake had been watching the two cats and said, "It seems like cats live in another world. They're not like other animals."

"No, they're not," Kate agreed. "Oh, look—pelicans."

Jake turned and saw that a feeding frenzy was going on out in the Gulf. It happened from time to time. A flight of pelicans would spot some fish surfacing, and the fun was on. The two watched as pelican after pelican would fold his wings and drop in a steep dive into the water—for all the world like a dive bomber. They hit the water, sometimes completely disappearing, and then surfaced with a fish. Sometimes the fish was big enough that they had to toss it into the air and get it going down their gullet head first. "Herons do that," Jake said. "I think they do it so the fish can't get out. Once they start down it's too late."

"They look like they're having such fun. It might be fun being a pelican," Kate said, watching them with delight.

"Not me. When I'm reincarnated I want to come back as a fighting bull."

"There's no such thing as reincarnation," Kate said sharply, but then grew curious. "You mean those bulls the bullfighters kill?"

"Them's the ones. Boy, do they have a life."

"There's something wrong with your mind, Jake. Nobody would want to be one of those bulls."

"I would."

"Why in the world would you want to be thrown out there? You know the bulls always lose. They don't have a chance."

Jake shook his head. "You don't understand. It's a *guy* thing."

"What do you mean a guy thing?"

"You don't know much about fighting bulls, do you?"

"I know it's cruel."

"Cruel! Let me tell you about the life of one of those prize bulls. They're raised especially for that task. They're bred to fight, but until they're old enough to fight they get the greenest grass, the best water—they get to have all the girlfriends they want. Those bulls get the best of everything. Plenty to eat, plenty of sex—all their lives." He grinned at her crookedly, looking more and more like a young Robert Mitchum. "They have one bad afternoon in their whole lifetime. Listen, Mary Katherine, I've had as many as ten bad days in a row. I've been beat up, shot, punched out, fired, insulted by masters of that art. No, those bulls have got it made. What a life!"

Jacques had been listening carefully to all this. *Say, Cleo, it sounds like those bulls do have it made.*

You have it made. You get everything they get, and you don't even have to fight for it. And you like it.

Well, I like to fight.

Well, maybe the bulls do, too.

Maybe so. That poor old Intruder, he sounds like he's had a hard life. He's probably done something wrong to deserve it, though. Anyway, I'm looking out for number one.

Jake said, "We'd better hurry. This is going to get cold."

"It's nice that Ocie's built them a house."

"It sure is. Ocie won't spend any money on himself. Still driving that old beat-up van, and if he's bought any new clothes, I can't tell it."

"He says it's God's money, not his, and God hasn't told him to buy any new clothes."

"Well, you'd think even God could see he needs new clothes."

"Don't be sacrilegious, Jake."

Jake stared at her. "I'm not. God knows he needs new clothes. If I know it, surely God does."

"Maybe Ocie doesn't need them. John the Baptist only wore a simple short robe with a leather belt."

"Well, John the Baptist didn't win the lottery."

The two kept trudging along, and soon the new house where Morgan Brice and Rhiannon lived appeared. "Jake, where do you take Jeremy when you two go off every day?"

"We go down to the fitness center and work out."

"There must be more to it than that."

"Well, there is," Jake admitted. "Have you noticed Slick comes in sometimes with a bruise on his face or a split lip?"

"Yes, I have, but he won't say anything to me about it."

"He will to me."

"Why doesn't he tell me?"

"It's another guy thing."

"I get so sick of that! I'm his *mother*."

"All right, I'll tell you," Jake relented. "He's getting beat up by a bully, and I'm working with him. Sort of a personal trainer."

Kate stopped in her tracks briefly. "Beat up? My Jeremy?" Jake nodded and Kate started walking again. Then she asked, "Are you teaching him that martial-arts stuff?"

"I'm working up to it," Jake said. "Got to get him built up physically first. We're doing a little bit. Working out with weights, stuff like that. You ought to come along sometime."

"Why? You think I need to be more physically fit?"

"Well, you may not need it, but it's a good place for women to go hunting."

"Hunting what?" Kate asked, puzzled.

"Why, men, of course," Jake said. "What else would a woman hunt? There's this babe there that's got a skintight Spandex workout suit. Now that woman's got real character!"

"Character? She's flaunting her figure at you!"

"Well, I've had worse things flaunted at me," Jake laughed. "Anyway, we could go shopping and buy you one of these suits. I've put in some time thinking about it."

"I'll just bet you have!"

"Anyhow, that's what Slick and I are doing."

"I'm not sure I like that, Jake."

"You'd rather have him get pounded?"

"Well...no, I guess not. I just don't want him to be—"

Jake shot her a quick look. "Like me? Is that what you were going to say?"

"That's...that's not what I meant. But life is so hard for young people. There's drugs and violence and sex available everywhere. I don't want Jeremy to get caught up in that."

"Don't worry, Mary Katherine. I'll help all I can. I won't let him turn into a thug like me."

They reached the house just as Jake made this promise, and the door opened before they could even knock. "Come on in," Rhiannon said. "What did you bring to eat, Jake?"

"Crawfish etouffée and a cake that Mary Katherine says sounds awful."

"What kind is it?" Rhiannon asked.

"It's a sour cream–walnut cheesecake."

"I never had that," Rhiannon said eagerly.

"Neither have I," Jake said. "I'm just trying out the recipe. We may have to feed it to the gulls."

The two went into the house, and Morgan met them, moving very slowly. "Good to see you," he said to Jake and Kate.

"We brought you some crawfish etouffée," Jake said. "I can't eat the stuff myself, but I know you and Rhiannon like it."

"Sure do. Rhiannon, set the table."

"I'll help you, Rhiannon," Kate said. She commented on how beautiful the new house was, and soon the table was set. Jake refused to eat any of the etouffé, and Kate ate just enough to be polite. They were both conscious that Morgan didn't look well, and when Jake got up and moved the dishes to the sink she followed him, whispering, "Take Rhiannon out, Jake. I need to talk to Morgan alone."

"Okay," Jake said. Then he turned to the girl and said, "Hey, Rhiannon, let's go outside and see if we can find something on the beach. Maybe a pirate's treasure."

"That's silly," Rhiannon said. "Don't be ridiculous."

Still, Rhiannon eagerly followed Jake out.

As soon as the two were gone, Kate said, "I've got some good news, Morgan. I'm getting some tutors lined up for Rhiannon. Beverly has a degree from Oxford. Knows English literature backward and forward. He can teach her literature. Jake is a history nut. He can teach her history. I don't know anything much, but I'll find some more tutors to cover all the necessary subjects."

Morgan blinked with surprise. "Why, that's wonderful, Kate!" Then he frowned. "But I don't think that new superintendent will go for it. He's a hard man to convince."

"I'll send Jake to make him an offer. He'll make him an offer he can't refuse."

Morgan suddenly laughed, and she saw that the good looks of a man wasted by disease were still there. "Like, do this or I'll break both of your knees?"

"Well, it worked in *The Godfather.*"

"Yes, it did, but I hope it doesn't come to that," Morgan said. He leaned forward then and added, "I've been wanting to talk to you, Kate. You've seen how I look. I'm very sick and...I think I may die soon."

"Don't talk like that," Kate said.

"It's what I have to say Kate. And I'm worried about what will happen to Rhiannon. She doesn't have any close relatives except me."

Instantly Kate said without thinking, "Jake and I will take her, Morgan."

"You two aren't married."

"No, but that doesn't seem to matter so much. I'll tell you what. We'll have Beverly draw up a will. He'll make it so that we'll get Rhiannon if anything does happen to you."

"Rhiannon says you ought to marry either Jake or Bev," the old man said with a sly grin.

"She has no preference?" Kate smiled slightly.

"Do you?"

"Do I what?"

"Do you have a preference?"

"No, I really haven't thought much about it."

Morgan leaned back and studied her carefully. "You had a bad marriage, didn't you, Kate?"

Kate dropped her eyes and murmured, "It wasn't good, Morgan."

"I'm sorry."

"But I didn't mean to talk about this," she continued, switching to a brighter tone. "I'm the bearer of good news. We're going to work on the tutors, and then we'll find some way to twist that superintendent's arm. It'll work out all right, and don't worry about what'll happen to Rhiannon. Jake and I and Bev will see to it."

With that, Kate rose to leave. She leaned down and gave Morgan a kiss and said, "Promise me you won't worry."

Morgan nodded, but said nothing. Kate went outside and looked for Jake but saw only Rhiannon sitting in the sand. She walked up and said, "Where's Jake?"

Rhiannon looked up and said, "We were finding sand dollars, and his cell phone rang. He got some kind of a message, and then he said goodbye real grufflike and then took off running for the house."

"Did he seem worried?"

"I think he was," Rhiannon said.

"I'd better go find out what it's all about." She reached down and put her hand on Rhiannon's black, curly hair. "I'll see you later, honey. I'll come back to check on your granddad every day."

"He's not getting better, is he?"

"God's still in charge, Rhiannon. Never forget that. He's not going to leave you alone."

"I'll try to remember," Rhiannon said.

"Good!" Kate said. "Now I'd better find out what Jake's up to."

Kate hurried along the beach, and as soon as she got home, she saw that Jake's Harley was gone. She ran up the front steps, avoiding Bandit, who was begging for something to eat, and then she noticed a note on the table, weighed down by a saltshaker. She picked it up, and it was very brief: *Have to make a trip. Don't know when I'll be back.* It was signed *Jake*, but something else had been written and then erased. When she held the paper up to the light she saw what it was. *"Love,"* she whispered. "Love from Jake. But he just couldn't leave it in there."

Kate sat down at the table. As usual, several animals wandered in. Abigail came in with that odd, humpbacked gait of ferrets, clambered up, and tried to climb into Kate's lap. Kate picked her up and held her, and she lay there comfortably, apparently going to sleep.

Cleo and Jacques had been watching as usual. *Where do you suppose Jake went in such a hurry?* Cleo said.

He probably had something important to do.

Well, our Person is sad. She's going to miss him. I wish he hadn't gone off without saying goodbye to her, Jacques.

He wants to keep her guessing. Jacques yawned and licked his forepaw.

That's mean.

It's a guy thing, Cleo. Come on, he said. *Let's go eat some of that good stuff the neighbors put out for that stupid calico.*

That's stealing, Jacques.

That mangy cat doesn't deserve it—but I do. Come on, I may have to rough him up a little. I'll let you have a taste of his goodies.

Cleo looked at Kate, who was staring at the note. *She's worried.*

Hey, it's good for females to worry. It gives them something to do. Come on— you can watch me whack that sorry excuse for a cat and eat his food.

Seven

By the time Jake pulled his Harley into the outer limits of Jacksonville, the sun was dropping deep into the western sky. The motorcycle had developed a miss, and he had been forced to stop and take it to a shop. It would have been a minor problem except that he'd had to wait for the service, and now as he slowed down to the legal limit, he was worried. He kept his eyes peeled for a sign that would lead him to the Veteran's Hospital. He saw none, however, and spotting a black car with the words *Jacksonville Police* on the door, he pulled over to it and balanced on his bike while the officer inside rolled his window down.

"I need a little help, Officer."

"What's the trouble?" The speaker was a beefy man with a thick neck and a suspicious look in his eyes. Jake thought, *Once a cop, always a cop,* but he let none of this show in his tone. "I've just pulled in from Alabama looking for the Veteran's Hospital."

"You're on the right path," the officer said. "Go to the next stoplight, take a left, and as soon as you get to the first big intersection, turn right and stay on that road. You'll see the hospital on your left."

"Thanks a lot."

"You got somebody there?"

"Yeah, a friend of mine who was in the Delta Force with me," Jake answered.

"Delta Force? Hey, that was a rough outfit."

"They kicked me out because I was sissy."

"Yeah, I can see you're a real pansy all right," the officer grinned. " Good luck."

Jake followed the instructions and had no trouble. When he pulled up to the imposing white building set back off of the road and bordered by green grass, he found a spot and parked. Taking off his helmet, he fastened it to the machine, then turned and walked stiffly toward the front entrance. The ride from White Sands, though only a medium distance from Jacksonville, was enough to numb a man's legs.

Entering the building, he took a quick look around and spotted a fresh-faced young woman behind a desk. He walked over and said, "Excuse me, I'm trying to locate someone."

"That's what I'm here for. What's the name?" The woman was no more than twenty-five, with rosy cheeks and lips to match. She had the typical Florida tan, and Jake could see she would look good in a bikini.

"I've got a friend here," Jake said. "Name's Ty Hayden."

The young woman's fingers danced over the keyboard in front of her. "Would that be Tyler?"

"Yes, we just called him Ty."

Something ominous came into the woman's eyes as she read the screen, and when she looked up she said, "He's in intensive care. That's on the second floor. The elevator's right over there."

"Thanks."

"I hope he does well," the woman said. There was doubt in her voice that Jake didn't miss. He thanked her, then moved across the lobby. There were two people waiting for the elevator, a short, chunky woman in a white nurse's uniform and a tall rangy man in green scrubs. When Jake stepped into the elevator with the other two, he reached out and pushed the button marked "2." As they went up, he asked, "Either one of you know Tyler Hayden? He's in intensive care."

"I do," the nurse replied. "My name's Ann. Folks just call me Annie. Mr. Hayden is under my care. You family to Mr. Hayden?"

"Just a friend," Jake replied. "How is he doing?"

The woman hesitated, then said, "There's always a reason a person is in intensive care."

"Yes," Jake said.

The man in green said, "Dr. Wilson's who you want to see. He's in charge of your friend's case."

"He won't be on duty for about an hour," Annie said. "And besides, we're not supposed to let anybody in but family, and then only once every four hours for twenty minutes."

Jake considered this, then said with a wink, "My favorite thing is breaking rules, Annie. What's yours?"

Annie flashed him a brilliant smile and said, "I like to break rules, too. How about you, Dr. Schultz?"

The doctor thought a moment, looking Jake over, then said "Some rules need to be broken. Dr. Wilson's a good man," he said. "As for the rules, I think you can break this one, Annie."

● ● ●

Dr. James Wilson was a tall, thin man with the soft tones of Virginia in his voice. A Virginia accent had always pleased Jake, and he studied the physician's face carefully. Wilson had intelligent features with sharp, laser-like gray eyes. He spoke of Tyler's condition with very little hope. "It's his liver," he said. "Always a bad thing. We all have two lungs and two kidneys, but only one liver."

"Is there any hope at all, Doctor?" Jake asked.

Wilson looked down at the floor and took so long to answer that Jake knew he was trying to find a way to put the best face on a hard situation. "I don't think so, Mr. Novak. It's just a matter of time. He's been weaker every time I've seen him, and there's only one end to that. Do you know if he has any family?"

"I haven't been in touch with him for a few years," Jake said. "We were in the army together. We were real close back then."

"Well, he listed a wife but had no address for her," the doctor said. "He does have a daughter, I know that much."

"Has he had many visitors?" Jake asked.

Wilson shook his head, and sadness touched his tone. "No, not that I know of. You might as well be with him. He needs *someone* in his corner. And though we've got a rule about when you can go in and how long you can stay, you can forget that."

"Thanks, Doc," Jake said. "How...how long does he have?" The question was hard for Jake to ask, and it was equally hard for Dr. Wilson to answer.

"A few days, Mr. Novak—a week at most. You may as well go in now. Come along."

Jake followed the doctor through a pair of double doors marked *Intensive Care.* There were six rooms, the doors opened on all of them, with a multisided station in the center of the area. It was quiet, with only the humming of machines and the hushed tones of the nurses. In only one of them was there a visitor, an elderly lady sitting beside a man attached to tubes and wires.

"Right in here."

Jake walked in, and it took all he had to hide the reaction he felt. He was barely aware that the nurse called Annie had stepped inside and that Dr. Wilson was instructing her to let Jake stay as long as he wanted to. Jake moved closer, and was shocked to see that the strong, vibrant man he had known was now literally a disaster. Yellow jaundice had colored his face, and he was connected to tubes that were connected to machines. He was down to nothing but skin and bones and nerves.

"He doesn't look good," Annie said, "but I'm glad you came."

"You've had patients like this before?" Jake asked.

"Oh, yes, quite a few. It always breaks my heart. Look," she said, "here's a chair. Pull it up to his bed. He might not wake up for a few hours. I'll bring you some coffee, or you can go down to the cafeteria."

"Thanks, Annie."

Annie studied Novak's wedge-shaped face carefully. She was impressed with the strength in the muscular body, and there was determination of a rare sort in the face that was now turned down to his friend. "He's no relation at all to you?"

Jake started to say no, but then said, "He saved my life once. Does that count?"

"I think it does. You sit down. If you need anything, just push that button over there or step out. I'll be at the desk. Is coffee all right?"

"Black with no sugar."

● ● ●

The time passed slowly. Jake was a man of action, and very few tortures could be devised that would hurt him more than to sit absolutely still, able to do nothing at all. He had sat there for over three hours with Annie coming in several times with coffee. Once she had reached over and put her hand on Ty's head and stroked his hair in a gesture of affection. "He's a good man, Jake."

"How can you tell that? You hardly know him."

"We talked quite a bit before he took a downturn. I know he's done some bad things in his life. He told me that himself, but he's a good man."

"Yes, he is," Jake agreed. "I'd do anything to help him, but there isn't anything, is there?"

"Maybe there will be," Annie said. "Did you know your friend is a Christian man? Hasn't been one long, but he's saved now." She turned to him and asked, "Are you a man of God, Jake?"

"No. I'm that lost sheep that Jesus talked about." His tone was flat.

Annie replied in the gentlest of tones, "It's never too late to be found." She didn't belabor the point, and Jake was grateful for that. He had been pressured before by high-powered evangelists and people who wanted to "save" him, and felt they could do it only by applying intense pressure.

From time to time Jake dozed off. Finally he came awake with a start, and looking over quickly he saw that Ty's eyes were now open. "Hello, Ty," he said.

Ty smiled, a travesty of the former smile Jake knew so well. Now the flesh of his face was sunken, and the eyes that looked at Jake out of cavernous hollows lacked the brightness they'd once had.

"You made it, man. Wasn't sure—you would."

Jake Novak wasn't a crying man, and so what was suddenly happening shocked him. He had known hard things before, but something about the helplessness of this man who had saved his life brought a tightness to his throat, and he blinked his eyes...his vision was growing watery. He resisted the impulse to pull out his handkerchief and blow his nose. Instead he snorted, swallowed, and said, "Hey, you owe me forty bucks. I've come to collect."

A faint smile touched Ty's eyes. "I don't owe you. You owe me."

"No, I don't. That bet, if you remember, was who could take that good-looking redhead out first."

"That's right, and I won."

"No, you didn't," Jake protested.

"You didn't know about it," Ty said. "She was smiling at you, but it was me she came to. We agreed not to tell you. You're such a sensitive soul, your feelings would have been hurt. Besides, you might have beaten me up."

Jake reached over and took his friend's hand, something utterly out of character for him. The two were both given to a jovial punch on the shoulder, or a Dutch rub, or an occasional high-five. But that day was gone, and now Jake felt the thinness of the hand, the weakness of it, that had been so strong.

Finally Ty said, "I have to say some things, Jake. You ever hear what the old comedian W.C. Fields said?"

"Fields? He never seemed funny to me."

"Me either, but I read two things he said that I've never forgotten. He was an alcoholic and didn't believe in God. One time a friend of his found him reading the Bible. The friend was surprised and asked him why. Fields said, 'I'm looking for loopholes.'" Ty shook his head slightly, "But he didn't find any. I tried to find a few myself, Jake, but I hit bottom. Two years ago I found God. I never thought I would."

Jake smiled. "What was the other thing he said?"

"The other thing was, 'Death is the fellow in the bright nightgown.' Strange thing to say."

"I don't get it," Jake said.

"I think he was trying to make death look better," Ty reasoned. "A fellow in a bright nightgown's not very scary. But death's not like that, Jake. You and I have been in some tight places, and we've seen some good friends go down, haven't we?"

"Yeah, we have."

"Back then I was scared to death, Jake, but I tried to cover up my fear."

"Me, too, Ty. Me too."

"Well, I'm not afraid of dying now, Jake. But I don't want to die with some things undone. Now there's one thing I'd like to do, but I don't know how."

"Maybe I can help," Jake offered, leaning forward.

"I always hated to ask favors," Ty said.

"Shoot, let me hear it," Jake said. "If it can be done, I'll do it. You know that, buddy."

Ty tightened his grip on Jake's hand and began slowly. "You know I had a daughter back when I was in high school—Sarita."

"Yeah, you'd talk about her sometimes," Jake responded.

"Her mom and I weren't married, and I wasn't interested in being a dad. So when her mom—Marie—and I broke up, Marie took Sarita." Ty paused a bit, breathing harder. "Well, about five years ago I was trying to go straight and do the right thing. I got in touch with Marie and—believe it or not—we ended up getting married." He smiled and said, "I loved her, Jake...but then she died, and I took a nosedive." He paused again. "To make a long story short, I failed Marie, and then I failed Sarita."

"You never failed us when we were in the Delta Force," Jake said. "I won't fail you, Ty. What do you want me to do?"

"I want you to look out for Sarita, Jake."

The two mens' eyes held each other, each realizing the enormity of the request.

Then Jake said, "You know I'll do it, Ty."

"Don't be so quick to agree, buddy. She's a terrible mess! Only sixteen, but she's already been in all kinds of trouble."

"Has she been in to see you?" Jake asked.

"No."

There was a world of sadness in that one single monosyllable, and Jake followed up quickly with, "What's her address, Ty?"

"It's written down on that notebook in the drawer."

Jake moved quickly, opened the drawer, and found a notebook. He noted the address, committed it to memory, and said, "I'll take care of it."

"I wish..." Suddenly Ty went limp. Jake whirled and went to the door. "Annie," he cried out, "come here!"

Annie came off her stool and was across the floor with astonishing quickness. She went over to Ty and examined his vital signs.

"Is he dead?" Jake asked.

"No, he does this," she answered. "What did he say to you, Jake?"

"He said he wanted me to do him a favor. He's got a daughter. He wants me to look out for her."

"Well, there you are. You wanted to do something for him."

"And I will."

"Mr. Novak, he won't wake up for another four hours, maybe six or eight."

"I'll be back as soon as I can," Jake said. He walked over to her and put his hand out. She took it and looked up at him with surprise. "Thanks for taking such good care of him," he said.

"*God's* taking care of him, and He wants to take care of you, too." She shook her head. "I'll watch out for Ty. You go find his girl."

● ● ●

Jake pulled his Harley up in front of a dilapidated old house. It had evidently been a business of some kind before being converted into apartments. Shutting the engine off, he attached the helmet and walked to the front door of the closest apartment. He knocked on it, and an elderly woman in a ratty-looking orchid robe smoking a cigarette, opened it and stared at him. "Whatcha want?"

"I'm looking for Sarita Hayden."

"Upstairs. Number two." She hesitated and said, "How's her daddy?"

"Not good. You know them?"

"Of course I know them," the woman said. "Ty's a good man, but that girl of his ain't much. She ain't been around for a day or two."

Jake thought for a moment, then said, "If she comes back, would you call me at the Veteran's Hospital? I'm trying to find her for Ty."

"It won't do you no good," the woman said, exhaling a puff of smoke.

"Maybe not, but I'd appreciate the call," Jake said.

The woman just nodded and started to close the door. Then she added, "Tell Ty that Mamie said hello."

"I'll do that," Jake said.

After waiting a moment, Jake went up the stairs and knocked on the door the old woman had indicated. There was no sound, and after several moments he slipped out his credit card and pried open the lock. When he stepped inside, he stopped. The place was a wreck—dirty dishes everywhere, clothes on the floor, the smell of marijuana so strong no one could miss it. Nobody was home, just as Mamie had said, so he turned and left, careful to relock the door. He then knocked on the door across the hall, and a fat man wearing a pair of frayed, skintight jeans and a dirty undershirt appeared. "Yeah, what is it?" he asked.

"I'm looking for Sarita Hayden."

"She's in jail," the man said matter-of-factly.

"What for?"

"I don't know what for, but I was here when the cops took her. You kin to Ty?"

"Just a friend."

"How's he doing?"

"He's not going to make it."

The man's eyes widened, and he made a face. "That's tough. He ain't a bad guy, him."

"If I miss Sarita," Jake said, "and you see her, would you call the Veteran's Hospital? Just give the number of Ty's room, and I'll get the message."

"What do you want her for?"

"Ty asked me to look out for her."

The man exhaled. "Lotsa luck," he said as he closed the door.

● ● ●

The precinct office looked like all other police precincts. Very institutional. The cops looked bored or angry for the most part. Jake approached the officer who was apparently in charge and said, "I need to talk to somebody about Sarita Hayden."

"What about her?"

"I'd like to know what she's in for."

The officer's name was Marx, according to his name badge and, like the others, he looked uninterested and merely said, "She was busted with a crowd for smoking pot."

"Is that all?" Jake asked, surprised.

"That's enough," the officer said. "It's against the law."

"You arrest everybody who smokes pot, you're going to have to open up a jail on the moon," Jake answered. "Where are you going to put them all?"

"What are you, a wise guy? She broke the law."

Jake decided to take a bold tack. "I want you to release her and let me take her with me."

Marx laughed harshly. "That's likely, ain't it? You could be anybody—a pimp, a white slaver. Get out of here."

Jake was undaunted. He handed the officer a card. "Call the homicide division in Chicago. Here's the number. Ask for Lieutenant Harv Morgan. Ask him if you can trust Jake Novak."

Marx stared, and then he suddenly laughed harshly. "Okay, come with me." Jake followed him to a room that contained a single desk, a coffee machine on a shaky table, and a telephone. Marx picked up the phone, got information, and then made the call. When he was connected, he looked at the card again and said, "Let me speak to Lieutenant Harv Morgan."

Jake stood silently and watched as Marx drummed on the table. Finally Marx said, "Lieutenant Morgan, this is Jerry Marx. I'm with the Jacksonville, Florida, police force. We got a situation here. There's a guy calls himself Jake Novak. He wants to take a prisoner off our hands, but I don't know him. What do you know about him?"

Marx sat there silently, and Jake could hear the faint voice of his old boss. He wondered if he had done the right thing. He hadn't always gotten along with Harvey Morgan, but he trusted him.

"Thanks, Lieutenant Morgan." Marx put the phone down and gave Jake a level look. "He called you a vile name I don't want to repeat. He said you were the most insubordinate cop he ever saw—but he said if you tell me you'll do something, you'll do it."

Jake grinned with satisfaction. "That's the nicest thing Harv ever said about me," he said. "I'm surprised the lieutenant didn't tell you a few of my other shortcomings."

Evidently Morgan had said the right thing, for Marx said, "Okay, you can take the girl."

● ● ●

Jake was seated against the wall when Sarita Hayden came in. He knew her at once. If she had decided to make herself look as cheap as she possibly could, this is what she would have come up with. She wore a skimpy miniskirt and a skintight T-shirt; her lips were scarlet outlined with a black pencil, it seemed. She had on heavy eye shadow, and her eyelashes looked gummy with mascara. Marx motioned Jake over and said, "This is Jake Novak. He's going to be responsible for you."

"I don't know him," Sarita spat.

"Well, you've got your choice, Missy. You can go back in jail, or you can go with him. What do you want to do?"

Jake saw the temptation in the girl's face to tell him to take a hike, but the memory of the cell, perhaps, changed her mind. "Okay, I'll go with him."

"Then come on and I'll get your stuff," the officer said.

Five minutes later, Jake and Sarita were outside the police station. Jake walked over to the Harley and put on his helmet. "I don't have an extra helmet," he said apologetically.

"Who are you?" Sarita asked. "Why did you get me out?"

"I'm a friend of your father's," Jake said. "We were in the army together."

"I don't want to see him." Sarita's lips drew into a line. "He ain't ever done nothin' for me." She began to curse her father.

"Shut up, Sarita," Jake said. Something about the big man intimidated Sarita, and she fell silent.

"Nice to meet someone like you," Jake said, "who's never made a mistake." When Sarita opened her mouth to reply, Jake reached out and took her by the arm. "He's dying, Sarita. You can't do much with a dead man no matter how much you try. If you don't go, you'll come to your senses some day and wish you'd been different with him. But it's up to you. You can go back to your cell, or you can go with me to see my friend."

Again there was a war in Sarita's face, and she finally relented and muttered, "I don't want to go back to that stinkin' jail."

"When we get there, you be nice to your dad," Jake warned. "If you aren't, I'll make you wish you had been."

"I ain't afraid of you," Sarita said unconvincingly.

"That's your first mistake. Now," Jake straddled the motorcycle, "get on and hang on. If you fall off, that's tough."

Sarita got on behind Jake and immediately felt the motorcycle surge forward. Wildly she grabbed Jake around the waist. And began to plan how she could get away from him.

Eight

Sarita swung herself off the Harley and stood watching as the man who called himself Jake Novak shut off the engine, removed his helmet, and came over to stand beside her. There was something frightening about him. She was accustomed to being around hard cases, but this felt like tiptoeing around a land mine. She wasn't going to show fear, however.

As he started walking toward the front doors of the hospital, she had to lengthen her stride to keep up with him. "Why'd they let you take me?"

"They know I'm okay," Jake said, quickening his pace. "Trust is a wonderful thing."

"Are you a cop or something?" Sarita asked.

"Not anymore."

Sarita was accustomed to men coming on to her, but Novak didn't even glance at her as he walked rapidly along the walk. She said, "They say you're okay? Well, I don't say it. You stay away from me."

Without looking Jake said, chopping his words off short, "Nothing would give me greater pleasure, kid."

"Yeah, I'm warning you."

Jake did turn to look at her then, though without breaking stride. "Nothing I can think of would be worse than putting the moves on a sorry kid who has to be forced to go see her dying father." He turned then and faced her, and once again she felt the aura of danger that seemed to emanate from this big man. "You say one cross word to your dad, I'll take you back to jail, and I'll be a witness against you. I'll tell them you tried to escape. Cops hang together. They'll believe me and not you. You got that?"

Sarita didn't answer, but she nodded imperceptibly.

"Come on, then."

The elevator rose jerkily. It seemed to cough and sputter, and when the door opened up there was a creaking sound. Sarita followed Novak as he turned right and moved down the hall. They came to double doors that were locked, and she watched as the big man punched a button. A voice said, "What is it?"

"Jake Novak to see Ty Hayden."

"Come in."

There was a buzz, and Novak pushed his way through the doors. Sarita had to hurry before they closed. She was feeling very uneasy in the hospital. It had strange smells, and as they pushed their way forward, she saw a woman being moved on a gurney. Her face was the color of a biscuit gone bad, and the man who pushed her seemed no more concerned than if he'd been hauling a load of fertilizer.

"What's wrong with her?" Sarita whispered.

"She's probably dying," Jake said.

The starkness of the remark struck at Sarita. She found herself wishing she were back in the jail, as bad as it would be.

As they entered the intensive care unit, Annie greeted them and asked, "Is this Ty's daughter?"

"Yes, her name is Sarita." Jake turned and said, "Sarita, this is Annie. She's been very good to your dad."

Sarita tried to say thank you, but she couldn't seem to speak. The atmosphere of the hospital seemed worse than the back streets of Miami for some reason.

"How is he, Annie?" Jake asked.

"He's awake. You can both go in."

Sarita stayed behind Jake as they entered the room. Then she stopped and watched as Jake went over to the bed. She had one clear look at her father's face before Jake's body blocked her view, and shock ran through her body. She hadn't seen him since he had been taken to the hospital two weeks earlier. He had been looking pale and yellowish even then, but now the sight of him frightened her.

"Brought you a visitor, Ty. Come on, Sarita."

Jake turned, and although he'd been smiling at Ty, when he turned to Ty's daughter there was no smile on his face. He didn't speak again, but Sarita knew she had no choice. She moved forward to the other side of the bed, feeling how Jake was watching her with those strange hazel-colored eyes of his. She forced herself to look down at her father, and saw he was trying to smile. "I've been...worried about you, Sarita."

"I've been all right," she offered without emotion.

"There wasn't much food when I left."

"It's all right. I'm getting plenty to eat."

A strange, muted silence seemed to fall over the room, then Ty reached his hand out, and glancing at Novak Sarita knew that she had no choice. She took the hand, shocked at how thin and weak it was. "I made out my life insurance to you, honey. It's not much—wish it were more."

Sarita tried to think of something to say, but absolutely nothing came to her mind. It was as if all her nerves were blocked off. She hadn't been so frightened since the time she had been trapped in an alley by two hulking dope addicts. She had managed to escape that, but there was no escaping now.

Suddenly her father's hand went limp. Sarita gasped. It dropped to the bed when she released it. She gave a frightened look at Novak, and asked, "Is he...is he dead?"

"No, he passed out," Jake said. "It comes on him suddenly like that sometimes."

"I don't know what to say to him," Sarita said.

"That's not too hard. Say you love him."

"But I don't."

"I know that, but it's what he needs to hear. It would mean a lot to him."

"It would be a lie."

"That's right. A fine, sweet, upstanding girl like you who never does anything wrong can't tell a lie. I can see virtue written all over you, babe."

Ordinarily Sarita would have lashed out, but the silence of the man on the bed seemed to exert some kind of force she had never known before. Not only that, but Jake's eyes were fixed on her.

"I never said I was perfect," she replied.

For a moment she tried to face Novak down, but it was hopeless. He was big, and she suspected he would use that strength if he had to. "I wish I weren't here."

"So does your dad, but he is, and so are you. And you've done worse things than tell a lie."

Sarita didn't answer. Finally she turned her back to her father and walked over to the chair and sat down in it. Novak didn't move but stood staring down into the face of her father. His face wasn't handsome, but there was an aura of strength and even hardness that was unmistakable.

Annie came in and said, "You'll have to leave now. We have to attend to Mr. Hayden."

"Come along, Sarita," Jake said.

As Sarita passed the nurse, she noticed the woman watching her. Once again she tried to think of something to say, but she couldn't think of a single thing.

"Can I bring you something back from the cafeteria, Annie?" Jake asked.

"Bring me one of them cream puffs with the little sprinkles on top," Annie said with a grin.

"You got it."

Sarita followed Jake out of ICU, down the hall to the elevator. Neither of them spoke a word. From time to time she would cast a glance at him, and once she had the wild impulse simply to run away, but she knew she couldn't move fast enough to get away from the man.

The cafeteria was almost empty. Jake took a tray and selected the pork chops with carrots and beans and rolls. Sarita felt a sudden hunger, and she chose meat loaf and a baked potato. She picked up two of the rolls and asked, "Can I have some pie?"

"You can get anything you want," Jake answered.

Jake paid the cashier, and Sarita followed him to a table along the back wall and sat down across from him. He paid her no more attention than he paid to the light fixtures in the ceiling or the paint on the walls. She ate quickly but noticed that Novak was only picking at his food. When she had finished the pie, she said, "What are you doing here in Jacksonville? I never saw you with my dad before."

"I owe him something."

"Yeah? Like what?"

"It goes way back to our Delta Force days. We made a jump behind enemy lines. We got trapped. I got a slug in the back, and your dad carried me until he got me away from the enemy patrols. By himself, he could have made it easily, but he wouldn't leave me. If they had caught us, they would have taken us both apart an inch at a time."

"I never heard him talk about that," Sarita said.

"It's not something one likes to remember or talk about."

Sarita put some butter on the roll and took a bite. She lifted her eyes and said, "He never did anything like that for me."

Jake paused. "No, I guess he didn't, but he's tried for the last couple years, hasn't he?"

Sarita didn't answer at first. Then she said, "He didn't pay attention to me most of my life. I had to make it without a dad. You know what that's like?"

Ignoring the question, Novak said, "And your mother—she was always good to you, was she?"

"Who's been telling you about my mother?"

Novak drank the last of his coffee, and without answering went over and refilled it. He came back and then turned his eyes on her. "You've had a tough time, kid. Your mother wasn't good to you, was she?"

Memories of the misery she had known living with her mother flashed through Sarita's mind. She remembered the time she had been left alone, locked up for four days. The food had run out, and her mother had finally come staggering home blind drunk, with her face puffy from a beating she had taken from some man.

"I know you've had a tough time, Sarita," Jake said. "I can understand why you'd have some hard feelings against your folks." He lifted the coffee cup, sipped, and then said lightly, "People fuss about bad coffee, but even the worst cup of coffee I ever had was real good."

Sarita wondered what that had to do with what they were talking about. She said bitterly, "Yes, I had a terrible time, and I hated my mother, and I hate him."

It was as if Jake didn't hear her. "There was a soldier named Randy Foss," he continued. "When I went in the Delta Force he treated me about as bad as you can treat a man, and I hated him for it. But then one day we went on a mission and this guy I hated so much—he fell on a grenade for us. He saved my life and your dad's life, too. Randy did some rough things to us, but when the chips were down, he gave us his life." He suddenly leaned forward and put his hands flat, palms down, pressing against the Formica. "I'd give anything if I could tell Randy how much I appreciate what he did for me, but I can't. Dead is forever, you know?"

Sarita felt a shiver run down her spine. She squirmed a little. Finally Jake said, "You need to go to the bathroom?"

"Yes. Are you going to go in with me to make sure I don't run away?"

"You won't run away. You've got better sense than that."

"What makes you think so?"

"Because if you run away, I'll find you, and I'll turn you in with a report that the sergeant won't like. Then I'll tell it again to the judge."

Sarita felt trapped. Her mind battered itself looking for a way of escape. But she knew she held a losing hand. "Okay. I'll tell him that I love him."

"Make it look good," Jake said.

Sarita smirked. "I can fool men. I've been doing it for some time now."

Jake didn't comment on this. They returned to the hospital room, but Ty was still asleep. The two sat there for two slow hours, when finally Ty woke up. At once Sarita went to him. He whispered her name, and she glanced at Jake and then turned to her father and stammered, "I love you, Dad. I'm sorry I've been so mean." She looked back at Jake, who nodded.

"That's all right—honey," Ty said. "I won't be around to help you anymore, but God will take care of you. I've prayed hard for you."

"Sure. Don't worry about it," Sarita said.

A few moments later, Ty passed out again.

"That was fine, Sarita," Jake said.

Sarita returned to a chair beside Jake. "It was a lie."

"He didn't know that."

"Are you going to tell him I was in jail?"

"No."

Time moved slowly, and Ty awakened twice more. The second time his mind was clear. Sarita was asleep, and Ty asked Jake, "You'll look after Sarita?"

"You bet I will," Jake promised.

Ty smiled knowingly. "I already had a lawyer make out a paper making you Sarita's guardian until she's of age."

"How'd you know I'd do it?" Jake asked.

"You always were an old softy."

The two men said little after that. Somehow Jake knew this was the end, and when Dr. Wilson came in on his rounds, he took one look and said, "Bring his daughter over here."

Sarita jumped when she heard her name and stood up. Jake went over to the bedside. Ty said, "Goodbye, buddy. I love you."

Ty was too weak to lift his hand, but Jake lifted his friend's hand, and as Sarita approached, he put her hand in her father's. Then Ty said to his daughter, "I won't be here to look after you, honey, but Jake will be."

That was the last thing Ty Hayden said, and thirty minutes later Jake and Sarita had stepped away from the bed and stood with their backs against the wall. Dr. Wilson was there, and after checking the still form, he turned and said, "I'm sorry. He's gone."

Sarita didn't move, but Jake went over and laid his hand on Ty's chest. He said nothing, but Sarita saw something she hadn't expected: tears trickling down Jake's cheeks. In her world, men did not cry. She was sure Novak didn't either, as a rule, but when he turned away from his friend she saw deep sorrow engraved in his features. She followed him out of the room quietly. He pulled out a handkerchief, blew his nose, wiped his face, and then said, "You did the right thing, Sarita. You'll never regret what you did today."

Nine

Lew Ketchell had given up many years ago on finding any grace in life. He had a profound contempt for most things, including his employer, Harrison Phelps. Now as he leaned back in his chair overhearing Phelps bark into the telephone, it occurred to Ketchell that working for a man like Phelps identified his own character.

At the age of thirty-eight Phelps was getting a paunch, but tailored clothes can hide many sins. His blond hair was thinning rapidly. He hired a hairdresser to cover up this flaw by pulling his hair from the back over the front—which fooled no one. And now his face had turned a flattering beet-red. His language was straight out of the gutter that had been his roots.

Ketchell pulled a package of cigarettes out of his shirt pocket, shook one out, and lit it with a kitchen match that he struck on the tile floor. He was a mild-looking man, which was deceptive, for Lew Ketchell was anything but mild.

He sucked the smoke into his lungs and remembered that his doctor had told him years before that he was a good candidate for lung cancer. Ketchell had never been able to get too excited about it—he'd heard worse threats than this from the killers that swarmed the mean streets of his youth.

He himself was a killer. He had lost his job as a homicide detective for killing other men on three distinct occasions. The howl that had gone up from the newspapers had disgusted him, and he had told his boss, the chief of detectives, "They want law and order, but they want to do it with a whisk broom." His lanky boss had said, "There's something wrong with you, Lew. You've got the makings of a good cop, but you've got the morals of a cobra."

Ketchell ignored Harrison Phelps's gutter language. He turned back to the book he was reading and didn't look up when he heard Phelps shout into the phone, "You'll do what I tell you or else!" and then slam the receiver down.

Phelps then turned to Ketchell and said, "Lew, you may have to go to Pittsburgh and take care of that idiot Martel."

"You want me to whack him?" Ketchell asked, not even lifting his eyes from his book.

"Make him an offer he can't refuse."

Ketchell smirked at his boss's cliché.

Again Phelps cursed. He came over and glared down at Ketchell. "What are you reading?"

"A book by a scientist named Stephen Hawking."

Phelps had risen to the top of the financial world by cutthroat methods. He had pulled every sort of financial shenanigan he could get away with, and he had made many enemies. He had hired Lew Ketchell to protect his life, but now as he looked down, he saw that Ketchell was the one man who did not fear him. Phelps did not trust anyone who read a great deal, and Ketchell read almost constantly.

"What's that book about?" he demanded.

"The cosmos. Universe. Stuff like that."

It was the kind of answer Ketchell would give, and the kind that Harrison Phelps hated. "Why do you waste your time on that junk?"

Slowly Ketchell lifted his head, and his eyes locked on the eyes of his employer, like a fighter pilot who locks in on a target, finger on the trigger. One impulse, one single motion, could set the rocket on its way to death and devastation. "Why do you care anything about cats?"

The question angered Phelps. "I'm not letting her get away with it, Lew!"

"Her" in this case was Phelps's ex-wife, Eileen. She had remarried and now was Eileen Saban. She was the one person who had gotten the best of Phelps in a financial war, for when she had divorced him, she and a battery of high-priced Chicago lawyers had taken Phelps for almost half of what he had—including a cat. It was the one losing battle of Phelps's life, and he was determined to get even. The cat in question was a prizewinning Russian blue, and Eileen had demanded it as part of the divorce settlement. Phelps didn't care two pins for the cat, but the idea of losing something valuable to

Eileen was unbearable. "Let it go, Harry." Ketchell shrugged his thin shoulders. "You need a hobby. Why don't you take up needlepoint or something else harmless?"

If anybody else had been this insolent to Phelps, they would have been fired on the spot, but Phelps knew that, although he both hated and envied Lew Ketchell, he needed him. "Listen, she's not getting away with it, that's all. She's entered the cat in the show down on the Gulf Coast. That's why I bought one that's going to beat her."

"And when it does, what will that get you?"

"Never you mind! It's none of your business, Lew. Your business is to do what I tell you."

"You're just making a fool out of yourself, Harrison."

"Shut up and listen to me!" the man snapped. "I want you to go tell Eileen that I want that cat back, and if she dares enter it in the show, it'll be too bad for her."

"You'd take it out on the cat?"

"Let's just say that cat's going to have a very short life if Eileen doesn't pull him out of the competition."

"Maybe she won't listen. You want me to whack her if she doesn't?"

Phelps knew that Lew Ketchell was taunting him, but his lips set in a determined line, and he said, "You do what I tell you, Lew. If you can't handle it, I can get a dozen like you. I want you to put the fear of death into that woman! You hear me?"

"Like I say, if you want to make a fool out of yourself, that's your business." Ketchell got to his feet, put the bookmark in his book, and left the room.

● ● ●

Eileen Saban was having a drink with Hannah Monroe. Eileen was a petite blonde with green eyes who practically advertised sensuality with every move of her body and every costume she had. She liked men, and it delighted her to take them, use them up, and throw them away. She had done this exact thing to Harrison Phelps, and winning her divorce case had delighted her beyond anything that had ever come into her life. She had won enough money through the settlement that she would never have to worry about finances again. She looked at Hannah, leaned back and said, "I'm going to get that ex-husband of mine, Hannah."

"Why do you bother?" Hannah Monroe, at the age of sixty-two, was a well-known breeder of cats. She had her own reasons for despising Harrison Phelps, who more or less had to buy his prizes for cats. Her reply was uncharacteristically indifferent though, and now as she took a drink of the cocktail before her, there was something not right. Even Eileen Saban could see that.

"What's wrong with you, Hannah?"

Hannah shrugged, then said without emotion, "Nothing—except I happen to be dying."

Eileen stared. "What are you talking about?"

"I just told you. I'm dying," Hannah repeated.

Eileen shook her head in disgust. "You're always trying to dramatize things."

"Death is fairly dramatic, my dear," Hannah said dryly. "As a matter of fact, I have one of the fastest-growing kinds of cancer. I'll be dead in a month."

Usually Eileen Saban had a comeback for anything, but she realized with a shock that Hannah Monroe was telling her the truth.

"But they can do—"

"They can do *nothing*. It's gotten beyond that." She finished the cocktail and waved her hand at a waiter to order another, then turned to Eileen. "How does it feel to be having a drink with a dead woman?"

Eileen swallowed hard and downed her own drink. She tried to think of some way to respond to what Hannah had just told her, but she could think of nothing.

"What would you do if you knew you were going to die in a month, Eileen?"

Eileen thought for a second, then said, "I'd shoot that ex-husband of mine right in the brain—if he had one!"

"What a lowly ambition! You wouldn't want to do anything *good*? Try to make peace with God or anything like that?"

"You don't know how I hate that man," Eileen said.

"Eileen, I never thought I'd hear myself say this, but life really is too short to go around hating people."

"Nobody's ever hurt you like that man hurt me."

Hannah didn't answer. Indeed, the world had become a narrow, rather dark place since the doctor had given her the stark news regarding her cancer.

Her first reaction had been anger. That had been followed by despair, and now she passed her days drinking, trying to blunt the news.

Finally Eileen said, "Let's go for a walk on the beach. It'll make you feel better."

"No, it won't, but I'll go. It may be my last walk on the beach." Hannah picked up her glass and stared at it thoughtfully. "Everybody has their last drink, their last sunset, their last good cry. The difference between you and me, Eileen, is I know that's happening to me and you don't. Pity. Why do you hate Harrison so much? Other people have gone through divorces."

Eileen couldn't answer. Her hatred for Phelps was without reason. It was just part of her. So instead of answering, she just said, "Come on, let's go walk on the beach."

● ● ●

Ketchell had been shadowing Eileen Saban for several long hours, standing in the sun mostly and waiting for a chance to talk to her alone. Wiping the sweat off his forehead, he followed the two women as they left the restaurant and walked down to the beach. The beach itself was white sand, and just to the north of it were the wallows and small rises and gullies that were thick with sea oats. Ketchell wasn't an outdoor man and, already overheated, he now found himself gasping for breath. He knew something was wrong with his lungs, and the doctor's words echoed in his mind: *You're going to have lung cancer if you don't stop smoking so much, Mr. Ketchell.* He shoved that warning away as he might have shoved away a person that intruded on his life.

The two women hadn't gone more than a hundred yards away from the wooden boardwalk that went from the fancy condo down to the beach, when Ketchell noticed Hannah Monroe turn and go back toward the boardwalk. He watched as Eileen watched the woman go with some expression Ketchell couldn't understand. Then she turned and continued her walk.

Quickly Ketchell moved out of the gully that had half hidden him and increased his pace toward the woman. The surf was loud, and he knew that right now she couldn't hear him. He had gotten about ten yards from her when he called out, "Eileen." As the woman turned, Ketchell took a perverse pleasure in the fear in her eyes.

"What do you want, Lew?" she asked guardedly.

"I want to talk to you."

"I don't want to talk to you. Now leave me alone."

"I can't do that. My lord and master sent me with a message."

Eileen had always been afraid of Lew Ketchell. She knew he was a man without scruples. Of course her husband was similar in that respect, but Ketchell had a feral quality, and she knew of at least two men he had killed since being released from the police force. She now tried to bluff, as she had always done before. "Still shooting up and killing people for Harrison, Lew?"

Ketchell had always rather admired Eileen. He had watched the marriage disintegrate, and though most people would have folded under Harrison Phelps's acid tongue and violent ways, to her credit, Eileen had not, and he admired that courage.

"I do what the boss tells me," he said.

"You're crazy to stay with Harrison, Lew. He'll toss you aside when he uses you up, just like he does everyone."

Ketchell was near exhaustion. He had received a sunburn when he first came to the coast two days earlier, and now he felt that strange sensation of burning up and being packed in ice. He had no desire to continue the conversation. He said, "Eileen, just give the cat back to Harrison. What do you care about a cat?"

"I'm not letting him win, Lew."

"You know how he is."

"I certainly do."

Ketchell pulled out his handkerchief and wiped his forehead. His tongue felt dry and his lips like toast. "You know, Eileen," he remarked quietly, "I always felt sorry for you. I don't admire too many people. I don't like many either, but I like you as well as any. Get out of this thing. I know you think I'm a killer, but Harrison is, too. Oh, he's a coward, but he'll kill you some way. He'll have me do it, or if I don't make it, someone else will, or he'll even do it himself."

Eileen Saban couldn't speak, for she knew that Lew Ketchell, in his way, was a wise man. He had seen a lot of life, and she knew what he said was the truth. One didn't stay married long to Harrison Phelps without learning he was a cruel predator who delighted in making his victims suffer.

She said, "Just stay away from me, Lew," and then turned and walked back toward the condo.

Ketchell watched her go, and then was surprised by a voice that said, "You're a bad man."

Ketchell's hand went behind him toward the Glock automatic on the belt in the middle of his back. It was concealed by his colorful Hawaiian shirt, and he had his hand on the weapon, when he saw a girl of no more than ten sitting in a gully of white sand. She was almost hidden by the sea oats, and now she arose.

"How long have you been there, kid?"

"You're a bad man," the girl repeated.

"What's your name?"

"Rhiannon Morgan."

If Rhiannon had been a man, she would have been in danger of being shot and buried in the sand at once. But Ketchell was staring at the young girl. "What do you mean I'm a bad man?"

"You kill people. You're sanguineous."

"How do you know a big word like that?"

"It means 'bloodthirsty.'"

Lew was almost amused at the girl. A surf casting rod lay at her feet beside a bucket of bait. "The lady and I were just kidding, that's all."

The girl came forward, and Ketchell saw that there was no fear in her. She came so close he could see the flecks of green in her eyes. "You're sick," she said.

"I don't feel too good, that's the truth."

"You're about to get heatstroke. Sit down here."

"You going to doctor me?" he kidded. "Let me see your medical degree."

"I know what to do for heatstroke," Rhiannon said.

Lew Ketchell found Rhiannon amusing. He sat down in the sand, and the girl took a large bandanna out of her pocket. She went down and dipped it in the water, came back, and began to bathe his face. "Why did you become a bad man?"

"I guess I was just born bad. Some people are, you know."

"I know that. The Bible says, 'All have sinned and fall short of the glory of God.'"

More and more the young girl intrigued Lew Ketchell. He had had almost no contact with children, and the girl had no fear of him, which puzzled him. Finally he began to feel better, and she said, "Come on."

"Come on where?"

"Up there. I live there. You need to get out of this heat, and you need to drink something cool."

Determined to find out how much the girl had heard of the conversation, Lew got up and followed. She picked up the bucket of bait in one hand and the rod in the other. "You carry the bait," Rhiannon said.

"All right."

The two walked slowly down the beach, and when they came to what appeared to be a brand-new house she said, "I live here. Come on in."

"What about your mom and dad? What will they think about you bringing a stranger home? Don't they tell you not to talk to strangers?"

"I live with my granddad." She ignored his latter question, and putting the bucket and the rod on the porch, she opened the door, and Lew followed her in. She said, "Granddad, where are you?"

"I'm in here, honey," Morgan answered.

Lew followed the girl in, looking around carefully. The house had the smell of new wood and new paint. When he stepped inside a long, high-ceilinged room, he saw a white-haired man sitting in a recliner. The television was across the room, but it was turned off, and the man had a book on his lap.

"He's having a heatstroke," Rhiannon explained.

"Well, you better cool him off and get all the fluid down him you can," Morgan said.

"I didn't mean to come here and be any trouble," Lew said.

"Sit down," Rhiannon said.

"Is she always this bossy?"

"She is with me. I'm Morgan Brice. This is my granddaughter, Rhiannon."

"Rhiannon? I'm Lew Ketchell. I don't want to be a bother."

"You've got a bad sunburn there, and heatstroke can get you pretty good. Just sit down. It'll pass."

Ketchell took the seat that Brice indicated. He noticed that the walls were lined with books, and he was scanning some of the titles, when Rhiannon came back with a bowl of ice water. She dipped a face towel in it and put it around his neck. She dipped a washcloth and then began to bathe his brow with it.

"You're down for a vacation, Mr. Ketchell?"

"Business, more or less."

"You'd better be careful of the sun. If you're not used to it, it can be bad."

Ketchell's quick attention had fastened on the old man's face. He saw the signs of illness there. The body was thin, and Ketchell wondered how bad the sickness was, but he didn't know how to ask. "This is some granddaughter you have here, Mr. Brice."

"Yes, she takes good care of me."

"He's the only family I've got," Rhiannon said. "My parents died some time ago." Now that the cold cloths were in place, she dragged a chair out and sat directly in front of Ketchell. Ketchell was wondering if the girl would say anything to her grandfather about what she had heard, but she said nothing.

"Why aren't you in school?" Ketchell asked.

"I am in school."

"What do you mean?"

"My granddad teaches me. He knows more than any old schoolteacher."

"No, that's not altogether true," Brice said. "Rhiannon, get something cool for him to drink."

"Do you like Dr. Pepper?" Rhiannon asked.

"I'd take anything cool," Ketchell answered.

"I like Dr. Pepper best." She went over to a refrigerator and pulled out two cans. She came back and said, "Here, drink this. It'll cool you off."

Ketchell took it, and for the next thirty minutes he sat listening to the intriguing young girl. He knew she would be a potent witness if he ever went on trial for killing Eileen Saban. No jury could doubt she would be telling the exact truth.

Finally he removed the towels and said, "Well, I'll be getting along. I'm feeling much better. Thanks for the drink and for the hospitality, Mr. Brice... and you too, Rhiannon."

"Stay out of the sun," Morgan advised.

"I'll do that."

As Ketchell stepped outside and headed back to his car, he noticed Rhiannon was following him. He turned and said, "You didn't tell your grandfather what happened."

"No, I didn't."

"Why not?"

"He's sick. He doesn't need any more problems."

"What's wrong with him?"

"He's got a heart problem, and he's going to die unless God works a miracle."

Ketchell blinked at the bluntness of the words. "I don't believe in miracles, kid."

"I know that."

"How do you know that?"

"I just do. You know there's a poet who says a mouse is miracle enough to stagger sextillions of infidels. And all the scientists in the world couldn't make one mouse."

The girl's logic amused Lew. "You're a smart kid."

"Yes, I am," she said placidly. "I always have been."

Lew studied her. "Well, I'll see you around."

"You'll have to come here if you do," Rhiannon said.

"Uh, do what?" Ketchell said.

"If you see me around," she said patiently.

Lew was still uncertain as to what to do about the girl. She had overheard his talk about killing, and Lew didn't need that kind of testimony being spouted before any jury.

"Tell you what," he said. "Suppose I bring you and your grandfather some takeout for dinner."

"Okay."

"What do you like?"

"We like Chinese." She stopped and said, "Get lots of it. I eat a lot."

"I'll get plenty." He turned to leave.

"Don't kill anybody, Mr. Ketchell," Rhiannon said as she watched him go.

Lew was nonplussed. It was as if she said, "Have a nice day." When he got to his car, he looked back as she went back into her house.

"That kid could be trouble," he said aloud. He would come back to bring the Chinese food and pump her some more.

Ten

The courtroom where Jake sat with Sarita had all the charm of a Greyhound bus station. Simply being in a courtroom brought unpleasant memories flooding into Jake's mind. He had sat in too many of them while he served as a homicide officer, and it had become his settled conviction that all courtrooms had the smell of fear. Most of the people who came before a judge emanated fright, and although today's business wasn't a matter of life and death, Jake wished fervently it would soon be over.

He sat back on the walnut bench worn smooth by thousands of people before him, who had come to watch their family struggle through the legal maze, all of them filled with fear. Jake had decided long ago it was because a courtroom, along with a doctor's office, was a setting where human beings felt totally helpless.

Sarita shifted slightly, and Jake turned and glanced toward her. Her face was set in a sullen, frozen look as she glared up at the judge, and Jake wondered, not for the first time, how in the world he was going to handle her.

Involuntarily the memory of Ty's funeral came to him. It had been only the day before and, as always, it was a trying experience. Jake had managed to contact four of the members of their Delta Force squad, and they had all looked beaten down and tired, as if life itself were more difficult than the special forces had been. The church had been half full, and the pastor had done a good job. He had talked with Jake considerably and had managed to bring up Ty's good military record. He had spoken of Ty's early life as not being exemplary and identified him as a late bloomer who had served God faithfully during the last three years of his life.

Jake pushed the memory of the graveside service away. He forced himself to think of the lawyer who, like all lawyers, had managed to make a neat profit from getting Sarita's case prepared to go before the judge. The thought troubled him, and he shook his head slightly. Sarita caught the motion and looked at him, but her lips were set in a firm line beneath the layers of lipstick.

Jake heard the bailiff call out Sarita's name, and he got up at once and went up to stand before the judge with her.

Judge Samuel Pence was a stern-looking man, but only in his midthirties, Jake judged. His eyes were level and direct, and he had the trim look of an athlete, unusual to find on the bench. From what Jake could pick up, he was as close as you could come to a hanging judge. Of course no one was actually hanged anymore, but Judge Samuel Pence looked at least tough enough to hang a guilty man without a blink.

Pence was looking over the papers before him. Then he looked up and said, "You are Sarita Hayden? I have reviewed your case, and have decided to approve you, Mr. Novak, as the guardian of Sarita Hayden."

"Thank you, Your Honor," Jake said.

Pence's eyes narrowed. Jake had found out that he had been a SEAL before law school, and now he looked every bit as daunting as one of those heroic figures. "You're not ideal, Mr. Novak, but you have financial stability and recommendations from some good people in the military and from the Chicago Police Department. I must warn you that you're taking on a very difficult task. Parents determined to raise children have a difficult time today, but this young woman will be even more difficult." He looked at Sarita daring her to speak, but she said nothing—for which Jake was devoutly thankful. "This young woman will be a burden to you, and I'm going to inform the juvenile authorities in Mobile, Alabama, to monitor your behavior." Again there was a silence, and Jake felt like the king in the Bible of whom the writing on the wall said, *Thou art weighed in the balances, and art found wanting.*

"If you take advantage of this young woman, you will be brought back to this courtroom, Mr. Novak, and you will find me *quite* unpleasant."

Suddenly Sarita said, "I don't want to go with him, Judge."

Pence stared at the girl. "What would happen to you if you didn't go with him, young lady?"

"I could take care of myself."

"Oh really?" the judge said. "Well, young lady I have your records here, and they plainly reveal that you have never taken care of yourself. You have nine charges against you, none of them as serious as they might have been, but they indicate that you are a rebel. So I will give you a choice. You can either go to a juvenile institution—a prison, you would call it—or you can go with Mr. Novak until you are of age. It's your choice."

The silence seemed thick enough to cut with a knife, and Sarita's face was touched with anger, but she said, "I'll go with him."

"I think that's a very wise choice. This young woman is committed to your charge, Mr. Novak. The papers are all in order, but as I have warned you, I will have the authorities monitoring your case."

"Thank you, Judge Pence. I'll do my very best for Sarita."

"See that you do!"

● ● ●

Jake hadn't wanted Sarita to appear in court wearing the motorcycle-riding outfit he had bought her. It consisted of a pair of jeans, boots, a jacket, and a helmet, but those seemed inappropriate in a court of law. However, the outfit she had chosen to wear was probably no better, Jake thought as he pulled the Harley up in front of the apartment house. He shut the engine off and waited until Sarita got off of the seat. He suddenly turned when she ran across to a young man who had apparently been waiting.

"Manny!" Sarita cried.

"It's me all right, babe." Manny was a hulking young man in his mid-twenties with a scarred-up face. Jake approached slowly, his eyes filling with disapproval as Sarita reached up, pulled Manny's head down, and kissed him. Jake was aware she was deliberately sending him a message—one he didn't particularly care to hear.

"Who's this guy?" Manny said, seeing Jake.

Before Sarita could answer, Jake said, "I'm her guardian, Manny. Now, as her guardian, and in my office as such, I'm telling you to move along."

Manny at once moved toward Jake. Jake stood there, apparently uncon-cerned. "Move along, Manny," he repeated. "Save yourself a trip to the dentist."

Manny laughed. "From you? I could take you with one hand tied behind my back."

"Well, go ahead and tie it, and let's get this over with. I can see you're never going to be happy until I administer a beating."

"Watch out for him, Manny," Sarita said. "He's been a policeman and in the army."

"Well, soldier boy," Manny warned, "*you* move along. *I'll* take care of Sarita."

Jake took one step forward, and his arm shot out so quickly to strike Manny in the throat that Sarita had trouble following the motion.

Manny made a noise that sounded like *goggle* and fell back a step.

"I think you probably have business somewhere else, so go on and peddle your papers."

Manny was choking. Sarita cried out, "What have you done to him, Novak?"

"He's not going to die. I shouldn't be that lucky." Jake reached forward, grabbed Manny's hand in a come-along, turned him around, and then gave him a shove with his foot. Manny cartwheeled forward, trying to regain his balance, but fell headlong. He got slowly to his feet. He tried to speak, but that seemed to be beyond him.

"Come along, Sarita." She didn't move, and he took her arm and led her into the building.

"You think you're so tough," Sarita said. "I know guys that can take you."

"And I know guys that can take them. Now, get your stuff ready. We're leaving in fifteen minutes."

Sarita glared at him and jerked her arm away. "Don't you put your hands on me!"

"Why would I want to do that? You look like a witch in that rig. Now, fifteen minutes. I'll come along to see you're on time."

● ● ●

Exactly fourteen minutes later the two were getting on the motorcycle. Jake had packed up some of Ty's belongings—books and other things that Sarita might want some day if she ever came to her senses. Sarita had thrown her clothes into two bags that would fit on the Harley. The two had gone downstairs, and Sarita looked around to see if Manny was there, but he had disappeared.

Jake stuffed her clothing into his saddlebags, mounted, and said, "Now, get on."

Sarita got on, and Jake left so fast that she was thrown backward. She reached out and grabbed him, putting her arms around him, which she hated.

"We'll make it as far as we can, and then put up for the night," Jake shouted.

● ● ●

Sarita was exhausted by the time they pulled off the road. She had never gone on a long motorcycle ride before, only short hops. She had clung to Novak on the back of the Harley, and now as she got off, she was stiff as a plank. Without a word Jake removed the key and said, "I'll go get us a place to stay."

Sarita watched him go. She was boiling inside and felt somehow she had been cheated by the way the man had treated her. When he came back, she said, "I'm not staying in the same room with you, Novak."

Novak handed her a card. "You're in room two-twelve. I'm across the hall. I'm going to get something to eat. You can do that, or you can go to bed."

Sarita wanted to throw the key back at him, but her hungry stomach restrained her.

"Go put your stuff in your room," Jake ordered. "The restaurant's nearly empty."

Ten minutes later they were seated, and Sarita was eating chicken-fried steak while Jake ate a salad. Neither of them spoke. Finally Sarita asked, "What's it like, this place where you're taking me?"

"It's a nice place, Sarita. You'll like it."

"No, I won't."

"Well, then you won't. What do you care what it looks like if you've determined not to like it?"

Sarita wasn't accustomed to guys like Jake. She had been fully a woman since she was fourteen, and now at the age of sixteen she had firm ideas about the nature of men and what they expected from women.

Jake took his cup of coffee, sipped it, and said, "To make a long story short, about a year ago an old lady died. She left her place on the beach to two distant relatives. I'm one of them. The other is a lady named Mary Katherine Forrest. She has a twelve-year-old son named Jeremy." He went on to explain the conditions of the will and saw that Sarita was listening carefully.

"Where am I going to stay?" Sarita asked when Jake finished.

"Not long ago we took a man in who was in bad shape. There's a big storage room downstairs that we converted into a room. It has a shower and everything. It's a little bit rough, but Mary Katherine will make it nicer for you."

"You're sleeping with her, right?"

Jake didn't answer for a time. Then he said, "No, I'm not."

He got to his feet and said, "I'm going to bed. We'll leave at eight in the morning."

Sarita watched Jake as he went and paid the bill, then left the restaurant. She lingered for a while but finally went to her room. She locked the door and stared at it for a minute. *Sooner or later he'll try to get in here with me. I'll have that judge put him in jail.* The thought pleased her, and she took a long hot shower and then got into bed. As the silence closed in on her, finally she said aloud, "If I don't like it there, I'll run away. Nobody tells me what to do!"

Eleven

Dawn had come to the Gulf Coast, and Bandit the coon had been prowling all night. He knew the location of every garbage can on the beach and had a nightly route that took him to each one. He usually left them turned over and empty, but the pickings had been slim tonight. Now he had come into the kitchen and found Jacques and Cleo watching him carefully.

Look at that dumb coon, Cleo, Jacques smirked. *What are coons good for, anyway?*

I'm sure they're good for something.

Well, you're right. I know in Arkansas they have a regular coon festival. Everybody goes and they eat the things. I'd sure hate to eat one of them. They wouldn't be very tasty. They'll eat anything. That means they're scavengers.

Catfish are scavengers, Cleo said. *You don't mind eating them.*

That's different. Jacques was hungry himself, and he watched as the coon moved along the cabinet doors. Jake had installed child locks on them for the sole purpose of keeping Bandit and various other critters out. Somebody, however, had failed to latch one of the lower cabinet doors, and Bandit opened it and looked quite pleased.

Look at that. Isn't he clever!

He's dumb as last year's bird's nest, Jacques said. He did, however, get up and walk over. Bandit had begun to toss cans out, and Jacques studied them. *I wish we had a can opener.*

Jacques, that coon is going to get us in trouble.

Nah, we'll put all the blame on him. Let's see if we can get something to eat out of this mess.

For the next half hour the cabinet was raided. Bandit pulled out anything that had any possibility of becoming food for hungry coons—and cats. Most of it was inedible, but he did discover that the right side of the cabinet was filled with pet treats. Jacques watched as Bandit cleverly opened package after package and sampled them.

I'm going to try some of that stuff.

You'll get in trouble.

No I won't. Come on. We deserve it.

I don't know why you think that.

Because everyone knows cats are superior beings.

Cleo was enticed, and soon the floor was littered with empty bags. The pet food had all been sampled, and Bandit had managed to open several liter-sized bottles of cold drinks. Most of it spilled onto the floor, and Jacques watched as the coon lapped it up.

That stuff looks pretty good. He went over and tried it and then spit. *Man, that tastes awful!*

At that instant a sound came from the other end of the condo. At once Jacques moved and leaped up to the top of one of the cabinets. Cleo watched him with amazement and then turned to see Mary Katherine coming into the kitchen wearing her dressing gown.

"Bandit, what have you done?" the Person said. *The Person*—that was how the cats always spoke of Mary Katherine Forrest. They called Jeremy *the Boy,* and Jacques always called Jake *the Intruder.*

Mary Katherine went over and shook her finger at Bandit. "Bad coon! Bad! Bad! Bad!"

Yes, he's a bad coon, Person. Throw his rear out of here!

Jacques, don't be mean.

Well, it's all his fault. He's the one that opened the cabinet and poured everything out. I hope she beats him with a boat paddle.

Bandit scurried out without a backward look, and Mary Katherine had started cleaning up the mess, when Jeremy appeared. He was wearing a pair of shorts and a T-shirt, and flip-flops.

"Wow—Bandit struck again, huh, Mom?"

"Yep. He got into one of the cabinets, and look at the mess he's made."

Jeremy laughed. "That coon's pretty smart."

Smart? Jacques said arching his back and glaring at the boy. *He's stupid, that's what he is. I'm the one that's smart around here.*

Mary Katherine suddenly looked up and stared at Jacques. "I'll bet you had something to do with this, Jacques."

Why, I'm innocent, he meowed. *I never do anything wrong. It's that coon that causes all the trouble.*

"We're going to have to be sure these cabinet doors are locked." As the two began cleaning up the mess, Jeremy continued. "Where did you say Jake went?"

"He didn't say. He just said he had some business to take care of."

"Will he come back, do you think?"

Kate shot a quick glance at her son. She knew he had bonded with Jake and was very close to a father–son relationship. As a matter of fact, he was much closer to Jake than she was.

"I'm sure he'll come back."

"When do you think?"

"I don't know, Jeremy." She tied the top of a garbage bag and said, "Jeremy, I've been wanting to ask you, what do you and Jake do at the fitness center?"

"Oh, he's just getting me into shape, Mom."

"Well, that's good, I suppose. But don't worry. Jake will be back. It may have had something to do with the book he's writing." She added, "I'm going to take some food down to the Brices. Will you finish cleaning up here?"

"Sure, Mom."

Kate quickly put a bowl of lasagna into one bag and stuffed another one with a cherry pie she had baked. It wasn't as good as Jake could do, but she refused to admit that. She left the room, and Jacques said, *Come on, Cleo. I may want to taste whatever it is she's got in that bag.*

Kate stepped outside and started down the beach. She was aware of the two cats following her. "Go home," she said. Cleo started to go back, but Jacques simply ignored her. "You are one awful cat, Jacques."

No, I'm not. I'm wonderful. You've never appreciated my finer qualities.

I don't think she's ever seen any of those, Cleo responded.

Kate proceeded along the beach, pleased as always at this time of day when the earth was beginning to warm up. The whispering of the surf always gave her pleasure. It was something she had never heard when she had lived in Memphis. She had been more likely to hear gunshots in the middle of the night. And now as she walked along, she thanked the Lord fervently that she had gotten Jeremy out of that place. When she reached the Brice house, she figured Morgan would not be up. She would just simply step inside and leave the food on the table. She knocked tentatively and then heard footsteps. The door opened, and Rhiannon stood there wearing an oversized T-shirt, which served as her nightgown.

"Hello, Rhiannon. I brought a lunch for you and your grandfather."

"Good. I bet it won't be as good as Jake's though."

A grimace touched Kate's lips, and she said, "Probably not, but I did the best I could."

"Come on in. Granddad's not awake yet."

Kate put the groceries on the table and said, "Maybe you better put this lasagna in the refrigerator."

Rhiannon looked down at Jacques and Cleo. "Yeah, I better. That big cat eats everything. I never saw such a greedy cat."

Well, rain on you, girl, Jacques expressed this with every fiber in his body. He had a way of doing that, of speaking with body language as clearly as any words that could be uttered.

"Have you had breakfast?" Rhiannon asked.

"Well, as a matter of fact, I haven't," Kate said.

"I'll fix you some. I like to cook breakfast."

"Well, that would be nice." Kate sat down at the table and watched as Rhiannon pulled a big frying pan out of a cabinet and set it on the stove. She pulled out a carton of eggs and asked, "How many can you eat?"

"One will be plenty."

"No, you better have two. They're not the big size. I always have two myself."

"Maybe I should then," Kate said.

As Rhiannon made toast and fried bacon and then eggs, Kate asked about her grandfather.

A shadow fell over the girl's face. "He's not very good."

When the meal was ready the two sat down, and Kate asked the blessing. Rhiannon said, "Amen," and proceeded to eat. As always, she ate as if she hadn't had a meal in days.

"You shouldn't eat so fast, Rhiannon," Kate said.

"Why not?"

"I don't know. I suppose it's bad for your digestion."

"It doesn't hurt me. I've always eaten like this."

The two finished their meal, washed the dishes, and then Kate said, "I guess I'd better get home. Jake's not there to fix Jeremy's breakfast, and the animals have to be fed."

Rhiannon walked out on the porch and said suddenly, "I hate to tell you, but I'm kind of scared."

At once Kate stood still. She walked over and said, "Sit down here and let's talk about it."

The two sat down on the deck chairs, and Kate encouraged Rhiannon to talk.

"I don't want to go to school," the girl said.

"You don't like school?"

"I'm always the smartest one in my class, and the other kids hate me for it."

Kate smiled. "I never had that problem."

"No, but you're pretty and that makes up for it. I'm not pretty, but I am smart."

Kate reached over and put her hand on the girl's cheek. "You are so pretty. You have a beautiful complexion and black curly hair and nice eyes."

"I wish I was blonde and had long hair that could be braided."

"Well, I don't," Kate said. "I like you just like you are."

For a time she sat there, and finally Rhiannon said, "I'm worried about Granddad. He's really not doing well."

Kate hesitated, not knowing exactly how to answer. She had noticed the same thing. "I'm sure the Lord's going to take care of him. We're all praying for him at church and at home, too."

"I know. I read in the Bible where it said not believing God is a terrible sin."

"Where does it say that?"

"It's in Hebrews, chapter three, the twelfth verse. It says, 'Take heed, brethren, lest there be in any of you an evil heart of unbelief, in departing from the living God.'"

"That's kind of a scary verse, isn't it? We always think of awful things like murder and stealing as being the terrible sins, but it sounds like unbelief is even worse."

"I like it though, that chapter. It's just like a big red stop sign. The Hebrews who got to the Promised Land and couldn't go in because they wouldn't believe God. But you and I are going to believe God, aren't we, Kate?"

"We sure are for your grandfather. Suppose we pray right now?"

"Okay." The two joined hands, and Kate said a quick prayer, and when she looked up she saw that there were tears in Rhiannon's eyes. Rhiannon was not a crying young girl, and Kate put her arm around her and hugged her. "It's going to be all right. We're going to believe God."

Suddenly Rhiannon stiffened and said, "Look, there comes that man."

"What man?"

"I found him on the beach the other day," Rhiannon said. "He almost had a heatstroke, so he came here, and I put cool towels on his face and gave him lots of cold water."

● ● ●

The sun had dropped into the west, the sunset turning the Gulf crimson, as Lew Ketchell moved toward the Brice house. Indeed, Ketchell had thought constantly of how the girl named Rhiannon had overheard his conversation with Eileen Saban. He wasn't a man to take chances unnecessarily, and he had felt it would be good to have another talk with the girl to see if she really understood all that had been said. Now as he walked up to the porch, he said, "Hello there, Rhiannon."

"Did you bring Chinese?"

"Yes, like I promised you."

"Most people don't keep their promises," Rhiannon said.

Ketchell smiled at Mary Katherine, who was standing by Rhiannon. He had met her only once, briefly, at the meeting of the cat owners, and he said, "Miss Forrest, isn't it?"

"Yes, and you're Mr. Ketchell, I believe."

Rhiannon went forward at once and took the two sacks, each with a dragon imprinted on the side. "Did you get fried rice?" she asked.

"Sure did. I got a little of everything."

Rhiannon turned suddenly and said to Kate, "He's a bad man, but I guess even a bad man can do good things."

Kate smiled, then said, "Well, I really must run. I'll leave you to your Chinese food. Good seeing you again, Mr. Ketchell."

Ketchell nodded, then turned his attention to Rhiannon. The young girl might be a danger to him, but she was certainly an original. "You ought not to tell people I'm bad."

"Well, you are, aren't you?"

"There are lots of men worse than me."

Rhiannon looked at Ketchell, and he felt an uneasiness at the innocence he saw there.

"What's the worst thing you ever did?" Rhiannon asked bluntly.

Lew Ketchell suddenly laughed aloud and said, "The worst thing I ever did was to suck my thumb when I was young like you."

"That's a story," Rhiannon said.

"What's the worst thing *you* ever did, Rhiannon?" Ketchell asked.

Rhiannon grew thoughtful. She put both arms around the sack and hugged it. Finally she said, "I hated God for letting my parents die in a car wreck."

It wasn't what Ketchell expected. "Well, I don't blame you. I guess I'd hate Him, too, if that happened to me."

"I don't hate Him now though. I told Him I was sorry, and that makes it all right."

"So when you do something wrong, all you have to do is tell God you're sorry and that takes care of it?"

"That's what the Bible says in John chapter one verses nine and ten. It says, 'If we confess our sins, He is faithful and just to forgive us our sins, and to cleanse us from all unrighteousness.' You're a bad man, but you could do that, and it would be all right again."

"Too late for me, Rhiannon." Ketchell said quietly.

"It's never too late," Rhiannon said. "Why don't you come on in and eat supper with us?"

Ketchell had come for this very reason, but he felt strangely intimidated by this young girl. He had never met such innocence and such honesty in one package. "All right," he said, "if it would be all right with your granddad."

"He loves Chinese food, and he likes company. He likes being copacetic. "

"And you like big words, don't you?"

"I like all words. Some short words are good and so are some long ones."

"You must do pretty well in school."

"I don't go to school. My granddad teaches me. But now that he's sick, Kate's getting some people to tutor me. Maybe you could tutor me. What do you know a lot about?" Rhiannon asked Ketchell directly.

"Not a whole lot about anything."

"I know everything up to J."

"What do you mean up to J?"

"I'm reading through the encyclopedia, and I'm in the J volume right now."

She took a huge bite of fried rice and stuffed a fried shrimp into her mouth. "You want to test me?"

"You mean something up to J?"

"That's right."

"Okay, what's a 'janissary'? I read the word in a poem by Robert Frost, but I haven't had time to look it up yet."

Speaking around the food in her mouth, Rhiannon said, "A janissary was a Turkish soldier, a member of an elite corps in the standing army of the Ottoman Empire."

"Hey, that's pretty good." Despite himself Lew Ketchell found himself fascinated by Rhiannon. He decided she was no threat to him—instead, she appealed to something deep down inside that he hadn't felt for years.

"If you like poetry, maybe you can tutor me in that," Rhiannon suggested.

"I wouldn't mind," Ketchell said, and to his surprise found himself speaking of the poetry he had been reading lately.

Jacques and Cleo had followed all this carefully—at least, Jacques had. Cleo had curled up in a corner and was asleep, but Jacques was studying Ketchell. *You know, Cleo, that guy is pretty bad.*

Cleo yawned, opened her golden eyes and stared at him. *How can you tell?*

I'm pretty bad myself. It takes a bad one to know another bad one, but I do lots of good things, too.

Cleo yawned and looked at Jacques with disbelief. *I don't remember you ever doing anything good.*

You know that robin I caught this morning?

I certainly do.

Well, I didn't torture him like some cats do. I just killed him dead instantly. That was a good thing.

Ugh! I can't stand it when you talk like that!

It's cat talk, sugar. You ought to get with the program.

Twelve

For Kate, fixing dinner for guests was almost like an exquisite torture devised by savage Indians. She looked over what she had prepared and saw that everything not burned was only half-cooked. She had managed to dirty every dish and pot in the kitchen, it seemed, which only reminded her how Jake could cook and keep a kitchen clean at the same time.

"Well, such as it is, it's on the table. Let's eat," she said.

Jeremy, Ocie, Enola, and Bev were there, and when Ocie sat down in front of some of the meat that had been burned, he said, "Sister, it looks to me like we got us a burnt offering here." When Kate gave him a hurt look, he laughed. "It's all right. I like well-done meat."

The meal actually wasn't bad, as evidenced by the seconds Ocie, Jeremy, and Bev helped themselves to. Jeremy watched as Ocie took a bottle of his special hot sauce and liberally anointed his meal with it. "Doesn't that stuff burn your mouth, Ocie?" he asked in awe. "I can hardly take a drop of it."

"Nah. It stirs up the digestive juices and makes the taste buds come alive, son. It's the reason I've lived so long. Lots of my special hot sauce—and I always sleep with my head pointed north."

Everyone laughed and Bev said, "That's interesting. I never heard that was particularly healthful."

"That's the trouble with you limeys. You spend so much time on unimportant stuff you don't have time for the real big things."

Bev had been at a meeting with Kate concerning a financial gift that Ocie had given. He had put it in legal language and established a fund for the youth work so there would always be money available for the programs Ocie wanted to support.

Enola said, "Well, the cat show starts the day after tomorrow. It's going to be interesting."

"As far as I can tell," Kate said, "every one of the owners hates every other one of the owners except for Mary Beth Pickens. She's a really sweet young woman."

"She won't last long if she is," Ocie said. "Sweet people don't last long in this world. They get et up pretty quick."

"Aw, that's not right," Jeremy protested. "I know lots of sweet people who do well."

"They're the exception, son. Us sweet people usually don't come around very often."

By the time they were almost through eating, Jacques lifted his head. *There's somebody coming,* he said to Cleo. *I hope it's not the Intruder. It's been a relief not to have him around.*

He's a nice man, Jacques.

Nice! He kicked me halfway across the room.

Only because you clawed his leg.

Well, he gave me a look I didn't like. When people give me bad looks, I give them the old claw, and I'll do it again, too.

Kate turned suddenly. "Somebody's coming."

"Maybe it's Jake," Jeremy said eagerly. They all turned, and the front door opened, and they all started to greet Jake. But then they fell silent. Jake looked angry, and he was holding onto the arm of one of the most rebellious-looking young women any of them had ever seen.

"Try to hold the applause down," Jake said defiantly.

"Jake, it's good to see you," Kate said quickly and got to her feet. She came over and said, "And who is your friend?"

Jake gave Sarita a disgusted look. "This is Sarita Hayden. Sarita's going to be staying with us a while."

"Why—how nice," Kate said, obviously nonplussed. She was studying the young woman, who looked like a streetwalker. Her clothes were too tight, her dress was too short, her hair was ratted, and there was a sullen look on her face.

In an attempt to head off the most obvious question, Jake said, "Sarita's father just died."

"Oh, I'm so sorry, Sarita," Kate said. "How terrible for you."

"She's managed to hold up pretty well," Jake said sarcastically. "Her father was Tyler Hayden. We were together in the Delta Force. I owed him something so when he knew he was dying, he sent for me and asked me to look after Sarita."

"Yeah, Jake owns me now," Sarita said with a scowl.

Jake gritted his teeth. "I do not *own* you, Sarita. Nobody owns you."

"That's what the judge said. He said you'd be my boss until I was of age."

"That's right."

"So you were legally appointed this young lady's guardian, Jake?" Beverly asked.

"That's right," Sarita answered for Jake. "Like I said, he owns me."

"Oh, I don't think that's right, Sarita," Kate said, "and anyway, I'm glad he's brought you here. You're welcome here."

Ocie had been watching the young lady, and now he said, "Have you been born again, honey?"

"No, I haven't, and don't you dare come at me with any of your preaching," Sarita warned.

"You two must be hungry," Kate broke in. "There's plenty left."

Jake looked at the table and said, "This looks like the wreck of the *Titanic*. You must have cooked this mess yourself."

"Yes, I did!"

"Actually it's not bad," Bev said quickly.

"Are you hungry, Sarita?" Kate asked.

"Yes," Sarita said without smiling.

"Here, you sit down. I'll bring some fresh plates," Kate said. "Jeremy, you help." Jake and Sarita sat down. Jacques began to approach their chairs.

"Look out for that cat," Jake warned. "He's a monster."

"He doesn't really like anybody except me," Kate explained. "Jeremy, don't let Jacques scratch our guest."

But suddenly Jacques came up to Sarita and with one smooth motion leaped up into her lap. Sarita was taken off guard after hearing the dire warnings about Jacques, but she quickly reached out and stroked his head. Jacques began to purr.

"He's not a bad cat," Sarita said defiantly. "See how he likes me?"

Huh, Cleo said, *You've never done that before, Jacques.*

I like her. She's bad like me. Us bad cats have to stick together.

Everyone was staring at Sarita with the cat in her lap. They looked for all of the world like a calendar picture of a happy cat and his mistress. Bev shook his head, puzzled. "That cat hates me."

"He hates pretty well everybody," Ocie said.

"Well, I'm glad he likes you, Sarita," Kate said. "Maybe you two will become good friends."

Sarita ate hungrily, but Jake made no attempt to eat. Finally, when Sarita seemed finished, he said, "Come on. I'll show you where you'll be staying."

Sarita carefully placed Jacques on the floor, stroked his head, and said, "You're a good cat."

You bet your bird I'm a good cat, but only to people that deserve it. The rest of these wimps don't deserve anything—except for my Person, of course. Come on, Cleo, let's see that the young lady's room is suitable.

Sarita followed Jake, who led the way outside. Kate accompanied them. Jake said, "There's no direct entrance to the house from where you'll be staying, Sarita. For your meals you'll have to come this way."

Sarita didn't answer, but glanced curiously at Kate and asked abruptly, "You two live in the same house?"

"That's right," Kate said, knowing what was coming next. "We have to, according to our relative's will. Jake has an apartment upstairs, I'm downstairs."

"Has he ever come on to you?" Sarita asked.

"No," Kate simply said. She had been prepared for the question. "Everybody asks that, but Jake and I are just good friends."

Jake opened the door, stepped in, and said, "This is it."

Sarita walked inside with Jacques rubbing himself against her ankles. She reached down and picked him up and stared about the room. Jacques purred like a loud sewing machine, and Cleo, who had also followed along, said, *You never let anybody pick you up.*

Like I said, this gal and me, we're simpatico.

The room Sarita saw was rather large. It had been a double garage, and Jake had installed two windows to let in sunlight. There was a through-the-wall air conditioner.

"There's no kitchen here," Jake said. "We can get you a hot plate and a toaster oven just for snacks."

Sarita was silent, and Kate said, "This room was put together for a man, Sarita, but you and I can fix it up nice."

Sarita turned and said, "I don't like it. I'll run away the first chance I get."

"If you do, I'll just have to come after you," Jake said. Then he turned and left the room abruptly.

"I'm sorry about your father," Kate said. "He and Jake were good friends."

"Yeah, but that doesn't mean *I* have to be his friend."

Kate changed the subject and said as tactfully as she could, "Sarita, maybe you and I could go shopping. You could get some new clothes."

"What's the matter with these?" Sarita asked defiantly.

Everything was the matter with them, but Kate was wise enough to understand she couldn't change this girl overnight. "Well, I was thinking you might find something you'd like. It'd be fun to shop anyway. If you're tired, you could lie down and rest a while."

"I'm not tired."

"Well, you can either go back in the house with me, or you can go for a walk on the beach, or you can stay here if you want to. Tomorrow we'll go get some nicer things to fix this room up."

"I think I'll go walk on the beach," Sarita said.

"That's fine. I hope you enjoy it here, after you've had a chance to get to know us better. I'm really amazed at how Jacques has taken to you. He's really not a person cat. If he likes you, then you must be very special. Goodnight, Sarita."

Kate caught up with Jake as he was rounding the corner and said, "Jake, wait a minute." When he paused, she said, "I wish you had called and let us know what was going on."

"I suppose I should have called you or something, but it just didn't happen." He then went on to explain more about his regard for Sarita's father and what had happened while he was gone.

Kate said finally, "You really loved him, didn't you?"

"Yes, I did, but Mary Katherine, I want you to know that Sarita is my problem, not yours."

"No, Jake, she'll have to become part of the family," Kate said.

"Dream on, Mary Katherine," Jake said grimly. "You see what she's like."

"You're just tired and discouraged. Why don't you go take a shower and lie down and nap for a while."

Jake shrugged his shoulders. "I appreciate it, Mary Katherine. But it's going to be a tough go."

"You did the right thing, Jake, and I'm proud of you." She went over and laid her hand on his arm, feeling the corded muscles beneath her fingers. "She's scared, she's had a hard life, but there's hope for her."

"Well," Jake said, managing a faint smile, "that reminds me of that line from an Emily Dickinson poem: 'Hope is the thing with feathers that perches in the soul.'"

"That's a good line, and that's what we've got to have for Sarita—hope."

Jake turned and walked away without another word, and Kate moved toward the door, murmuring a prayer.

"Well, Lord, You can do all things, so please give this girl what she needs to make her into the young woman You want."

Thirteen

Jake picked up the Sawzall and revved the motor. At top speed it made a teeth-rattling whir that sent a group of gulls overhead into panic. Looking at the outline he had drawn on the end of what was now Sarita's room, he lifted the saw, and with a high-pitched whine, the blade bit into the wood. He made his top cut, sawing through two studs, then cut out the bottom, and finally the sides. When he had cut the second side, he gave the square a tremendous blow with the heel of his palm. He felt a glow of satisfaction as the square fell inward. He looked over at Trouble, who was watching him curiously. "My favorite tools are a Sawzall and a sledgehammer, Trouble. With those two tools I can destroy anything or build anything."

Trouble panted and barked happily, then came over and tried to sit on Jake's feet. "Get away. Go sit on Sarita's feet."

Sarita had demanded a window that faced the Gulf so she could watch the water. As he framed in the opening, Jake thought through the whole situation. He was determined to do anything in his power to help the girl find her way—which at this point in time seemed about as simple as inventing a perpetual-motion machine.

Jake picked up the window he'd bought and slapped it in. It fit tightly enough so that he had to pound it again with the heel of his hand until it reached the right place. Then picking up a hammer and a few nails, he proceeded to secure it. On the final nail he happened to glance at the green water rolling in onto the white sand, and smashed his thumb. He dropped the hammer and let out with a curse.

Jacques, who had come to watch, liked this. Turning to Cleo he said, *Listen to him. He's the one that's been teaching Bad Louie all those cuss words.*

I don't think so.

You always think the best of anybody. I always think the worst. Look at him. Isn't he a silly-looking thing jumping around?

So, do you still like the new Person, Jacques?

Yes, I like her. Jacques sat down, licked his paw, meditated for a moment, and then seemed to glow with satisfaction. *She's as mean as I am.*

I think she's scared.

What's to be scared of? She's got the Intruder hopping around trying to please her and not doing a very good job.

You need to be more understanding, Jacques.

*No, I don't. I understand too much as it is. I wish—*Suddenly Jacques stood straight up, and his back arched. *There he is. I'm going to get him this time.*

Cleo glanced down to see a huge cinnamon-colored tomcat coming along the beach. *He's not hurting you, Jacques. Leave him alone.*

No, he's not hurting me, but I'm hurting him.

With this threat hanging in the air, Jacques broke into a dead run, and Cleo followed as best she could. She saw the two collide like two meteorites. They were rolling over and over, clawing and yowling loud enough to wake the dead.

Jake whirled when he heard the cats fighting, and he plunged along the beach with Trouble beside him, barking. When he got to where the brawl was taking place, he was at a loss to know how to separate them. Cats have a much faster reaction time than humans, and he knew that to interfere would be to put himself in harm's way. He circled, looking for an opening to reach in and grab Jacques, but the two suddenly lurched over against his feet. Jacques reached out and gave him a claw that felt like liquid fire running down his calf. He kicked out and managed to catch the cinnamon cat, knocking him loose. Trouble immediately started barking and showing his fangs, and the tom took off with a yowl straight down the beach.

"Come here, Trouble. Leave that cat alone."

Jake looked down at his leg, which was bleeding freely from four furrowed gullies. "Now you see what you've done, you stupid cat! I need a full-time medic to keep me patched up from your dumb claws."

Jacques looked longingly at the cinnamon cat. *I would have killed him if you hadn't come along, Intruder.*

"Let's see your back. Oh, he got you a bad one there. You're going to have to have stitches."

Jacques said, *You lay a hand on me, and I'll decapitate you.*

Jake didn't understand the words, but he understood Jacques' pose. He turned, walked back up to the deck, and picked up an enormous bath towel. He returned to find Jacques trying to lick the out-of-reach wound. Before he could move Jake threw the towel over the cat and quickly pinioned him. He got the ends together. All the time Jacques was threatening Jake, *I will kill you! I'll make hamburger out of you!*

Jake tied the ends of the beach towel and carried the animated bundle to the house, to where the old van that Ocie had abandoned was parked, opened the back doors, and tossed Jacques in. He pulled out his handkerchief, wiped off the blood from his calf, and said to the toweled bundle, "I ought to throw you in the Gulf," but knew that he had no choice but to take Jacques to Enola's clinic.

● ● ●

Enola looked out the window when she heard the awful sound. She saw the battered white van pull up in front. She watched Jake as he got out, opened the back doors, and grabbed a turquoise-and-pink beach towel. By the thumping and moving, she knew he had an animal in there.

Enola stepped out the door. "What you got in there, Jake?"

"The Adolf Hitler of the cat world—Jacques," Jake replied, clearly amused.

"I see he got you on the leg. You'll have to have something for that."

"This dumb cat is going to have to have stitches," Jake said over Jacques' yowling and clawing.

"Bring him in here." Enola led the way to a stainless-steel table, and Jake put the bundle down.

"I don't know how you're going to treat him," Jake said. "It'd be like treating a crazed elephant."

"I'll have to calm him down."

Jake watched as Enola moved over to a large medicine cabinet, took a syringe, and filled it with a clear-looking fluid. "Hold him now. I'll shoot him right through this blanket."

"You might hit him in the eye," Jake commented.

"No I won't." Carefully she felt the blanket, found a satisfactory spot, and plunged the needle through. Jacques let out a banshee howl, and Jake had to hold him down forcefully.

"We'll have to wait a little bit, but not long. I gave him enough to knock out an elephant, so tell me what happened."

"He got into a fight with another cat," Jake said.

"Well, another happy day in the life of Jake Novak. Has this been your high point?"

Jake gave Enola a telling stare, then said, "This cat needs to be put down."

Enola laughed and said, "You've just lost a little blood, and you're unhappy. Be happy, Jake, like the song says. 'Don't worry—be happy'."

"Yeah, nothing easier than that," Jake groused. "You know, Enola, sometimes the world is good, and you feel alive. Things taste better, and colors are brighter, and it's just a pleasure to breathe the air and soak in the sun." Jake shook his head sadly. "And then you lose all that somehow, and you go around looking for a car to hit you so you won't have to go home."

"Jake, sit down there and let me see your leg," the vet said.

Jake sat down disconsolately in a chair and watched as Enola got the materials to put him together again. She took a bottle of yellowish liquid, soaked a cotton pad with it, and began applying it to his leg.

"Ow! That hurts!"

"Life hurts, Jake. Haven't you found that out?"

"What are you—a psychiatrist?"

"No, just a vet." She cleaned the wound and examined it critically. "Not going to need any stitches for that."

Enola put the medication away, washed her hands, and said to Jake, "So, your latest job is rescuing poor waifs off the street. You're like the head of Boys Town, Father What's-his-name. Well now—how are things with you, Father Jake, rescuer of children?" She smiled and pinched his arm. "How is the little tyke?"

"Don't you start on me, Enola!"

"Why, I'm just filled with admiration for you. I just love knights in shining armor who rescue damsels in distress. May I call you Sir Galahad?"

Jake said, "I can do without your opinions."

"Where is Sarita? You didn't leave her alone, I hope?"

"Kate took her shopping. She doesn't have any decent clothes."

"Yes, I saw what she was wearing when you brought her in. She might as well wear a sign around her neck—*I am a tramp.*"

Jake was silent, and Enola said, "You must have lost your mind, Jake. That girl is going to be nothing but trouble."

Jake sighed, and his shoulders drooped. "Her dad was a good guy. He saved my bacon when we were in the Delta Force. I wouldn't even be here if it weren't for Ty, so I've got to try."

Enola put her hand on his shoulder and said, "Jake, I admire you, really. Not many men would tackle a thing like this. Beneath that tough exterior I expect you've got a heart as soft as a marshmallow."

Jake gave a slightly sour grin. "Patch up Simba over there and we'll get out of your hair. I just wish you could give him enough dope to make him sleep for two weeks."

● ● ●

Kate's idea hadn't worked out well at all. She had conceived the plan to take Sarita shopping at the Tanger Mall in Foley, and instead of showing a spark of gratitude, Sarita had simply shrugged her shoulders at Kate's suggestions for clothes. Occasionally she'd respond with a sullen "I don't care."

On the way to the mall Sarita had said nothing. Kate had tried everything she could think of to get her to speak of her past, but evidently she didn't have the right key. Kate found a parking place, and as she and Sarita got out of the car, she heard her name being called.

She turned to see Beverly Devon-Hunt coming toward them. "Hello, Bev," she said. "What are you doing here?"

"I've finally decided my wardrobe is a bit lacking in American casual attire."

"Well, you've come to the right place. I believe you remember Sarita?"

"Yes, of course. How are you, Sarita?"

Sarita glanced at the Englishman and dully offered a "Hi."

"Mind if I accompany you two ladies?" Bev asked. "I assume you're shopping?"

"Men don't like shopping," Kate said. "At least my husband didn't, and Jake hates it."

"They weren't raised properly," Bev surmised. "Now, we worthless British nobility spend our life shopping. Attire is all to us." Bev's cornflower-blue eyes sparkled, and he looked quite handsome in his rather formal suit. He was absolutely trim, unlike Jake, who had smoothly rounded muscles. "Why, one of my ancestors in the Battle of Darcy insisted that the battle be put off until he could find a blue cornflower to put on his helmet. That's how important we of the nobility think our attire."

Despite herself Kate laughed. "I don't believe a word of that."

"It's the truth. On my honor."

"Well, I never saw a man yet who enjoyed seeing women shop, but you're welcome to come along."

"Thank you, Kate. Perhaps I can be of some assistance."

The trio began a pilgrimage, going into different stores. Sarita seemed to grow a bit more interested, but the selections she made were terrible. Kate figured at least they were better than what she wore, and let Sarita have her way on several of her choices. Bev watched the women carefully, making a few remarks, and then finally he picked out an outfit he thought was suitable. "Why don't you try this one on, Sarita? I think you'd look very well in it."

"But you're British—and you're a man," Sarita said. "You don't know anything about American clothes."

"On the contrary," Bev countered. "I've been studying all the authorities—like *Cosmopolitan* and *Vogue*. I think this outfit would say something about your sweet personality."

Sarita snickered. "Give me that," she said, snatching it from Bev's hand. She went off to the dressing room. Kate shook her head. "She's hard to please, Bev. I don't know how we're going to weather this."

"Oh, things will come out all right in the end," he said. "They always do."

"I'm pretty discouraged. She's so negative about everything."

"Oh, don't worry so much, Kate. All will be well."

At that moment Sarita came out, and at once Bev went to her and began praising her. "Now, *that* is what I call a boffo outfit. You look just tremendous, Sarita!"

Sarita shot a glance at Kate, then seemed half-amiable. She looked at herself in the mirror from all sides and said, "Well...it's not bad."

"Good, it just fits you," Bev said. "We'll take it."

The shopping went on for some time and ended with Beverly buying hot dogs all around, which he proclaimed an abomination only Americans could eat. But Kate noticed he ate two dogs, both heavily anointed with mustard.

As they were eating, he said, "Kate, I don't want you to forget, I still have you in mind."

Sarita picked upon this. "In mind for what? And why are you being so nice to me? You trying to impress Kate?"

"Indeed I am," Bev smiled. "I'm thinking of making her Lady Devon-Hunt."

Sarita was impressed in spite of herself. She turned to Kate and said, "You'd better take him, Kate. He's better than that scum-sucking Jake!"

● ● ●

Sarita went to the window Jake had installed and gazed out at the Gulf. It was late in the afternoon, and the sun striking the water brought glints like diamonds flashing. She watched for some time, listening to the gentle hissing of the waves as they came ashore, fascinated by the pelicans flying over the gulf in formation.

Finally she walked over to the closet and studied her new clothes. She had shown very little appreciation to Kate, but reaching out she touched the clothes and realized they were better than any she had ever had. Then she looked around the room and sensed a feeling of profound aloneness. Her world back home hadn't been good—no one had known this better than Sarita herself. She had fallen in with the wrong crowd. She'd had no parents for most of her life, and when her father had finally shown up to take an interest in her, she had put up walls and posted a "No Trespassing" sign.

Finally she turned and left her room. She walked around the house to the kitchen, where she saw Jake with what looked like every dish, pot, and pan in the kitchen out. She watched silently. He glanced her way, but his mind was clearly on the meal. "What are you cooking?" she finally asked.

"Chinese."

"Why don't you just order it?"

"Because I can do it better than they can. We're having egg rolls, egg drop soup, sweet and sour pork, and asparagus salad."

Despite herself Sarita was impressed at how efficiently Jake moved. She had already found out that Kate was no cook at all. All Kate could do was pop frozen meals into the oven.

"How do you know what goes into that stuff?" she asked

"I consult a cookbook, and then I add my own special touches." Jake turned and grinned at her. "I always think I can do things better than anybody else, Sarita. Of course, most of the time I find out I'm wrong about that."

Jeremy came in and plopped himself down at the island.

"What's for supper?" he asked.

"Chinese," Jake repeated.

"Why don't we just have it sent in?"

"That's what I said," Sarita replied. She seemingly couldn't avoid making fun of Jake. She liked to see him lose his temper. "That's what I told him. Only women are cooks. A man who cooks is a sissy."

Jeremy blinked his eyes with surprise. "You're crazy, Sarita! Jake was in the Delta Force. He was wounded and got a medal. They don't take sissies in that outfit!"

"Thanks for your sterling defense, Jeremy," Jake turned and winked. "I'll give you an extra bowl of soup for that."

Kate entered from her room and said, "Can I help, Jake?"

"Stay away," Jake warned. "I'm making a masterpiece here. Chinese. How does that sound?"

"I love it," Kate said. "Actually, I love any meal I don't have to cook myself."

"Well, we're in agreement there," Jake said. "I like any meal you don't have to cook too!"

As usual, the meal turned out to be excellent. Sarita had had takeout Chinese food, but never anything like this. The vegetables were crisp, the soup had a special flavor to it she had never tasted before, and the sweet and sour were blended just right. She said little at the dinner table, but she ate heartily.

After they were finished, Jeremy said, "I'll do the dishes, Jake."

"I'll help you," Sarita offered.

Everyone turned to look at her—it was the first positive thing she had said.

"Why are you staring at me?" she asked angrily.

"I always stare at nice-looking ladies," Jake said. "You don't have to help with the dishes."

"Look, I'm gonna earn my keep around here," Sarita said.

Sarita and Jeremy plunged in, and they cleaned the kitchen while Jake sat in an easy chair and read a book. After they had finished the dishes Jeremy said, "Let's play Scrabble."

"Jake always wins," Kate shrugged, "but it's all right with me."

"I'll tie half my brain in a knot or close one of my eyes," Jake grinned. "You like Scrabble, Sarita?"

"I think it's dumb."

Actually she liked Scrabble and was rather good at it, but she felt she was making herself too available to this unwanted world she had been forced into.

While the others gathered around the game table and began playing, she watched television, choosing three programs she hated and deliberately turning the TV on too loud to disturb the others.

They can't make me like it here, she thought. *I'll make them throw me out.*

● ● ●

Sarita had been unable to sleep. Finally she got up and went to the window and stared out. A bright moon was shining down, making a silvery track that seemed to lead over the horizon. It was warm, and she slipped out her door and onto the deck, wearing a pair of pj's that Kate had thought she would like. For a time she stood there watching the water.

Suddenly something touched her leg, and she turned around and saw that it was the big black cat.

"Hello, Jacques," Sarita said, relieved. "Nice night, isn't it?"

She began stroking his silky fur. "I hate this place, Jacques. What am I going to do?"

I agree. It's pretty bad, Girl Person, but you'll get three squares a day, maybe more.

"They all want me to be something, and I don't know how to be whatever it is they want."

Well, you have to learn how to cope with these Persons. Kate's all right, but the Intruder, Jake, he's no good at all. The Boy, he's not bad, but you can't let them run over you. I sure don't.

Sarita sensed that Jacques was speaking to her in some cat language, and she began laughing as he butted his head against her. Suddenly she became aware that someone had stepped out of the shadows, and her heart began to race. She jumped to her feet and saw it was Jake. He had a gun in his hand, and she said, "What are you doing with that?"

Jake was wearing a pair of shorts and a T-shirt, and he shoved the gun in the waistband of the shorts in the back. "I heard voices. Thought it might be burglars. What's the matter?" he said. "Couldn't you sleep?"

"No."

"I couldn't either." He came over and stood beside her and looked out at the Gulf. "This looks a lot better than the room I had in Chicago. That was really a drag."

Sarita wanted to say, *It was a drag where I was, too,* but instead she said, "I hate this place."

"Nothing I can do about that, Sarita. We're stuck together, you and me."

Sarita asked abruptly, "Didn't my dad leave an insurance policy?"

"Yes, he did."

"How much was it?"

"Fifty thousand dollars face benefit."

"I've got that much money?"

"No, you'll get it when you're eighteen."

"But what if I need something now?"

"I'm the administrator. If you want anything and I think it's good for you to have it, I'll see about it."

Sarita tensed. But then she remembered some of the tricks she'd already learned about how to soften men. She made herself relax and turned to Jake and said, "Jake, I know I've been mean, but I really do appreciate all you've done for me." She leaned against him and put her head on his chest. "I get scared sometimes."

"So do I," Jake said. "Anybody who doesn't get scared sometimes is a fool."

Sarita looked up at him. She had learned when men looked down into a woman's eyes it makes them vulnerable. She whispered, "I don't mean to be bad."

Just then a voice broke in. "I heard voices."

They turned to see Kate in her robe, holding a flashlight.

Sarita grew angry. "I came out here because I couldn't sleep," she said. "And then *he* came out and tried to put his hands on me. He tried to—"

Jake rolled his eyes. "Go to bed, Sarita," he simply said.

Sarita looked from Kate to Jake, then gave a short bow toward Jake and said in mock humility, "Yes, master." She then whipped away, rebellion stiffening her back.

Kate came over by Jake, and he said defensively, "She was lying."

"I know," Kate replied.

"She's a mixed-up kid, just a child really."

"She's not a child, Jake," Kate said. "I doubt if she ever was. You've got to be careful, Jake. If she should accuse you of molesting her, you'd have a hard time defending yourself."

"What can I do?" Jake asked. "I've got to help her. I promised Ty."

"I'll help you, but you mustn't ever let her get you into a situation like this again."

"It's kind of hard to avoid her." Jake grew quiet and stared out over the sea, then he turned to say, "I feel like I'm at my limit with this girl. I'm caught by my promise to Ty, and I don't know what to do."

"Sarita is a little bit hard to understand, Jake."

"Folsom Prison is filled with inmates who are hard to understand," he said wryly.

Fourteen

Harrison Phelps pulled a Havana out of his inner pocket, bit the end off, and spat it out. He extracted a platinum lighter from his pocket, and when the flame caught, he stuck it to the end and began sucking it in. When he had gotten his cigar going, he watched the blue smoke as it curled toward the ceiling, leaned back in his chair, and said with satisfaction, "Well, Lew, I'm going to be interviewed by a major television network. Ain't that something?"

"Still looking for respectability, are you, Harrison?"

"Well, a little respectability never hurt no one, did it?"

"I don't know. I never had any, but I know you won't get it by hugging a cat."

Phelps cast an angry look toward Lew Ketchell, who was sitting in a straight chair, his legs crossed, looking down at a book. "You've always got your nose in a book."

"You ought to try it sometime."

Phelps got up and began to pace the floor. Twice he started to say something to Ketchell, and finally he came and planted himself in front of the man. "So what have you done about Eileen and that cat she stole from me?"

Ketchell glanced up. "I gave her a warning, but she brushed it off."

"Well, make it stronger then."

"You want me to break her kneecaps, Harrison?"

"I want you to make her withdraw that cat from the show. I don't care how you do it."

"What difference does it make to you? I don't understand you. You've got everything you want that money can buy."

"She made me look like a fool, Lew."

"Women can do that. Get used to it."

"I *said*, I want you to make your warning a lot stronger."

"You want me to pull her fingernails out?"

"I don't care what you do!" Harrison Phelps snapped. "Just get her out of the show. I don't let people do me in, Lew. You know that."

"One day you'll be done in just like everybody else."

"Who's going to do it?"

"Death, of course."

Harrison was clearly agitated and took a deep puff off his cigar. "Why do you always have to talk about dying?"

"Well, it's something we all have to do. I don't think you've ever realized that." Ketchell lifted his eyes from the book and studied his employer carefully. "You've always been able to push people around, but you won't be able to push Mr. Death around."

"What do you mean, 'Mr. Death'?"

"It's in a poem you never read. A poet talked about Buffalo Bill, who was a great man in his own world, but he died and the poet asked, 'How do you like your blue-eyed boy, Mr. Death?'"

"I don't know why you read that junk," Harrison Phelps shouted. "You'd be better off if you never opened a rotten book. Now get out and do something about Eileen."

Lew got to his feet in a leisurely fashion and moved toward the door. He had smooth movements like a cat and made no sound as he crossed the room. At the door he turned around and said, "There was a man called Massinger once, Mr. Phelps. He said, 'Death has a thousand doors to let out life.' So I'd say you're wasting your time getting upset because people get the best of you." He thought for a moment and shook his head. "Death gets the best of all of us."

● ● ●

The civic center in White Sands had been overbuilt. The ambitious city fathers had assumed there would be huge crowds coming to the Gulf, and they had built a mammoth auditorium. It was practically empty now, except on the main floor in the center of all the thousands of seats. A few people had gathered. Cat owners had brought some of their contenders for "Best of Show," although the event wouldn't take place until the next day. Some reporters had also arrived, and Channel 5 had a cameraman scoping things out.

The cats were being held by their owners, placed on small platforms, or were still in their cages. Jake, Jeremy, and Sarita had all accompanied Kate to this meeting, which was mostly for publicity purposes. The three of them sat in the stands and watched Kate as she was combing Cleo out.

Sarita said, "This is dumb."

Jeremy said, "I don't think so. I think it's kind of fun. Look at those cats."

"Who cares what a cat looks like?"

"Quite a few people I'd say," Jake murmured. "Enough to get Channel 5 to get it on the local news."

Sarita moved restlessly and finally turned to study Jake. She hadn't yet been able to get to him, and this troubled her. A thought popped into her mind, and she said, "Did you know that Englishman Devon-Hunt is thinking about marrying Kate?"

Jake turned his head swiftly. "Won't ever happen," he said, his lips stiff.

"Why not?"

"She's got better taste than that."

Sarita laughed. She actually had a delightful laugh, and she looked very attractive in the outfit Devon-Hunt had picked out for her—a bright turquoise-colored pair of slim pants that ended just above the ankle, and a white cashmere twin sweater set with turquoise embroidery down the front.

"It'd be good for her," Sarita continued. "He's got money and even a title. She'd be Lady Kate then, I guess."

"That doesn't matter to her," Jeremy said quickly. "She wouldn't marry somebody unless she loved them."

Sarita laughed. "You're a romantic. People get married for all kinds of reasons."

"Not my mom," Jeremy said loyally.

At that moment Mason Craig, the emcee of the cat show, moved over to where Kate was brushing Cleo out. He was a smooth-looking man of forty with well-trimmed chestnut hair and a winning smile.

"Hey, let's go down and meet him," Jeremy said.

"Meet who?" Sarita asked.

"Mason Craig. He's a celebrity."

Jake grinned and followed Jeremy and Sarita to the main floor.

Soon they were standing beside Kate, who was now being questioned by Craig. He nodded toward them but continued to say, "And you've never entered the cat in a show before, Mrs. Forrest?"

"I never have. Never even thought of it."

"Well, that's unusual," Craig smiled, and his teeth gleamed against his tanned skin. "Most of these owners have pretty well built their lives around cats and cat shows."

"I think that's a mistake," Kate said firmly.

Craig was surprised. People didn't usually argue with him. "In what way, may I ask?"

"It's a mistake to build your life around anything that you're going to lose, and every one of these people will lose their cats one day," Kate said.

"Well, that's a rather pessimistic view," Craig said.

"But it's true, isn't it?"

Craig laughed. "I suppose it is, but please don't say that for our audience." He waved toward the camera recording the interview. "Better cut that out, Steve."

The cameraman, a tall black man with a broad smile, nodded, "Right, Mr. Craig."

Craig moved on to the next owner, who happened to be Harrison Phelps. Jeremy said, "You did fine, Mom. You'll be on television."

"I doubt it," Kate said. "I can see my future doesn't lie in entertainment."

Jake nodded, "Harrison Phelps will sing a different song."

"Who is he?" Sarita asked.

"He's a criminal trying to look like he's honest."

"A real criminal?"

"He's never gone to jail," Jake said. "He lets other people do that for him. He's a bad man to cross."

Mason Craig was well aware of Harrison Phelps' history. He was smiling but very polite as he said, "Well, it's not usually the kind of affair I'd expect to see you at, Mr. Phelps."

Phelps blinked and said innocently, "I'm just a businessman, really, but I do like cats."

"What do you think your chances are of winning best of show?" Craig asked.

"I always think I'm going to win."

"And you usually do," Craig said in a knowing tone.

Phelps shot Craig a quick smile. "It's a rough world, Mason. I've had to fight for everything I've got."

"Well, I want to wish you the best of luck," Craig said.

"Thank you."

Craig started to turn away, when he had another thought. "Oh, by the way, I didn't mention that your ex-wife is entering a Russian blue that's favored to win. I understand you once owned that cat."

Eileen Saban had approached, and she smiled cagily at her ex-husband and answered for him. "I got Blue Diamond as part of the divorce settlement. He's going to win, too."

"Why don't you butt in somewhere else, Eileen!" Phelps snapped.

"My, I see you haven't changed your sweet ways," Eileen said.

Craig stood there as the two took verbal potshots at one another, and finally he said, "Well, good luck to both of you."

"How about that, Jake?" Sarita said. "Those two hate each other."

"I guess there's a lot of that going around, Sarita. Come on. Let's mingle."

The small group walked around, and finally they came to a man and a woman at the end of the line. Jake said, "Hello, Mary Beth. Do you know everybody? I don't think you've met my young friends here. This is Sarita. This is Jeremy."

"Oh, I met your mother, Jeremy. She's a fine lady."

"We've just been listening to Mr. Phelps talking about how to win cat shows."

Anger touched Mary Beth's face. She had a sweet appearance with fine eyes and a sensitive mouth. "I don't think people like Phelps should be permitted to enter their animals."

"I guess they don't take characteristics of owners into consideration, just the cats," Jake shrugged.

A man standing on the other side of Mary Beth had been listening. He turned and said, "Hello there. I'm Gary Charterhouse."

"Are you new to White Sands, Mr. Charterhouse?" Mary Beth asked. "I don't think I've met you before."

The man was slow to speak, but said matter-of-factly, "I've been in prison, but I'm trying to put all that behind me."

"What were you up for?" Jake asked. "If I may be so bold."

"Assault with a deadly weapon."

"A gun?" Jake said.

"No, just my fist. I was a fighter, and they called these things a deadly weapon." Charterhouse grinned. The marks of the ring were on him. Scar tissue around his eyes drew them down into a squint, and one of his ears was puffy, a cauliflower job.

Mary Beth said, "Do you think your cat will win, Gary?"

"I hope so," the man said.

"Well, it's like a game," Mary Beth said. "Somebody wins, somebody loses, and if my cat loses, I'll handle it."

"I think you got the right idea there, Mary Beth," Jake said. He nodded to Charterhouse saying, "Good luck to you."

The three wandered around until the interviewing was finally over. They left the civic center and went home. When they got there Kate's eyes were gleaming and dancing with fun. "That show's going to be fun! I just love the cats."

"If we could leave the owners out of it, it wouldn't be a bad show," Jake said.

Jacques had been listening to all this. His stitches were itching, and he tried to claw them. He said to Cleo, who was now the center of attention, *Don't get all stuck up. If I were there, I'd win every prize they had.*

Jake glanced over at Jacques and said, "I bet Jacques is all in a snit because he didn't get to be the star." He laughed at Jacques, who glared at him, and went on, "If they ever have a show where they match cats in fights, I'll put you in it, Jacques. You might win something there."

Jacques hissed at Jake and turned around and left the room, his ears leaning back.

Kate picked up Cleo, who at once drooped across her shoulder and began purring. "You may not win, Cleo, but you'll be my favorite."

● ● ●

Jake was fixing banana pancakes when Ocie burst through the door the next morning. He had bought a big griddle that could do three pancakes at a time, and he was keeping it busy. The rest of the household—Kate, Sarita, and Jeremy—had already started eating and were devouring them as fast as Jake could cook them.

Ocie's eyes were wide as he came in without knocking. "Well, praise the Lord, something happened. Late-breaking bulletin here, folks."

"What is it?" Kate said, curious.

"Did you hear about the big catnapping?"

"You mean a kidnapping?" Jeremy said.

"No, I mean a *cat*napping. You know that Blue Diamond, that fancy cat Eileen Saban got from her husband when they split the blanket?"

"What about him?" Jake asked.

"Well, he's missing. Somebody catnapped him."

"How could that happen?" Kate asked.

"The woman left him at the civic center where they're having the show. There's a guard there of sorts, I guess, but he sure wasn't watching—because the cat was gone this morning."

"I'll bet she's spitting fire. That's a valuable cat," Jake said.

"She sure is," Ocie said. "Guess who the prime suspect is?"

"I'd guess Harrison Phelps," Jake said.

"You're right," Ocie beamed. "His ex-wife is claiming she's going to shoot him if he doesn't give her her cat back."

"Well, they'll never nail Phelps on that," Jake said. "He's too sharp to get involved personally." He thought for a moment and said, "He may have gotten Lew Ketchell to do the job."

"I never heard of a catnapping," Sarita said. "Wonder if they'll hold the cat for ransom?"

"I'd guess not," Jake said. "Whoever got him will keep him out of the show long enough so he can't compete. Everybody said he was an odds-on favorite. Sit down and have a pancake, Ocie."

"Well, praise the Lord, I don't mind if I do." As he sat down, the parrot, Bad Louie, flew in and perched on his shoulder. He croaked, "Praise the Lord," and then spat out an obscenity.

"You're just like lots of Christians, Bad Louie," Ocie scolded. "You got your good side and your bad side. Part of you redeemed, yet still just like most of us."

"Do you believe all that stuff about religion?" Sarita asked scornfully.

"I believe every bit of it, honey," the old man said. "It's all so. There ain't no other answer. Jesus is the way."

Sarita started to speak and then shook her head and muttered, "Well, I don't believe it."

"You will," Ocie said. "Your time's a-coming, no doubt about it. I got you right at the top of my prayer list."

Sarita barked out a laugh. "Mr. Plank, you're wasting your time praying for me. And God's time, too!"

Fifteen

Ray O'Dell, Chief of Police, White Sands, Alabama, had the palest blue eyes in the world. He was five-feet-ten, with brown hair that had a tendency to curl, which gave him a boyish look even at his age of fifty-three. O'Dell had been a rodeo performer specializing in bareback riding during his younger years and had won the all-around-cowboy award twice before he got sense enough to quit. He stared across the room at Harrison Phelps, and in a flat Oklahoma drawl said, "You've made it pretty plain, Mr. Phelps, that you and your wife have had differences over the cat she won in your divorce."

"It was pretty well public information when we got our divorce," Phelps replied. "Eileen made World War III out of it."

"I understand you probably remember the war correctly. She nicked you for quite a bit of coin."

Anger glinted in Phelps's eyes, and he snapped irritably, "The judge who made that decision should be disbarred. He was senile, and Eileen charmed him into getting at me. She's good at that."

"She says you're good at getting things you want, too," O'Dell remarked. "Especially, as I understand it, the missing cat was part of the settlement."

"That shows you the judge was nutty, doesn't it? Imagine making a cat part of a divorce action."

"I've heard of stranger things." Suddenly O'Dell said, "Did you take the cat, Mr. Phelps?"

"Of course not," Phelps said. "Why would I do a silly thing like that?"

"I read the records of your divorce," O'Dell said. "It seems you made several remarks about that cat, mainly that you were going to get him back again one way or another."

"That was just talk. I said a lot of things and so did she. Most of hers were unprintable."

Oralee Prather, the deputy serving under Ray O'Dell, listened as the two men talked. Oralee was twenty-six, short, stocky, and hard as a rock. Her skin was black as ebony, and those who doubted whether a woman could do her job and challenged her authority wound up with a knot on their head and their hands cuffed behind them. She was quick as a striking snake and had about as much mercy. It was fairly well talked about that she had her eye on being the next chief. She suddenly demanded, "Where were you last night, Mr. Phelps?"

"I was out having dinner at the Oyster House. After that I went to my condo and stayed there all night. I can give you witnesses for that."

Oralee said smoothly, "Are there any of these witnesses who don't work for you?"

Phelps gave Deputy Prather a withering look. "You're just dying to pin something on me, aren't you, Deputy?"

"As the old TV show put it, I just want to get the facts."

"Well, the facts are, I didn't take the cat. I'd be a fool if I did. I'm the logical suspect. Yeah, I made remarks about how I'd get even with her and get the cat back, but I'd go about it in legal ways."

"You haven't always been so careful, Mr. Phelps," O'Dell suggested gently. His eyes were slitted, the face of a man who had been out in the open sun and the weather a lot. "Several times you've almost gone to jail over your various pursuits."

"I'm just a businessman."

O'Dell grinned suddenly. "That's what Al Capone always said—'just a businessman.' He also said you can get more from somebody with a kind word and a gun than you can with a kind word alone."

"Am I under arrest?" Phelps demanded.

"Not at all," O'Dell said. "This is just routine questioning. We'll be talking to a lot of people. We'd like to get Mrs. Saban's cat back for her. She's pretty upset about it."

He took a toothpick out of his pocket, studied it, and stuck it in his mouth, then wiggled it up and down. "Where's your bodyguard, Mr. Phelps?"

"I don't know."

"Kind of careless, a bodyguard leaving the body he guards without any protection."

"I don't know where Lew went," Phelps repeated. "He just took off. Didn't say where he was going. He can't watch me all the time."

"When you see him, tell him we're looking for him."

"I'll tell him, but he didn't take the cat either."

"No, Lew's into bigger things than that, I suppose," O'Dell said. "This is a small town. It's not Chicago or Boston or New York. I know you don't think much of small towns, but I'd advise you that we can put you behind bars just as quick as the district attorney in New York. If we find you had anything to do with that theft, it'll be grand larceny. That cat is worth a lot of money."

Phelps laughed. "You won't find anything on me. I'm innocent. Can't you tell from the look on my face?"

Oralee burst out, "I can tell—"

"Never mind, Oralee," O'Dell said. "Just tell Ketchell we're looking for him, and we may be around to ask you some more questions."

"I'll be here. Come to the cat show tomorrow. You'll see me walk away with all the prizes. I don't like to get beat at anything."

● ● ●

Lew Ketchell usually stayed close to his boss, but something was troubling him, and he couldn't figure it out. He had left the condo, gone to a liquor store, and bought a pint of whiskey. Then he had gone down to the beach and sat listlessly watching the waves and drinking. He had a low tolerance to liquor and usually didn't drink at all, but of late his life had seemed to him empty and the liquor seemed to cut the pain. It surprised him that he had come to such a conclusion, but as he sat on the white sand and watched the sandpipers running along in front of the waves, he felt somehow that life had slipped through his hands. He had been raised in the toughest part of Philadelphia, filled with hard men and hard women. He had learned to survive by using his fists, a gun, a knife, or whatever was at hand. He had turned his skills into something he thought was useful when he had become an officer in the Philadelphia police force, but something in his nature couldn't be quelled, and after he had shot two suspects unnecessarily—or so the police commissioner determined—he had been fired from the force.

The world of violence had been the only world he knew, and now as Ketchell sat in the sand, dark thoughts surrounded him like a cloud. He had taken only a few gulps from the bottle but he looked hard at the amber-colored spirits, then stood up and tossed the bottle out into the Gulf with a single vicious heave. He went back to his car, and as he drove along the beach highway, he suddenly saw a small girl running. He recognized Rhiannon Brice, the girl who had said that he was a bad man. Pulling over, he stepped out of the car, leaving the engine running. "What's the matter, kid?"

"It's my granddad. He's really sick. I can't wake him up."

"Get in the car. We'll have a look."

"All right, but hurry."

Rhiannon climbed into the front seat. Ketchell drove down to where the new house sat. He got out of the car quickly, but Rhiannon was even quicker. She was running and saying, "Hurry! Hurry!"

When they got inside, she ran at once through the house, and Ketchell followed her. He took one look at the old man on the bed and reached out and checked his pulse. It felt weak and terribly erratic.

"We've got to get him to the hospital," he said. He pulled out his cell phone and hit 9-1-1.

When the voice answered, he said, "We've got a man unconscious. It's near the beach. What's this address, kid?"

"8221 Beach Highway."

Ketchell repeated the address and then said, "Hurry up!"

He closed the phone, stuck it back in his pocket, and saw that Rhiannon had gone over to her grandfather and was holding his hand. Her eyes were fixed on the old man's face, and Ketchell remembered that the old man was the only relative she had. A helpless feeling came over him, and he wanted to say something to give some encouragement to the child but did not know what to say.

Suddenly Rhiannon took her right hand away and held it out. Automatically Lew Ketchell took it. "You've got to help me pray for my granddad," she said.

Ketchell's eyes blinked, and he stammered, "Why—why, I can't do that. I ain't a praying man."

"You've *got* to help me. There's nobody else."

"Kid, it wouldn't do any good."

"It *might*."

"No, God wouldn't listen to me. Why should He? I never listened to Him."

Her hand seemed very small in his. He closed on it more strongly than he'd intended. He saw that her face was pale and her lips were trembling. "Please, let's pray," she said.

Lew Ketchell suddenly felt fear, something alien to his nature. He couldn't say a word. Finally he said huskily, "You pray out loud, kid. I'll pray to myself."

"All right." Rhiannon's grip was firm and tight on his and felt very small and fragile. Ketchell didn't close his eyes, but watched Rhiannon's face. She closed her eyes, and her lips moved, and her voice was thin and unsteady as she said, "Dear God, I'm asking You to help my grandfather. Me and Mr. Lew here, we're asking. I know he's a bad man, and I've been a bad girl, but You hear bad people sometimes. You heard that thief on the cross, and he was a bad man, and so I ask You to help us even if we're not good and perfect like you'd like for us to be..."

Lew Ketchell had never heard anything like this. Rhiannon continued to pray, and he held onto her hand. Her voice seemed to go deep down inside him, and Ketchell, who usually kept a firm guard over letting anyone get inside of him, found himself moved and somehow even more afraid. It was a fear he had never known before. This child, with her innocence and her desperate prayer to God, touched him, and although he didn't pray, he held her hand tightly and finally knelt down beside her and put his arm around her. She leaned against him and continued to pray in a piping voice, and Lew Ketchell, the toughest man Harrison Phelps could find to be his bodyguard, found himself strangely weak and vulnerable.

● ● ●

Kate and Jeremy were feeding the pets. They were followed carefully by Jacques, who wanted to sample everybody's meal. Jeremy reached down and gave him some of the birdseed that went into Romeo and Juliet's cage. The lovebirds were fighting, as usual, having, so it seemed, no affection at all for one another.

Jacques tasted one of the seeds, spat it out, and turned to Cleo. *I don't know how birds can eat this stuff.*

I guess it's good for them, Cleo said. She wasn't hungry, for she and Jacques had just had a good sampling of canned tuna, and she said, *It was so much fun being at the cat show. I got to see lots of other nice kitties.*

I should have been there. I'm the one that ought to be in that show.

I wish you were, but you're all beat up, Jacques. You look awful.

I got these scars honorably, Cleo. I'm going to get some more, too. You see if I don't.

At that moment the doorbell rang, and Kate said, "I'll get it, Jeremy." She went to the door and was surprised to find the man she had last met at the Brices'. "Mr. Ketchell," she said in surprise. "What brings you here?"

"Got some trouble, Mrs. Forrest. It's Mr. Brice, Rhiannon's granddad."

Alarm shot through Kate's nerves. "What is it?"

"Ma'am, he's pretty sick. He's in the hospital. His granddaughter's in the waiting room, but I think she needs a woman with her. You're the only one I could think of. She mentioned you a time or two."

"I'll be ready in just a minute," Kate said.

Kate disappeared, and as she did, Jake came through the door and saw Ketchell standing there. "What's going on? And who are you?"

"Name's Lew Ketchell. I work for Harrison Phelps. I've, uh, become a friend...well, Rhiannon Brice has become my friend. She, uh, called me in to help with her granddad. They just took him into the hospital—he's had some kind of heart attack or something. I came to get Mrs. Forrest to sit with her. I thought she might need a woman there."

"Is it bad?" Jake asked, wondering how anyone associated with Harrison Phelps could care about an old man and his granddaughter.

"He looks bad, but I don't know about things like that."

"I'm going to go, too," Jake said. He turned and ran through the house and around to Sarita's room. He knocked on the door, and she opened it at once. "What do you want?" she said.

"Rhiannon's granddad is in the hospital. He's had some kind of a heart attack. I want to go to the hospital."

"I've had enough of hospitals lately. You go without me."

Jake hesitated. He knew he shouldn't leave Sarita alone, not at this early stage. "I'll stay here, then," Jake said. "They can call me if they need me." He turned and walked back in the house just as Kate was putting on a sweater.

"Call me as soon as you find out something, Mary Katherine," Jake said.

"Of course," Kate said.

As soon as Kate and Lew Ketchell left, Jake went into the kitchen, poured a cup of coffee, and sat down. Just then, Jeremy came in all wet, drying his hair. He had been out swimming, and he said, "Boy, the water is chilly today."

Jake didn't say anything. He seemed far away to Jeremy, who had learned to read him pretty well. Sitting down, Jeremy studied Jake's expression and said, "Is something wrong?"

"Well, sort of."

"What is it?"

"It's Mr. Brice. He's in the hospital. Your mom's gone to be with Rhiannon."

Jeremy didn't answer for a moment. "Is he going to be all right?"

"I don't know," Jake answered. "It must be pretty serious. We'll just have to wait until your mom calls us."

"Gosh, I hope he's all right. He's all Rhiannon's got. She'd be all alone."

"Yes, she would."

"If something does happen to Mr. Brice, if he...doesn't make it, do you think she could come and stay with us?"

"I don't know, Slick. That would be up to the court, I guess."

"You wouldn't mind, would you?"

"No, I wouldn't mind." Jake glanced at the clock. "Are you hungry, Slick?"

"A little, I guess."

"Why don't I make us one of my mysterious omelets?"

"Okay. I'll go dry off and come back."

As soon as Jeremy left, Jake began throwing the omelet together. Sarita came in and asked, "Is the kid's granddad going to be all right?"

"I don't know, Sarita. I'm making Jeremy an omelet. You want one?"

"What's in it?"

"I can't tell you."

"Can't tell me? Why not?"

"Because it's called Jake's mysterious omelet. Nobody really knows what I put in it. I invented it myself."

"Oh, come on!"

"Sit down and watch if you want to. Maybe you can figure it out."

Sarita plopped herself down, and Jeremy entered the room. They watched as Jake put the omelets together. He was throwing in eggs and bell peppers and bacon and cheese of all kinds, and it seemed as if he was simply just going through the refrigerator, adding whatever came to hand. Sarita wondered at the smoothness with which the man worked. He was big and strong, and yet somehow there was a deftness in his touch. At one point he glanced up and said, "That's a nice outfit, Sarita."

"Yeah, it looks real good on you," Jeremy agreed.

"It's all right—for old ladies," Sarita said.

Jake finished the omelets and put them into three portions. "That's all you get. If you want something else, you'll have to have a piece of toast."

Sarita sniffed her omelet. "How do I know I can trust what you put in here?" she said. She tasted it cautiously, and her eyes flew open. "Hey, this is good!"

"Jake's mysterious omelet will raise people from the dead," Jake said.

Sarita ate hungrily, pausing only to ask, "You ever married?"

"Nope."

"Why not?" Sarita asked.

"Well, I nearly got married once, but it didn't work out," Jake admitted.

Sarita shrugged. "Maybe that's just as well."

Jacques jumped up on the island, and Jake said, "Get off the table, you mangy critter!"

"He likes omelets," Jeremy said. He broke off a fragment of his and began to feed Jacques.

"Jake's mysterious omelets may be poison for cats," Jake grinned. "Wouldn't that be something. I'd sing at his funeral and dance, too."

You know what you can do with your song and dance, Intruder.

"It seems like that cat's talking to you," Sarita said, looking puzzled. "Cats can't talk."

"Jacques can," Jeremy said. "He doesn't say it in words, but you can just look at him and tell what he means."

You're darn tootin'. Just look at me give the Intruder the evil eye here.

Sure enough Sarita saw this and said, "He doesn't like you, does he, Jake?"

"No. Hard to believe, isn't it?"

After they ate, Jeremy said, "You want to go fishing Sarita?"

"I guess so," she said. "Anything to break the monotony of this dump."

Jake watched them go and then turned and found Jacques staring at him. "You monster. Why don't you go and kill something."

You better watch out. You may be my next victim. Jacques yawned, stretched, and went over to the cabinet where the tuna was stored and clawed the door, leaving his mark. Jake couldn't help laughing. "You dig four trenches into my leg, and you have the nerve to ask for a reward?"

I deserve it, Intruder.

Jake opened the door, dug out a can of tuna, and opened it. "Come on, Cleo, you can have half of this."

He opened the can, dumped the contents equally into two saucers, and put one down for Cleo, who began eating it daintily. He held it up and said, "All right, Jacques, say pretty please."

I'll say something you don't like if you don't give me my tuna.

Bad Louie, at that moment, flew through the room. He circled Jake and lit near the tuna. He looked up at Jake and said in his harsh, croaking voice, "Love one another."

Jake laughed. "That's Mary Katherine's influence. You're forgetting how to cuss, Louie." He set the tuna down, and Jacques spit at him. *Don't be so slow next time.* The cat dug in.

● ● ●

Kate and Lew were sitting beside Rhiannon in the waiting room. Lew's eyes were on the floor, his head bowed.

"Do you think the doctor will come and tell us something soon?" Rhiannon asked.

"I'm sure he will," Kate said.

Rhiannon turned to face her and said, "My granddad's going to get well. Lew and I prayed for him, didn't we, Lew?"

Ketchell glanced up and met Kate's gaze and felt his face redden, something that never happened to him. To be caught blushing over the remark of a ten-year-old. "She did the praying," Lew said. "God wouldn't listen to a mug like me."

"Oh, I think He might," Kate said.

"Like Rhiannon says, I'm a bad man, Mrs. Forrest."

"Good!" Kate exclaimed emphatically. She saw the surprise on Lew Ketchell's face and said, "Jesus is the friend of bad men. If you're a bad man, that means He's your friend. And let me tell you, it's good to have Him for a friend."

Ketchell's brow furrowed. "I don't see how anybody who lived two thousand years ago could mean anything to people like us today."

Rhiannon said, "That's because He rose from the dead. Didn't you know that, Lew?"

"I heard about it—a long time ago."

"Jesus never turned anybody away except hypocrites," Kate said. "And you're sure not a hypocrite, are you, Lew? You know you're a bad man, and you don't make any excuses for it."

Lew was surprised to find himself smiling. "I guess that's pretty much what I am. I think—"

At that moment the doctor in charge, Dr. Darrin Manti, walked into the room.

"How is he, Dr. Manti?" Kate asked quickly.

Manti ran his hand over his short haircut and shook his head. "He had a heart attack...he's doing as well as can be expected."

"Is he going to be all right, Doctor?" Rhiannon asked, looking up at the tall, lean physician.

"I'm doing all I can to help him, young lady," the doctor said. "I'm afraid he's got a very weak heart."

Rhiannon said, "God's going to give him a new heart. It says so in Ezekiel 11:19, and I read in the *Encyclopedia Britannica* about how doctors are able to give sick people new hearts."

Manti studied the young girl and nodded, "Heart transplants. Yes, we do that sometimes."

"I want my granddad to have one. Please."

"Well," Dr. Manti said doubtfully, "there's a long line of people who want a transplant. He'd have to wait his turn. And he may be too sick for it to help him. We just don't know yet."

Lew said nothing, but when Kate and Rhiannon went in to see Morgan, he caught the doctor. "How about it, Doc? Give it to me with the bark on it."

"Are you a relative?" the doctor asked.

"Just a good friend." This wasn't exactly true, but Lew found himself willing to stretch the point to find out what he wanted to know.

"I'm afraid he's not going to make it unless a miracle happens."

"So no transplant?"

"As I said, there are a lot of people on the list. He'd have to take his place in line. And he's very weak." Manti shook his head and said, "I feel sorry for the little girl."

Ketchell said, "Me, too," and watched as the doctor walked away. He sat down in the chair and considered the matter. He remembered how the girl had asked him to pray, and despite himself the moment had seemed to come alive for him. *Imagine the kid thinking I could talk to God.*

Sixteen

"Jacques—will you please behave yourself!"

Kate stood in the center of the floor with her hands on her hips, staring at Jacques, who was in the midst of some sort of fit of rage. He had run around the room and slashed at Bandit the coon, who had scurried away and hit the dog door whimpering.

Cleo was sitting on the table next to her carrier. Kate had brushed her until there wasn't a hair out of place, and now Cleo looked over at Jacques and said, *How do I look, Jacques?*

You look like a cat.

Jacques, you're not mad at me because I'm in the cat show, are you?

It's all a bunch of phony baloney!

Cleo stood up and stretched and studied Jacques carefully. *I believe you're jealous because everybody's paying attention to me and none to you.*

Jacques' golden eyes seemed to glow like coals of fire. He glanced around the room at all of the bipeds that had been admiring Cleo and bared his fangs. *What do I care if they pay attention to you or not?* He suddenly reached over and made a wild pass at Miss Boo the rabbit. Miss Boo turned a backward somersault and ran squeaking from the room.

"Jacques, I'm going to lock you in the closet if you don't leave your friends alone," Kate warned.

Friends? What friends? I don't have any friends here. You're all against me.

Jake leaned against the wall and grinned. He was wearing a pair of L.L. Bean chinos—light olive color—and a vintage red polo shirt. This was his idea of formal dress, his equivalent of a tuxedo. "Suck it up, Jacques," he said. "Get used to it. You're playing second fiddle around here. From now on Cleo's the star."

Jacques advanced, his eyes glowing golden as he approached Jake. *I'll make mincemeat out of you, Intruder!*

Kate moved over between the two and shook her finger. "Jacques, we're going to be back pretty soon. I'll give you an extra treat when I get back. Now you be *nice*." She looked up at Jake, and a worried expression crossed her face. "I hate to go to this show and leave Rhiannon all alone." Kate had insisted that Rhiannon come home from the hospital with her and stay at their house. She had made up a bed for her on a cot in her bedroom.

Beverly had come over to join them on their way to the show, taking them in his Rolls. "I'll come back to check on Rhiannon after I drop you off at the show," he said.

Sarita chimed in, "I'll come back with you. I'm not interested in a cat show."

Kate felt a sense of relief. "All right," she said. "That would be so sweet of you both." She turned to Sarita and said, "Remember, Rhiannon's only ten years old, Sarita. She talks like a dictionary, but she's just a little girl inside. See if you can cheer her up a little bit."

"I guess I can try."

"All right," Kate said. "Let's go."

The party left the house, and as soon as Kate got to the Rolls, Jacques was there waiting to pounce in with her.

"Jake, don't let him in," Kate said. "He'll rip that upholstery up, the mood he's in."

Jake caught Jacques by surprise, coming up behind him and grabbing him. Jacques immediately began yowling as if his claws were being ripped out. Jake simply laughed. He had a chokehold on the cat by the ruff of his neck and held him close to his body with an iron forearm—where none of the claws could reach him. Jake walked over toward the beach, and when he saw that the Rolls was ready, he tossed Jacques down and said, "Go for a swim in the Gulf, Jacques. Just swim out as far as you can. Don't bother to come back."

Jake ran back and slid into the backseat of the Rolls just as Bev started the engine and pulled away.

Kate reached over and put her hand on Bev's arm. "It's so nice of you to do this, Bev, and then to go sit with Rhiannon."

"Oh, I'm a nice chap." He turned and grinned, with a smooth handsomeness to his face that Kate liked.

Then she said doubtfully, "You know, I really wish I hadn't agreed to enter Cleo in this show, but I promised Enola."

"It'll be good for you," Jake said. "And I think Cleo likes all the attention. She's a pretty sweet cat." He reached over inside the carrier, and Cleo began licking his fingers. "If that were Jacques now," he grinned at Sarita, "I wouldn't have any fingers left. You know, it just occurred to me that she and Jacques balance out. Cleo's all good, and he's all evil."

"He is not!" Kate rushed to Jacques' defense. "He's just high-strung."

"Yeah? I've known three serial killers," Jake said. "All of them were high-strung."

The trip to the arena didn't take long. Jake picked up the carrier, while Kate turned to Bev and said, "Thanks again for taking care of Rhiannon."

"Call me on my cell phone," Bev said. "Sarita and I will come back and get you."

Kate stepped back, and the Rolls moved away smoothly and almost silently.

Jake and Kate walked side by side, Jake with the carrier in his right hand. He suddenly turned to look down at her. "Mary Katherine, I've got to give you a warning."

"A warning? What kind of a warning?"

"About Devon-Hunt."

"Why are you warning me about him?"

"He won't marry a commoner."

Kate turned to glare at Jake. "What do you mean by *that?*"

"Well, these limeys take their nobility seriously, you know. He's a ladies' man and is used to women swooning every time he walks into the room. You told me he had mentioned marriage to you, but it won't ever come to that."

"So, why is he courting me and talking to me about marriage, then?"

"He's a womanizer."

"He is not! I know a womanizer when I see one."

"You don't see them *right*. You don't see Bev right."

"What are you talking about?"

"You know what the Pleiades is?"

"No. What's that?"

"A small group of stars, part of the constellation called Taurus. It's just a few million miles to the right of the Hyades."

"What in the world does all that have to do with the way Bev is talking to me about marriage?"

"I'm talking about you don't see him right. Just like you can't see the Pleiades if you look right at them. You see, the Pleiades is a small group of stars, some of them very faint, and if you look right at that little group, you can see the biggest star, but the rest kind of fade away. The way to look at the Pleiades," he said, "is not to look at them directly. You turn your gaze just to the right of them or the left. Then, for some reason or other, you can see the whole group. But if you look right at it, you never can."

"So what does that all mean?"

"Well, you're looking right at old Bev. He looks good when you look at him directly, but just turn your eyes away a little bit, and some things about him will come clear."

"What kind of things are you talking about?"

"Oh, you know that noble blood in England. It's about played out. Look at the royal household. Nothing but a mess. Divorces and fights and all sorts of scandals. Mark Twain said the British would be better off to get rid of their monarchs and keep cats." Jake grinned at her and winked roguishly. "He said it would be a lot cheaper, and the cats had much better morals."

Kate suddenly laughed. "You are a piece of work, Jake Novak! You'd say anything to get your own way, wouldn't you?"

Jake grinned. "Why, I've never made any secret about what I want, Mary Katherine. All I want is my own way. As long as I get that, I'll be as happy as a pig in mud."

As soon as they entered the arena, they made their way to the main floor, where the show was to be held. The stands were filling up, and the air was full of noisy talk and laughter. "Look, there's the stand with Cleo's name on it," Kate said.

They moved toward the three-foot-high table and set the carrier down. Kate opened the cage door, and Cleo came out. She looked calmly around, listening to the mewing and yowling of the many nearby cats being groomed by their owners, and then she sat down and began to give herself a bath.

"I think I'll snoop around a bit and see if I can learn anything more about the missing Blue Diamond," Jake said.

Kate watched him make his way into the stands and the thought came to her, *He doesn't realize what an attractive man he is.* Suddenly Kate heard her name called. She turned around to see Hannah Monroe, who had the station next to her. Hannah was holding a beautiful Burmese, stroking him softly. "Who was that good-looking man, Kate?"

"Oh, that's Jake Novak," Kate said.

"Is he your man?"

Kate couldn't help looking a bit disturbed, and a faint touch of color appeared in her cheeks. "No, he's not, although everybody certainly seems to think so."

Hannah smiled. "Why would they think that, if it's not so?"

"Well, we live in the same house," Kate said. "I know that sounds awfully sinful, but it's not." She went on to explain how she and Jake had come to share the beach house. As she was speaking, she was noticing that Hannah Monroe seemed very tired. She was in her early sixties, Kate had discovered, and had been showing cats for many years. The two women stood there talking, and finally Kate said to Hannah, "You know, I didn't really want to enter Cleo here in the show, but Enola, our vet, talked me into it. I've heard you've been in lots of these shows, haven't you?"

"Quite a few," Hannah admitted, "but this is my last one."

"Oh, you're giving it up?"

Something changed in Hannah's face. "Yes, I am," she said. She hesitated and then said, "It's not a choice."

"What do you mean?"

"I mean I won't be around long enough to be in another show, if things go as my doctors say."

Shock ran along Kate's nerves. She couldn't think of a single comment that made sense. She moistened her lips and finally said quietly, "I'm sorry. Are they sure? Isn't there any hope?"

"The doctors make doctor noises, but I've learned to read those things. This is my last show. That's why I'd like to win. Something to go out with. I've never shown Bathsheba," she said as she continued to stroke the beautiful Burmese. "She's been a pet. I want her to win so badly."

Kate tried to think of some tactful way of telling this woman about Christ, but she couldn't figure out a way to ask her if she was ready to meet God. Finally she blurted out, "I don't know any other way to say this, Hannah, but how do you stand with God? Are you ready to meet Him?"

"I've never believed in God," Hannah replied.

"You should think about it."

"Are you a preacher of some kind, Kate?"

"Oh, not at all," Kate said. "I'm just a believer in Jesus." She hesitated then said, "I know people don't like to be pushed about their religious beliefs, but I wonder if we could have tea some time, and I could tell you what God has done in my life. No pressure."

At first Kate thought the woman was going to refuse. She saw it plainly in Hannah's eyes, but then Hannah shrugged and said, "That would be nice."

"Good. Give me your number, and I'll call and see when it would be good. You probably wouldn't like my house. It's full of animals. We're really running a menagerie there."

"You can come to my place," Hannah said, pulling out a card with her number written on the back.

The two women then began grooming their cats.

Olga Ivanov was on the opposite side of Hannah, just to the right of Kate's station, with her Abyssinian. She moved closer to say, "How are you today, Mrs. Forrest?"

"Oh, I'm fine...and everybody calls me Kate."

"Well, then you can call me Olga. I like your cat. She's very attractive."

"She's a sweetheart, all right," Kate agreed.

"Ragdolls are like that," Olga said. "Abyssinian's aren't such sweetie pies. They're more like us models."

"I've seen your pictures in many magazines." Kate turned to face Olga, noting her model's body—tall and thin, with enormous brown eyes and high cheekbones, smooth auburn hair, and a wide mouth. "It must be a lot of fun being a model."

"Not really. Not after the first excitement is over."

"Olga, I feel so out of place here. I never should have entered Cleo, and I'm sure she'll get eliminated fairly quickly. Then we can go home."

"What makes you so sure, Kate?"

Kate laughed, mischief dancing in her eyes. "I guess because I'm an expert in elimination. My first one came when I was thirteen years old. I was desperately in love with a boy named Harold Schultz. My best friend was a girl named Agnes Feltman, and guess what happened?"

"Agnes got your man."

"Yes. I didn't mind, though, when I found out that I was six months older than he was." Kate went on telling about some of her other rejections, and finally Olga said, "I wouldn't count Cleo out. Judges are notoriously erratic. None more than our own beloved judge Raina Bettencourt."

"Do you know her well?"

"Oh, heavens yes. She knows as much about cats as anybody in the world, but some of her choices are strange. You've got as good a chance as anyone else, I think."

"I don't really care about winning all that much, but I figured I'd try it this once."

● ● ●

Jake was in the stands, moving among the people, and finally ventured back down to the floor and asked one of the men who seemed to be in charge, "Is there a watchman around here, buddy?"

"Sure," the man replied. "That's him right over there. See that skinny dark fellow? His name is Lonnie Doucett."

"Thanks."

Jake moved over to where the man was leaning against a pillar and asked, "Hey, you Lonnie Doucett?"

"That's me," the guy said without looking at Jake.

"I'm Jake Novak," Jake said to Doucett, who then turned to give him a suspicious look. "I'm doing a little detective work."

"You a cop?" Doucett asked.

"Not on the force. Just private stuff. Mind if I ask you a few questions about how that cat got stolen?"

"The police asked me that. I'll tell you like I told them. I don't know nothin'."

"You were on duty that night."

"Yeah, most of the cats stay here during the night. My job's to check them, and I did."

"Were you asleep?"

"No."

"Were you drunk?"

"No. I took a coffee break. Went out to get some fresh air, and I didn't even notice when I got back the cat was gone."

"Was the cage door open?"

"It was locked. I looked in like always, just glancing in, you know, so that I see if the cat's there. Only there ain't no cat. Not a real one."

Jake stared at the man. "What do you mean, not a real one?"

"Well, when Mrs. Saban came the next morning, she opened the carrier and found a stuffed toy."

"Then whoever took the cat had a key."

"Maybe he did."

"Who else has a key?"

"The owner and me. That's all."

"Well, I'm sure she didn't steal her own cat. You say you didn't."

"Me, I didn't do nothin'."

"Then somebody had a key made or else is a pretty good lock-picker."

"Wasn't me. I told you that already." Doucett turned around and walked off, his back stiff with resentment.

Jake noticed Eileen Saban sitting in one of the front seats. The seat next to her was empty, so he sat down and said, "Jake Novak."

"Oh, I remember you, Novak," Mrs. Saban said.

"I'm sorry to hear about your cat," Jake said. "I was talking to Doucett. You have a key, he has a key. Nobody else. You didn't steal your own cat, and he vows he didn't. He'd be stupid if he did. But somebody got Blue Diamond. Who would do such a thing?"

"Harrison, of course. My ex."

"How much is the cat worth?"

Eileen shrugged. "Not much, considering he can never be shown again. Everybody knows him, and Harrison couldn't use him as stud either because he's my cat. Everybody who wants to breed Russian blues knows Blue Diamond is the best. You get fantastic fees for that." Her eyes flashed, and she looked out in the ring where Harrison stood. "I'd like to kill him!"

"I wouldn't do that if I were you," Jake warned. "You wouldn't like the women's prison in this state."

Jake noticed Chief O'Dell walk in. He excused himself from Mrs. Saban, walked over, and said, "Hello, Chief."

"Hello, Novak." O'Dell had a dour look. "I've been catching flak from Mrs. Saban. She says it's my job to find that stupid cat."

"It had to be either the woman herself," Jake said, "which doesn't make sense—or Doucett—or else somebody had a key from somewhere."

"Or else somebody's a good lock-picker." O'Dell's eyes were fixed on

Harrison Phelps. "The only one I can think of who would gain anything would be Phelps. He's made no secret about how much he hates his ex-wife for getting that cat in the divorce settlement."

"If I know Phelps, it'd be hard to prove," Jake said. "He probably has a hundred professional witnesses lined up."

"I don't know what he's doing here anyhow. He doesn't care anything about cats."

Jake shook his head, and his lips drew together in a tight line. "He's one of those who can't afford to lose. Eileen made a fool out of him in court, and the story was taken up by all the tabloids. He feels he's got to prove he's a better man than she is a woman. He probably did take the cat, but it's going to be hard to prove."

"Well, cats are cats to me," O'Dell said. "These people go crazy over them." O'Dell suddenly looked over. "They're going to start the preliminary round. If you hear anything, Novak, let me know. I sure could use the help."

"Sure thing, Chief."

Raina Bettencourt was wearing a long, sage-colored dress that glittered as she walked. Her hair was short, pure silver, and her face was rather plain. Jake had picked up from the other owners that she had never married. Her life had been devoted to cats.

Jake took a seat and watched the proceedings. Raina judged the cats slowly and never let herself be hurried.

Kate stood stiffly as Bettencourt approached. She had watched the judge spend a great deal of time over several cats, but when she came to Cleo she simply ran her hand down over Cleo's back and under her stomach, and then without a word moved on.

Suddenly tears came to Kate's eyes. *She could have been nicer than that. I know Cleo's not going to win, but she could have at least spent a little more time.*

She felt defeated somehow. All the time she had said it didn't matter whether she won or not, but now she found herself wishing that Cleo could have at least advanced toward the final round.

She saw Raina stop at several cats, and finally she moved to a table, where she picked up three ribbons. As Raina walked back down the line of cats and their owners, Kate leaned over and said, "Don't be sad, Cleo. You're *my* prizewinner, even if that woman doesn't think so."

"Congratulations."

Kate looked up, startled, and saw Raina Bettencourt, a smile on her lips. She was holding out a ribbon. Not realizing at first what it was, Kate took it. "The most beautiful Ragdoll I've ever seen in all of my years of judging. Congratulations," she said again.

Kate stood there amid the applause, watching as Raina distributed the other two ribbons. She happened to glance up and see Harrison Phelps glaring at her, his eyes small and glowing like furnaces. She remembered someone saying that he couldn't bear to lose anything...and now he had lost to her.

Olga came over and said, "Congratulations. You *should* have won. Cleo is a magnificant animal." She paused, then said, "You'll be in the finals now. Phelps doesn't like it. Watch out for that man."

● ● ●

On their way home, Kate sat silently in the front seat of the Rolls, holding Cleo in her lap and stroking her. She couldn't get her mind off what Olga had said. Finally, when they got to the house, Jake said, "Let's have a celebration. We'll drink to Cleo, queen of cats."

"Look at Jacques," Beverly said. "I don't think he'll be joining the party."

Jeremy laughed. "He's *jealous*. Look at him."

Jealous! You better keep quiet, boy, or you better close the door to your bedroom tonight.

Jacques moved over in front of Cleo, who was glowing. *I won, Jacques. See the ribbon our Person has?*

Who cares? It's just a piece of cloth.

Can't you even be a little bit happy? I would be glad if you won a prize. When you got that gold medal saying you were the world's greatest detective, I bragged on you about that, didn't I?

That's different. Males are supposed to be bragged on.

And what are females *supposed to do?*

They're supposed to stay home and take care of their males.

Kate bent over and began to stroke Jacques. "Don't be mad, Jacques. You're still the number-one guy around here."

You bet your booty I am, and everybody better keep that in mind. Jacques glared at Jake.

Kate stood up and said, "How was Morgan, Bev?"

"About the same."

"Rhiannon is scared," Sarita said. "She doesn't say it, but I could see it in her."

"I understand that," Kate said sadly. "He's all she's got."

"That man who works for Harrison Phelps was there," Bev said.

"You mean Lew Ketchell?" Jake asked with surprise. "What was he doing there?"

"I don't know," Devon-Hunt said. "He didn't say much. Rhiannon talked to him more than I did. Funny thing. They've kind of bonded. Seem like an odd couple don't you think?"

"I guess when you're scared, you take what you can get," Sarita said knowingly.

Seventeen

The next morning Jake was scrambling eggs, adding different ingredients to it. It seemed to Kate that he made scrambled eggs different every time.

"Don't put too many of those jalapeños in there, Jake," Kate warned.

"Jalapeño peppers are good for you," Jake said. "They clear out your sinuses."

"They clear out everything. And they make my tongue tingle."

At that moment Rhiannon came out from Kate's bedroom, fully dressed.

"Why, hello, Rhiannon," Kate said. "I thought you'd sleep in this morning."

Rhiannon's eyes were puffy as if she had been crying, and she said nothing but slipped up onto one of the tall chairs at the island. "What are you making, Jake?" she asked.

"Scrambled eggs à la Novak. It's my own invention. You're going to love it."

Rhiannon said, "What's that you're putting in there?"

"Something to make it taste better." Jake stirred the eggs, then he lifted the skillet, came over, and scooped out a healthy portion on the plate in front of Rhiannon. "Eat that. It'll make you healthy, wealthy, and wise."

"I'm not very hungry," Rhiannon answered.

"You know, I feel that way sometimes, but then I start eating, and I get hungry as I go."

Jake divided the rest of the eggs among himself, Kate, and Jeremy. "Kate, you get the blessing out of the way while I get the rolls and butter," he said.

Kate knew he deliberately said things like this to aggravate her, but she began to ask a simple blessing as Jake was rattling pots and pans and silverware. When she said, "Amen," Rhiannon said at once, "It's not polite to make noise when people pray."

"Oh, God doesn't mind that," Jake said.

"How do you know?" Rhiannon challenged. "Are you and God copacetic?"

Jake laughed. "Not really. That's Kate's department. I've designated all my religion to her."

"That's not sensible," Rhiannon said. "You have to do your own religion."

"That's right," Jeremy said. "You tell him." He was grinning widely, and then he said, "Jake, what did you put in these eggs?"

"I forget," Jake said truthfully. "I just throw stuff in hoping it'll turn out all right."

"It usually does," Jeremy said. He took another bite, and then said with his mouth full, "We going to the gym again today?"

"That's what we agreed on, isn't it, Slick?"

"What do you do at the gym?" Rhiannon asked between bites.

"Jake's teaching me how to fight," Jeremy announced.

Rhiannon took a bite out of one of the rolls she had slathered liberally with butter and asked, "Why do you want to fight?"

"There's a big bully been beating up on me. Jake's gonna teach me how to break his neck."

Before Kate could protest, Jake said, "Now, Jeremy, I never said anything like that."

"I should hope not!" Kate said indignantly. "The very idea!"

"Let's change the subject," Jake said. "This is just a guy thing between me and Jeremy."

They finished their breakfast, and Kate said, "Come along, Rhiannon. Let's go to the hospital."

The two left, and Jeremy began helping clean up the kitchen. "Rhiannon's real sad," he said. "She's scared, too."

"Sure she is," Jake agreed.

"Would you be scared if you were in her shoes?"

"Now, Jeremy," Jake said, "be sensible. I'm a twenty-nine-year-old professional thug, and Rhiannon's a ten-year-old girl. I'm not scared of some things, and I am scared of others."

Immediately Jeremy asked, "What are you scared of?"

"Snakes."

Jeremy laughed. "You sure are! Anything else?"

"Well, several things, I suppose, but what about you, Slick? What are you scared of?"

"I'm really scared of airplanes," Jeremy admitted. "I only flew once on a trip with my mom, but it scared me."

"Oh, don't worry about it," Jake said. "The airliners can kill you, but they can't hurt you."

Jeremy grinned. "You make this stuff up as you go along, Jake?"

"It just flows out of me. A natural-born poet. Come on—let's go teach you how to break somebody's neck."

● ● ●

Harrison Phelps was eating breakfast in his suite. As his young female chef passed by, he made a grab at her, but she quickly moved away. "You keep your hands to yourself, Mr. Phelps," she said.

Phelps shrugged and went back to eating his breakfast.

Lew Ketchell picked at his food, and finally Phelps said, "What's the matter with you? You not hungry, Lew?"

"Not much," the man admitted.

"Hey, you see the tabloids? About me stealing a cat? What a laugh!"

"Well, you've stolen everything else. Why not a cat?"

"Very funny."

"Not much you can do about the tabloids. They'll write anything to sell more copies."

At that moment the doorbell rang, and Ketchell opened the door and recognized the man at once. "Hello, Ocie," he said.

"Got to see Mr. Harrison Phelps."

Lew Ketchell's eyes flashed with amusement. "Come on in. I'm sure he'll be glad to see you." He stepped back, and Ocie entered. Ocie was wearing a pair of disreputable blue jeans and an olive drab shirt with *U.S. Marine* across the chest. "You steal that shirt from the marines, Ocie?" Lew asked.

"Nah, I found it at a yard sale."

"With all your money you could buy new clothes."

"Don't need 'em. A waste of money."

Ketchell led the tall, gangly man in and said, "Mr. Phelps, have you ever met Mr. Ocie Plank?"

"No, who is he?" Phelps asked, clearly irritated by the interruption.

Ocie didn't give Ketchell a chance to answer. "Have you been born again, Mr. Phelps?" he asked.

Harrison Phelp's eyes flew open. "*What!*" he barked. "What are you talking about?"

"I'm asking if you've ever hit the glory road? Have you ever had your sins washed away? Are you bound for heaven?"

Phelps leaned back in his chair and closed his eyes. "Ketchell, why did you let this nutcase in?"

"This is a rich nutcase, Harrison. He won ten million dollars in the Florida Lottery."

"So he's a rich nutcase. Big deal. Get him out of here!"

Ocie grinned. "You better listen to me, son. Your number is coming up."

Instantly Harrison Phelps straightened up. He was a man who had been threatened in many ways, and he had learned to never overlook possible danger. "What do you mean, my number's up?" he asked, his eyes narrowed.

"Why, I mean what you think I mean. You're going to die."

"You check this guy, Lew? Is he carrying?"

"No," Ocie laughed. "I ain't carrying nothing but the word of God." Ocie pulled out a battered New Testament. "Let me read you a few verses here."

Lew Ketchell was highly amused. But Phelps, whose face had grown fiery red, shouted, "Get this idiot out of here!"

"I'm going, son," Ocie said. "I'm going. But remember it's appointed unto man once to die, but after that the judgment. Get ready to meet God, because you're going to."

Lew put his hand on Ocie and winked at him when he turned. "Come on, Ocie. I guess that's enough preaching for one day."

The two moved outside. Lew closed the door behind him and said, "It's too late for him, Ocie. Better go after somebody else."

"No, it ain't too late for nobody. Not for you either, Lew. How about we just kneel down right here and pray and get you right with God?"

"Not today, Ocie."

Ocie didn't take offense but said, "God's going to get you one day. I'm gonna see to that."

"Too late, Ocie. Way too late."

"It ain't too late, I tell you. Why, if a man fell out of an airplane and got right on his way to the ground, he could leave the plane a sinner and hit the ground a believing Christian."

"You believe in deathbed repentances?" Lew asked, still amused.

"It ain't the best way, but that thief on the cross proved it can happen."

Hardened man that he was, Lew Ketchell felt a strange softness in his heart for this old man who was so blatant with his testimony about Jesus. He hated to go back inside and listen to Harrison's raving, for he had no doubt that whatever softness that had ever been in Harrison Phelps had hardened long ago.

● ● ●

Kate and Rhiannon were sitting in the hospital waiting room when Ocie entered, followed by Dr. Manti.

"I'm telling you, Doctor," Ocie said, "if you just let me go in there and anoint Morgan with oil, he'd get up off that sickbed."

Manti didn't know whether to be angry or to laugh. He finally decided on the latter and said, "I just can't let you in to see Mr. Brice right now. Maybe he'll feel better tomorrow."

"He'd sure feel better if I could anoint him with oil," Ocie said. "I really need to go get two or three more brethren, and we'll all gather around him and lay hands on him."

Kate approached the men and said, "Ocie, I expect you'd better do as Dr. Manti says."

Ocie shook his head. "Now, Mary Katherine, don't you be losing your faith." Then turning to Rhiannon, he asked, "How you doing, honey?"

"Okay, I guess," Rhiannon replied. "Thanks for coming to pray for my granddad."

"Well, I ain't giving up," Ocie said. "This young doctor fellow, he's about as stubborn as a blue-nosed mule." Suddenly he turned back to the doctor and said, "Have you been regenerated by the blood of Jesus, son?"

Manti blinked with surprise. "Well—not really."

"There ain't no 'not really' about it. You have or you ain't. Which is it?"

"I guess it ain't," Manti said. "I mean, isn't." He smiled at Kate and said to her and Rhiannon, "Come along. You wait out here, Mr. Plank."

As they walked down the hall, the doctor asked, "What's wrong with that man?"

"Well, he's just an enthusiastic Christian," Kate said. "He has a good heart."

"That's right," Rhiannon said. "He won the Medal of Honor, too."

Manti's eyes opened with surprise. "He did? Well, that's some brand of religion he got."

He led them down the hall and then into a room. "Your grandfather may not be awake yet. You'll just have to wait," he said. "Stay as long as you please."

"Thank you, Dr. Manti," Kate said.

The two went over and stood beside the bed, Kate on the left, and Rhiannon on the right. Morgan was breathing heavily and shallowly. His eyes opened, and the first person he saw was Rhiannon. "Hello, honey," he whispered.

"Hello, Granddad." Rhiannon reached out and put her hand on his cheek. "I'm sorry you're so sick."

"Well, I am too, but things like that happen."

"Kate brought me here. We've been praying for you, and Ocie Plank's praying for you, too."

Kate watched as the old man and the young girl spoke. The bond between them was stronger than any she had ever seen. She was shocked when she heard Morgan say, "Honey, you may have to do without me."

"No!" Rhiannon said firmly. "You're going to live. God's going to give you a new heart."

Morgan smiled. "That would be good. Would you go see if the nurse would give you some water to bring me? I'm a little thirsty."

"There's water over here," Rhiannon said.

"I need some ice in it, honey."

"All right. I'll be right back."

As soon as Rhiannon was out of the room, Morgan turned his head. "Kate, I hate to ask favors."

"Don't be afraid. What is it?"

"Rhiannon will be alone if I don't make it."

Kate saw the trouble in Morgan Brice's fine old eyes. "No, she won't be alone," she said. "She'll be my little girl."

Tears came into Morgan Brice's eyes. He reached his hand out, and Kate took it. She felt tears in her own eyes. "I've always wanted a little girl, but she's believing for a new heart for you. That's the desire of my own heart also, so we're going to believe that, Morgan."

"God can do great things, but if I don't get that new heart, I can rest easy now. You've made me feel much better, Mary Katherine Forrest."

●　●　●

Jake was sitting at his computer banging away, his face screwed up into a puzzled expression. Jacques was sitting on the table watching. "Don't you try to slash me, Jacques," Jake said giving the cat a threatening look. "I'll make mincemeat out of you."

Jacques ignored the statement. He was still miffed over all the attention being paid to Cleo, and there was no other human available but the Intruder. *You just get on with your stupid story writing, bub.*

Jake leaned back. He had an impulse to reach out and stroke Jacques' head, but he knew that was trusting too much in the big cat's temper. His mind was wandering, thinking about the catnapping, and thus he wasn't concentrating on his book. When he heard the door slam and heard footsteps, he looked toward the landing. Sarita came in, and suddenly Jake straightened up. She was dressed fairly modestly but Kate had made it plain that he shouldn't be alone with her behind closed doors, and Jake had agreed. Quickly he stood up and said, "Hey, Sarita, let's go for a walk on the beach. I need a break."

"All right," Sarita said.

The two went down to the beach, followed closely by Jacques. They left by the back door, and Trouble stepped back as Jacques made a pass at him with his steel-like claws. Sarita said, "That dog could bite Jacques' head off. I wonder why he doesn't?"

"That's a male thing. Jacques has got his bluff in on Trouble. I've seen guys weighing a hundred and thirty pounds push two-hundred-pound bullies around."

The two walked along, and Jake gave Sarita a little lecture about the Gulf and the tides. He had difficulty talking to her, but today she didn't seem as filled with animosity as she had in the past.

Finally Sarita said, "Jake, do you believe all that religious stuff Kate talks about?"

Jake, for a moment, couldn't think of an answer. "What's happened to her, has never happened to me, Sarita," he said, "but Kate's religion is real."

After another long silence, Sarita said, "I wouldn't want you to know all the bad things I've done, Jake."

"And neither would I want you to know all the bad things I've done."

They watched as a fisherman pulled in a small fish, took it off the hook, and tossed it over to a blue heron standing nearby. The heron speared it with his bill, flipped it in the air, and swallowed it headfirst. They watched the lump go down his throat, and finally, as they moved on, Sarita asked, "Do you believe in hell?"

"It's in the Bible."

"I don't want to go there if there is a place like that."

For once in his life Jake wished he had something to say, but all he could think to say was, "You'd better talk to Kate about that. I know what she'd say."

"What?"

"She'd say you don't have to. It's up to you."

They walked for half an hour down the beach and turned and came back. It was the closest Jake had ever been with Sarita. He saw that something was troubling the girl, and she didn't know how to express it. When they got close to the house, he said, "Look, there's Chief O'Dell. He's waiting for us."

"You haven't done anything to get arrested for, have you, Jake?"

"Probably lots of things, but I doubt that's it."

"Hello, Jake. Hello, miss," O'Dell said. His face was troubled, and he said, "There's been another catnapping."

Jake straightened up, alarms going off in his mind. "Who was it?"

"Somebody broke into the condo Olga Ivanov is renting, while she was gone. Probably better that she was. They swiped her cat."

"Who had a key to her place?" Jake asked.

"Just her and the condo owners, of course. Nobody saw anybody go in. Nobody saw nothin'." O'Dell looked a bit dejected.

"What are you going to do, Chief?" Jake asked.

"What can I do? We're not the Chicago Police Department. Just got a skeleton staff here."

"Do you mind if I go talk to Miss Ivanov?"

"I wish you would, Jake. Let me know if you find out anything."

● ● ●

Olga Ivanov knew nothing. After Blue Diamond had been stolen, she had brought her own cat home because she was afraid to leave him at the arena.

"Do you have any enemies?" Jake asked.

She smiled and said, "Don't we all?"

As Jake left Olga's, his cell phone rang. It was Lew Ketchell. "Hey, Novak. Phelps wants to see you," he said.

"What about?"

"I'll let him tell you that. Can you come over now?"

"I'll be right there."

Jake made his way to the Phelps condo just a short way down the beach. When he went up to the top floor and rang the bell, Ketchell said, "Come on in. Thanks for coming."

"You don't know what this is about?"

"He doesn't tell me everything."

Phelps was out on the balcony. He was wearing only a pair of shorts, and his pale body looked like that of a slug. "Novak, sit down. You want something to drink?"

"No, I'm good. What's this about, Mr. Phelps?"

Phelps turned and said, "I want to hire you."

Jake was taken aback. "What do you want me for? You've got Lew here."

"I want you to protect all the cats in the show. I don't want no more of them to get stolen."

"I didn't know you had that big a heart, Harrison."

"I ain't got a big heart. The cops and the papers think I'm the catnapper. I'm going to show them I'm not the bad guy. How much you charge?"

Jake mentioned a figure, and Phelps shrugged. "That'll be fine. Lew, tell the papers and them paparazzi folks that I'm bound to get at the bottom of this. That I'm an innocent man."

"They'll be happy to hear that, Mr. Phelps," Lew said with a wink to Jake.

● ● ●

Jake went next to the arena, where he found the guard Lonnie Doucett eating lunch. He said, "Lonnie, Mr. Phelps has hired me to see that nothing happens to any more cats."

"Good. I'm tired of them asking me—like *I* stole the dumb cats. What would I do with a cat?"

"Doucett, you watch until midnight. I'll come on then and take the morning shift," Jake said.

"That'll be cool with me." Lonnie shook his head. "This guy is clever. He can open locks like they was made out of butter or somethin'." Lonnie looked at Jake. "You gonna be packin'?" he asked curiously.

"Yes. I'm going to bring the biggest gun I've got and maybe a hand grenade or two."

"Good. You blow him to bits, this cat stealer!"

Eighteen

The house sounded strangely empty, the morning silence broken by the bubbling of the fish tanks and the faint voice of Bad Louie practicing his profanities. Kate had been working hard. Jake had such a low opinion of her housekeeping abilities that it hurt her. She knew she was a bad housekeeper, and she knew she would never be as good a cook as Jake. Recently, however, she had been trying to pick up after herself and Jeremy more consistently.

She was taking a break, drinking a cup of coffee and staring out at the Gulf. A big ship of some kind was making its way across the horizon, and Kate watched, thinking how wonderfully different it was here from the life she'd had in Memphis. There she and Jeremy had lived in a tough part of town in a walk-up apartment. There had been no view at all. Now the sight of the green water and the blue sky and the white clouds gave her intense pleasure.

Her thoughts were disturbed as the doorbell rang. Opening the door, she found Bev standing there. He was wearing taupe-colored gabardine trousers, a dark russet plaid shirt, and a pair of light British tan calfskin loafers. As always, every hair was in place, and he looked like he had stepped out of *Esquire* magazine.

"Hello, Bev," Kate said. "Come on in."

"I just stopped by on the chance you might have coffee time with me," Bev said.

"Coffee? For a Brit? How about if I fix you some tea?" Kate suggested.

"No," Bev said, stepping inside. "I'm becoming a Yankee, you know. Coffee will be fine."

"Good, then. I just made some. Sit down. And Jake baked some delicious banana-nut muffins. If I ate all I wanted, I'd weigh two hundred pounds in no time at all."

Bev sat down at the table, and Kate put a cup of steaming black coffee in a white mug and filled a plate with the muffins. She watched as Bev added cream and sugar, and said, "Jake would say you were ruining his coffee."

"I'm sure he would think so," Bev agreed. He tasted the muffins and shook his head. "Jake could make a fortune as a chef in some fancy restaurant."

"Somehow I can't see Jake being a chef. He likes to cook, but just for himself."

"And for you, of course."

"Well, we try to show our appreciation. My cooking is mostly frozen dinners."

Looking out the window, Bev said, "The Gulf is so much prettier than the ocean, at least the gray and dreary one England's sitting in. Look at that green! It's kind of a turquoise, isn't it?"

"It seems to change color," Kate agreed, "and at night when the moon shines on it, it makes kind of a silvery pathway."

"The Vikings call that the Whale's Way. They had kind of a poetic turn, the Vikings did. That and smashing people's heads seem to be their contribution to history."

As they talked, Kate was aware of a sense of comfort she felt with Bev. She did not feel the tension she had often felt with other men.

"Kate, I've been wondering," Devon asked, "how Mr. Brice's finances are. Do you know?"

"Well, I don't think he has much," Kate said. "Ocie built him that house, and he was very successful with a book he wrote, but that was years ago. Why are you asking?"

"Well, it occurred to me that he might need some help with his medical expenses, and I'd like to be the one to do that."

"Why, Bev, what a sweet thing! How generous of you."

"No, Kate. It's just that I've got more money than I can possibly use." He paused to take a sip of the coffee. He put it down and nibbled at the muffin before adding, "Money isn't much. It pretty much prevents a person from giving in the best kind of way."

"I don't understand you," Kate said. "Rich men have more to give."

"And they have a lot to give from. The best kind of giving, Kate, is when you give sacrificially."

Kate was surprised at Bev's insight. She had often thought this herself, but she had never thought to hear it from a wealthy man. "You're exactly right about that, I guess," Kate agreed. "I've never been rich."

"Well, the one part of the Bible that's always impressed me is the story of when Jesus was watching at the gate of the temple. There was a box there that people put money into as their gift, and Jesus watched them going by. You know the story. He watched them proudly putting large sums into the box, and then a poor widow came by. She had two 'mites.' I don't know how much that was, but it was all she had. And the Bible says she put those two mites in as a gift, and you remember what Jesus said?"

"He said this poor widow had cast in more than them all."

"You do know your Bible, Kate! Exactly right. A rich man could never really do that."

"A few men have given away very large sums," Kate said.

"Yes, I know. Andrew Carnegie gave away millions, but when he died he still had a few million around. This widow didn't have a million dollars in the bank—or even a hundred. So," he grinned suddenly saying, "I suppose I could give everything away, but I haven't the nerve for it. I'm spoiled to the bone, Kate. Most rich men are."

"I think you're very generous, Bev," Kate countered. "You know the rich young ruler that came to Jesus, and he asked Jesus the way to live, and Jesus said to sell everything and give it to the poor."

"I've often thought about that," Bev said. "Did he ever tell anybody else that?"

"No, he was the only one. So I think that was what the theologians would call a descriptive matter rather a prescriptive matter."

"I don't follow you."

"I think that the young man had made money his God, and for him, at least, it was necessary for him to give it up. So, the Gospels are just describing that situation. They're not prescribing it, saying that everybody should do this. At least that's what I think."

"You know, I've never been able to talk with anybody about the Bible, about God and things like that," Bev observed, "except you, and Ocie, of course. Of course with Ocie it's like talking to a shotgun. He just raises it and *bam*—lets you have it. But it's not like that with you."

"I'm glad that we can talk about these things," Kate said.

Beverly suddenly shifted his shoulders and ran his hand across his hair. "You know, I've been thinking more and more about how my life is slipping by. My parents are having a fit for me to get married and have children. I feel like, somehow or other, I'm a kind of a stud in their sight."

"What an awful thing to say. I'm sure they don't mean it like that."

"No, they don't really. But they want grandchildren, and naturally they want the name to be carried on." He hesitated which was strange for him. Bev had a gift for words, but Kate saw that he was having difficulty putting his thoughts into words.

"What is it, Bev?"

"Well, I told you once that I was looking for a wife. Do you think I would make a good husband?"

Kate Forrest knew that this was not a casual remark. Bev had once before proposed marriage to her. She had learned a great deal about Beverly in the brief time she had known him. He did joke quite a bit, but there was a seriousness beneath that she had learned to recognize. "I think you could be a wonderful husband. Of course nobody knows for sure about that."

"Well, you should know about it. You were married."

Kate hesitated. Beverly had been totally honest with her, and she suddenly felt she could do no less than show him the same kind of honesty. "This may sound strange to you, Bev." She hesitated, licked her lips nervously and then looked down at her hands. "I was in love with my husband, but I didn't love him—not in the best way."

Beverly stared at her. "I don't understand what you mean."

"I don't know if I can say it right. I was in love with him, and that word has been cheapened by Hollywood and romantic novels. It seems to imply that there's an excitement between a man and a woman, that there's passion and a desire to hold onto that person so you can be with them. Feeling that you *must* have them."

"Well, isn't that a good thing?"

"I think it is," Kate said slowly, "at one stage. During the early stages when we're coming into the consciousness that we're drawn to someone. I speak for myself, of course, but I was drawn to Victor. I felt like that, and I'm ashamed to admit it. I was as bad as any of the heroines in romance novels. I thought about him all the time and cried sometimes when I thought I would never have him, and when we first were married, all of the things in the Hollywood movies seemed to be true."

Devon-Hunt waited for her to go on, and finally he asked gently, "Well, didn't it last?"

"I don't think love can ever last in that form. Really loving someone is deeper than that. It means wanting to share the hard times with them, not just the good times. It means caring for them when it's not easy. It's a strange kind of partnership. It means even the loved one's faults become something to live with, because love that can do that is more than just the explosive, shooting-star sort of thing between Clark Gable and one of his leading ladies. You notice the books that end with the line, 'And they got married and lived happily ever after'?"

"And you don't believe that."

"It hasn't been true for many people, I know. If I were writing a book, I would say they got married—and then they started learning to live with each other even when it was hard...until finally they really became as one."

Bev reached over and put his hand on Kate's. "I've never heard anybody talk like that. I believe I could spend the rest of my life listening to you talk, Kate."

Bev began to move slowly toward her. A quick breath stirred her breast. Kate knew he was going to kiss her. She didn't stop him, for she was uncertain of her own feelings. As he put his hands on her shoulders she tilted her head back, and the two kissed. Kate enjoyed the luxury of the caress and knew there was a need in her for something from a man—for love, for security. For that one moment they were on the very edge of the same mystery every other man and woman faced with each other.

Bev, too, had been stirred by the moment. He was usually so self-assured and certain, but that was not in him now. All he could think to say was, "I feel a great deal for you, Kate. A great deal."

● ● ●

Bev's offer to pay Morgan's medical expenses moved Kate deeply. That evening after dinner, she planned a trip to the hospital to inquire about the bill. Jake went along. As they entered the hospital, Kate ended her explanation by saying, "So Beverly has offered to pay all of Morgan's expenses."

"Well, that's good," Jake said. "He's a good man."

"You really think so?" Kate asked, remembering Jake's previous objections to Bev.

"Well, I don't think he's as good as you think he is," Jake said without smiling.

They entered the hospital and found Dr. Manti before they went in for their visit.

"I've got to tell you," Manti said, "unless he gets a new heart, I don't think he can make it for long. He's very fragile."

"What are the chances of that, Doc?" Jake said.

"We did put him on the waiting list, but of course, there are several ahead of him. I suppose he has a chance of a lucky draw."

"You make it sound like a card game," Kate said.

Manti shrugged his thin shoulders. "It *is* a little like gambling. If you need a new heart, you put your name into a computer. There are always more recipients than there are hearts to give, so somebody has some sort of scale, and they try to get the hearts to the most deserving."

"How can they decide that?"

"Well, if someone had terminal cancer, it wouldn't be sensible to give him a new heart instead of giving it to a young woman of twenty-five who has her life before her," he said. "I put Mr. Brice's name in the computer— that's really all I can do."

"All right, Doctor, thank you," Kate said, suddenly depressed. She and Jake next went to the business office, but were unable to speak to the person in charge. So they sat with Morgan while he slept. Then Jake's phone went off. He got up and walked out, and Kate sat there alone. He came back almost at once and said, "I've got to leave, Kate. Can you call Bev and ask him to take you home?"

"Yes, of course. But what's going on?"

"I just got a call from a bartender at a dive down on the beach called the Blue Parrot. Sarita's there. I don't know how she got there, but she is, and she's getting into trouble."

"I'll go with you," Kate said. "She'll need us both."

The two left the hospital and drove down to the beach.

"Have you ever been in this place?" Kate asked.

"Not this one, but lots of others just like it. Nothing but trouble." He hesitated. "You better stay in the car."

"No, I'm going in with you," Kate insisted.

The inside of the Blue Parrot was dark and thick with smoke. The air was filled with loud laughter and raucous music. Two couples were dancing on the small floor, clinging to each other.

Jake said, "There she is. You stay back."

Kate did hang back, and she saw Jake go over to a table where Sarita was sitting with four men. They were bikers, three of them in their forties or even older, and one younger—in his early twenties if that much. He was the loudest of the four. Jake walked up to them as if he were going to the line at Wal-Mart. He stopped at the table and said, "Hello, Sarita."

Sarita was clearly drunk. Her voice slurred as she said, "Hey, Jake, join the party. This is Jake. He's the one that looks out for me."

"Well, you don't need him," the young man said. He had blond hair and a nice, even tan; his shoulders were broad, and he was obviously proud of his strength. "Let's go over to the bar. I'll buy you a drink."

"Can't do it, Jack. I've got to take Sarita home," Jake told him evenly. "Sorry to break up the party."

"You want to go with him, Sarita?"

"No, Charlie, I wanna stay here."

"Sorry, Sarita, it's past your bedtime." Jake moved smoothly and easily, and as he did, the four men stood up. One of them, the oldest apparently, said, "You better get out of here, bub. It ain't a good day to go to the hospital."

"Sarita, can you walk or do you want me to carry you?" Jake asked, ignoring the man.

Sarita started to speak but found she couldn't form the words. She got up and walked unsteadily over to Jake. The young blond man scowled. "You can't take her."

"I believe I can," Jake said calmly. "You'll be better off if you let me do this the easy way."

The young man let out a bellow and lunged. Kate wasn't able to see how Jake did it, but he snatched up a chair while the young man was lunging at him and brought it down over his head. The young man collapsed to the floor. The other three stared, and then the oldest said, "Get him!" They lunged forward—but stopped as suddenly as if they had run into a concrete wall. They were facing the muzzle of Jake's nine-millimeter Glock. And Jake didn't flinch.

"Hey, no guns!" the oldest man gasped. "Watch it with that thing!"

"The party's over. You fellows better take care of your friend. He needs some stitches."

The three just stared at Jake, and the older man began cursing under his breath. "Let's get him out of here," he said. The three lifted their comrade, but Jake hadn't waited. "Come on, Sarita." Kate came over and helped stabilize the girl.

Jake put away the Glock, and when they got outside, Kate helped Sarita into the backseat. Then she looked at Jake. "Would you have shot them?"

"I knew I wouldn't have to. They're not really bad guys. They're just wannabes."

When they arrived home, Kate helped Sarita to her room. Jacques followed them along with Cleo, and as soon as Kate closed the door, Sarita started crying. "I hate myself when I do things like this. Now all of you will hate me, too."

"No, we won't." Kate said as she put her arms around the trembling girl.

Jacques watched all this and sniffed. *I don't know why bipeds get so uptight about stuff.*

She's sad, Jacques. Look at her. She's crying and whimpering.

Yes, she's crying and whimpering, but when I stole that yellow cat's food and made ribbons out of his ears, did I shed any tears? Not likely. What I say is, take what's in front of you. The world was made for me. I deserve the best, and that's the way it is. You won't hear me crying over any of this stuff.

Jake was waiting for Kate to come out of Sarita's room to assure him that the girl was all right.

"Don't be mad at her, Jake," Kate said as she closed the door behind her. "Not now."

"I'm not mad," Jake said. "I've taken too many falls myself to hold it against anybody else."

"I'll keep an eye on her tonight," Kate said.

"You'll have to. I've got to go out. I told Doucett I'd take the midnight watch. Keep the doors locked, Kate. Don't open for anybody but me."

● ● ●

At the convention center, everything was dark except for a few lights glowing in the arena. Jake entered and looked around for Lonnie Doucett, but he didn't see the man at first. But then he saw two feet sticking out from under one of the judging tables. He rushed over and saw with relief that Doucett was alive. He was unconscious, however, and Jake began trying to bring him around. It took some time, as apparently he had been drugged.

While Doucett was waking up, Jake made the rounds of the cats, and he discovered that one of the cages was open. The big Bengal belonging to Gary Charterhouse, the truck driver, was gone.

On a hunch, Jake opened Doucett's thermos of coffee. The liquid didn't smell right, and it had a strange taste when Jake touched a little to his tongue.

Jake pulled the watchman into a sitting position. He still hadn't come to. In the meantime he called Chief O'Dell and gave him the news. O'Dell cursed and said he'd be right there.

As Jake put away his cell phone, he looked down at the unconscious man and thought, *Well, Lonnie, you sure spit in the soup this time. The papers will have a field day. And that fellow Charterhouse will be on the warpath.*

Nineteen

Jeremy circled Jake, his left hand extended with the fist closed, his right held back. He stared at the shield made out of foam rubber Jake was holding. He imagined that the face that Jake had drawn on the figure was that bully, Carl Bailey.

Jake was watching Jeremy steadily, and could see that Jeremy's arms were getting so tired he could hardly hold them up. For the last half hour, with only short breaks, he had been going around, striking out at the figure. Jake had said little, but Jeremy had been determined not to give up. He suddenly threw his weight forward as Jake had taught him, from the heels down, and followed through with the hardest blow he could imagine. It struck just below the chin, and Jake cried out, "Hey, Slick, that was just right!"

Jeremy felt a glow of pride. He and Jake had been coming to the fitness center for only two weeks, and Jeremy could remember how feebly he had struck when they had first started. Jake hadn't let up on him, though—and now, although Jeremy still felt a twinge of fear when he thought of the bulky form of Carl Bailey, he was excited by Jake's praise.

"That *was* pretty good, wasn't it?"

"*Extra* good! What do you say we leave on a high note?"

"Okay, Jake."

The two donned light shirts over their gym clothes. As they walked along, Jeremy asked, "Do you think I can whip Carl Bailey now, Jake?"

"Not a chance," Jake replied.

Jeremy hadn't expected that answer. He shot a glance at Jake and said, "But—I thought I was doing good."

"You are doing good, but he's a lot bigger than you are, and he's probably got more confidence than you. The first time you fight someone who's better than you or bigger than you or has more experience, you're probably going to get your plow cleaned."

Jeremy said nothing until they reached the Harley. As Jake was putting on his helmet, he burst out, "Well, shoot, what's the use of all this?"

Jake turned, and his eyes narrowed. He said seriously, "You know how you learn something, Slick?"

"What do you mean?"

"How do you learn to do anything? For instance, do you remember the first time you tried to ride a bicycle?"

"Yeah."

"What happened?"

"I fell down and scraped all the skin off my knee."

"Oh, you didn't just get on it and start out like somebody on the Tour de France?"

"Not hardly!"

"You kept falling down, didn't you? But one day you found out you could go ten feet before falling. The next day twenty. Then one day you got on it and just took off, didn't you?"

"That's right, Jake. That's the way it happened."

Jake put his hands on the boy's shoulders and squeezed them. He had gradually gained great affection for Jeremy, and now he said earnestly, "Son, you learn by failing. Those that get up after they're knocked flat on their back, they're the ones who are going to make it. You'll probably get creamed when you fight Bailey, but you'll leave him something to remember you by. And the next time after that you'll be bigger and stronger and faster, and *he'll* be the one that gets creamed."

Jeremy didn't answer until they were both on the motorcycle. He held onto Jake and said, "I'm going to do what you say, Jake. I'm going to give it my best shot."

"That's the way to talk, Slick."

Jeremy was thrown back as Jake accelerated, but found that the fear that he had felt for Carl Bailey had somehow dissipated, and he was actually looking forward to the inevitable fight—even if he did get whipped!

● ● ●

Lew Ketchell entered the waiting room of the ICU ward and saw at once that Rhiannon was all alone. She looked sad sitting there, and he walked over quickly to her side. He couldn't understand why he was drawn to this girl when he had had nothing to do with children for years.

He sat down in the chair beside her saying, "Look what I got—Chinese. Good soup, and some shrimp with the good dip." Rhiannon looked up. Her eyes revealed fatigue, and Lew surmised she had been sleeping little. "Plunge in, here. Let's eat it up."

"All right, Lew."

"Do you always call adults by their first names?"

"Not always. Just the ones I like."

"Oh, I made the grade then. Glad to hear it. Here, try some of this dip."

The two sat there eating, until finally Rhiannon looked up and studied Lew in that strange way she had. Ketchell felt as though he were being examined by a jury or even a judge. This youngster made him feel so strange…"I asked Jake about you, Lew, and he said you were a thug," Rhiannon said before she took another bite of shrimp.

Lew managed to grin. "He got that right. I am a thug."

"Well, Jake calls himself that too, so don't feel bad." She popped another shrimp into her mouth, and after swallowing it said, "Jake is teaching Jeremy how to fight. There's a big guy in his class called Carl Bailey who's been beating up on him."

"That's a real drag! I got some of that when I was growing up. Some even after I *was* grown up."

The two sat there talking. Finally the nurse approached and said, "Rhiannon, you can see your grandfather now."

"Thanks, Millie."

Lew got up, and the two walked down the hall to Morgan's room. They entered, and Lew got a glance at Morgan Brice. It frightened him, somehow, the helplessness of the man being kept alive by artificial means. It didn't seem right, but yet he knew it had to be. Rhiannon went to her grandfather's bed and took his hand. "Hello, Granddad," she said.

"Hello, honey. How are you today?"

"I'm fine. Do you feel any better?"

"I'm all right."

Lew simply stood there, knowing that Morgan Brice was *not* all right.

There was a shadow over the man, and Lew recognized it as the shadow of death. He had seen men die, usually in violent ways. He had seen them alive one moment and then fall to the pavement the next, filled with big-caliber slugs—alive one moment, dead the next. He had learned to accept that kind of death, but this was different. Somehow Morgan Brice's plight was a frightening thing.

Ketchell was wondering why, when suddenly he heard Morgan say, "Rhiannon, would you go tell the nurse I need some juice, please."

"All right, Granddad."

As soon as the girl was gone, Morgan whispered, "Mr. Ketchell, I wanted to thank you."

"Everybody calls me Lew."

"Well then, Lew, I appreciate the attention you've shown to Rhiannon. She's told me all about it."

"I don't understand it myself, Mr. Brice. I'm not much for kids, but she's so different."

"She is, isn't she?" Morgan lay still with only his fingers twitching for a moment, and finally he said, "If I don't make it, she'll have a hard time. Kate Forrest says she'll take her in, though."

"That's good—but maybe you'll make it. Rhiannon would be lost without you. Maybe I can help, too."

Lew's offer came out almost without his volition, but at once Morgan Brice's eyes lifted, and the old man whispered, "But you won't be here, will you?"

Lew hesitated and tried to think of a proper answer to that, for he knew that he had no ties in White Sands, Alabama. "I don't know," he said slowly. "I've never really known where I was going to be next."

A silence fell over the two men, then Morgan said, "I've been thinking, Lew, about my life. How I missed some chances to do some things I should have, and how I did some things I shouldn't have. You know, I've never heard of anyone who was in my condition...about to face God...regretting that they didn't spend more time at the office or make more money. Most of them regret they didn't do the right things."

Lew blinked with surprise at Morgan's frankness. "What kind of right things?"

"Mostly your family, people you love and who love you. I've been lying here wishing I had done the things God admires, the things that give God pleasure."

Lew was silent for a time, and then he said just before Rhiannon entered, "I never thought about dying all that much."

Rhiannon came over and said, "I got you some orange juice." She put it to the sick man's lips, and he held it with one hand, and when he'd drunk half of it, he said, "That's enough for now. Just put it on the table." Then he said, "What have you learned today? You've kept up with your studies, haven't you?"

"Oh, sure. I'm still working through the J volume."

"The J volume," Lew said. "What's that?"

"Oh, it's a volume of the *Encyclopedia Brittanica*," Rhiannon explained. "I'm reading it and learning things that start with J. I learned today about 'Juggernaut.'"

"Does it have some special meaning?" Lew asked. "I thought it was just another word."

"Well, it's kind of an idol for the Hindus over in India. The most interesting thing about it was the fact that they have a great big image of Juggernaut, and they put it on a wagon so heavy that it takes a lot of people who worship him to move it. Every July they drag it to the country house of the god, and you know what?"

"What?"

"Some people throw themselves under that thing so they get crushed."

"Why would they do a nutty thing like that?"

"I don't know. The book didn't say," Rhiannon shrugged. "I guess they think it pleases Juggernaut." She suddenly turned and put her eyes on Lew. "That's not like Jesus. He didn't want people to be crushed. He wanted people to live. Isn't that right, Granddad?"

"That's right. He said, 'I am come that they might have life and they might have it more abundantly.'"

The machines were humming as Lew Ketchell stood beside the dying man's bed. He felt strange, as if he were in another world. He couldn't grasp what he was feeling about this dying old man, and this odd ten-year-old with the mind of an adult but still with a child's weaknesses. He felt like someone in a fantasy movie, almost out of the world and in a strange new realm—and the longer he stood there, the more he wondered what had brought him to this place in his life.

● ● ●

Jacques, I'm telling you it was wonderful! There were so many beautiful cats there!

Beautiful cats? There couldn't have been all that many beautiful cats.

But there were, though, all kinds. Some shorthairs, some longhairs, some no-hairs.

A cat with no hair? That's obscene! Cats are supposed to have hair.

Well, this one didn't.

The two cats had been fed, and Jacques had eaten himself almost senseless. His eyes were half-lidded as he and Cleo lay on the rug in front of the coffee table. She continued to speak with interest about how much she had enjoyed the show.

I wouldn't want to go to a show like that, yawned Jacques. *That's no way to have a cat show.*

Cleo turned to face Jacques. *What do you mean, no way to have a cat show? What other way could there be?*

Lots of ways. They could give points for cats that killed the most things—like one point for a sparrow, five for a redbird, ten for a mockingbird. And maybe even baby rabbits. That would be something. They could be fifty points.

That's awful, Jacques! Why can't you think of something nice?

Well, Jacques yawned and stretched his forearms out, flexing his claws, *there's me. I'm nice.*

No, you're mean. You're always thinking about killing something or scratching somebody.

Hey, it's the law of the jungle, kid. Grow up!

● ● ●

When Jeremy came in from school, Kate at once noticed a skinned spot on his right cheekbone and that his ear was red. "What happened to your face? And your ear's all red."

Jeremy was beaming. "I got my licks in on old Carl Bailey, Mom. I got him right in the throat with my knuckles, and just like Jake said, old Carl started gagging, so I whomped him good. Of course he got over it and gave me some licks too, but he's the one that's scared of me now. I may whip him again tomorrow."

Kate gave Jeremy a look and said, "You don't want to become like him, do you, Jeremy?"

Jeremy suddenly paused. "I never thought about it."

"That's what he does, beats up on people. Is that what you want to do?"

"No, not really, but a fellow's got to learn how to take care of himself." Jeremy thought for a moment then added, "Look at the Bible. David was a fighter, and he was a man after God's own heart. And Abraham went to war when his nephew Lot was captured by some bad tribesmen. And there was Joshua. He was a mighty warrior. Those guys fought."

Kate wished at that instant she were a theologian, but she knew she was not. She went over and put her arm around Jeremy and said, "I can't answer that. I know there are times when Christians are called upon to fight. For example, if there's a war, they're supposed to protect their homes and their country. Policemen have to sometimes use violence to protect us, but we have to be careful about when and why we must fight."

"I don't understand why it was right for David and Joshua."

A thought came to Kate that had never occurred to her, and she said quickly, "In the Old Testament, son, God was creating a race for the specific purpose of bringing the Messiah into the world."

"Sure—Jesus."

"That's right. So, Israel was created so they could carry on their race down to the time when the Messiah would be born. But in order to do that they had to survive. That meant sometimes they had to fight. But in the New Testament it's different. Jesus was born. The Messiah did come, so now the days of the Old Testament had passed away. Israel had fulfilled its destiny. Now Jesus brings a new kind of life. He said to forgive your enemies."

"Oh, Mom, that's hard to do!"

"I know it is, son. It was hard for Jesus to go to the cross, too. We're going to church tonight, you and me and Jake. Maybe your question can be answered there."

"Who's going to be preaching?"

"Dale Scott."

Jeremy's eyes flew open. "You mean the major-league MVP?"

"That's right, and he's going to be available for questions. You can ask him anything you want to."

"Oh, boy, that'll be great, Mom!"

● ● ●

Jake said, "This is one time I'm looking forward to going to church. I always thought Dale Scott was the best shortstop who ever lived. I guess Pastor Bates still has some connections with folks in the big leagues."

"Mom says we can talk to him, Jake, and ask him questions. Look, I got my baseball. I'm going to get an autograph."

As they started to leave, Jake suddenly walked over and closed the cat door and locked it. "I don't want Cleo getting out," he said. "We'll lock the doors, too."

Kate knew he was apprehensive about Cleo. She didn't say anything else, and finally they stepped outside. Trouble was ready to go, wagging his tail and whining.

"No, you stay here, Trouble," Jake said. "You take care of things here, and I'll bring you something good when we come back."

● ● ●

On the way home from the meeting, Jeremy talked like a magpie. "Gosh, he's just like a regular guy—Dale Scott!"

"I thought so, too," Jake said. "He talks good, but not as good as he fields a ball. That guy is poetry in motion. He makes the hard plays look easy. You know, Slick, that's the difference between a great ballplayer and a merely good one. The good ones make the hard ones look easy, the bad ones make the easy ones look hard."

Kate felt a warm glow. She had glanced at Jake during Dale Scott's testimony and could tell it meant something to Jake. Several times she'd prayed silently, *Oh, God, let this ballplayer say something and do something that'll bring Jake close to You.* She had become accustomed to praying like this. After the service, when they had gotten in the line to shake the hand of the speaker, Jake said, "I saw you make that triple play against Cincinnati. Never saw anything like it."

Dale Scott was not as large a man as Jake, but there was something alive and almost electric about his movements and also in his eyes. "Well, brother, that was a real thrill," Scott had said. "There was a time when the biggest thrill in my life was making a play like that or getting a timely hit, but as I tried to say tonight, serving the Lord Jesus is where I get my kicks now."

As they pulled into the driveway, Kate thought how good it was for Jeremy to have someone like Jake around—and men like Dale Scott to admire. As they got out of the car, Jeremy was still excitedly chattering about the meeting.

Suddenly Jake put his arm out so abruptly that Kate ran into it. "Hold on," he said.

"What, Jake?"

Jake didn't answer. He took three more steps and then knelt to one knee. Jeremy ran forward. "It's Trouble!" he cried. "What's wrong with him, Jake? Is he dead?"

Jake was feeling for a pulse in the dog's throat. "No, he's not dead. He's unconscious. Something wrong here." He turned and ran over to where the Harley was parked, reached into the saddlebag, and came out with a small pistol. "Wait here," he said.

Kate put her arm around Jeremy, and they watched as Jake entered the house. "We left that door locked," Jeremy whispered, "but Jake went right in."

Jake entered, and the first thing he saw was that there was no sign of Cleo. She would always come to whoever entered the door. He then saw Jacques lying on the floor. He quickly went to him, bent over, and saw that the cat's mouth was open and he was breathing. Quickly he checked all the rooms. "You got away with it," he said between gritted teeth. He went to the door. "You can come in now," he called.

As soon as Kate came in, she saw Jacques. "What's wrong with Jacques?"

"I think he had a rap on the head." The three bent over the still form of the cat, and Kate said, "Look, his claws are bloody."

"That's right," Jake said grimly. "He got a piece of somebody."

"Look at this," Jeremy said. "It's a piece of cloth."

Jake picked up the tiny scrap and studied it. "It's a piece of a shirt, I think, blue and white checks." He turned and said, "You call Enola. Get her over here as quick as she can come, Kate. I'll call the chief."

Jake called the police station on his cell phone and was glad to find O'Dell still there. "We've got another missing cat over here, O'Dell."

"I'll be right out," O'Dell said after a pause. "We've got to get this guy."

Jake turned and found Kate sitting on the floor, holding Jacques on her lap and crying.

"I'm sorry. I can't help it. Crying, I mean."

"It's okay," Jake said, his mouth drawn into a tight line. "If it weren't so unmanly I'd cry myself."

They sat there, and sooner than seemed possible Enola arrived. They heard the brakes squeal on her Hummer, and Jake went out to meet her and take her to Trouble. She looked at the big dog's eyes and said, "He's all right, but it appears he's been drugged."

"The catnapper struck again, Enola," Jake said.

Enola looked at him, her eyes flying open. "Oh no—Cleo?"

"Yes—she's gone. I shouldn't have left her alone like this. Jacques, I think, tried to protect her. His claws are bloody, and we found a fragment of a shirt nearby."

Enola followed him inside and quickly knelt down beside Jacques. Jake said, "Don't wipe that blood off his claws."

"Why not?" Enola said.

"We can get a DNA test off it, and then when we catch this guy, we'll have something to match it to."

Jake glanced over at Kate. The sight of her tears made him angry. He felt like somebody had struck at the sanctity of the one thing in his life that had come to mean something.

"You think you can catch him, Jake, and find Cleo?" Jeremy asked.

Jake put his hand on the boy's shoulders. "All I have to do is find the guy with fresh cat scratches and a blue-and-white shirt with a chunk out of it. It shouldn't be hard. Only twenty thousand men in this area I'll have to check." He grimaced, then looked down at the boy and said, "I'll get him, Jeremy. It's a promise."

Twenty

What is this stuff? Yuck! How can anybody eat it?

Jake had put a dollop of oatmeal out for Jacques, watched him sample it and now grinned broadly. "There you go, Jacques. Eat up. It'll be good for you."

Jacques showed his displeasure by trying to cover up the oatmeal. Then he arched his back and hissed at Jake. *I ought to give your nose a decoration! Feeding an upstanding feline like me garbage like that.*

Kate had been watching the little drama, and now she had to smile. "You ought not to torment Jacques like that, Jake. Why don't you try to make friends with him?"

"I'd just as soon try to make friends with a brown recluse spider."

Jeremy was wolfing his oatmeal down. He had watched Jake make it, but had been unable to see all the ingredients that had been added to it. "Hey, this is the best oatmeal I've ever had, Jake. Mom, why didn't you ever make good oatmeal like this?"

"I have other talents besides oatmeal," Kate said defensively.

"Come on, Jake," Jeremy said. "Tell me what you put in it. I can taste the cinnamon, but what else is in it?"

"I never reveal my secrets to the common herd," Jake said proudly. "If you'll be a good boy for the next ten years, then I may teach you how to make oatmeal."

Jeremy took three huge bites of the golden cinnamon toast before him and said, "You know what? Rhiannon says she's going to pray for Cleo to be found with no harm done to her. Do you think it's okay to pray for animals, Mom?"

"Of course, I do," Kate answered.

"Does it say so somewhere in the Bible?" Jeremy continued. "I don't remember anybody ever praying for an animal."

"Well, I can't remember a specific verse." Kate was also enjoying her oatmeal. "But I remember a poem my mother used to say to me. As a matter of fact, she made a needlepoint of it, and I had it hung in my room."

"You know a poem?" Jake said with feigned amazement. "I am shocked! Shocked at finding poetry in our establishment!"

"You hush, Jake. I haven't thought of it in a long time, but I must have read it every day of my life when I was growing up."

"How does it go, Mom?"

"Like this," Kate began:

All things bright and beautiful,
All creatures great and small,
All things wise and wonderful,
The Lord God made them all.

Jake was smearing fig preserves on his French toast. He liked it an inch thick, which made Kate a little nauseous since it was so sweet. Jake cocked his head to one side and said, "That's where James Herriot got the titles for his books. You know, the veterinarian. He wrote *All Things Bright and Beautiful.*"

Jeremy finished the last of his oatmeal and said, "Is there any more?"

"Yes, but I'm saving it for myself," Jake said.

"Ah, come on, Jake. Half it with me."

"Well, since you're such a good boy, I can afford to do that." He got the remainder of the oatmeal and divided it evenly between himself and Jeremy. "You don't get any, Mary Katherine. You haven't been a good girl." He ignored the face that Kate made at him and said, "About this oatmeal, Slick, you've got to learn that most food doesn't have any spizaringtum."

"What's that?"

"You know, razzmatazz."

"I don't know any of those words."

"What do they teach you kids in school these days? Anyway, oatmeal without spice is like a woman without pizzazz."

Kate straightened up. "What do you mean by that—a woman without pizzazz?"

"I don't know what else to call it. Some women are dull, flat, tasteless, uninteresting, boring—while others have *fire*. They know what love is all about, and they know most of all, Slick, how to put a man at his best."

"How do they do that?" Jeremy said, his eyes wide.

"Why, it's easy. They always make life comfortable for him. They give him everything he wants. As a matter of fact, they even look ahead and figure out what he's *going* to want, and when he wants it all he has to do is reach out and take it because she's put it there. They make a fuss over him and tell him what a wonderful guy he is, and they pay no attention to his faults. They just keep him happy. A real woman like that, why, a guy can't get home from the office quick enough."

"You are insane, Jake Novak!" Kate exclaimed. "That's *not* the way a real woman acts."

"Oh, I'm sorry," Jake said in mock apology. "I forgot you were here, Mary Katherine. I didn't mean to hurt your feelings." He reached over and patted her shoulder. "Don't worry. I'm going to work on you. You'll have all these qualities—and lots of pizzazz—when I finish training you."

"Get your grubby hands off me!" Kate brushed his hand from her shoulder.

Jake grinned, then said, "Well, folks, I think I'll do a little detecting today."

"You gotta find Cleo," Jeremy said. "We can't do without her. She's almost like a member of the family."

Those were exactly Kate's feelings. She loved the two cats, and now she gave Jake an appealing look. "Please, Jake, do the best you can."

"I will. Try not to worry about it. Can I trust you to clean the kitchen up, Mary Katherine?"

Kate ignored him and turned to Jeremy, "We'll pray for Cleo. It's all right to pray for anything that you love..."

● ● ●

Lew was having a late breakfast with Harrison Phelps, when the doorbell rang. "Who can that be this time of the day?"

Harrison Phelps scowled. "Why don't you go see? It would be easier than straining your brain wondering."

Lew stared at Phelps for a moment as if he intended to respond, but then gave it up as a lost cause. He made his way through the condo to the door, and was surprised to find Jake standing there.

"Hello, Novak," he said. "You out selling subscriptions to the daily paper?"

"Been thinking about taking that up to make a little pocket money, Lew, but right now I need to see your boss."

"Come on in. He's having breakfast. He's in his usual charming mood, so don't get overwhelmed by the warmth he's about to shower on you."

"Is he always like that?"

"Only when he's awake." As they moved back toward the balcony, Lew asked, "Have you heard any more about how the little girl is?"

Jake shook his head. "I just can't tell, Lew. She's so blasted sure that God's going to heal her grandfather. You know, if God doesn't do it, I think she'll lose it."

"What do you mean 'lose it'?"

"I mean she's got the most simple faith in God of anybody I've ever seen. Of course, she's only a child, but she's so grown-up in some ways! I don't want to see her change."

Lew stopped suddenly and turned to face Novak. Jake was surprised. He and Ketchell were not cut from the same bolt of cloth, but now as he studied the smaller man's expression, he saw that something was working inside of him. "What is it, Lew?"

Ketchell stood there for a moment, and then he said, "That little girl has gotten to me. I can't make out what it is."

"She's an unusual child," Jake agreed. "Uses words long as a piece of rope. Calls all the grown-ups by their first names. She says whatever's on her mind, too."

"Yeah, I like that in her." Ketchell grinned. "Maybe that's what's made me so interested in how she comes out of this." He hesitated, then looked down at his feet. When when he looked up, there was something like pain in his dark-blue eyes. "I had a little girl once."

This admission caught Jake by surprise again. "I never knew that, Lew."

"No, you wouldn't—I wasn't married to her mother. My girl's name was Alice."

"Where is she?"

Again that momentary hesitation. "She died when she was three."

"I'm sorry to hear that," Jake said, genuinely moved. "Hit you hard, I'd guess."

"I've thought about it every day, wishing I could have done better for her. She was only three, but she loved me. Maybe she was the only one that ever did."

"Hard to lose someone like that, Lew."

"Maybe if I'd married her mother, I could have done things differently." Suddenly a veil fell over Lew Ketchell's eyes, and he said almost brusquely, "Well, that's the way it happens. Come on and meet Mr. Personality."

Jake followed Ketchell out to the most spacious balcony he had ever seen on any condo. Harrison Phelps was sitting at the table with a full breakfast spread out before him, gnawing at a roll. "What do you want, Novak?" he barked.

"Need a little talk, Phelps."

"You want some breakfast?"

"No, I'm good. Got some news you probably haven't heard."

"Must be bad or you wouldn't be here. What is it?"

"Another cat's been stolen."

Phelps suddenly laughed harshly. "Good. It cuts down on the competition. I hope it was a prizewinner."

"It was Mary Katherine Forrest's cat."

"That's your woman?" Phelps wiped some egg off his face with a sudden motion of his hand. He had small eyes, almost piggish, and now he put them on Jake. "Why are you telling me this?"

"I thought you might be interested, you being such a cat lover and all."

"Another competitor out of the way."

"A little bit hard on these people, aren't you, Phelps?"

"You want me to cry over a stupid cat, Novak? Get real."

"What about *your* cat? What if *he* gets stolen?"

"He won't. That's what I got Lew for. He takes care of my chores, hauls my garbage out, takes care of all the things I don't wanna mess with. You get that, Lew? You keep a double watch on that fancy cat of mine. And you, Novak, were supposed to keep an eye on the cats at the arena."

Novak sat there studying Harrison Phelps. Suddenly a motion caught his eye. He saw that Ketchell had stepped forward and was eyeing Phelps with an intense expression.

"I've always known it, but let me get this straight, Harrison. You don't care about anyone, do you?"

"Sure I do, Lew. I care about me."

Ketchell's face seemed rigid. There was something more than curiosity in his eyes. Jake had been in tight situations before, and there had always been that moment of eerie silence just before violence. He had heard soldiers say it; he had seen it in the military, too, just before everything busted loose—automatic weapons, bombs, and everything else. He put his attention on Lew. If there were any violence, the bodyguard would be the source of it. He couldn't imagine what was going on in the man's mind, so he watched him carefully.

"I've been with you for quite a few years," Ketchell said. "You don't care about me, do you?"

The question caught Phelps off guard. "You *work* for me."

"So if I wear out, Harrison, and can't do my job? You'd throw me out like an old coat, wouldn't you?"

Phelps shrugged and began eating the eggs in front of him. "You know what the world's like, Lew. You're no different from me. You use things up and throw them away. That's life."

The silence grew more intense, and for some reason Jake found his muscles tensing. His gaze was fixed on Lew Ketchell, for he saw that something had transpired inside the smaller man. But the moment passed, and Lew seemed to relax. It was as if he had come to some sort of decision on a matter that had been troubling him.

"Pay me off, Phelps."

Phelps jerked his head up, his small eyes widening with surprise. "What do you mean, 'pay me off'?"

"Pay me what you owe me. I'm through with you."

Phelps could not have been more shocked if Ketchell had told him he was going to jump off the balcony. "You can't walk out and leave me like this!"

"Yeah, I can," Lew said. "I'm not going to wait for you to throw me away, Phelps. I'm throwing *you* away. Now write me out a check and take care of your own cat."

"Why, you—" Phelps rose to his feet, his face flushed with anger. "You're nothing but a two-bit hood! I can buy a dozen like you!"

"Yeah, sure, and they'll be real friends to you, won't they? For the last time, give me my money. If you do, I won't throw you off this balcony."

Something in Ketchell's voice froze Harrison Phelps. He suddenly saw that the man before him was utterly capable of doing what he said. "Sure," he blurted out, "I'll write you out a check." He reached into his pocket, pulled out a checkbook, and scribbled in it. "I guess you're expecting some severance pay."

"No, I'm not."

Harrison's eyes locked with Ketchell's, and Jake felt the tension of the moment. Then Phelps signed the check, ripped it out of the book. "There. Now get out of here. You'll come crawling back, Lew."

"Don't hold your breath. You through here, Novak?"

"Sure."

Ketchell turned and walked through the condo, Jake beside him. As soon as they were outside, Ketchell turned and seemed to expel a deep breath. "I guess I must be losing it, Novak. Throwing away a good job like that."

Something about the way Ketchell had walked away from Harrison Phelps pleased Jake. "Maybe not. I had to walk away from something once. Thought I had something going, but it didn't work out. So I walked away." He hesitated, then said, "What will you do now, Lew?"

"Don't know, but whatever I do it'll be better than I had with that creep."

'Well, if you're interested in a little short-term work, I need some help."

"What kind of help?"

"Your kind. I've got to find those cats. Mary Katherine loves that cat of hers, and I'm sure the other owners do, too. Somebody's been doing this. Everybody thinks it's Harrison Phelps, or rather they think you're doing it for Harrison Phelps."

"I wish it had been. That'd be easy enough, but it's not him."

"We've got to have twenty-four hour surveillance on those animals. Doucett and I can do eight each, but that leaves another shift."

"Sure, I'll lend a hand."

"The money will be all right. It's coming from your old boss, as you know."

"Right now I'm flush, and I'd just as soon completely cut the ties with Phelps. Maybe someday I'll come and ask for a handout. You know," he looked out over the Gulf and said thoughtfully, "You know, maybe after we catch this catnapper, I'll head out. Go down to Belize and do some snorkeling. Maybe you'd like to go with me, Jake."

"I've been there. Most fun I ever had was snorkeling in that big reef down there. We'll talk about it later. Come on. We'll go set everything up. The shift's up with Lonnie Doucett."

● ● ●

Chief Ray O'Dell looked around at the people gathered in the large room. He had called a meeting of the owners of the cats, and the room was crowded. His pale eyes went around, touching on each face, and he said crisply, "Sorry to call you people all in here, but we've had another catnapping."

A buzz went around the room, and Gary Charterhouse, the tall lanky truck driver from Oklahoma said, "Whose cat was taken this time?"

"It was mine," Kate spoke up. "Whoever's doing this broke into my house and took the cat from my home."

"Didn't you have any protection?" Olga Ivanov said. "After mine was taken, I'd think all of the owners would take extra precautions."

"Had a pit bull that was outside, and he was drugged." Jake had told her not to mention the fact that Jacques had scratched the intruder. He had told her he might spring that as a surprise. She glanced over to where he was standing against the wall with Lew Ketchell and continued, "I've got to have my cat back. It's not just a show thing with me, she's my friend."

"I want mine back too, Chief O'Dell," Olga said. She looked as if she had dressed for a fashion show—her sleek black outfit set off her enormous black eyes.

"Me, too," Charterhouse said, bitter anger in his eyes. "I'll kill whoever took my cat."

"Harrison Phelps. He's right here in this room," Eileen Saban said. She pointed at her ex-husband and said, "Harrison did it."

"Shut your mouth, Eileen!" Phelps said angrily. "I had nothing to do with it!"

"You hired somebody. Probably Lew there."

"No, it didn't happen that way," Jake said quickly. "Lew's helping us now to find the guy that did this. He didn't like his boss's attitude."

"He did it, I tell you!" Eileen Saban screamed. "Just like he did with those men in Detroit. When they crossed him, he had them all killed!"

"I could sue you for that, Eileen!" Phelps shouted.

"Go ahead and sue. You sued me for divorce and lost half of everything you had. Try it again and see where it gets you!"

"All right, that's enough of that," O'Dell said. "So far we don't have all that many leads, but I want to tell you that if you leave your cats at the arena, we'll have an armed guard on duty at all times. But if you take your cat home, you could lose it just like Mrs. Forrest did."

The chief then answered several questions from the owners. Finally, Raina Bettencourt, the judge, who had also attended the meeting, spoke. "It might be better to call off the show," she said calmly.

A wave of protest went up, and Hannah Monroe said, "I don't think that would be right, Raina."

Kate gazed at Hannah's pale face. Now that she knew the woman was dying of some disease she wouldn't even mention, she felt a wave of compassion and wished heartily that the woman knew the Lord. Hannah Monroe had money, but what did that matter to her now?

Hannah said, "I can't attend many more of these shows in my condition, but I'd like my cat to have a chance to be best in the show."

Raina Bettencourt stared at the woman. "Even if you take the chance of losing your cat, Hannah?"

Hannah smiled, and there was an enigma in her expression that Kate noticed at once, and she was sure Jake had seen the same thing. "We all lose, Raina. We lose everything sooner or later, so I'd like to do this even though I know it's not something that'll last forever. It's something I need right now in my life."

Mary Beth Pickens suddenly spoke up. "Well, I'm withdrawing." She drew herself up and said, "I thought rodeo was a rough way to make a living, but I never saw *anything* like this. You can have your cat show! I'm taking my cat and getting out of here and going back to riding the barrels."

O'Dell saw that there was little more to be gained, so he dismissed the meeting. He walked over to Jake and Lew and said, "Well, it's up to you guys. We can't do anything about the people who keep their cats in their suites or hotels. You need some extra guards?"

"I think we can handle it between the three of us," Jake said.

"All right. Holler if you need help."

Jake turned to Lew. "Come on. Let's go set up the shift with Doucett."

The two men left and walked toward the entrance where Jake had seen Doucett lounging, listening to the talk. "Hello, Lonnie," he said.

"Hey, Novak, what's happening?"

"You heard the meeting. Have you got a gun?"

"Yeah, I've got a piece."

"Good. I'll have O'Dell give you a special permit."

"It's that Harrison Phelps, I think." He stared at Ketchell and said, "And I don't trust you neither, man."

"Good. Don't trust anybody," Ketchell smiled politely.

"You gonna let him get around those cats? He'll steal all of them. Don't you know what he is, Novak? Ain't nothing but a big-city crook."

"I've reformed," Ketchell said. "I'm going to become a monk in a monastery and spend the rest of my life saying prayers, Doucett."

Doucett glared at Ketchell and then said, "You get me that permit. Somebody try to get a cat, I'll put a bullet hole in his head."

"Just be sure you shoot the right one," Lew said sarcastically.

"You take the rest of the day, Doucett," Jake broke in. "Lew, you come on at four and stay until midnight. I'll take over then."

● ● ●

Night had fallen, and Jake had been up in his room most of the time. Finally he came downstairs. Kate was fixing a meal for him to take with him. "I did the best I could," she said. "I thought you might get hungry after midnight. There's a jug of your special decaf coffee."

"Well, that's right thoughtful of you, ma'am." He stood there for a moment and said, "I can't get over the change in Lew Ketchell. He's one of the hard ones."

"I think Rhiannon's got something to do with it," Kate said. "He's become attached to her, strangely enough. He's gone to the hospital to sit with her, and she keeps asking him to pray with her." She smiled and said, "I bet that came as a shock to him."

"He told me about it."

"I wish he could change his life. He could if he wanted to."

"I'm not so sure about that," Jake said.

"Don't you think people can change, Jake?"

"Some people can, but you know we've lived a pretty hard life, me and Lew both. Some things get ground into you. It's hard to walk away from them."

Mary Katherine wanted to quote Scripture or ask Jake to pray, but she knew this wasn't the moment. It was strange how at times it was so easy to say something, while at other times it was like the Holy Spirit was indicating, *Don't speak*. She was learning that there was a time to speak out and a time to keep quiet and pray.

"Well, I'll see you sometime in the morning," Jake said. "Keep the doors locked. You've got that thirty-two. If anybody tries to come in, shoot them."

"I don't think I could do that, Jake."

"Try, will you? Of course, since Cleo's gone, I'm not expecting any more trouble."

Jake turned and left without another word. Kate sat and read for a while, then went out on the balcony, with Jacques following her. He hopped up in her lap purring, and she said, "You're not a dainty little kitten any more, Jacques." She stroked his fur, and Jacques flexed his paws and touched her, but gently.

Kate was still sitting there when the phone rang. She answered and heard Bev's voice ask, "Is it too late for me to come by, Kate?"

"It's pretty late, Beverly," Kate said, glancing at her watch.

"I know, but this is important."

"Well, I haven't gone to bed yet," Kate said. "Come on over."

"Good. I'll be there in two minutes."

Wondering what could bring Bev here at this hour, Kate left the balcony and waited until the doorbell rang. When she opened it, Bev stood there. He looked a little bit rumpled, which was very strange for him. "Come in, Bev."

"Thanks. I know it's late."

"Would you care for some coffee?"

"Not really. I need to talk."

There was a strange tension in Beverly that troubled Kate. He was usually so smooth, easygoing, and urbane, but now he seemed nervous. "You want to go out on the balcony?" she asked.

"No, I've got something to say to you, and I'd just as soon say it here."

"Something bothering you, Bev?"

"Yes." A sudden decisiveness touched Beverly Devon-Hunt. He plunged his hand into his pocket, pulled out a box, and said, "I usually do pretty well with words, but I've been kind of, as you Americans say, 'shook up.'"

Kate reached out and took the small box. It was a jeweler's box, she saw, a deep blue. She opened it, blinked with surprise, and uttered a little gasp. "Bev!" she exclaimed and could say no more. She was staring down at a diamond ring, a solitaire, larger than any she had ever seen. Instantly she looked up and saw that Bev was struggling for words. "I've talked a little bit to you about what I want, getting married and having a family." Bev bit his lower lip and said, "To tell you the truth, I've been feeling more and more attracted to you, Kate, and I couldn't sleep tonight. So, I've come to ask you to marry me."

Kate forgot the box momentarily. She was more interested in the face of the man than she was in the stone that glittered under the overhead lights. "Why, Bev, of course it's always an honor when a good man asks a woman to marry him, to share his life with him, but—" Desperately she tried to think of some way to explain how she felt and finally knew that there was no perfect way to do it. "I'm not really thinking of getting married. I've got a son to raise."

"I know, and I could help with that. It's always expensive. He could have the best schools, and if it means anything, I could adopt him legally. He'd have a title."

The enormity of what Beverly Devon-Hunt was saying began to weigh heavily on Kate. She knew she had to say this quickly. She closed the box and said, "We haven't known each other long enough. I—" She hesitated and said, "I made a mistake in my first marriage. I married Vic when I thought I had the kind of love a woman should have for a man she spends her life with, and I found out I wasn't right about that. He wasn't the man I thought he was, and I agreed too quickly."

"So you're afraid to try again. Is that it?"

"I never thought of it like that, Bev, but that's certainly part of it. But the other thing that you probably won't understand is I've got the idea that God moves in our lives, that He has certain things He wants us to do. I have to be sure, Bev, that the man that I marry, if I ever do, is the one man in the whole world that God wants me to live with for the rest of my life."

Bev took the box from her, held it loosely at his side. "I was afraid you'd say that. But I must tell you one thing."

"What's that?"

"I know I seem like a rather flighty sort of fellow...a poor little rich man with nothing but his money, who's spent his life rather foolishly...but I'm a very stubborn man, Kate, and I must warn you you haven't heard the last of this." Kate was caught off guard when Bev suddenly reached forward, pulled her to him, kissed her, and then stepped back. "Sooner or later I'm going to catch you at a weak moment, and you're going to say yes, and we're going to spend our whole lives together just like you want."

Kate had no chance to answer for he turned and walked away. Without looking back he shut the door. Kate felt weak, and she sat down as if she had lost all her strength. She knew she had much praying to do to find out what God thought about all this.

Twenty-one

The hot sun beat down on Jake as he moved away from one of the houses that lined the beach close to their own house. It had occurred to him that the catnapper had almost certainly come in a vehicle. He would have had to take Cleo in a carrier.

As Jake moved along, he thought of how slim his chances were of finding anything. From his days in the police department, he knew that most people's idea of what a policeman's life was like was totally out of line with reality. People had seen too many TV cops and had come to think that it was one moment of excitement after another, when in reality boredom was an occupational hazard for most policemen. Who could find it exciting to go from door to door to door asking people who didn't want to be interrupted and who didn't know anything if they had seen something? Usually it had taken all of Jake's patience to do such donkey work. Now, however, he was grasping at straws.

"It's a pretty small window," he muttered as he trudged along the sand toward the next house. "Whoever took Cleo did it while we were at church. We were only gone for a couple of hours. I think we've pretty well crossed Phelps out. Lew would have done it for him, but I'm sure Lew's becoming a straight arrow."

With a sigh he turned toward an aqua-colored house, a color that turned his stomach as a rule, and marched up to the front door. He rang the bell three times, and a woman with hair like white straw—and wearing a revealing swimsuit when she should have been wearing a poncho to cover the bulges—smiled at him. "Well, hello," she said. "Won't you come in?"

"Thank you, ma'am. I'd like to," Jake lied smoothly, "but I'm looking for some information."

"Well, aren't you just the one—and a big fellow, too! Come on in, and we'll talk about it over a drink. You do drink on duty, don't you?"

"No, ma'am, I can't afford to."

"Heavens! Why not?" she said. Her lips were painted so thickly that all reality was gone, and her mascara was thick enough to form the mortar between bricks. Jake managed to fight off the attraction she seemed to feel she was offering and said, "I'm just wondering if yesterday evening you saw a vehicle of some sort you were not accustomed to."

She said, "Well, darlin', all kinds of cars come and go here. What did it look like?"

"I just don't know exactly. Just some vehicle you ordinarily wouldn't see."

The woman tapped a finger on her lower lip and shut her eyes for a moment. The alcohol on her breath was like mace, but he managed to stand it.

"Well, there was a white jeep parked right out there. The man went swimming in the ocean. I went down and joined him. We had a great time."

Somehow Jake didn't feel that the driver of the white jeep was the man he was looking for. "Thanks very much, ma'am. I appreciate it."

"Sure you won't come in for a drink?"

"No, that's the best offer I've had in years, but I've got to be working. Have a glorious day, ma'am."

"I surely will if a good-looking man like you comes along again."

● ● ●

Lew was going through the same boring routine as Jake. He knew the drill, and trudged from house to house asking questions. As he had expected, he had gotten no response. Finally, when he had covered his mile along the Beach Road, he gave it up, and he expected Jake had done the same. Most people had given him the same answer. "We don't watch the beach. People come and go. That's what a beach is for."

Trudging back through the sand, Lew got into his black Lincoln and headed for the hospital, his mind working on the missing cats and how to find some kind of clue. He dodged through Gulf Shores and headed towards

South Baldwin Hospital, and at some point he gave up wondering about cats and started thinking about Rhiannon Brice and her grandfather. He parked the car in a slot marked *For Doctors Only*, muttered, "What can they do to me?" and went inside. He made his way to the ICU, where he found that Rhiannon was just coming out.

"How is he today, Rhiannon?"

"Not too good. His color is all bad."

"You want to go get something to eat?" Lew asked.

"I guess so, but I want to come back later."

"What would you like? Chinese? Mexican?"

"I want a beef enchilada, a hard taco, and lots of refried beans."

"I know just the spot."

He took her out to the car and drove to downtown Gulf Shores, where he parked in a business center. He led her to a small restaurant that didn't even have a name on it.

"Why don't they have a name?" Rhiannon said. "That's ludicrous."

"Well, I think it's called The Tequila. There's not much décor here, but the food is good." The two went inside and took a booth, and soon the orders had been taken and the food brought. Lew watched Rhiannon as she ate methodically. She took no pleasure in the meal that he could see. It wasn't like her, for usually she ate hungrily, grabbing at everything.

"Jake and I have been looking for Mrs. Forrest's cat," Lew said.

"You mean Kate?"

"Yes, I call her Mrs. Forrest. Do you always call grown people by their first name?"

"You already asked me that. Yes."

Lew grinned at the brevity of her reply. With this girl there were no gray areas. Everything was either *yes* or *no*. He waited for her to mention her grandfather, and when she finally slowed down and was drinking her Coke out of a huge red glass, she said, "Have you been praying for my granddad?"

"Well, I think about him a lot."

"You got to *pray* more, Lew. How we going to get my granddad well if people don't pray? Ocie says he's going to be healed. Jake says he doesn't know about things like this."

"I guess I don't either," Lew said without thinking. "I wish it was me instead of him. His life's worth something and mine's not."

Rhiannon looked at him with her strangely colored eyes. "Would you give your life for somebody else?"

"I don't know if I would or not. I guess there was one person I would have."

"Who was that?" Rhiannon asked.

"A little girl named Alice."

Rhiannon watched him steadily. "Who was she?"

"She was my daughter, Rhiannon."

"I thought you never got married."

"I never did. Her mother and I weren't married. I guess you think that's pretty bad."

"Yes."

Once again Lew was caught by the directness of Rhiannon Brice. "Well, it was. I wasn't living the right kind of life, but I would have died for her."

"You know, the Bible says something about dying for somebody else. My granddad asked me to learn it by heart. Do you want to hear it?"

"Sure."

Rhiannon spoke the words easily: "For when we were yet without strength, in due time Christ died for the ungodly. For scarcely for a righteous man will one die: yet peradventure for a good man some would even dare to die. But God commendeth his love toward us, in that, while we were yet sinners, Christ died for us." She turned and gave Ketchell a nod. "Isn't that good, Lew?"

"Yeah, I guess so." Lew had listened to the girl as she quoted the Scripture marveling again at her intelligence and memory, wondering how one small head could hold so much information.

"I'd die for my granddad."

"I'm sure you would, Rhiannon."

"Well, Jesus loved you enough to die for you, so maybe you'll find somebody you'd die for somewhere sometime."

Lew Ketchell stared at the girl not knowing how to answer that. "I hope I do," he said. "You ready to go back to the hospital?"

"Yes."

• • •

Jake stopped alongside the highway, for an idea had occurred to him, and as it took shape, he slowly made a decision. He kicked the Harley into action and went to the condo where he knew Raina Bettencourt was staying. He had to go through the gate, and when he gave his name, the guard passed him on in. *I could be a serial killer, and he'd let me in anyway,* Jake thought as he made his way up the stairs to Raina's condo. When he rang the bell, she answered the door almost at once. "Hello, Mrs. Bettencourt, we've met before."

"Yes, you're Novak. Mary Katherine's houseguest."

"That's my usual designation, I guess," Jake said. "Do you have a minute or two?"

"Come in." She stepped back, and Jake followed her in. The interior was beautiful, done in pastels and an almost glistening white. She led him to a table and said, "You want something to drink?"

"Some water would go down mighty good."

"We always serve water." She went and got a glass of ice water and came back and then sat down. "Have you come to talk about the missing cats?"

"Yes, I have."

"I heard you say that you and Ketchell have been working on it. I hope you can stop any more kidnappings, or *catnappings* as everyone calls them now."

"I've got an idea, Mrs. Bettencourt, but it would take your help. I don't know if you'd like the idea or not."

"Tell me what it is, Mr. Novak, and I'll tell you whether I like it or not."

Jake had thought steadily on his way to the condo, but it was a lot to ask of someone. She sat there listening as he explained carefully, and finally, to his surprise, she nodded and said, "It sounds like a good thing. I'll do it."

Jake felt a sigh of relief. "I'm glad to hear that. I get turned down so many times that when somebody agrees with me, I almost want to faint."

Raina Bettencourt laughed. "They used to have a fainting couch in Victorian days. Women, when they passed out, could gracefully recline on them. Of course, they had to be sure they fainted within falling distance. But please don't faint. I think your idea is a good one."

Jake left feeling somehow that he had accomplished something—although he couldn't say exactly what. He went back to the house, parked the Harley, and walked up the steps toward the deck. He found Kate sitting in a lawn chair staring out at the Gulf.

Jake sat down beside her, relaxing for the first time that day. The sibilant whisperings of the waves as they came in were soothing, and the breeze cooled his face. The sun was hot, but there was a good breeze that carried a flight of gray pelicans overhead in their familiar V-formation.

"Jake," Kate had been thinking about Bev's visit, and now she said, "Bev came last night after you left."

"Kind of late, wasn't it?"

"Yes, it was. Jeremy had already gone to bed, but I couldn't sleep worrying about Cleo."

"What did the man with a hyphen want?"

"He—he wanted me to marry him."

Jake's head swiveled so quickly that Kate flinched. "What'd you tell him?"

"I told him I wasn't thinking of marriage right now."

"Good!"

"What do you mean *good*?" Kate said almost angrily. "It could be a good marriage."

"You can't know that."

"You just don't like Bev, do you?"

"I like him fine, but you two are not made for each other, as they say in Hollywood."

"Oh, so when did you get your degree in sociology and marriage counseling, Mr. Novak?"

"Do you love the guy?" Jake demanded abruptly. It was almost as if he had pointed a gun at her head.

"I told him I had made one mistake in marriage, and I needed a lot of time to think about another one."

"You made a mistake marrying your husband? You never told me that."

"I have a few secrets, Jake, just as you do, I'm sure."

"What was wrong with your marriage? Wasn't he a stand-up guy?"

"Oh, he was good in a lot of ways. He was very good with Jeremy, but—" She broke off not knowing how to explain how it had been with her and Vic. "I think I went into marriage with the wrong idea." She wanted to say more, but Jake was studying her so intensely she couldn't. "Anyway, Bev had a ring. The biggest diamond I ever saw, and he said if I married him he'd adopt Jeremy, and Jeremy would be nobility. He would have a title."

"Sir Jeremy. Well, you think Jeremy would want that?"

"I don't think so," Kate said. "And anyway, I couldn't marry a man just for what he could do for Jeremy...although if I ever did marry, it would be someone who was good with him."

Jake got up and gave her a critical look. "Don't do it, Kate," he said abruptly, then turned around and walked into the house.

Kate stared after him almost angrily. "Why don't you just say what you mean, Novak?" she called out, but was fairly sure he didn't hear her or he paid her no attention. She sat back on the lawn chair and watched the Gulf again, but her thoughts were not on the waves that broke on the white beach.

Twenty-two

"Take a gander at this, Mary Katherine."

Kate looked up from the book she was reading and took the newspaper that Jake handed her. It was the latest issue of the *Mobile Register*. She looked at the headline that said, "Judge Picks Winners Before Show."

She read the first few lines and looked up with surprise. "Why, this says Mrs. Bettencourt is telling who the favorites are. She shouldn't do that!"

"Well, she's helping us out a little bit." Jake leaned against the wall and gave her the details. "I had a big idea. I have about fifty great ideas an hour with gusts up to ninety-five. Most of them are gone with the wind, but I think this one will work."

"What idea did you have?"

"I wanted the catnapper to strike again, so I had Mrs. Bettencourt make up this story. These cats are not the ones she's picked to win. She told me plainly she never makes that decision beforehand. Only on the floor."

Suddenly Kate's lips parted. "I see. You mean the catnapper will try to steal one of these cats."

"I'm hoping tonight. If we wait until the show's over, everybody will be scattered. We'll never catch him."

"And we'll never get Cleo back or the other cats."

"That's about the story. It's now or never."

"Do you think it'll work, Jake?"

"It's the only show in town, and I'll tell you one thing. It wouldn't hurt if you put some extra prayers in there that we'll catch this bird. I'd hate to think of him getting away with all this."

"I didn't know you believed in prayer."

Jake rubbed his chin thoughtfully and said, "Well, I believe in *your* prayers."

"God doesn't play favorites, Jake."

"You're wrong there. I think He does. I think His favorites are those who are faithful to Him."

Kate suddenly smiled and got to her feet. She put her hand on his arm, feeling the hardness of the muscle. "That's the most theological remark I've ever heard you make, Jake Novak. Obeying God is close to loving Him, I think. "

"I think the catnapper will strike again some time after midnight. Lonnie Doucett is taking the day shift, and Lew's going to be on from four until midnight. I think he'll wait until two or three o'clock or something like that."

"Be careful, Jake."

"I'm always careful. You do the praying, and I'll do the rest of it."

"Where are you going now?"

"I've got a few things to take care of."

"Meanwhile, I'll be at the hospital."

"You might find Lew there, then." Jake said. "He told me he was going to visit Morgan before he went on the job. In fact, I think I'll swing by there myself."

"It's strange how Lew's taken to Rhiannon," Kate said. "You can tell he's a tough, hard man."

"Yes, he is. He tell you about his daughter?"

"No, I didn't know he had a daughter," Kate said.

"She died when she was only three, but he's never forgotten her. He thinks the girl would be something like Rhiannon."

"Jake, that reminds me...I've been meaning to tell you. I told Morgan something, Jake. I didn't talk to you about it, but maybe I should have."

"What was it?"

"I—I promised him that if he didn't make it, that we'd take Rhiannon into our family."

"Well, we've got an albino Burmese python, a profane parrot, lovebirds that hate each other, and a rebellious teenager. How much trouble could a ten-year-old girl be?"

She leaned over suddenly and hugged him. "I didn't know how you'd take it," she said.

"Well, if I get attention like this, I may do some more good things that you like." With that, he turned to leave. But then he turned around and said, "Remember, anybody who marries you has to have your father's consent."

"My father isn't living."

"I know, so I'm your surrogate dad."

"You are *not* my father!"

"Sure I am, Kate. You need a strong, parental figure. That's me. If the limey comes around, tell him to come to me. I'll slap him around a little bit and get the truth out of him." He laughed when he saw her make a face and turned. "I'll see you later."

● ● ●

Jake was right about Lew being at the hospital. He found him out in the waiting room. "They won't let but one person at a time in to see the old man, so I figured the girl ought to go," Lew said.

"I'm glad you're paying attention to Rhiannon," Jake remarked. "She needs all the support she can get."

"Yeah—well, I feel like a fool trying to tell her something. She knows everything."

"No, she doesn't. She's a scared ten-year-old, Lew, and I want you to know that I admire you for the way you've tried to help her."

Lew looked up at Novak with astonishment, then smiled sheepishly. "I never figured myself for a softy, but there's something about her."

"Yes, there is. Well, I just came by to check on things, but I've got a few things to do. Watch out for yourself. I don't think this guy will strike until early in the morning, maybe two or three, but you never can tell. You got your nine-millimeter?"

"Right here."

"Don't hesitate to use it."

"Okay, boss."

Lew watched as Jake left the waiting room, and then picked up a two-year-old issue of *Better Homes and Gardens*. He soon tossed the magazine aside, leaned back, and closed his eyes. As he did, he thought of his daughter. The memories hadn't grown fainter with the passage of time but stronger and more vivid. He had lain awake many a night wishing he had spent more time with her. He'd kept every picture he'd had of her and had them enlarged. And he realized as he sat there that Alice had been the only thing of value in his life. But somehow Rhiannon was taking her place, and he couldn't understand it.

He smiled slightly, and in a half-mocking tone murmured, "Well, God, that girl's made me pray once so I guess it didn't hurt. You know what I am. Can't change what I've done, but I'm asking You to take care of that old man. He means the world to Rhiannon. I can't do anything, but You can." He murmured in a barely audible voice, and an old woman at the other end of the waiting room looked up and stared at him curiously. Embarrassed, he picked up the *Better Homes and Gardens* and began to read how to plan a spring flower planting, which he was quite certain he would never do.

Finally Rhiannon came out and sat down beside him. "I'm glad you're here."

"How is he, Rhiannon?"

Rhiannon, for the first time, showed a weakness. Her lower lip trembled, and he saw tears form in her eyes. "I'm afraid, Lew."

Ketchell put his arm around the girl, and she suddenly threw her arms around him. "I'm afraid," she whispered. "I'm afraid he's going to die!"

Lew didn't know what to say, so he simply pulled her up on his lap and held her. She began to sob, and it was so unusual a thing for this sturdy, independent ten-year-old that Lew felt shaken by it. Finally, as the sobs lessened, he handed her his handkerchief, and she said, "I want us to pray for Granddad and for you."

"For me?"

"Yes. I'm going to pray for Granddad, and you're going to pray for yourself. That's the way people get saved, Lew."

"Honey, I've told you—it's too late for me."

Rhiannon shook her head, and a stubborn look set her lips in a straight cast. "No, it's *not* too late. I've told you before, Lew, about that man who died on the cross. He was a thug just like you, but he said, 'Jesus, Lord, remember me when thou comest into thy kingdom,' and Jesus told him He would. He said, 'Today shalt thou be with me in paradise.' So, that's all it takes. You believe in Jesus, don't you?"

"I guess I've shoved him out of my mind, but I've seen something in Mrs. Forrest and in you and in your granddad. I guess I have to say I do."

"I'm going to pray for Granddad, and then you're going to pray for yourself." Without further warning the girl bowed her head and prayed a prayer for her grandfather. It was a simple prayer of a child asking for something deeply desired, and Lew was moved by it more than he could say. She said, "Amen," and then she turned and said, "Now, you pray."

"I don't—I don't know what to say."

"Tell God you're a thug."

"He knows that."

"But you need to say it anyway. Didn't you know that? We're supposed to confess the bad things we've done. I do."

"Honey, it would take a long time to say all the bad things I've done."

Honey was the endearment Lew had used for Alice, and his heart constricted as Rhiannon's features seemed to be transformed into the features of his daughter.

"You don't have to say every one of them. Just tell God you've done a whole bunch of wrong things, and you're sorry for them all, and you don't want to do them any more. And then you tell Him that you want to be saved in the name of Jesus. You believe Jesus died on the cross. That's all it takes."

Lew Ketchell had done hard things before, but for some reason this was the toughest thing ever. He dropped his eyes, unable to meet Rhiannon's gaze, and when she grabbed his shirt and shook him, she said, "Go on. I want you to be saved. When I go to heaven, I wouldn't like it if you aren't there, Lew."

Lew Ketchell, professional thug, found tears had come into his eyes, and he did exactly as Rhiannon said because there was nothing else left to do. He said, "God, you know what a bad man I've been. I've done everything wrong that I can think of. I'm sorry that I've led that kind of life, and I ask you to forgive me for all that."

"Now tell Him you want to be saved by the blood of Jesus," Rhiannon instructed.

"Okay. God, I want to be a Christian. It's late, and it seems too easy, but I believe that Jesus died on the cross, and this child says that I can be changed from what I am. So, in the name of Jesus I ask You to save me."

"Amen," Rhiannon said. "Now, you're a Christian."

"Wait a minute. Aren't I supposed to do something?"

"Yes, you *are* supposed to do something. There's lots of stuff for you to do. I'm going to teach you how. We're going to go to a church, and you're going to stand up and tell people that you're a Christian now. You're going to get the preacher to baptize you. You're going to take the Lord's Supper.

Me and you are going to study the Bible together. It's going to be a lot of fun, Lew, it really is."

A lightness came to Lew then. He didn't know for sure if what he had done was real, or if it was just something this girl, with her imagination, had worked on him. He knew he felt he had done the right thing, if for no other reason than to make her happy. Still, he felt like, somehow, a chain had been broken that had been binding him, and he laughed and said, "Okay—you're the boss, honey."

"Good. Now, the first thing you have to do is memorize the Bible. I want you to memorize John 3:16."

"What does it say?"

The girl began saying the verse, and her face was so serious, and Lew Ketchell was glad that for the time being she had momentarily forgotten her granddad. He obediently repeated the verse, thinking about how strange it was that he, Lew Ketchell, would be learning Bible verses.

● ● ●

Jacques had mostly recovered from the blow on his head—except there was still a sore knot. He felt somehow that something was missing, and knew that it was Cleo. They had been together since early kitten-hood, and he felt something was wrong with life without her.

Where are you, Cleo? I don't know if I'm ever going to forgive you for getting yourself catnapped, and I don't know if that Intruder's got sense enough to find you or not. You know me—no confidence in these persons traipsing around here on only two legs. You want anything done right, do it yourself.

He escaped through the cat door, took a swipe at Trouble, who came to greet him, and then trotted off toward the road. He had some vague instinct he couldn't understand, but he knew he had to find Cleo and quickly. He hunted for over two hours, sniffing and trying to find something that would lead him to his companion. He saw a young cat, a shorthair, eating something out of a bowl. He marched over and said, *Get out of the way, freak!* The shorthair took one look at the huge black cat and nearly broke his back retreating.

Jacques licked his lips and sat down for a snack. Then, satisfied he turned and moved again, refreshed and ready to do more detective work.

• • •

It had been an unfruitful day for Jake. He was pinning all his hopes on finding the catnapper striking—stealing away some of the cats mentioned in the article. He arrived at the arena at a quarter till midnight. He parked the Harley and walked inside. The lights were on, but he saw no signs of Ketchell. "Lew?" he called out and waited, but there was no answer. The only sound was the mewing of cats, one yowling in a loud disconsolate voice.

Jake was disappointed. He wondered if he had been mistaken about Ketchell. He began to walk down the line of cages and saw that one of the carriers was missing. He quickly checked and found two other carriers were also gone. The three missing cats were among those that had been mentioned in the newspaper article. Jake started running down the aisle, and suddenly, behind the line of carriers, he saw a form. He pulled his gun, knowing it was too late. He moved between the carriers and stopped in his tracks. Lew Ketchell was on his side, clutching his stomach, and lying in a pool of blood.

Jake fell to his knees, holstering his weapon. "Lew, can you hear me?"

"He—he caught me off guard." The whisper was faint.

"Don't try to talk, Lew." Jake pulled out his cell phone, punched in 9-1-1, and as soon as he got someone, he said, "Get an ambulance to the convention center, at once. This is an emergency!"

After calling Chief O'Dell, he leaned down and said, "It's okay, Lew. Hang in there. Don't give up, buddy." He put his hand over the wound in his stomach to staunch the flow of blood, and as he sat there listening to the cats crying and the faint breathing of Lew Ketchell, he knew something had gone terribly wrong.

Twenty-three

The phone rang, breaking the silence of the night, and Kate jerked awake. For an instant she lay there in that twilight zone between deep sleep and awareness, then the phone rang again. Pulling herself into a sitting position, Kate groped in the darkness. She knocked the receiver off the cradle, fumbled for it, and put it to her ear. Her voice sounded thick in her ears as she said, "Yes, what is it?"

"This is Jake. We got a real problem, Mary Katherine."

Awareness washed through Kate, and she reached over and turned the light on, blinking like an owl at the sudden brilliance. "What's happened, Jake? Are you hurt?"

"No, it's not me. It's Lew Ketchell. He's hurt bad, Mary Katherine."

"How did it happen?"

"I don't know. I went to take over the midnight watch, and I found him. He'd been shot, and he almost died on the way to the hospital. They're doing all they can to keep him alive, but the doctors say he's not going to make it. He wants to see Rhiannon."

"I'll get her up. We'll be there as soon as we can get there."

"I'll be here. If you can, you'd better break the news to Rhiannon on the way so she'll be ready."

"You mean tell her he's going to die?"

"I think it'd be better. He looks terrible, and he's just hanging on by a whisker. He may be dead by the time you get here, so you'd better speed it up."

"We'll be there as quick as we can."

Slamming the phone down in the cradle, Mary Katherine threw the light

220

cover back and jumped out of the bed. She dressed quickly, and then went to Rhiannon, who was sleeping soundly on the cot that she had made for her. Bending over, Kate said, "Rhiannon, wake up, dear."

Rhiannon stirred, mumbled something, and Kate shook her lightly. "You've got to wake up, Rhiannon."

"What's the matter?" Rhiannon's eyes were only barely open, and Kate pulled her up into a sitting position.

"We've got to go to the hospital. Your friend Mr. Ketchell has been badly hurt."

Rhiannon passed her hand across her face and blinked her eyes until they opened widely. "What's the matter with him?"

"He was shot. Come on and get dressed. We've got to hurry."

It took only a matter of two or three minutes to get Rhiannon dressed. She was wearing only a pair of shorts and a purplish T-shirt and sandals.

"I'll go tell Jeremy what's happened." Leaving her bedroom, she went across to Jeremy's room. She knocked loudly then entered. "Jeremy, wake up."

Jeremy came out of his sleep quickly and looked frightened. "What is it, Mom? What's the matter?"

"Mr. Ketchell, he's been shot. I've got to take Rhiannon to the hospital."

"I'll go with you."

"No, I want you to stay here. Take care of the animals and stay by the phone. I'll call you as soon as I know something."

"All right, Mom."

Quickly Kate wheeled and found Rhiannon coming out. "We'd better hurry," she said. They moved outside. The air was cool, although not cold. As they got to the beach highway, Kate turned west and headed for South Baldwin Hospital in Foley.

"Is he going to be all right?" Rhiannon asked.

Kate had tried to figure out how to tell Rhiannon, but there was never an easy way. The child was so mature in some ways, and one became so accustomed to her grown-up talk and use of long, complicated words that it was easy to forget how young she was and how vulnerable. She breathed a quick prayer and then said, "He's been very badly hurt, Rhiannon. Jake said he almost died on the way to the hospital." She hesitated and then said, "I don't think he's going to be able to survive."

Rhiannon said nothing, and this troubled Kate. She didn't know what more to say, so she reached out with her right hand and put it on Rhiannon's neck. Rhiannon was strangely quiet, and she remained so as they pulled into the parking lot of South Baldwin Hospital.

Kate got out, and by the time she came around the car Rhiannon was outside. "We'd better hurry, hon." They had come to the ER entrance, and as soon as they went in, she found Jake waiting for them. His face was set in an expression between anger and distress. It was the closest she had ever seen Jake Novak to losing it. His lips were tight, and he seemed to bite his words off. "You'd better hurry. He wants to see you, Rhiannon."

Turning, he led the way to where Lew Ketchell lay on a bed. A doctor was bending over him. He looked up and said, "Is this family?"

Before Kate could answer, Rhiannon said, "Yes."

"I'm Dr. Roberts. You can come and try to talk to him. He fades in and out." He shook his head with a finality that left no doubt in Kate's mind.

Jake stood back and watched the small girl as she went to Lew's side. He saw her reach out and put her hand on his hair and brush it back. Then Jake's cell phone rang, and he ducked out of the emergency room to take the call.

"This is Jake," he said.

"This is Oralee Prather. We had a call you might be interested in, Novak."

"What is it?"

"A woman called in about a huge black cat prowling around her place. She's afraid of it. She said it was the biggest cat she had ever seen. It sounds like that cat that belongs to Kate Forrest."

"Did you see him?"

"Yeah, I got here to the location, and he was prowling around. I tried to get him, but he wouldn't play ball with me. I couldn't handle him with bare hands."

"That's just as well. He can be pretty rough. Can you get animal control?"

"Not this time of the night. They don't work around the clock."

"Okay. I'll be right there. Where are you?" He listened as Officer Prather gave him the instructions.

He turned, went back inside, and said to a nurse, "Would you tell Mrs. Forrest that I had to leave? I'll be back as soon as I can."

He left the ER to get onto his Harley and start out. *I wonder what in the world Jacques could be doing in that part of town so far away from our house,* he thought. He shook his head.

● ● ●

Kate watched Rhiannon, wondering what was going on in her mind as she stood beside Lew. If the girl had been a typical ten-year-old, she would have gone over and put her arm around her, but there was a streak of independence in Rhiannon Brice like a bar of steel. *Maybe later,* Kate thought.

"Are there any other relatives?" Kate turned to face Dr. Roberts, who was standing back watching Rhiannon as she stroked the wounded man's hair.

"I really don't know, Doctor."

"Well, I don't think there's time, but if you think of one, you ought to get a call in."

Kate lowered her voice and pulled Dr. Roberts outside. "Is there any hope at all?"

"No. I'm sorry to be so blunt, but he lost so much blood, and the bullet tore him up so badly inside. He was shot twice. It's a miracle he made it this far. As a matter of fact, if Mr. Novak had been a minute or two later, he'd have been dead." Roberts shook his head and said, "Nothing I can do."

"Will he regain consciousness?"

"He's come to twice. He may again, or he may not."

Roberts left the room abruptly, and Kate moved to stand on the other side of Ketchell's bed. She realized how little she knew about him. She was aware he had led a hard life and had strayed outside the law more than once. Jake had told her that much. She had sensed in Jake a kind of reluctant admiration for Lew Ketchell. He had told her once, "I could have gone the way Lew did just as easy. I mean, I could have become a bad guy. Don't know why that didn't happen."

Suddenly Kate noticed Ketchell twist his head slightly, and then his eyes came open.

Rhiannon leaned forward at once and said, "Hi, Lew. Can you hear me?"

The voice of Ketchell was faint and weak, a fluttering thing. "Hi, honey."

It was all the wounded man could manage, and Rhiannon reached out and took his hand. "You've got to get better, Lew."

"Not...this time." For a moment his eyes fluttered, and Kate feared he was dying. He had great difficulty breathing, and his voice grew even fainter. "I...I want to...do something." It was hard to hear him, but Rhiannon understood well. "What is it, Lew?" she asked.

"I want your granddad...to have...my heart."

Kate straightened up, alarm running through her. She turned at once and left the room. Dr. Roberts was across the room, and she said, "Doctor, Mr. Ketchell wants to donate his heart to Rhiannon's grandfather. Morgan Brice is his name. He's in this hospital."

Roberts wheeled and ran across the room. He jerked open a drawer and pulled out a form. He wrote on it rapidly and said, "Have him sign this. It gives us authority to take his heart, and it designates who the heart will go to. If we don't have this, someone else will have better claim on it."

Roberts picked up the phone and said, "We'll have to fly him to Dallas with Mr. Brice."

Kate hurried back and leaned over. "Mr. Ketchell, you want Mr. Brice to have your heart?"

"Yes." The answer was almost too quiet for Kate to catch, but she leaned over and said, "You'll have to sign this. I'll guide your hand." She had the paper on a clipboard and a pen in her free hand. She held the clipboard steady so Ketchell could see it, then put the pen in his hand. "Just write it as best you can."

Kate watched as Ketchell's hand moved. It was a scratchy, wavy signature, but it was a signature.

Kate turned and ran outside. "Here it is, Doctor."

"There'll be a plane here within thirty minutes. We've got to have him out to the airport. Both men will have to go."

"Can I go, too?" Rhiannon said.

"No, you wouldn't have anybody to take care of you."

"I'll go with her," Kate said quickly.

"I don't see why not. There's plenty of room. I'll call and make the arrangements."

Rhiannon turned and ran back, and she stood beside Lew Ketchell. Kate, on the other side of the bed, reached out and took his free hand. "It's a wonderful thing you're doing, Mr. Ketchell."

"I want...to help her. I need to."

Kate's eyes were dim with tears, but she saw that Rhiannon wasn't crying. Her eyes were fixed on Lew Ketchell's face, and she said, "You know what,

Lew? After you give my granddad your heart, every time I see him, I'll be seeing you. Every time I hug him or give him a kiss, it'll be you I'm kissing. I'll be your little girl."

Rhiannon's words brought Lew Ketchell's eyes up, and Kate saw that he was smiling. "That's...good," he said. "I'd like that."

The eyes were fluttering, and Rhiannon said, "Now, we're going to call on Jesus, and He'll meet you."

Rhiannon began to pray, and Kate saw Lew Ketchell's lips move as he whispered something, and she hoped fervently it was a prayer to God.

● ● ●

Both men had been placed on stretchers and tied down inside the jet. The attendant turned and said, "We'll have to fasten you in until we take off."

"That'll be fine." Kate got into her seat and Rhiannon into hers, and the attendant checked their safety belts. He then moved forward and took his own seat. The engines picked up speed, and the plane began to move. Kate watched out the window as the ground rushed by, and in the darkness they rose and left the earth. Once they were airborne and the plane had steadied, the attendant came over and checked the vital signs of both men. He said to Kate, "Mr. Ketchell's barely hanging on. Mr. Brice seems to be stable." He looked at the two men and said, "Never had anything quite like this before. If I understand it, Mr. Ketchell's giving his heart to Mr. Brice."

"That's right," Kate said.

Rhiannon came to stand beside Ketchell, and the attendant asked, "Is that your dad, honey?"

Rhiannon looked up and without hesitation said, "Yes, he is."

● ● ●

Lew had been in a coma when they arrived at the Dallas hospital. Morgan remained weak, but stable. He looked up at his granddaughter beside his bed and said, "This doesn't seem right, taking a life from another man."

Kate, standing behind Rhiannon, said, "It's not like that, Morgan. Lew Ketchell is dying, and there's nothing the doctors can do about it. But he wanted you to have his heart."

Rhiannon said, "He's going to be with Jesus, Granddad, but he'll still be with us in your new heart."

Morgan smiled at the girl, and she reached out and touched his hair. Just then two orderlies came rushing in with a doctor following. "Mr. Ketchell just died, but he had a strong heart," the doctor said. "We're going to do the operation right now."

Kate was grieved over Lew's death, and she was concerned about how Rhiannon would take it. The two sat together for what seemed like hours. Once Rhiannon even dropped off to sleep. But the sun was rising when the doctor finally came out. His mask was dangling from around his neck, and he pulled off his green operating cap. Kate and Rhiannon got up, and when Kate saw his smile, her heart gave a leap.

"It was a good operation," the doctor said. "Mr. Brice is in recovery and doing well. That's your granddad, is it, sweetheart?"

"Yes," Rhiannon said through tears.

"Well, thanks are certainly due to the donor. It was a great gift for one person to give another. I hope you never forget it."

Rhiannon looked up and said firmly, "I never will."

Kate put her arm around Rhiannon, and the two stood there as the doctor explained the recovery process. Kate was filled with joy at the thought of Morgan's new lease on life, but there was a sadness there, too, that one man had to die for another to live.

Twenty-four

While the drama in Dallas was unfolding, Jake was involved in a drama of his own. When he had exited the brightly lit ER at South Baldwin Hospital into the darkness of the night, he was met by Ocie Plank.

"I've got bad news, Ocie," Jake said. "You know Lew Ketchell?"

"Sure, I know him. What about him?"

"He was shot earlier tonight. Don't think he's going to make it."

"Maybe I'd better go in and pray for him—but where are you going?"

"I just got a call from Oralee Prather. She says a large black cat has been reported in a neighborhood over close to the landfill. I expect it's Jacques."

"That's a pretty seedy neighborhood, ain't it?"

"Yeah, but I've got to go see about him."

"Good. I'll just go along."

"I thought you wanted to pray for Ketchell."

"I can pray on the back of this here machine. Just get 'er goin'." Jake got on the Harley and was about to start it, when Ocie grabbed his arm. He leaned forward and said, "We better pray before we go that it's the right cat, and that we catch this fellow doin' all this mischief. He's a killer, ain't he?"

"Yes, he is, but I don't know about praying."

Ocie shook Jake's arm, which irritated Jake greatly. "Your dad prayed before we hit the beach at Normandy. You reckon you're a better man than your dad?"

"No, I'm not." He reached back into his saddlebag, pulled out his thirty-two, and said, "Stick that in your belt. And watch out—it's loaded."

Ocie took the gun, hefted it in his hand for the balance, and shook his head. "It ain't big enough to do more than annoy a feller."

"Get him between the eyes, Ocie. That'll annoy him. Now, say your prayer and get on."

"I can pray on the way." Ocie swung on behind Jake, who started the engine and guided the Harley out of the parking lot. As soon as he hit the highway, he gunned it, ignoring speed laws. He figured if a squad car took after him, he'd claim official business.

Ocie hung on tight, and once he yelled, "There ain't no sense in getting us killed, son!" But Jake didn't respond, so Ocie concentrated on praying and holding on as tight as he could. Jake took every shortcut he knew, and soon he was at the part of town Oralee had described. It was filled mostly with framed shacks built years ago by people who wanted to live close to the beach but couldn't afford a richer place. Some of them were unoccupied now and falling down. Sooner or later this would no doubt be a fancy subdivision, but not now.

The Harley's headlights outlined Oralee, and Jake pulled up to a stop. He waited until Ocie got off, then shut off the engine and put the kickstand down.

"You got here pretty quick," Oralee said. Her eyes were watchful in her smooth ebony face, and she waved a flashlight. "Your fool cat ran away from me, Novak. He's somewhere around here, though. I'm pretty sure it's that cat you're looking for. Not many cats that big and black."

"Thanks, Officer Prather."

"I've got a call I have to go on. You two can handle this?"

"I guess we can corral one black cat," Ocie said. "Are you born again, Officer Prather?"

"You asked me that the last three times we met. No, I'm not, so don't keep pestering me."

"Jesus loves you," Ocie called out as Officer Prather moved quickly back and entered the squad car.

As soon as she left, Jake fished a small flashlight out of the saddlebag. "Don't have a spare. We'll have to go together."

The two men started searching. It was an unappetizing part of town, to say the least. The landfill wasn't far away, and the smell was rank. One by one they began to check the houses, beginning with the one where Oralee had indicated she had seen the cat. He moved right and found nothing, and Jake said, "Let's try the other way, Ocie."

"Right with you, son."

They worked their way back, and as they approached a two-story house, Jake stopped and flashed the light around. Suddenly something touched his right leg. He let out a grunt and jumped in the air a foot.

He turned the light on the ground, and looking down, he saw Jacques staring up at him.

Well, it's about time you got here—I knew you'd be a flop at this, the cat meowed.

Ocie laughed. "I didn't jump that much when I landed at Normandy. You're mighty goosey, ain't you, son?"

Jacques was glaring at Jake in his usual unamiable manner. *You two bipeds are sure worthless detectives. Here I've gone to all the trouble to solve this case, and you're stumbling around in the night. I don't know why I put up with you.*

"You mangy critter," Jake said angrily. "I've got important things to do. Now, you come on. I'm taking you home."

Jake reached down, but with that incredible feline reflex, Jacques moved smoothly away. *You ain't taking me no place, you featherbrained biped! Follow me, you dumb flatfoot, if you got enough sense.*

Jacques moved around to the front of the house and began clawing at the front door.

"What's that cat doing?" Ocie asked curiously. "He wants in that house."

Jake's mind was working quickly. "I don't have much use for Jacques, but I'll say this. His hearing is about twenty times better than ours, and his sense of smell is probably a hundred times better."

You got that right, Intruder, so quit fooling around. I've done my job. Let's see if you can do yours. Won't be as good as a cat could do, but you're all I have to work with.

Jake had often worked on hunches, and this was one of them. "I think there's something in there. Jacques is a pest, but he wouldn't be clawing at that door for nothing."

You're mighty right, except the "pest" part. Now, get at it! I can't do everything for myself.

Jake tried the front door, which was locked. He moved around to the side of the house, closely followed by Ocie, and by Jacques, who was complaining all the way. Jake tried a window and found that it was unlocked. He opened it, but before he could move, Jacques had leaped up, landed on the sill, and disappeared into the darkness of the interior.

"Well, that tore the rag off the bush, didn't it, Jake?" Ocie said.

"Here, I'll go first," Jake said.

"Well, you'll have to help me in. That's a little bit high for a fellow my age."

The window was actually rather low, and Jake had no trouble getting through it. He turned around and gave Ocie a hand, and then the two of them looked around. "It kind of looks like a pigpen, don't it?"

The main room of the downstairs was evidently the entertainment room. There was an old television set, a stereo, a battered couch, and a recliner. It looked like a fishing camp. Jake flashed the light around and saw that the kitchen sink was full of dirty dishes. Empty containers from fast-food places littered the floor, and the smell was strong.

Jake moved around quietly, followed by Ocie, checking the bathroom and the bedroom. Nothing.

Up here, you dummy!

Actually this was a yowl from Jacques, who was on the stairs looking down at the two men. *Do I got to carry you up these stairs? Yikes, what a pair of noodles!*

"We check the upstairs," Jake said. The two men went up, Jacques going before them. At the top landing there were two doors, both closed. Jacques looked at one, reached out, and raked his claws down it. *Open this door.*

Jake suddenly heard a sound. He moved forward, opened the door, and threw the light switch on. There were four cats, one of them Cleo. She came forward at once and shoved her head against Jacques' head. *You came for me, Jacques. I knew you would!*

Of course you knew I would, Cleo. Are you okay?

Yes, we've had something to eat, but we all want out of here.

"What are we going to do now, Jake?" Ocie asked.

"Whoever stole these cats will come back," Jake said. "Sooner or later he'll open that front door. He's the one who shot Lew, and he's going down for it." He picked up Cleo and stepped outside, and Jacques followed. *Where you going with my partner?* he yowled.

Jake shut the door on the other cats, who began moaning and crying.

"We're going to wait for the great catnapper."

As they went downstairs, Jake pulled out his phone. He punched in the number of Chief O'Dell, who, by some miracle, picked up at once. "Chief, we found the cats. I think we've also got a line on the guy that shot Lew Ketchell."

"I just heard about that, Novak. I also heard they're flying Ketchell and Mr. Brice to Dallas. But where are you?"

Jake gave the directions, then mentioned that Oralee Prather had led them here. "She's a good cop, O'Dell. She needs to hear what a good job she did."

"Yeah, I'll tell her. What are you going to do?"

"Ocie and I are going to sit here, and sooner or later that guy is coming. Whoever opens that door is the guy we want."

"Don't shoot him, Novak."

"I won't, Chief. I won't give him a medal, but I promise I won't shoot him unless he makes me. Now don't come roaring out here with your sirens blasting. I don't know how much manpower you got or how long it'll take, but we don't want to scare him off."

"Don't tell me how to run my business, Novak," O'Dell said huffily. "We'll be there, and you won't be able to see us till we want you to."

"Right. Sorry about that, Chief."

Jake put his phone away and began prowling around the house. It didn't take long before he found what he was looking for. "Look at this."

"It looks like a shirt," Ocie said.

"It *is* a shirt. A blue-and-white checked shirt. And look—there's a piece missing here. Jacques there took a plug out of it when the guy stole Cleo."

The two men settled down. The fridge was well stocked with liquor, but also with bottled water and soft drinks. Time seemed to crawl along. Jake knew that it might be a long stakeout, but it reminded him of the times he had had to be silent when he was with the Delta Force. When the enemy is all around you, you don't move, you don't blink, you don't breathe. You make yourself into a rock. And whoever had been stealing the cats would walk through that door, and they'd have him.

● ● ●

The wait wasn't as long as they had thought. Both Ocie and Jake heard the footsteps on the porch. Both drew their weapons. The lights were off, and their eyes had become accustomed to the darkness. The door swung open, and a figure stood there. Then the door closed, there was the click of a light switch, and the room was flooded with light.

"Hold it right there, Doucett." Jake pointed his Glock right at the convention center's watchman, who stood looking as if he might turn and flee. "Don't even *think* about it, Lonnie. You may not get the death penalty, but I can arrange it right now if you want it."

Lonnie Doucett seemed to droop. He looked down. "Look, I didn't mean to shoot him," he said, looking up a bit and holding his hands high.

"We can talk about your excuses later. Stand right there—I'm going to check you for a weapon. Put your hands against the wall." Jake waited until Lonnie did as he was told, and Jake then found the forty-five stuck in his belt in the small of his back. "I expect this will match well with the slug you got Ketchell with."

Lonnie turned around. All his confidence had seeped out. Words tumbled out of his mouth. "I didn't mean to shoot the guy. I didn't go there for that. I was just going to take some cats."

"But you did shoot him, didn't you?"

"He scared me. I didn't know he was near. He pulled his gun and hollered, and when I saw he had his gun out I just fired. Didn't even aim at him."

"You didn't aim at him *twice*, but you got him both times. Don't give me that. I'm going to see to it that you get all the law can give."

Lonnie looked desperate. His face was beaded with perspiration, and he wiped it off with the back of his sleeve. "Look, all this wasn't my idea. You don't think I'd steal a bunch of mangy cats. What would I do with them?"

"Whose idea was it?"

Jake moved closer and caught Lonnie's glance. He held it. "Who put you up to this, and why?"

The words tumbled out of Lonnie Doucett's lips, and finally Jake pulled out his phone and punched in a number. When a voice came, he said, "You can come in and get him, Chief."

In just moments O'Dell and Oralee Prather came through the door. They took a look at Doucett, and Jake held out the forty-five. "He was carrying this. I expect it will match the slugs taken out of Lew Ketchell. Also, his DNA will match what we took off Jacques' claws—and besides that, we found this shirt. It's the one he wore when he stole Cleo, and we found the patch on the floor."

O'Dell was beaming with satisfaction. "I just love to catch guys like you, Doucett. We're going to put you where the dogs won't bite you, and you won't come out until you're an old, old man—if ever."

Jake said, "Let Officer Prather take him in, Chief. We've got one more call to make, and you need to be there."

"One more call?"

"Yes, and I don't look forward to it."

● ● ●

Jake rang the doorbell and waited for what seemed like a long time. As Ocie shuffled his feet, Jake rang it again, and finally, on the third try, the door opened a mere crack. "We need to talk to you, Mrs. Monroe," he said.

Hannah Monroe was wearing a robe, and her face was pale as paste. She hesitated and then opened the door. She gave O'Dell a strange look, saying, "I can guess why you're here, Chief. You know it was me, don't you?"

"Yes, we do—but we don't know why. Why in the world would you hire a thug like Lonnie Doucett to steal cats?"

"Because I'm dying."

The three men stared at the woman, and it was Jake who asked, "What do you mean *dying?*"

"I mean what I said. There's nothing the doctors can do. I have only a few weeks left." She suddenly swayed, and Jake took her arm.

"Sit down, Mrs. Monroe," he said, and guided her over to a chair. O'Dell moved forward and Ocie stood back while Jake spoke to her. "I didn't know about your illness. Are you sure?"

Hannah Monroe smiled. "A person would be sure of a thing like that, wouldn't they?"

"But I don't understand."

"I don't have any religion, Mr. Novak, do you?"

Jake shook his head. "Not much," he said.

"I envy your companion Miss Mary Katherine Forrest. She's got a firm belief in God."

"Yes, she does."

"I don't know why, but I never have. Even now that I know I won't be here any longer than a few weeks, I still can't believe."

"But why would you spend your last days stealing cats?"

"I've always loved cats. I love shows. I knew this would be the last one I could ever win, so I thought of weeding out the probable winners so that my cat could win." She looked up and shook her head slightly. "Foolish, isn't it—but most of the things I've done in my life have been foolish."

"I'm sorry, but you're going to have to answer for this."

"What are you going to do? Kill me? There's no chance of that. I'm not even going to live long enough for the first hearing, much less a long, drawn-out trial."

Jake didn't know how to answer this. He'd never encountered a situation quite like it.

"I'm going to have to arrest you, Mrs. Monroe," Chief O'Dell said as he came up to her.

"What's going to happen to my cat?" She picked up the cat that was pushing against her ankle and held him. "He's all I have."

O'Dell looked down at the floor and said, "You can take the cat with you, Mrs. Monroe."

"Thank you, Chief. That's very kind of you. I've got to find her a good home before I go. Maybe that nice veterinarian will help me."

"I need to tell you about Jesus," Ocie said. "He can help you."

"I'll have Enola come and see you, Mrs. Monroe," Jake said. He began to mention the fact that a human death had resulted from Mrs. Monroe's plots, but he found that he couldn't.

● ● ●

Jake arrived home with the cats and let them loose from their carriers. He leaned down and stroked Cleo as she looked around the room. "You glad to be home, sweetheart?"

Yes, I am, but where is my Person?

Jacques came and stood before Jake and looked up at him with his trademark arrogance. *If it weren't for this sorry biped, Cleo, I could have handled this a long time ago. After all, I am the world's greatest detective.*

Jake stared at the cat and said, "You are unbearable, Jacques."

No, you're unbearable. I'm a nice enough chap—when I get my own way.

Fifteen minutes later the phone rang, and Jake picked it up, and Mary Katherine's voice spoke. "It's good news, Jake. Well...good and bad. Lew is gone, but they did the transplant, and Morgan is doing fine."

"I'll bet Rhiannon is happy," Jake said.

"Oh, yes—she says she'll always have Lew there. That every time she hugs her grandfather she'll be hugging him, that she's his little girl. When Mr. Ketchell left us, that was the last thing he heard."

"Not a bad thing to go out on," Jake murmured softly.

Twenty-five

The day of the finals at the cat show had come. That afternoon Jake took Mary Katherine's call and listened as she told him how well Morgan was doing. She ended by saying, "Of course, I guess, the recipient of a heart transplant always has to be careful. I think there are certain medications he has to take so his body won't reject the heart, but he's going to be all right."

"That's good news," Jake said. "When will you be coming back?"

"It's too soon to move him now. Probably some time next week—and, Jake, I want you to find a place to bury Lew Ketchell. I want his grave to be in White Sands. Rhiannon and Morgan both have asked for that."

"I'll take care of it," Jake promised. "There's a nice cemetery out on 98 with big trees. I'll handle it."

"Well," she said, regret tinging her voice, "The finals are tonight, and I won't be there. But that's all right. I never really was excited about it anyhow."

"I wish you were here," Jake said.

After goodbyes, Jake hung up the phone and went to the kitchen to cook a soufflé. It was one of his own inventions and, after a while of struggling, he poured the whole thing down the garbage disposal in disgust. "I heard that Edison tried more than a thousand times before he found something that worked in a lightbulb. I guess I can mess up a soufflé once in a while."

"Jake, are you talking to yourself?"

Jake turned around to see that Bev had come in, accompanied by Sarita and Jeremy.

"I guess so. I knew it would come to that sooner or later. We artists are driven to it eventually."

Bev was dressed impeccably as always. He wore a pair of olive-toned country cord trousers, a sandwashed poplin shirt with tiny checks of yellow, and a tropical-weight blazer of dark khaki.

"Don't you ever get tired of that foppish attire you put on, Beverly?" Jake asked with some irritation.

"No, when I leave my place I always dress as if I were going to be carried directly to the funeral home."

"Well, it's true we won't have to do anything to you if you drop dead. You look ready to bury."

Bev could not be teased, however.

Jeremy said, "Jake, you know you're going to have to take Cleo and show her. The finals are tonight."

"Not me," Jake said. "I'm no cat handler."

"But, Jake, you have to," Jeremy said with emotion. "I mean, after all, we're a family, and Mom can't be here—so it's up to you."

"I'm not doing it, and that's final," Jake said.

"Not to worry," Bev said breezily. "I'll do it for Kate."

Jake suddenly turned and glared at him. "I'm handling Cleo and that's final."

"But you said—"

"Didn't you hear me, Mr. Hyphen? I'm handling the cat."

Sarita suddenly spoke up. "No, Jake, *I'm* showing Cleo."

"Hey," Jeremy said, his eyes brightening, "that'll be great! You're better-looking than both of these guys put together."

"I should hope so," Sarita sniffed. She suddenly smiled. "There's not much to showing a cat. You're just holding her still while the judge looks at her. Maybe some good-looking guy will see me and ask me out."

"He'll have to ask my permission first," Jake warned.

"Yes, Father," Sarita said mockingly, and smiled, tapping her chin with her finger. "I wonder what I should wear tonight?"

● ● ●

The show had taken longer than usual. Jake had watched until his brain seemed numb. There had been breeds of cats he had never even heard of, such as a Munchkin, a Singapura, a Turkish Van, and about thirty others.

Jake was sitting beside Jeremy and Beverly, who said, "The woman who was put in jail—her cat's not here."

"No, she feels pretty much down," Jake said. "Her life was nearly over before, and now it's surely finished. I think she's grieving over Lew Ketchell's death."

"She feels responsible, I take it?"

"Well, she *is* responsible. Of course, she didn't tell Doucett to shoot anybody and never dreamed it would come to a violent end. Just snatching the cats was all she wanted to do."

"I'm sorry for her," Jeremy said. "She's old and going to die, and that's bad."

"Maybe you could go visit her in jail," Jake said.

"I wouldn't know what to say to her."

"I don't think we have to say much of anything. Just let her know we're her friends."

"I'll bet Mom will go," Jeremy nodded. "She told me Mrs. Monroe wasn't a Christian, but Mom's already praying for her. She told me over the phone."

"I hope it works out for her," Bev said sadly. "Seems like such a waste."

Raina and two other judges had completed their evaluation of the finalists—a Bengal, a strange breed called a Snowshoe, a Ragamuffin, a Ragdoll—which, of course, Cleo represented—a Maine Coon, a Devon Rex, and a Sphynx. Jake found himself wishing—desperately almost—that Cleo would win. Despite himself he had grown attached to the cat. He knew it would please Kate, despite her protests that it didn't really matter.

Finally Raina Bettencourt walked away.

"She's going over to get the ribbons," Bev said, excitement gleaming in his eyes. "Cleo's got a good chance."

Everyone in the arena watched as Judge Bettencourt picked up three ribbons representing Best in Show, second place, and third place. She walked over and gave third place to the Sphynx. There was loud applause, but of course the handler looked disappointed. The second place went to the Maine Coon, which Jake thought was a fine-looking cat.

Everyone was holding their breath by then, and Judge Bettencourt milked the moment. She stood looking at the remainders—and then she walked over and gave the Best of Show ribbon to Sarita, standing with Cleo. "Congratulations, you have a beautiful animal."

There was loud applause, and Jake heard Ocie give a screeching yell: "Praise God! Hallelujah! Glory be to God and the Lamb forever!"

"I think Ocie turned his wolf loose," Jake grinned. "Let's go down and congratulate the winner."

They made their way to the main floor, where Sarita was surrounded by photographers and admirers, some of them obviously admiring her more than the cat. She had chosen to wear a long-point Di Roma skirt that reached down to her heels, an embroidered turtleneck sweater that fit her closely, and a pair of black patent-leather boots with high heels. Jake went over and hugged her. "You look beautiful, darlin'."

"Thank you, Jake. I'm so glad Cleo won. Won't Kate be happy!"

"I beg your pardon, miss." Sarita turned to look at a young man in his early twenties, tall with auburn hair. "I'd like to interview you."

"Are you a reporter?" she asked.

"Freelancer. Maybe we could go out for coffee and talk about your cat."

"You'll have to ask my grandfather," Sarita said with a grin.

"Your grandfather? Where is he?"

"Right here," she said, pointing to Jake. "This is my grandfather. What do you think, Grandpa?"

Jake almost smiled, but he said, "He's too young. You need a mature man, somebody in their forties. Sorry, bub."

Sarita giggled, and then Enola came up and gave Sarita a hug. She turned to Jake and said, "Congratulations, you're co-owner of this beautiful cat. Here's your reward." She put her arms around Jake, pulled his head down and kissed him. The kiss went on far longer than the peck Jake had been expecting, and when she backed up, she winked and said, "Now, we can celebrate. Maybe I'll have a special reward for you."

Sarita pulled Jake aside and whispered, "She's after you, Jake."

"And that's bad?"

"Yes! She's a predator," Sarita said. "You stay away from her, you hear me?"

"I guess you'll have to look out for me, Sarita," Jake said in mock humility. "I'm just a poor country boy trying to make it in this world."

"Yeah, I know all about that," Sarita scoffed.

"You know," Jake said thoughtfully, "your dad would have been so proud of you tonight."

"Do you think so?"

"Sure he would, just like I am. Come on. Let's go out and celebrate."

● ● ●

Two weeks had passed, and finally Morgan Brice was well enough to make the trip back to the Gulf Coast. He flew in on a special flight, Jake discovered, paid for by an anonymous friend.

"Either you or Bev had to pay for that," Jake said to Ocie. "Kate said by the time she called to order the plane, it had already been taken care of."

"I almost had to shoot that limey to get him to let me pay the bill," Ocie said. "We cut cards for it, and he lost."

"Yeah, and I bet you cheated," Jake said.

"He never caught me," Ocie grinned. "It ain't cheatin' if you don't get caught."

The two were waiting as the plane taxied up. The first one off the plane was Rhiannon, who ran straight to Jake. He picked her up and hugged her, and she kissed him on the cheek, something she had never done before. "You found Jacques and Cleo. You're a hero."

"Well, actually Jacques found Cleo," Jake said. "I guess we'll have to get him another medal to hang around his neck."

Jake glanced over Rhiannon's shoulder and saw Bev advance toward Kate, who had just stepped out of the airplane. He held out his arms, and Jake glared as Kate embraced him. The two were laughing. He put Rhiannon down and called to Kate, "Wait a minute. *I'm* your hero. *I* saved your cats. What about me?"

Kate winked at Bev and suddenly stuck out her hand. "Shake, partner. That's what I do. I always shake hands with heroes."

Jake didn't have time to respond, for they were bringing Morgan off the plane on a stretcher. The three visitors hovered around him, and Rhiannon said, "He's going home at last."

"Are you sure he doesn't need to be in the hospital?" Jake asked.

"Oh, that's all taken care of," Rhiannon said. "Bev fixed our living room up like a hospital room, with a special bed, and he's paid for nursing around the clock."

"Isn't that wonderful, Jake?" Kate said as she put her hand on Bev's arm. "Thank you so much."

"No trouble at all," the Brit said.

Ocie had been watching Jake's face while this went on. He leaned over and whispered, "I kind of like that limey, don't you?"

"Not much."

Rhiannon and Kate rode with Morgan Brice in the ambulance, while Bev, Jake, and Jeremy watched them pull away.

"Well," Bev said, "that turned out rather well, I think."

"You didn't have to pay for all that stuff to take care of her grandfather," Jake said. "I could have done that."

"Oh, I wanted to," Bev said. "It's only money. All in a day's work. Well, I really must run. See you soon. Ta-ta."

Jake watched him go off and said to Ocie and Jeremy, "That fellow makes a pest out of himself."

"Aw, come on. He's done a lot for Rhiannon."

"Yeah, he's made Mary Katherine happy too, ain't he, Jake?" Ocie nudged Jake with his elbow.

"Keep your elbow to yourself, Ocie, or I'll cut you off at the neck." He turned and walked away, his back stiff.

"What's the matter with him?" Jeremy said with surprise. "He acts mad."

"Jake Novak's like a bear with a sore tail. Hard to figure him out, but I think I got his number. Come on. I'll explain it to you..."

● ● ●

By the time the week was gone, Jake was thoroughly sick of Beverly Devon-Hunt. The man was always underfoot, and Jake had become more and more short-tempered. On Thursday Bev took Kate to see Morgan Brice, and then the two went out for dinner afterward and then on to a Shakespeare play in Mobile.

Jake paced the floor, and finally at two o'clock, when the two came in, Jake was waiting for them. "What do you mean keeping her out this late, Devon-Hunt?"

"What?" Bev was totally taken off guard. "Why, the play lasted a long time, then we had something to eat afterward."

"You don't have to explain anything to him, Beverly," Kate said. "He's not my keeper."

But Jake wasn't finished. "Limey, why don't you take your stupid hyphen and go bother some other woman?"

Bev was a man of moderate temper, but two red marks appeared on his cheeks as his fair skin flushed. "I don't recall that you have any reason to tell me what to do, Novak."

The two men began arguing, with Kate trying to calm them down. Jacques the Ripper appeared and sat down to watch with enjoyment. Cleo was beside him.

Oh, I hope they don't hurt each other, she said.

I'm sure they will, Cleo. I hope they beat each other to a pulp, especially that Intruder. He needs to get his comeuppance.

Look at them. They're about to have a fight!

If I were Devon-Hunt, I would have brought a blackjack and slapped the Intruder right upside the head! What few brains he had would be scrambled, and that would take care of him. I hope the Englishman beats the soup out of him.

But Jacques' desire was never to be answered. Jake reached out his hand and pushed Beverly, who responded by hitting Jake in the mouth. It stopped Jake but not before he came across with a mighty right hand that caught Bev high in the head. It split his eyebrow and opened a cut that dripped blood all over his white shirt as he fell backward and lay still.

I do love to see a couple of bipeds hurting each other, Jacques said with obvious relish. *It makes me all nice and warm inside.*

Kate shrieked, then glared at Jake and said, "You common thug! Look what you've done!"

"He hit me first," Jake said.

"You sound like a bully in the school yard!" Kate sat down on the floor and pulled Bev up until his head was against her chest. "Look how he's bleeding."

"I didn't hit him all that hard," Jake said.

"You did it on purpose! I hate you, Jake! Go away!"

At that instant, Jake saw Beverly Devon-Hunt's eyes open and a smile touch his face. Bev winked at him but didn't move a muscle. "He's faking," Jake roared. "There's nothing wrong with him!"

"I think he's unconscious!" Kate said with alarm.

"He is not! He's putting it on, just looking for your sympathy." Jake started to grab Beverly and jerk him upright, but Kate slapped at him with her free hand. "Get away, Jake! Go on off and beat up some other helpless victim!"

Jake stared at the two, and when Beverly winked at him again with even a more superior smile, he uttered a frightful obscenity, turned, and stomped out the door. Sarita walked over and said, "I guess I'd better go talk to him. He might drown himself."

"Tell him I don't care if he does," Kate said. "Jeremy, get some cold water so I can bathe Bev's head."

Sarita slipped out the door, and she ran lightly until she caught up with Jake. "Where you going?"

"I don't know. I'm so mad I could spit nails."

"You sure have a funny way of trying to win a woman's love, Jake Novak."

Jake stopped and turned to face her. "I'm not trying to win anybody's love."

"Oh, come on now," Sarita said. "I can see you're gone on Kate. Your voice changes when you speak to her, and you watch her when she doesn't think you're looking."

Jake said nothing.

Sarita took his arm and said, "I'll walk with you. I need to give you some pointers on what women really like. First of all, they don't like bullies. You have to beat Devon-Hunt with other things than your fist..."

Later Sarita found Kate standing in the kitchen staring out the window. "Where's the victim?" she asked.

"Bev came to, and he went home," Kate said absently.

"It wasn't really all Jake's fault, Kate," Sarita said.

"Of course it was," Kate said. "He's been in the Delta Force. He knows how to fight. Bev never hit anybody in his life."

"Let me tell you something about Jake," Sarita said. She came over and stood beside Kate and looked her in the eyes. "Jake will never fail a woman. He will never take advantage of one." She smiled slyly and said, "I've tried to make him do just that. You know, Kate, I think Jake is the only good man I ever met. And besides that Bev was faking it."

"He was not!"

"Sure he was. You couldn't see it, but his eyes opened, and he grinned and winked at Jake."

"I don't—I don't believe that."

"I saw it with my own eyes. I don't blame him for it. He can't fight Jake physically so he has to impress you some other way—and he did, didn't he? You babied him and probably talked real sweet to him and encouraged him."

Indeed, Kate had done all these things, and she was silent for a moment. "I thought he was hurt."

"Jake's hurt far worse."

"He didn't have a scratch on him," Kate said.

"Kate, believe it or not, Jake is a sensitive guy. I know he's big and tough and hard, but there's something soft on the inside of him like a marshmallow."

"You're quite the expert on men, aren't you?" Kate said bitterly, but still there was uncertainty in her voice. "So you really think Jake got hurt?"

"I know he did. You should have listened to him out there. He's really sorry he hit Bev. He's used to fighting big strong men who can ward off blows and give as good as they take. He said he felt like he had hit Rhiannon."

"He said that?"

"He sure did. I know he's a tough guy, but you hurt him pretty bad."

Kate didn't answer. She finally said, "Good night, Sarita," and went off to her room.

Sarita watched her and said to Jacques, "You liked all that, didn't you, Jacques?"

I sure did, babe. Just wasn't quite enough blood to suit me. I wish the limey would have picked up a chair and broke it over the Intruder's head. Now that would have been something!

● ● ●

Kate did not go to bed. She couldn't sleep. She thought over and over about the evening, and finally she got up and went out on the deck. She saw Jake trudging down the beach toward the house. The moon was bright, and as he came up the steps, she said, "Jake, can I talk to you?"

Jake stopped abruptly, the moonlight illuminating his face. "What do you want now?"

"Just to talk." She got up and came over to face him.

"There's nothing to talk about."

"Yes, there is," Kate said. She reached out and put her hand on his arm. "It makes me feel good that two very fine men would find me attractive enough to fight over."

Jake was looking down at her, and for a moment he couldn't speak. Suddenly the heat of something timeless and thoughtless brushed against him, and he knew this woman had a power to stir him, to deepen his hungers...and somehow this increased his sense of loneliness.

"I didn't mean to hurt Bev—or maybe I did. I don't know anymore."

"He shouldn't have tried to fight you. Fighting is your business. It's your strength. He should have been using his weapons."

"What weapons?"

"Oh, he's good-looking. He has a title."

"And he has a hyphen," Jake said grimly. "Don't forget that."

"Yes, he does." Kate's strong and self-assertive pride suddenly dropped away. She straightened and looked up at him, her lips opening slightly. Her hand came up uncertainly, and she laid it flat against his chest. A rose color stained her features strongly, and at that moment there was a sweetness to her and a fragrance that Jake had never seen before in any woman.

"He's got all that," Kate said, "but you've got an earthy charm, Jake. Women like a little caveman in their men. Didn't you know that?"

Jake reached out and pulled her toward him gently and then kissed her firmly on the lips. "That what you mean?" he said.

Kate nodded and put her hands on his chest, but he held her tightly. "You know what I think?" she said. "I think the two of you have enough qualities for *one* good husband!"

Jacques and Cleo had come out to watch. Now Cleo said, *Isn't that beautiful?*

You know, for bipeds, that's all right. He suddenly got up, stretched, and cast a look at the two figures that formed one shadow together as they held each other. *I'm going to go out and find me a good-looking lady cat. I feel romantic.* He turned to go and said, *As a matter of fact, I may find three or four lady cats. So long, Cleo.*

Cleo watched Jacques as he went padding off into the night then turned back and watched the pair. *They're so sweet,* she purred, and she watched to her heart's content.

THE END

If you enjoyed *When the Cat's Away,*
be sure and pick up the previous adventures of Jacques & Cleo,
Cat Detectives...

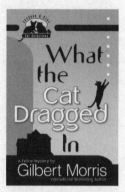

What the Cat Dragged In

In their debut mystery, Jacques and Cleo and their owner—or rather, the human *they* own—Kate Forrest, and her son, Jeremy, move to a beautiful beach house in White Sands, Alabama, left to Kate by a distant relative.

The catch is that *another* distant relative, wannabe novelist (and bona-fide cat-hater) Jake Novak, has also inherited an interest in the house. Undeterred, Kate and Jeremy move into the downstairs quarters and Jake takes the apartment upstairs.

Then, when a murder occurs, everyone is stumped—but feline sleuths Jacques and Cleo come to the rescue and reveal the identity of the killer.

The Cat's Pajamas

Hollywood comes into the lives of the newest residents of White Sands, Alabama. Jake Novak and Kate Forrest have settled into the beautiful beach house left to them by a distant relative. Cat-hating Jake busies himself working on his novel in his upstairs apartment, while Kate gets involved in a beach ministry to young people.

When New Leaf Productions arrives to film a movie, the locals are fascinated by the glamour of the actors. But when a cast member is murdered, followed quickly by a second killing, the town of White Sands becomes worried.

Jacques the Ripper has already solved one murder, and when he and Cleo are recruited to be in the movie, Jacques throws himself into nosing around for clues—and a murderer.

About Gilbert Morris...

Gilbert Morris has been a favorite novelist with readers for many years. His books include the Christy Award–winning *Edge of Honor,* and popular series such as the House of Winslow, the Appomattox Saga, and the Wakefield Dynasty. Mr. Morris lives in Gulf Shores, Alabama, with his wife, Johnnie.

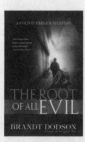

INTRODUCING...
A SMART CHICK MYSTERY SERIES BY MINDY STARNS CLARK, FEATURING HOUSEHOLD HINT WRITER JO TULIP

The Trouble with Tulip
ISBN-13: 978-0-7369-1485-7
ISBN-10: 0-7369-1485-4

Josephine Tulip is definitely a smart chick, a twenty-first century female MacGyver who writes a helpful hints column and solves mysteries in her spare time. Her best friend, Danny, is a talented photographer who longs to succeed in his career...perhaps a cover photo on *National Geographic*?

When Jo's neighbor is accused of murder, Jo realizes the police have the wrong suspect. As she and Danny analyze clues, follow leads, and fall in and out of trouble, she recovers from a broken heart—and he discovers that he has feelings for her. Will Danny have the courage to reveal them, or will he continue to hide them behind a facade of friendship?

Blind Dates Can Be Murder
ISBN-13: 978-0-7369-1486-4
ISBN-10: 0-7369-1486-2

Blind dates give everyone the shivers...with or without a murder attached to them. Jo Tulip is a sassy single woman full of household hints and handy advice for every situation. Her first romantic outing in months is a blind date—okay, a candidate for the Hall of Fame of Awful Blind Dates—but things go from bad to worse when the date drops dead and Jo finds herself smack in the middle of a murder investigation.

With the help of her best friend, Danny, and faith in God, Jo attempts to solve one exciting mystery while facing another: Why is love always so complicated?

Elementary, My Dear Watkins
ISBN-13: 978-0-7369-1487-1
ISBN-10: 0-7369-1487-0

Mindy Starns Clark's first two books in the Smart Chick Mystery series—*The Trouble with Tulip* and *Blind Dates Can Be Murder*—are followed with more love and adventure in this final, suspense-filled book.

When someone tries to push Jo Tulip in front of a New York train, her ex-fiancé, Bradford, suffers an injury while saving her—and the unintentional sleuth is thrown onto the tracks of a very personal mystery.

Jo's boyfriend, Danny Watkins, is away in Paris, so she begins a solo investigation of her near murder. What secret was Bradford about to share before he took the fall? And when Jo uncovers clues tied to Europe, can she and Danny work together in time to save her life?

Widows and Orphans

ISBN-13: 978-0-7369-1914-2
ISBN-10: 0-7369-1914-7

Widows and Orphans is the debut novel in the Rachael Flynn Mystery series by critically acclaimed author Susan Meissner. The perfect series for readers who enjoy CBA authors Dee Henderson, Angela Hunt, and Brandilyn Collins.

When her ultra-ministry-minded brother, Joshua, confesses to murder, lawyer Rachael Flynn begs him to let her represent him, certain that he is innocent. But Joshua refuses her offer of counsel.

As Rachael works on the case, she begins to suspect that Josh knows who the real killer is, but she is unable to get him to cooperate with his defense. Why won't he talk to her? What is Josh hiding?

The answer is revealed in a stunning conclusion that will have readers eager for the second book in this gripping series.

Sticks and Stones

ISBN-13: 978-0-7369-1915-9
ISBN-10: 0-7369-1915-5

Critically acclaimed author Susan Meissner's Rachael Flynn Mystery series started with the popular *Widows and Orphans*. In the second serving of intrigue, *Sticks and Stones,* lawyer Rachael Flynn receives an unsigned, heart-stopping letter:

> *They're going to find a body at the Prairie Bluff construction site. He deserved what he got, but it wasn't supposed to happen. It was an accident.*

When the body is uncovered, Rachael and Detective Will Pendleton discover that the fifteen-year-old victim, Randall Buckett, was buried twenty-five years before. Are the letter writer and the killer the same person? Why would someone speak up now? And why are they telling Rachael?

HARVEST HOUSE PUBLISHERS

EUGENE, OREGON